Winter Roses

Anita Mills

AN ONYX BOOK

ONYX
Published by the Penguin Group
Penguin Books USA Inc., 375 Hudson Street,
New York, New York 10014, U.S.A.
Penguin Books Ltd, 27 Wrights Lane,
London W8 5TZ, England
Penguin Books Australia Ltd, Ringwood,
Victoria, Australia
Penguin Books Canada Ltd, 10 Alcorn Avenue,
Toronto, Ontario, Canada M4V 3B2
Penguin Books (N.Z.) Ltd, 182-190 Wairau Road,
Auckland 10, New Zealand

Penguin Books Ltd, Registered Offices:
Harmondsworth, Middlesex, England

First published by Onyx, an imprint of New American Library, a division
of Penguin Books USA Inc.

First Printing, February, 1992
10 9 8 7 6 5 4 3 2 1

A special thanks to
Dr. Theresa DaKay Stimson,
my reader for this work.

A special thanks to
Dr. Theresa DaKay Stimson,
my reader for this work.

Prologue

The Scottish Border Country:
September 28, 1127

The rumbling sound of carts and the muted jangle of mailed riders broke the peace of the starless night as they crossed the Cheviot Hills. Behind them a dozen archers walked, their tools of trade on their backs. Above, the moon was nearly hidden behind a bank of clouds, affording cover on this, the eve of Michaelmas. It was, William of Dunashie reflected grimly, as good a night for their purpose as he'd ever seen. It was the night they'd regain his half-brother's stolen patrimony.

Ahead, the keep of Dunashie rose from the crest of the mound, an aged stronghold built on the rubble of an ancient Celtic fortress. Within its timbered walls there stood but one thatched-roof stone tower, and without there was but a single narrow ditch of stagnant water to reflect the hazy moon. For all that he'd wanted the place, 'twould seem that Hamon of Blackleith had done little to it. It appeared much as it had been when William had left it more than sixteen years before.

The tall, black-haired boy beside him reined in and stood in his stirrups to contemplate the task before them. William followed his gaze, thinking 'twas almost too easy: And they did it right, the fool who ruled within would yield to them this night what the courts had refused. Looking back to the boy, William felt a surge of pride. Though he'd celebrated his sixteenth birth anniversary but the day before, Giles of Moray already showed the purpose of a man. Aye, the exile, the attempted assassinations, and finally the futile court case, had tempered the youth, hardening him until he was a warrior worth following.

"What think you, Will?" the boy asked. "Is it as you would remember?"

William looked again at the timbered walls. "Aye."

For a moment Giles' face was sober, then he half-turned in his saddle to smile at Will. "But for you, brother, I'd not have lived to see it."

"Nay, I did but what Iain of Dunashie asked of me."

"You undervalue yourself—you were but five years the elder yet you kept me safe, even in King Henry's court," Giles reminded him.

Embarrassed, William looked away, spitting at the ground. " 'Twas my lot to serve ye," he protested. "The old laird said, 'I canna leave ye anything, ye know, fer yer dam was but a village lass I took to my bed, but I'd hae ye look ter the babe as has the right.' 'Twas the last he spoke ter me ere they hanged him," he recalled bitterly. "E'en as young as I was, I couldna fergit his words."

"E'en so, there's not many bastards as faithful to the legitimate heir. I owe you for what you have done for me, Will," the boy said solemnly.

"Nay, but ye were worthy of the service." William leaned over and spat again to cover the rise of emotion he felt. "And now 'tis ye as brings us home."

"What think you—is aught different that you can tell?"

The bigger man studied the wall. "Well, there's

naught ter say Hamon of Blackleith's nae changed the place a bit, but I canna see it.''

Hamon of Blackleith. The name hung between them, for when the powerful family of Moray had executed Iain of Dunashie for forcibly wedding the Lady Judith, they'd given the unwanted product of the union for hostage to King Henry of England, leaving it to King Alexander of Scotland to bestow Dunashie on a liege man. And later it had been the courts of Alexander's successor, King David, that had upheld Hamon against a powerless boy.

"Hamon spit in my face, Will, and I'll see him dead for it.''

"Aye.''

"The fools sleep,'' Giles noted with grim satisfaction. "They know not we are come.''

William looked again to his half-brother with an equal grimness. "And may Hamon of Blackleith die knowin' 'twas ye as took it back.''

Between them, they'd gathered a motley band of malcontents from both sides of the border for the attempt. And now those who rode with them hoped to gain service with the next lord of Dunashie. At the rear of the column, some of them stood ready to fire the pitch vats for the assault. It was, William knew, going to be a brutal, bloody thing they did, but he told himself there was no other way. As long as Hamon breathed, he'd not yield Dunashie.

A wiry, toothless fellow, Robert of Langhorne, worked his flint, but Giles shook his head. "Nay, I'd have all in readiness first, Hob. I'd not give them time to raise a defense once we are seen. We are not enough to stand and fight.'' Nudging his horse to ride back amongst his men, he kept his voice low. "Lang Gib,'' he addressed the tall, lanky Gilbert of Kilburnie, "I'd have you cover the archers whilst they take to the trees above.'Twill be Wat's task to supply the pitch-wrapped arrows. And Willie and Ewan will ride beneath, holding their brands high to light them.''

William knew why he'd been chosen: At six feet and

seven English inches he was taller than the others, taller even than Lang Gib by a full head. "Wee Willie" he'd been called derisively at the English court, and the name had stuck. But this night at least he would not curse his size.

He watched almost dispassionately as the men dipped the wrapped ends of torches and arrows into the thick pitch. The archers moved to the trees that spread their limbs almost to the malodorous moat, then climbed high to position themselves within firing distance of the wooden walls. When all was ready, the toothless one gave the raven's call. Inside, all was quiet.

The mounted columns separated to ring the wall. Will took the torch he was handed, and for the first time since he'd proposed the plan his body felt taut. This was no meaningless skirmish for another master—this was the battle for the keep of his birth. This was the fulfillment of his promise to his sire. This night Giles of Moray would hold Dunashie, or they would die.

Above them a lone sentry walked the wall, his horn lantern flickering like a small, distant star. The poor fool didn't know it was a target he carried.

Finally Giles nodded, lifting his hand to signal it was time. William rode back to where the hot coals were held within the vented iron kettle. Tipping the lid over, he thrust his brand within, holding it until the flame flared and the pitch caught the fire. The sentry above turned just as an archer's arrow caught him, and he fell, his last cry muted by the splash when he hit the water.

William spurred his horse and, holding his flaming torch high above his head, he rode beneath the trees. The archers leaned their brands down to catch the fire. Ahead of him, he could see Giles flinging his own torch over the wall to the thatch that covered the stable. Others followed him, and soon the curling smoke attested to a dozen or more fires within. The taunts of the circling, shouting borderers mingled with the cacophony of animals afraid of the flames on the other side.

The thatch was like tinder, and within minutes every roof from the granary to the tower was ablaze. The courtyard, which had been so silent before, was filled with the shouts and the choking coughs of those who scrambled from their pallets. And above the din women screamed, crying for God's deliverance from the smoke and the fire. Will closed his ears to the pitiful cries, for there was none to aid them now.

In one final, desperate attempt to escape the burning keep, those within ran for the gate, pushing against it even as the heavy chains creaked and rattled to lift it. Several men worked frantically to turn the pulleys, lowering the bridge. Behind them the courtyard was orange with the unchecked fires, and the light silhouetted hastily mounted knights, their mail hanging unhooked from their shoulders. At their head, the fat baron cursed the gate men for their slowness.

" 'Tis Hamon!'' Giles yelled.

Will rode for the drawbridge as it made its slow descent down, shouting, "Move the pitch cart to block their escape!"

Above the frightful din Giles called to Hob, "Burn it! Now!"

The cart rolled forward, and just as the wooden bridge struck the pilings Hob pushed the vat over, spilling the pitch onto the wood. Will leaned over to fire it, and those who rode out faced a wall of shooting flames. Panicked horses reared, and men blasphemed as they were thrown into the burning pitch. Living torches, they struggled to rise, then curled over as they were consumed.

"Watch out!" Will shouted hoarsely, as the huge-girthed man he'd recognized for Hamon rode through the fire. "Giles! 'Tis he!"

But his younger brother spurred forward, taunting the usurper, shouting through the smoking hell, "Behold, the boy you dispossessed is become a man! Use your spit to put out the fire!"

"Nay, ye'll not live to take it—ye've built yer funeral pyre!" the baron snarled. "Ye'll die fer this!"

William knew fear as Hamon's sword flashed, its blade catching the glow of the disintegrating bridge. He threw his torch away and reached for his axe. "I'd take him fer ye!" he cried.

"Nay! He is mine!"

William saw Hamon's horse leap, gaining the hard-packed earth, while the baron leaned from his saddle to swing his sword so wide that he nearly lost his seat. The blow glanced from Giles' shield. William forced his attention to the others, telling himself he'd taught the boy to take care of himself.

More crowded behind Hamon, trying to escape before the bridge fell into the water. William shouted to Lang Gib, "We canna let any of Blackleith escape! For Moray of Dunashie! For Dunashie!" Even as he called out the battle cry he rode at them, swinging his axe furiously. The broad blade caught the first man out after Hamon, lifting him in his saddle and cleaving him cleanly upward from the ribs. His curse died in a look of surprise, then he toppled. His frightened horse dragged him away.

After that it was a mad melee: Many who would try the gate fell back from the flaming bridge, but some managed to force their neighing mounts across. Above, those trapped inside screamed piteously and tried to jump from the burning walls. There was no other time, no future, no past, as Will and Gib and the others hacked at those who dared the bridge. He'd let none aid Hamon. The din of battle was deafening, and then it was over, followed by a sudden, eerie silence broken only by the popping and cracking of the settling timbers.

When there was no more coming out, William turned to find his brother. Giles stood over the fallen baron as Will came up behind him.

"I'd be shriven," Hamon gasped. "I'd have God's mercy. In the name of the Virgin, I'd have a priest."

While William watched, Giles struck the final blow.

Hamon's legs lifted, jerked, then his body went limp and his head lolled. "Nay, Hamon, but 'tis all the mercy you will have of me," the boy said softly. "I'd see your soul in Hell ere I called a priest for you."

They'd done it—they'd won. William's throat ached and tears streamed down his face as Giles turned to him. Wordlessly the boy clasped him, holding his mailed arms with bloody hands.

"I've brought you home, Will—Dunashie is ours."

"I never doubted you would—never." Still overwhelmed with what he felt, Will stepped back and smiled crookedly. " 'Tis yers, my lord."

"Aye." They both turned to survey the flames that licked the night sky. "And there'll be none to want it now—'tis but ashes."

" 'Tis a lesson fer ye—when ye build it again, make it stone," William murmured.

The borderers moved among the fallen, stripping anything of value they found, as William and Giles surveyed the destruction and death they'd wrought. It had been a bitter struggle, but it was over. Even if he willed it, King David could not give Dunashie back to Hamon.

"My lord, these are all as survive."

As he spoke, Lang Gib prodded several sullen people forward. Grimed with soot, their clothes wet from the foul water in the ditch, they looked down rather than at Giles of Moray. The boy approached a girl, scarce twelve.

"Art of Hamon's family?"

She shook her head, then her face crumpled. Covering her face as though she could blot out what she'd seen, she wept loudly. Behind her a man cried, "They are all dead—Lady Margaret even! Sweet Jesu, but you have burned us in our beds! May God consign your souls to Hell for it!"

But Giles was watching the girl, and he felt the need to justify what he'd done. "Demoiselle, he took what was mine." Abruptly, he swung around. "How many were inside?"

"Thirty-six that called Hamon lord," the man muttered, "and we are all that live."

"And the others?" Giles wanted to know. "How many as were born here?"

He shrugged. "No more'n an English dozen."

"Any of his blood among you?"

The man's arm tightened on the half-naked boy beside him. "Nay, they all perished. You have murdered all. All," he repeated. "E'en the women and the bairns is dead."

William counted but six survivors. Turning away, he studied the still burning wall. The awful smell of cooked flesh assaulted his nose, sickening him, and guilt washed over him. Then he shook it off. "The guilt is Hamon's," he said aloud, "and may God curse him for it, fer 'twas him as stole Dunashie from ye."

"Aye," Giles agreed grimly.

It was decided to send the young girl, Aveline de Guelle, back to her father. The others Giles intended to let go, allowing them to seek refuge where they would. But as he and Will walked away, the one who had dared to raise his voice a moment ago spat at them.

"Butcher! Art naught but a butcher! May ye burn in Hell for this!" The other men and the boy joined in, chanting, "Butcher! Butcher! Art but a craven butcher, as burns women and babes in their beds!"

Giles stopped still, his jaws working to control the surge of anger he felt. And then he shook his head. "Will," he said evenly, "hang them." With that he walked on, leaving his brother to carry out the order.

It was an unpleasant task. Battle was one thing—a man testing his skill against another—but hanging was something Will did not relish. He looked to Lang Gib. "You heard him, did ye not?"

"Aye," Gib acknowledged grimly.

Will started to walk away also, then turned to look at the frightened youth. "How are ye called, boy?"

"My lord, I would ye spared him," the man who'd first angered Giles pleaded. "He has but ten years!"

"Who is he?"

The man hesitated, then cast a warning look at the child. "He is mine nephew."

"Ye dinna answer me, boy—how are ye called?"

The youth swallowed visibly, then shook his head mutely.

"He is Walter, my lord."

"I dinna ask ye—and I am no more lord than ye," Will snapped. For a long moment he considered the boy, thinking he could not let Gib hang a child. And remembering how it had been when his own sire had been hanged before his eyes, he nodded. "Aye. Come with me then, for 'tisna anything fer ye to watch."

The boy hung back, clinging to his uncle. The man looked up at William. "I'd hae a farewell wi' him."

"Aye." Will's eyes traveled to where Hob already looped a rope over a stout limb. "I'll walk apart a little that ye may speak, but I'd nae gie ye o'erlong."

The man waited until Will had turned his back, then he held the boy's arm, speaking low and urgently. " 'Tis the last of yer blood ye are, and I'd nae hae ye fergit it—d'ye ken me?"

Tears welled and spilled from young Walter's eyes as he nodded. "I'd die wi' ye!" he cried fervently.

"Nay, 'tis ye as must remember—'tis ye as must make Giles of Moray pay for what he does this day," his uncle whispered. "For yer sire's memory, ye must live." Leaning down, he embraced the boy. "Ye ken me?" he asked again.

"Aye."

It had been long enough. Will beckoned to the boy. "Walter." When the child shook his head, he caught him beneath the arm and pulled him away. "Here now . . . I told ye . . . tis no sight fer ye."

"Where do you take me?" the boy whimpered, his eyes now wide with his fear.

"D'ye have any kinsmen beyond these walls?"

"Nay."

William peered down at the grimed face and felt pity for the lad. "And Giles does not mind it, I'd take

ye ter the brothers at Kelso,'' he offered gently.
''They'll have a care fer ye.''

''I'd nae be a priest!''

'' 'Tis better than a hanging,'' William countered.
''Ye'll have a roof above ye, and food fer yer stomach.'' His troubled eyes traveled up the burning timbers once more. ''God willing, ye'll fergit this.''

''Never!''

The boy spoke the word with such vehemence that
it gave Will pause. ''Ye'd best. 'Tis a better life I'd gie
ye than that of a villein, ye know, and if Giles—''

''I hate him! I hate the Butcher!'' Tears spilled over
onto the grimy cheeks, streaking them. ''Hang me with
them!''

''Nay.'' Will motioned to the one called Wat.
''Here, you keep the boy from harm, will ye? I'd ask
Giles' permission to take him to Kelso,'' he told him,
starting away.

''Bastard! Bloody bastard!''

He stopped, but did not turn around. ''Aye. Call us
'Butcher' and 'Bastard,' if ye will, but Dunashie's ours
this day.''

Much later, when the flames were no more than
tongues tasting the charred remnants of what had been
Dunashie, Will broached the matter of the boy, saying,
''I spared the boy, ye know.''

Giles' earlier anger had been overcome by his guilt.
He nodded. ''Tell him he can stay here.''

Will shook his head. ''Ye'll nae want one as hates
ye in yer service, ye know. And ye dinna mind it, I'd
take him to the monks.''

''Aye.'' Giles' black eyes were red-rimmed from
the smoke. ''I've killed enough children this night.''

''Ye couldna know none would escape.''

''If I had, 'twould have made no difference. Dunashie is my birthright, Will. Nay, but I have offered
prayers for the innocent and damned the rest.''

''Aye. Ye canna count the cost of justice.'' William's mouth twisted crookedly, and his eyes were red-

dened from more than the fire. " 'Tis proud of ye I am, and I'd hae ye know it."

That elicited a smile from the boy. "You know, Will, 'twill not always be Dunashie. I mean to rise before the world, and when I do I'll not forget the service you have given me. One day, William of Dunashie, you will rule a keep of your own. One day I'll see you a lord also."

"Ye'd best rise yerself, ere ye promise to raise a bastard before the world." Then, realizing how he sounded, he cuffed his young brother on the shoulder. "But if ye do, I'll hold ye to it."

"Ah, Will, but 'tis the first of all we shall have." Giles turned to throw his arm around him. "I tell you what you told me at Henry's court: 'I'd nae have ye doubt yerself,' you said to me. Do you remember it?"

"As I recall, 'twas said to keep ye from weeping in yer pallet."

"Aye, we were but two boys then." Giles drew in a deep breath, then let it out. "But this night we are become men."

Chapter One

"Aidan! You must flee, and quickly!"

"Wha—what?" Still dazed from sleep, the young man sat up slowly from his straw pallet. The girl before him thrust his tunic into his hands. Baffled, he stared at it for a moment. "Should not be up . . . ought to be abed," he mumbled thickly. "Your babe . . . Elias . . ."

"There is not time to explain. Sweet Mary, but can you not hurry?" As she leaned over him, the veil fell away from her bruised face.

"God's blood, lady!" His eyes widened, and he came awake fully. "Who . . . ?" But even as he asked, he knew it had been Elias. "Jesu," he muttered.

"Get you dressed," she whispered, turning away.

"But *why?* What did ye to deserve this?"

She shook her head. " 'Tis the babe. He would kill you for it, and naught I can say . . . Dear God, there is not the time—you must go now, sir! And you would live, you must leave *now!*"

Ignoring the urgency in her words he stared still,

unable to comprehend. "Me? But I have done nothing, and—"

" 'Tis enough that he believes you have sired my babe," she answered bitterly. " 'Tis enough that you have smiled at me—that you have shown me kindness here."

A look of utter incredulity passed over his face. "He thinks *what?* By the rood of God, nay!" As her words sank in, he hastened to pull open the neck of the garment, diving into it. "Nay, but 'tis beyond belief! Who dares to carry such a tale?" His voice was muffled as he tugged the tunic down over his naked body. Moving quickly now, he pulled on his chausses and tied them at his waist. When he would have reached for his garters, she shook her head.

"There is not the time, and you'd leave alive."

"But I canna understand how 'tis he could think that I . . . that ye . . ."

"The babe is not whole, and Elias would have one to blame for it." She looked up, toward the sound of the shouting men above them. "Go with God, Aidan." She picked up his sword and handed it to him.

"But 'tis a lie!" Even as he said it he girded his sword belt about his waist, then bent to pull on his boots. "Nay, I'd face him, and tell him that whoever accuses me lies."

"Think you he cares for that? Mine own innocence protected me not!" She bit her bruised and blackened lip to still its trembling, then she dared to touch his muscled arm. "Nay, but I'd not have your blood on my soul!"

He cursed himself inwardly, for had not his lord's own son warned him that Elias of Woolford was blindly jealous of his young wife? But he'd done nothing beyond show her kindness. . . . Nay, 'twas not true, and he knew it. He'd dared to admire her openly—he'd dared to speak with her when others would not. For the briefest moment, he'd even allowed himself to touch the softness of her hair. If there had been any sin 'twas his, for he'd dared to dream of the old man's

wife. Now, he looked on her battered face and felt an
intense anger toward Elias of Woolford.

"Nay, but I'd nae leave ye to face him alone, lady.
I'd tell him you are blameless."

"He'd kill you ere you spoke a word," she cut in
flatly, "and 'twould serve nothing."

And now even as he tarried, the grizzled Elias
emerged from the stairway above, calling out, "There
is the whore's son! Afore God, I'll hear from his own
lips that he has lain with my wife! We have caught
them together!"

Still Aidan hesitated until she pushed him, hissing,
"Now! Save yourself whilst you can! They'll hang you
and you do not go!" Hating himself for it, he made
the decision to run, heaving his body out the narrow
arrow slit and dropping to the ground below, then
breaking into a run for the stable.

To gain him time, Arabella moved to face her
drunken husband. Clenching her hands for courage,
she dared to beg for the borderer's life. "Nay, my
lord, but I swear by the Blessed Virgin that we are
blameless! Put me aside if 'tis your will, but I pray
you will not kill one who is innocent!"

Elias of Woolford reeled unsteadily. "Innocent!"
he snorted derisively. "Innocent! Mine eyes have seen
his innocence! God marks your babe for your sin!

Behind him his sons glowered at her, and Donald
muttered, "Ye can tend to her later.'Tis Ayrie as es-
capes."

She dropped to her knees before Elias and held out
her hands. "I am willing to swear on the True Cross
that I have been naught but a good and faithful wife
to you, my lord."

" 'Tis not my babe you have borne me, Arabella of
Byrum," Elias growled. " 'Tis the devil's changeling
you would have me claim, and I'll not do it! Woolford
wears the horns for no man!" He reached to shove her
aside, cursing as Aidan rode from the stable. "After
the whoremaker!" he shouted furiously. "One hundred pennies to the man who takes him!"

In desperation Arabella caught at his sleeve, hanging on. "Nay! Sweet Mary, but are you so blind that you cannot see the truth? Is there no proof I can offer?" she cried.

He shook free of her, casting her roughly against the stone wall. "When I am done with Aidan of Ayrie, wife, I will punish you also," he promised. "There'll be none other to want you when I am done—I swear it!"

Screaming and cursing, he followed his sons down the winding stairs, leaving her to watch helplessly at the slit. But as Elias reached the courtyard, Aidan leaned to strike furiously at the frayed ropes that held the drawbridge, cutting them with his sword blade. And before the wooden platform banged against the pilings on the other side of the flooded ditch he had spurred his horse onto it, forcing the beast to jump to the slippery bank. For an awful moment the animal seemed to lose its footing, but then it struggled up and pawed its way onto solid ground. Before the others could gain their mounts, Aidan of Ayrie had disappeared into the foggy rain.

Forgotten in the din of men scrambling for mounts, Arabella clung to the cold stone for support. "God aid you, Aidan, for a smile was your only folly," she whispered. "If there was any sin 'twas mine, for I wished for your kindness, and more." And as she spoke the cold rain mingled with her tears, streaking her battered face. She did not move until her tiring woman came after her.

"Och, and ye ought ter be abed, my lady," Ena chided. " 'Twas a hard birthing and a hard beating,"

"What difference does it make?" Arabella asked dully. "The babe is not whole, and he means to kill me for it."

As the rain continued to beat steadily against the shuttered arrow slits that served for windows, Arabella smoothed the soft, downy hair on the small head that lay at her breast. Looking down on the wee, sleeping face, she felt a surge of tenderness for this babe, for her less-than-perfect son. But she was alone in that, for she'd not missed the furtive glances, nor had she missed the number of servants who'd made the sign of the Cross when they thought she would not know it. Even the stout village girl who'd been brought in to wet-nurse the babe had recoiled when she'd seen him, and Arabella had sent her back, saying she would give suck herself. And Ena, for all that she had served her, would not hold him until he'd been wrapped and his deformity hidden from sight.

"The Devil's mark," indeed. If anything, her son's twisted, useless leg had been caused by all the beatings Arabella had endured at her husband's hands. She could not count the times she'd wanted to send to her father and her brothers for aid, but she'd known what Nigel of Byrum would tell her: that it was a woman's lot to be obedient, and a man's right to chasten her when she erred. But she'd not erred, and it had made no difference. Elias had chastened her for every glance, every kind word she had dared to bestow, until finally she was isolated from every man at Woolford. And still the beatings had not stopped.

But the matter of Aidan of Ayrie was more serious than any other, for her son's birthright was now being questioned. Were it not for that, she'd have welcomed being set aside. But now there was no possibility of that, for Elias' pride would suffer. Nay, but he'd beat her to death without reason, then pay a fine to her father for it. And she dared not think what he would do to her poor, innocent babe.

They were gone for many hours, for so long that night waned into dreary dawn and finally into yet another grey, rainy day, and all the while Arabella sat there, holding her son, praying that an innocent man would escape her husband's unreasoning wrath. But she had little real hope of that, for the burns that lay between Woolford and Ayrie were flooded with two weeks and more of the ceaseless rain.

"My lady."

She looked up to see Father Bertrand standing before her, his hands clasped over the crucifix he wore. His gaze dropped to the babe at her breast, and he cleared his throat.

"I thought mayhap you would want to name him," he said quietly. "I have brought water from the River Jordan."

She caressed the soft hair again, and nodded. "I'd name him James, for my mother's father." Lifting her eyes to his again, she added, "I am innocent—'tis Woolford's son I have borne."

"Aye."

"Ever have I tried to please the husband I have been given," she continued bitterly, "but I cannot."

"Aye." He opened the small vial he'd concealed in his palm and held it out for her to see. " 'Tis sacred— I had it of a man who traveled to the Holy Land." Even as he spoke, he leaned over her to drip several drops of the precious water onto the babe's forehead, letting it course downward. At first the slate-colored eyes blinked, then the tiny face screwed into an expression of outrage and the babe wailed indignantly. Wetting his thumb in the water, the priest made the sign of the Cross over the small head.

"I baptise thee, James of Woolford, in the name of the Father, the Son, and the Holy Spirit, that you may serve Him in this world and the next. Amen."

"And may He cause His countenance to shine upon you with His mercy, wee Jamie," Arabella murmured softly, as she leaned to kiss the wet face.

As the old priest looked down on her bent head, he felt a great sadness for her. It was not right that Nigel of Byrum had given her at fifteen to a man of fifty-four, and so Bertrand would tell him if ever he saw the lord of Byrum again. Aye, as Elias' fleshly abilities had begun to wane his jealousy had soared until it knew no bounds, and he had beaten her far too often for her imagined transgressions. And now, having convinced himself that he had not sired this lame child, he would probably kill her—after he tortured Aidan of

Ayrie into confessing to that which had not been done.
And at best he would let the babe starve.

Not that he did not blame young Aidan for what had
happened. The fool had been incautious in his admiration of his lord's wife. And more than once, despite
a dozen warnings, he'd dared to lavish praise on the
girl in the presence of Elias' sons. Indeed, had his
father not been Duncan of Ayrie, Aidan would have
been sent away long ago. Now Elias was too blinded
by unreasoning fury to spare him.

At first Bertrand thought 'twas the sound of harder
rain he heard, but then he saw Arabella stiffen. "Mayhap if he were to see you in chapel on your knees . . ."
he offered helplessly. "Mayhap . . ."

"He would take it as proof of my guilt," she said
tonelessly. Rising, she held her son close for a moment, then laid him within the cradle Elias had com-
missioned before the babe had been born. "He'd say
I prayed that Aidan of Ayrie might escape. And that
at least would be the truth."

Bertrand fingered the Cross at his breast nervously.
"Would you that I stayed with you?"

"That he could accuse you of lying with me also?
Nay, I—"

There were trampling footsteps on the stairs, then
the door burst inward to admit Milo of Woolford,
Elias' youngest son from the earlier marriage. "Father," he addressed Bertrand breathlessly, "I pray you
will come! Donald would have you shrive Papa, though
he is dead."

"Dead?" Arabella asked faintly, sinking into her
chair. "Elias is *dead?"*

Without looking at her, Milo nodded. "Ayrie's
whelp swam the flooded river, but Papa's horse reared,
throwing him into the water."

"Sweet Mary. And Aidan of Ayrie?" she dared to
ask also.

"For now, he has escaped capture."

Relief washed over her with the realization that Elias
of Woolford had come home for the last time, that no

longer would he humiliate and beat her. He was *dead*.
Aware that Milo finally had turned to her, she bowed
her head to murmur, "May God show Elias the mercy
that he showed me."

"Amen," he agreed, not understanding her meaning.

Pleading the exhaustion of childbed, Arabella did
not witness Elias' interment beneath the chapel floor
at Woolford. It did not matter: His grown sons behaved as though she were not there now, anyway, as
Donald assumed the lordship of the keep. It was not
until nearly a week after the funeral mass that all three
of Elias' surviving sons climbed to the solar to see
her.

Hugh, the middle one, walked to stand over young
James' cradle, peering intently at the blinking babe.
"I don't know. . . . Mayhap . . . ," he ventured fi-
nally.

"It matters not," Donald snapped. Without pre-
amble, he turned to Arabella to announce, "We are
here to decide how best to provide for you, madam."

For an awful moment she felt a cold sickness descend. Had there been no child she would have been
sent back to her father, but now . . . now Donald could
choose to send her to a convent. And he would be
expected to keep Jamie.

His eyes swept the tapestries that blew against the
walls of the solar. " 'Tis time I slept here," he decided.

"Aye." She clasped her hands tightly in front of
her, not knowing how best to appeal to him. There
was too much of Elias in him to risk setting him against
her. "It is your right as lord here."

That pleased him. A faint smile crossed his mouth,
then fled. "And your sire does not require your dowry,
you may return to him."

She ought to have known he would not want to send
her to the nuns, for then he'd be expected to endow
the convent that took her. But he'd not mentioned Ja-

mie. "And James of Woolford. . . ? And my
son. . . ?" she dared to ask.

The brothers exchanged brief glances, then Hugh
looked away. "Your bastard goes with you," Donald
answered. "I've no use for a lame brat."

"He is not my bastard," she responded evenly. "He
shares the blood of Woolford with you. Whether you
believe it or no, I have never lain with any but your
father."

"Aye," Hugh agreed, "there's none—" He
stopped, quailing beneath the look his older brother
gave him.

"I say he is Aidan of Ayrie's bastard," Donald
stated flatly. "And you would take him with you, you'll
not dispute it."

He walked closer and lifted the blanket from the
babe, staring downward on the tiny leg that turned so
much the stubby foot lay over. His lip curled in dis-
dain, and when he looked up Arabella could see Elias
in his eyes. "I share no blood with *this,*" he declared
contemptuously.

"Nay, you'll not deny him. I will . . ."

Donald's eyes narrowed. "Would you make me keep
him for you?" he demanded. "And you do, the brat
will come to hate you for it. And you do, he'll not
prosper here."

The threat was clear: If she made any claim on
Woolford for her son, Donald would treat him cruelly.
And if she did not, it was as much as admitting to the
falsehood that her babe was Ayrie's bastard. While she
considered the impossible choice, he looked again to
her babe. "Nay, but my sire never got *that* of you,"
he said contemptuously. "This brat's Devil-born. And
'tis witchcraft to consort with the Devil, madam," he
added ominously. His eyes met hers and held, waiting.

"Then try me for it! You cannot accuse both the
Devil and Ayrie!"

Hugh moved between them and laid a hand on her
arm. "And you leave with the babe, we'll not accuse
you."

"I cannot deny my son's birthright of Woolford."

"Birthright?" Donald snorted. "You behold three others before him, and I am possessed of two sons. And he *were* born of my sire, I'd not spare more than a hundred marks for him!'Twould be the Church, and they'll not take *that!*"

She turned to Hugh. "And you: Will you not hold for my son? Will you not protect one of your blood?" For answer, he looked away. "And you also, Milo?" she asked softly, seeking the youngest. "Do you deny your father's flesh?"

There was only silence in the room. Finally, she sighed and nodded. "Aye, I'd not leave him amongst you. All I ask is escort to Byrum for myself and my son."

After they'd left, she sat staring into the embers that glowed in the brazier. It was done—her awful, terrifying marriage to Elias of Woolford was done. She had survived the countless beatings, and she was free. Not even the knowledge that she returned home to a father who would not want her, who would be angered when he saw Jamie, could dampen the surge of exhilaration she felt. *She was free.* And God willing, she would never have to submit to the cruelty of a husband again.

Chapter Two

"But Papa—*nay!*"

" 'Tis settled between us, Bella—the lord of Dunashie brings his brother Tuesday next, and I'll nae hear otherwise!"

Arabella clasped her hands tightly before her and tried not to reveal the terror she felt at her father's words. She would wed again, he told her, this time the half-brother of Giles of Moray. And every tale she'd ever heard of the Butcher and the Bastard came to mind, chilling her blood, for there was none who did not know that they'd burned Hamon of Blackleith and all his family in their beds, or that the Butcher had been tried for the murder of his wife. And it was said that the Bastard of Dunashie had aided his brother in the commission of those terrible acts.

"Well?" Nigel of Byrum regarded his daughter with thinly veiled dislike, then he sneered. "Art not pleased, Bella?" he challenged. " 'Tis as well as I could do fer ye, ye ken.'Tis but yer good fortune they've nae heard the tale, else e'en a bastard like Wil-

liam of Dunashie wouldna take a whoring wife. Nay,
but for all ye did, I'll profit of ye yet."

"How can I be pleased?" she cried. "How can I
be pleased? Papa, 'tis said the Bastard is a giant!"

"Ye be nae wee thing yerself!" he retorted. "And
the Bastard's more like than most to accept ye. Ye can
hope 'tis enough that he weds one of gentle birth."
Turning away from the fear in her eyes, he continued
matter-of-factly, "Lord Giles enfiefs his brother with
Blackleith, Bella, so 'tisna like ye were going to be
nae more than another woman in the Lady Elizabeth's
house. Ye'll be mistress o' yer own keep, wi' a husband ter warm yer bones and—"

"Papa—I . . . I cannot!"

For a brief moment his expression grew pained, then
he went on as though she'd not spoken. "They've nae
asked a dowry fer ye, beyond two hundred o' King
David's pennies, ye ken. Nay, ye'll do yer duty ter yer
house, daughter, for I've need of the Butcher's aid
against the thievin' English."

"Was it not enough that I went to Elias?" she cried.
"Was it not enough I suffered four years? Papa, look
at me: 'Tis your flesh you sell!" For once, she dared
to pull at his sleeve. "Please, Papa—I beg you! I'd not
do this!"

It did no good. His face told her his patience was
strained, that he would not listen. " 'Tis for me to
decide where you are wed, and I'll have no puling
o'er it, d'ye hear? 'Tis as good a match as I can get for
ye, I tell ye!"

"He is the Butcher's brother!"

" 'Tis why I have chosen him! I've nae need of a
saft man, ye foolish hinny!"

"I'd not go to another husband, Papa. I pray you—"

"Ye pray me, ye pray me," he gibed scornfully. "I
look ter yer welfare—aye, and the welfare of the misbegotten brat ye've brought home ter me—and 'tis the
gratitude I get of ye! I made ye lady to Woolford—a
rich place on the English side, it was—and ye couldna
keep it! Four years ye lay with Elias, and ye've nae

but a curst bairn ter show fer it! Aye, and 'tis said ye played him false wi' Ayrie's son ter get that, e'en!''

'' 'Tis a lie!''

"Ye'll be thankful, Bella, that there's the Bastard willing ter take ye. There's nae many as would have a woman of twenty-five, e'en if ye'd borne Elias a whole son," he reasoned more calmly. "By the time he hears the tale told of ye, mayhap ye'll have borne William one."

"I'd rather wither than wed," she muttered bitterly. "Think you I have forgotten how 'twas with Elias? Two babes I lost ere I bore Jamie to him, and if I carried them not 'twas because he beat me until I could scarce stand! Papa, he beat me for naught: 'Twas my Scots tongue, he said . . . 'twas that the serving boy brushed my sleeve when he poured the wine . . . 'twas that any between six and sixty smiled upon me!''

'' 'Twas his right!'' His eyes met hers defensively. "And if Donald is believed, ye deserved it for whoring with Ayrie's son."

"Jamie is born of Elias! Can you not understand 'twas Elias' vanity that denied him? 'Twas Jamie's leg, Papa! Aidan of Ayrie's only sin was a smile to me!''

"And I believed ye, I'd send the brat back ter Woolford that they may feed him," he grumbled. "What need have I fer one the Devil's marked?"

The threat hung between them, frightening her. "Nay—Papa, I beg you will not! Donald has no love for him!"

"Think ye any man will look on him and still want ye?" he asked. " 'Please, Papa','' he mimicked cruelly. "Nay, Bella, but 'tis ye who will please me in this. I'd have the Butcher's favor, and God willing he'll nae see nor hear of the boy ere 'tis too late to draw back."

'' 'Tis the brother, not the Butcher who takes me," she retorted recklessly. "And I'd tell him. I'd—"

He raised his hand as though he would strike her, making her cringe. "Seven babes yer mother bore me,

and nae one son left fer hold fer me! I need the
Butcher, Bella!''

"I'd nay do it!''

He hit her then with his open palm, staggering her.
'' 'Twould seem Elias beat ye nae enough, Arabella
of Byrum, for ye've nae learned yet ter mind yer
tongue! Cost me this alliance with the lord of Dunashie, and ye'll find my hand as heavy as Woolford's!''
As she rubbed her cheek, he brushed her hand away
and caught her chin, forcing her to look into his angry
eyes. "Ye'll gather yer bride clothes, Bella, and put a
smile on yer face ere William of Dunashie comes fer
ye, d'ye hear? For if ye willna do it, I'll send yer
bastard back to Woolford.''

For a long moment she stared through welling
tears, then she swallowed the lump that rose in her
throat. Despite his grip on her chin, she managed to
nod. Satisfied, he released her.

"Ye'll nae speak of the brat to William o' Dunashie,
d'ye hear? If he draws back from this marriage, I'll
see you rue the day ye were birthed, Bella!''

As his steps receded on the stone stairs hot tears
scalded her eyes, and she sank down on a low bench,
her whole body shaking from the desperation she felt.
There was no end to the fear, no end at all, for she
had but the choice of being beaten yet again by a husband or a father, and as she saw it, 'twas no choice at
all. Sweet Mary, but she'd been born for naught but
misery. She'd go to this giant bastard—or she'd lose
her son. Sometimes it seemed to her that God had
abandoned her, that there was no reason she lived.

There was a scraping behind her, then the little boy
crawled across the floor, dragging his twisted limb
slowly, painfully through the rushes. He laid his small
hand over her knee and stared up fearfully. Forcing a
smile, Arabella reached to stroke the pale hair,
smoothing it against the bony, frail back. And the
child, the only thing she had to show for the four years
of hell Elias of Woolford had given her, somehow
managed to smile back.

They were wrong, all of them, Arabella thought as she gathered him close: Jamie of Woolford was God's gift rather than His curse. Despite his deformity, her son had the face of an angel. She sat there, stroking the soft curls, trying not to betray her terror to a child already afraid of everything. Here then was her only reason for living. Without her, Jamie would surely perish.

But she could not face another brutish husband, she could not. Merciful Mary, but if this one should prove to be like the last, she would not survive. And yet as she regarded the tousled blond head she now pressed against her breast, she knew that she had little chance of escaping the Bastard of Dunashie. But she had to, for what if he discovered the truth about Jamie? At best, he'd send the boy away. At worst, he'd be cruel to Jamie for what the child could not help. And already her son had learned to fear the loathing in men's eyes.

"Sweet Jamie," she crooned softly, "so saft and fair, Sweet Jamie, with the golden hair . . . Sweet Jamie . . ."

For answer her son snuggled closer, his frail arms clinging to her. She loved James of Woolford with an almost desperate intensity, for by his sweetness the pale, frail, boy belied the violence that had gotten him. There was nothing in the child's smile to remind Arabella of Elias or those terrible years at Woolford.

Send him to Donald? Never. Like Elias, Donald would never be brought to see this child as anything but proof of God's punishment for Arabella's imagined sins. Nay, in Donald of Woolford's keep, there would be none to care if he starved.

Her thoughts turned again to the Bastard of Dunashie. If she accepted him as husband she would again be hopelessly trapped, forced to endure whatever he would do to her and her son. Nay, she was trapped already. Utter despair overwhelmed her as she looked down on the small, fair head. "Art God's angel come to life," she murmured.

"Don't want ter be an angel," he protested, his voice muffled against the wool of her gown. "I want but two good legs."

But she was no longer listening. For in that moment it was as though God had revealed another choice to her. She'd flee Byrum ere the Bastard came there, she'd flee to the Convent of St. Andrew but a few leagues away. And surely, when the nuns saw her son, they would be moved to pity and let her stay. Nay, if she and Jamie could but cross two leagues of hill and burn unaided, they would be safe from this William of Dunashie. They would have peace and kindness. No longer would she have to fear the heavy hand of a father or a husband.

Saying only that she would distribute the stale bread her father grudgingly gave for alms, Arabella of Byrum managed to cross the lowered bridge into the village below, carrying her undersized son on her hip. Even as she walked, she held her breath lest she be discovered.

The narrow lane wound between small, one-roomed huts fashioned mostly of clay and turf, their thatched roofs brown beneath the cloudy sky, until it reached the single stone house that served the family of Byrum's bailiff. The narrow ditch that drained the offal downhill into the castle moat stank in the unseasonable warmth, for the weather felt more like August than September.

Two stout villeins gathered rushes from the bank. Seeing the lord's daughter they stood back respectfully whilst she passed, then spat after Jamie when she could not see them. A village boy gibed derisively about "the Devil's foot" under his breath, but stopped when he noted the basket of alms she carried. Instead, he called out loudly to his mother. The woman emerged from a hut, wiping dirty hands on her skirts, ready to receive the dry bread.

It was the jest of the village that Nigel of Byrum gave only that which could not be eaten without a day's

soaking in water or ale, and Arabella knew it. Even as
the woman took her half-loaf, she made honking
sounds that were answered by several geese. They
waddled from inside the hut also, then pecked at the
crust she threw down to them.

"Where is Sim's Jock?" Arabella asked, trying to
sound casually interested.

The woman jerked her head toward where a man
worked to load his hay cart. "Jock gaes ter Cockrell,"
she muttered succintly. "Fer the laird."

"Oh . . . aye."

The villein's wife managed a tired smile at Arabella
before her gaze dropped to the child on her shoulder.
And as was usual, her smile froze. Her hand crept to
her breast, as though she would sign the Cross there
against the evil spirit that had made the crippled boy.
Arabella felt the familiar rise of anger, but bit back
bitter words. These folk did but take their lead from
their lord's contempt of his grandson. Besides, Arabella had the greater need of goodwill now.

"God smiles on the weak, and even our Savior bade
the children to come to him," she said stiffly, stepping
past the woman. Smoothing her hands against the skirt
of her woolen gown, she walked toward Sim's Jock.

"Lady," Jock acknowledged her, as he continued
to pitch the hay from his allotted pile.

She bit her lip to stifle the sudden fear she felt, then
blurted out, "Would you take myself and my son with
you today—to Cockrell?" Then, realizing he'd stopped
to stare, she held out a small English coin. "I'd pay."

His pale eyes traveled over her as she waited nervously for his answer, then he shook his head. Her
heart was pounding, and yet it seemed that she did not
breathe. "Jock, I pray you. . . . For the sake of Jamie,
I cannot stay," she pleaded desperately. "He means
to send him away."

The man's eyes rested on James of Woolford for a
moment, and it was clear from the expression in them
that he too was repelled by her son. She passed her
tongue over her parched lips to wet them. "If not for

him, then for me. Jock, I brought medicine for your boy when he was fevered,'' she reminded him.

"Aye, and he'd nae ha lived without it,'' Jock admitted freely, "but—"

"I love my son even as you love yours.'' As she spoke, she nuzzled Jamie with her chin. "Despite what any thinks, God gave him to me that I would love him.'' Before he could deny her, she pressed the coin into the man's dirty hand. " 'Twill buy your boy lessons with the priest mayhap. . . . Or a piece of silk for your wife.'' She groped desperately for something that might tempt him. "Aye, or a piece of iron for your plow even. Jock—"

He looked down at the small coin in his palm, and dared to dream briefly. Then he shook his head. "Lord Nigel'd know as where I got it, and I'd nae keep it,'' he muttered.

"Hide it. Later, when 'tis forgotten that I am gone, send Jock's Sim to lessons. Mayhap he could learn to clerk,'' she ventured, trying not to recall the crudity of the lad.

"Ain't no villein's son—"

"Yours would be the first. Jock's Sim could bring you honor, Jock,'' she persisted.

He turned to stare where his boy bundled the stems of straw, struggling with them, and he dared to see him in a clean tunic, his nails pared, his hair combed, carrying the rolls of a clerk. Jock's Sim a clerk for his lordship, paid in pennies for his labor, sitting in the warmth of the lord's fire. What Auld Sim would have given to see such a thing, a grandson who did not toil in the fields. He looked again to the coin in his hand, and he wavered.

"Save my son, Jock, and I'd save yours.''

This time the man's pale eyes lifted to the wall that loomed above the village, squinting as he considered the sentries there. "I canna risk it—nae now.''

"I pray you, Jock. . . .''

His gaze dropped and he spat on the ground. "But if ye were ter get into th' cart o'er the hill, I'd take ye. I'd nae have any ter carry th' tale, fer there's still Annie and young Sim and the others ter feed, ye know.''

She looked to the castle wall also, wondering if any would note that she walked beyond the village itself. Surely none would think she could escape, or even that she would dare to try. "We'd have to be hidden—mayhap beneath the straw." Her mind raced ahead excitedly. "And I'd have to visit others, that we are not suspected."

"Aye." His leathery face scanned the sky, then he spat again. "I canna tarry past the high sun, fer I'd be back ere 'tis dark. And ye'll have ter get down ere we come ter Cockrell, fer the straw stays there." He stabbed viciously with the pitchfork, lifting another load to the cart. " 'Tis the laird's due, though what's ter feed mine own puir beasts, I canna say. A man canna plow with a starvin' ox," he muttered. "And a cow nae gives milk when she doesna eat." For a moment, he dared to meet her eyes. " 'Tis a hard laird God gives the people of Byrum, my lady."

She looked away. "Aye. And 'tis a hard sire He gives me also."

"And ye can get there, I'd take ye up in the field beyond the burn. They canna see ye there."

"Can I walk from the Cockrell road to the abbey, do you think?"

He eyed the soft shoes she wore with misgiving, then nodded. "Ye'll have sair enow feet, but aye, ye can alone. 'Tis the boy ye'll need to worrit o'er. 'Tis overfar ter carry 'im."

"There is no help for that." She managed to smile at him. "I thank you, Sim's Jock," she said sincerely. "I would that I had more to give you."

He stopped and leaned on the pitchfork to rest. "Nay. And Sim can learn, 'tis my thanks ter ye."

The rocks bruised the soles of her feet through her shoes, but she dared not leave the road that wound through the tree-covered hills lest she be lost. Already

the sun was setting, and the mists between the hills
bore the rosy hue of the western sky. But a league
more, the last man she'd passed had said, and yet
surely she'd come further than that.

Jamie weighed heavily against her shoulder, hanging on tightly, his eyes on the road they'd traveled. For
two hours of walking and more she'd talked brightly
to him, lest she betray her own worry to him, but her
determined cheer was deserting her with the descend-
ing darkness. She shifted her son to the other side,
then began to sing softly, taking what comfort she
could in the sound of her own voice. The frail child
seemed to weigh at least five stone instead of a little
more than two.

Already the peat fires from distant huts gave forth
their musty smoke, as villeins sat to eat ere they sought
their beds. And still the abbey did not loom ahead.
Her legs and back ached with every step, until she
thought she could not stand it. Finally, too weary to
go on, she set the boy down and leaned against the
sturdy trunk of a tree. Loosening the woolen girdle
wrapped at her waist, she took out the last of the stale
bread she'd carried into the village in what seemed to
have been another day. The child's eyes were luminous
in the dusky light as he reached for the crust.

"Eat slowly, and 'twill seem as though there is
more."

She sank down beside the little boy and gnawed
at the hard hunk of bread, trying not to despair.
Surely they could not be so very far away from sanc-
tuary. She closed her eyes briefly to dream of the
peace behind the cloistered walls. Strangely she'd
never before considered it, but now it seemed the
right thing to do: She would give herself to God, and
the nuns would take Jamie also. Let the Bastard find
another wife—never again would she have to cower,
afraid for her life.

"I'm nae verra hungry." Jamie's small hand pressed
the rest of his bread into hers as she looked down on
him.

It was a lie, and she knew it. In his own way, the little boy sought to give her enough to eat. "Nay, but 'tis yours, lovey—and you do not finish it, you'll not grow."

As soon as she had said it she wished back the words, for he flinched visibly. Already he was a full head shorter than other boys his age, and that, combined with his infirmity, made him the butt of their taunts. Where once he'd tried to drag the leg despite his falls, their derision had taken such a toll that he no longer even struggled to walk. Instead he clung, a pale, thin child, to her and Ena. She blinked back the tears that burned her eyes and reached to smooth his fair hair against his head, saying, "Nay, but I was going to give you mine."

He eyed her doubtfully, then took back the remainder of the crust, cramming it into his mouth as she once again stared helplessly into the darkening distance.

"Mama, will they like me there?" he asked, his words nearly lost in the mouthful of bread.

"Oh, Jamie! They are of God. Of course—" She stopped and listened intently. It was then that she heard it, and all else was forgotten. Somewhere over the gentle roll of hills bells had begun to ring, summoning the sisters and the brothers to observe Compline at their separate chapter houses. She struggled to stand on her sore, aching feet and reached a hand to her son.

"Come, lovey—we must get there ere they are all gone to bed." She leaned over to hoist him again to her shoulder.

"I would I wasna useless to ye," he whispered wistfully, as he settled his head against her neck. Then, sighing, he added, "Will they laugh at me, d'ye think?"

"Nay." Her arm squeezed him quickly. "Nuns do not laugh at such things," she promised. "And you are not useless, Jamie—God gave you to me that I would have someone to love."

Gathering new strength from the sound of the bells,

she stumbled on. A jagged rock pressed beneath the arch of a foot, sending pain shooting upward, but she dared not stop now. Not now that she knew they neared the abbey. Soon she and Jamie would have a life of peace.

At first she thought the horses behind her belonged to hunters returning home for the night, but then she realized that there were too many of them, and that they were being ridden far too hard. Clasping Jamie close, she forgot her sore feet and tried to run for the woods ere she was overtaken. It was an impossible flight. As the horses bore down on her she fell, tumbling and rolling, trying to shield the child's body with her own.

Her father dismounted and walked slowly to where she lay, her head down to hide her tears. Beneath her Jamie struggled, pinned between her and the muddy ditch.

"Mama—mamaaaa!" he wailed.

"Where did ye think ter gae?" Nigel shouted above her.

And once again the awful terror closed around her heart, until she could not breathe. "Answer me!" Even as he spoke, he pulled her up roughly. "Answer me, ye foolish hinny! Where, I said—*where?*"

"Nay!" Jamie pushed frantically at Nigel's leg. "Nay! Ye'll nae . . . Mama dinna—"

Nigel shook loose angrily, kicking him to the ground. Arabella, for all her fear of her father, bent down to lift her son beneath Nigel's furious scowl. "Keep the brat away from me! Jesu, but 'tis a sufferance that I feed him!" he shouted at her. "Now, where is it you thought to go?" he demanded again.

"The nuns," she mumbled.

"Where?" he yelled, shaking her. "Afore God, I'd hear ye tell me!"

"The nuns!" she answered more defiantly. "I was taking Jamie to the nuns!"

"The nuns," he sneered. "And ye think they would welcome *that?* What would they want with ain as canna even walk? He is but a worthless mouth ter feed! Nay, but they would know him for the sign of your sin!''

"He is God's creature also!'' she cried, holding the boy against her. Jamie's arms tightened convulsively around her neck, and Arabella knew he was frightened. "He is God's creature also!'' she shouted again. " 'Tis not right what you do to him!''

"Afore God, I'll brook nae insolence from ye!'' he yelled, striking her. "And I had the time, I'd beat ye now rather than wait until I get ye home!'' As she reeled he dragged the little boy from her, shaking the terrified child before pushing him toward a man-at-arms. "She would take the brat ter the nuns, would she? Nay, 'tis too good for him—'tis ter Woolford he goes on the morrow!'' Leaning closer until his eyes glittered but inches from Arabella's, he gibed, "Or would ye that I sent him ter Ayrie? D'ye think Duncan would welcome Aidan's brat any more than I do? D'ye think he would welcome ain with the Devil's mark?''

It did no good to deny again that Jamie was Aidan's son, for there was none from Byrum as believed her. "Nay,'' she answered wearily. "You'll not send him, Papa, for if you do, I'll not wed this William of Dunashie. And you'll not hit me again, I think, for if you mark me he'll think me ugly.''

"The Bastard willna want him,'' he growled, concealing his triumph. Then, wanting her to confirm her defeat, he pressed her. "Ye'll wed with the Butcher's brother? I'd hear ye say it.''

"Aye.'' Her throat constricted, making speech nearly impossible, as she knelt to comfort her small child. "Come, Jamie,'' she whispered painfully. " 'Tis all right.''

"Ye are nae to speak of the brat ere ye are safely contracted, Bella,'' Nigel warned her sternly. "The boy stays from sight.'' Turning to the others, he added, "And if any amongst ye speaks of Ayrie's son before Moray or his brother, I'll hang ye. I'd nae have any betray my daughter's shame to them, d'ye hear?''

They rode back in stony silence, she hunched forward to shelter her son from the damp chill of the night. Beside her, her father ignored both of them. But he had what he'd wanted: She'd wed Giles of Moray's bastard brother, giving him the bond of blood between them he needed.

Telling herself that no matter what her husband would do to her, it could be no worse than what she'd endured at Elias' hands, she forced herself to acknowledge the inevitable. She would wed, and hope that this lord would die also. Hopefully this time she would bear an heir, and she'd not ever have to return to Byrum.

Chapter Three

It was still warm for September, but the clouds overhead promised a change. Torn between wishing for rain and cursing the probability of it, William of Dunashie removed his helmet to wipe his sweating forehead with the back of his hand. It did little good for a man to ride forth in his finery if the best he could do was either stink from the heat or be soaked to the skin.

He looked down to where the bright blue silk covered the mail on his forearm. Aye, he was arrayed as fine as a peacock, he knew, but would Arabella of Byrum not see the ill-bred bastard beneath? Despite the fancy clothes he wore, despite his newly shortened hair or his clean-shaven face, would she not recognize the new lord of Blackleith for what he was: a man better suited to serve than be served? And would she not think him unworthy of her? She had, after all, been wed before to an English lord of some substance. Beyond that he knew nothing of her, not even if she were short or tall, fat or lean, bonny or ill-favored. But it mattered not, he supposed, for there were not many as would wed a poor border bastard. Whatever she looked like, he would take her gratefully, and he would get his sons of her.

At first the thought of taking a wife, coupled with the news that Giles meant to invest him with even so small a keep as Blackleith, had elated him beyond measure. But now reality had set in and he had great misgivings about both. He'd neither led nor wed before, and at thirty-two he wondered if he was over old to begin either. Yet he dared not betray his doubts, for Giles was proud of what he'd done for his bastard brother.

He cast a sidewise glance at the man he'd served for twenty-seven of those thirty-two years, and he felt a surge of his own pride. They'd been through much together: the exile, Dunashie, Giles' miserable marriage to Aveline de Guelle, too many battles to count. . . . But now the boy he'd tended had grown to a man of great worth. Giles of Moray not only held Dunashie, but now he'd taken Count Guy of Rivaux's proud daughter for a wife, and he had risen in royal favor.

William's thoughts again turned inward. He was William, Lord of Blackleith, vassal to the lord of Dunashie. He was William, ruler of his own small demesne. He was William, who rode this day to see Nigel of Byrum's daughter.

"Art silent," Giles chided him, smiling.

"Och, but I was thinking how ye've risen, and 'tis proud I am of ye," Will answered. "And 'tis loath I am ter leave ye." His hazel eyes dared to meet his brother's black ones. "But then ye've no need fer me now, I suppose."

"Is that what ails you? Or is it that you fear Byrum's daughter will not be comely?"

"A wee bit o' both," Will admitted candidly. " 'Tis more like she'll nae think me favored, ye know. And 'tis bound to weigh with her that my dam was naught but a village lass."

Giles appeared to consider him, then his smile broadened to a grin. "You look well enough to me."

"Och, but yer not a woman, are ye?" Will retorted. " 'Tis to be hoped that she doesna cower and weep, as Aveline de Guelle did fer ye," he added glumly. "She hasna seen me, after all."

"Aveline hated and feared me for burning Dunashie, Will—'twas that she blamed me for killing Hamon of Blackleith and his family."

They both fell silent at that, for even eleven years later the burning still weighed on Giles' conscience. And with each silently passing league, William's misgivings grew. His experience with women was limited, with ladies nigh on nonexistent, although he'd learned to discourse with Elizabeth of Rivaux, he had to admit. But Giles' wife was different. Despite her sex 'twas easy to count her a man's equal, for she considered it her due. Yet for all he liked Elizabeth, he'd not have one of her high temper. Nay, there were none others like Rivaux's daughter, he consoled himself.

But still he worried. Feeling the pain of bastardy himself, he'd lain with none of the village girls, for he'd been loath to bring another bastard into the world. Nay, but when he'd burned until he could not stand it, he'd sought out only whores, saying that any babes they dropped could not be laid to him alone. It was the jest of Dunashie that the woman Berta charged him more than she did the others, all the while complaining that she was not made for a giant. Yet she always seemed glad enough of his money, and she never accused him of hurting her. But she'd been with so many, and had borne a swarm of bastards.'Twas hard to tell by her if his size would frighten another.

And that was another of his fears. What if the Lady Arabella was small? Giles had not seen her and could not say. All Nigel of Byrum had told him was that she was not barren, for there was a child born of her first union to Elias of Wolford. That she had been wed before relieved William somewhat. It would not be like taking a frightened virgin, he supposed. Unless his big body terrified her.

He looked down to the horse beneath him, the huge

bay he favored for traveling. Unlike others who chose
smaller beasts with easier paces for riding, he'd had to
have a war-horse gelded for the purpose. That too had
been a jest at Dunashie: Wee Willie would bow the
back of a palfrey, 'twas said. Overtall and weighing
eighteen stone, he was acutely aware of what an oddity
he was. He could not blame Byrum's daughter if she
quaked at the sight of him.

" 'Twould seem we are awaited,'' Giles observed
suddenly, breaking into William's almost morose reverie. "The bridge comes down."

Momentary panic assailed the big man as he looked
up the moss-covered wall. This then was Byrum, home
to the woman he would wed. Resolutely, he squared
his broad shoulders and reached to smooth his thick
hair. Of all that had ever been said of him, there'd
been none to call him coward. And one mere woman
could not be worse than the many warriors he'd faced
in battle, he reassured himself. Yet despite his resolve
to see the matter through, this day he'd rather have
ridden to war, for at least he knew how to fight.

"One small matter, Will,'' Giles murmured for his
ears alone. "Ere the Lady Arabella marks you for
naught but a border lout, you'd best speak as you
learned at Henry's court. She is more like to have a
care for that than for your size."

"Then 'tis time she gains an ear fer the Scots
tongue,'' Will retorted. "If I wouldna change that e'en
fer King Henry, I'll nae change it fer a Scots-born
woman.'' But even as he said it, he was not entirely
sure. How much he would be willing to please his
bride depended on how pleased he was with her.

Arabella knelt on the high wall to watch the approaching mesnie anxiously. At first they were little
more than specks in the distance, filing in a line over
the hills, and then they moved slowly, almost sedately
into view. She judged there must be fifty or more of
them.

They stopped and reformed into neat columns, three

abreast, then one broke from their ranks to ride forward, shouting loudly, "Behold, 'tis the lord of Dunashie as comes!"

"Enter and welcome!" her father's seneschal called out from further down the wall.

"Mama, they are come," Jamie murmured nervously, clutching the cloth at her shoulder.

"Aye." Exhaling slowly to hide her fear from her son, she held him closer and tried to discern which man was the Butcher and which the Bastard, for both were said to be exceedingly tall. Two men rode at the front, one whose face was obscured by the helm he wore, the other bare-headed, his dark red hair cropped short like a Norman's. As there were those who called the Butcher "Black Giles," she surmised the red-headed one must be the Bastard, and her heart sank like a rock within her breast. Merciful Mary, but even from the distance she could tell he was the biggest man she'd ever seen.

"By the rood but they are big, Mama," Jamie observed with wonder.

"Aye," Arabella half whispered through lips parched with dread.

The thought that here was one who could probably kill her with one blow came unbidden to her mind. She froze there, unable to think of aught else. If she angered him, he would kill her. And as the knowledge chilled her, she realized also that he was not nearly as old as she'd thought. She'd not outlive this man.

"Your lord father would not have you come down ere he sends for you, my lady," a boy spoke behind her. "And he said the lord of Blackleith is not to see the child."

"Aye," she answered hollowly, tearing her gaze from William of Dunashie. She wiped her clammy palms against her gown and nodded. "Take James to Ena, I pray you, and ask that he be kept from my father's sight."

"Mama . . ."

"Nay, I'd meet him first, Jamie," she said quickly.

"I'd tell him you go to Blackleith with me, else I'd not go." She forced a smile as she smoothed the unruly blond curls. "Go on. Tonight I will tell you of this William of Dunashie."

"He will be displeased, won't he?" he asked timidly. For a moment, his eyes sparkled with tears. "He won't want me. . . . I know it."

" 'Tis to be hoped that he is a kind man, Jamie. I have prayed 'tis so. He cannot be worse than Papa, after all," she added without conviction.

After they'd disappeared down the inner steps, Arabella tried to compose her thoughts ere she was summoned. For a moment she clung to the hope that the Bastard would not find her pleasing, that he would draw back from the marriage. But in her heart she knew that even had she been an infant or a crone, he'd still take her—it mattered not at all what she thought or wanted. She was merely the bond between two families, nothing more. Her body and her blood were but the seal upon an alliance between the family that held Dunashie and her own.

When she dared to look down again the mesnie was already inside the courtyard, and the ostlers were taking reins from the riders. The one she'd marked for the Bastard still sat astride his huge horse, waiting for his brother to dismount first. He was directly beneath her, scarce thirty feet below now, and she tried to study him dispassionately, seeing thighs that reminded her of trees and broad, powerful shoulders beneath silk and mail. He looked up, scanning the wall, giving her a glimpse of his face. It was impassive, grim almost, and rather forbidding. He looked less a man come to wed than one come on unpleasant business. She drew back before he could see her, then watched from behind the stone as he swung down.

From behind him a squire took the lord of Dunashie's helmet and heavy gloves, as her father moved to greet the Butcher he'd once called an "upstart." Now, after spending a week readying Byrum to receive the man who'd wed Rivaux's daughter, Nigel was bowing obsequiously to Giles of Moray.

" 'Twas a pleasant journey?" he asked, his voice carrying upward.

"Well enough. Mine enemies were elsewhere."

"Nay, ye grow too great for enemies," Nigel said smoothly. "There's nae a man as dares face ye in the field."

"And many who do not fear my back. But it does not matter, for we are safely arrived." The Butcher turned to the redhaired giant, beckoning him forward. "My lord of Byrum, I give you William of Dunashie, my brother. He now holds Blackleith of me."

"Aye. I bid ye both welcome for myself and my daughter.'Tis not every day a father celebrates the betrothal of his eldest girl, my lords." His eyes moved upward to the Bastard's face. "She is most pleased with the match."

"I see her not."

"Ah, she orders supper fer ye. Would ye see her now, or when ye sit down to the meal?"

The big man looked up to the wall where she hid, then back to her father. And again his face was grim. "Now. I'd see her ere I sup."

"Oh . . . aye. She is all I have told your brother, and so ye'll see. Come inside that I may send for her.'Tis pleased ye'll be with her, I promise ye," Nigel added emphatically. "Comely and biddable, and what more could a man ask?" he added when William's expression did not lighten.

"She is a widow?"

"Aye, and if she seems overquiet ter ye, 'tis that she has mourned Elias of Woolford overlong.'Tis time and more that she wed again," Arabella heard Nigel say as he guided them through the tower door. "Ye'll be pleased wi' her," he repeated, "for she has been schooled to meekness."

"Still, I'd see her with mine own eyes."

Her stomach knotted, and she had to close her eyes against the awful nausea she felt. Mother Mary, but she'd not go to this man. She leaned her head against the cool stone and waited for her father's summons. For a moment she considered taking Jamie down with her in defiance of Nigel, but she knew if the Bastard refused her when he saw her son, then her father would send the boy to Woolford. Nay, but she *had* to please William of Dunashie.

It was not long ere a serving boy appeared behind her on the wall. "My lady . . ." He waited until she turned to him to deliver his unwelcome message.

"Lord Nigel would have you come to him in the solar."

There was no help for it, and she knew it. She rose with effort, still hoping against hope that somehow the Bastard would discover a reason not to take her, and smoothed the skirt of her best gown. Following the boy down the dark, winding inner stairs, she prayed silently, fervently: *Let him find me unpleasing. Let him decide I am not what he would have. Sweet Jesu, let him refuse to take me. And let Nigel not blame me for it.*

The room that had once been her mother's work place as well as bedchamber was well furnished by Scottish standards, with cushioned benches and low tables along one wall. As she entered it, all three men rose from where they drank of her father's mead to face her, but it was Nigel who came to get her. His fingers closed tightly over her arm as though to warn her, and he thrust her forward, saying, "Behold Arabella of Byrum, my lords."

The Butcher smiled pleasantly, but his brother drained his mead and placed the cup on the table ere he acknowledged the presentation with a nod. Then both walked closer. Nigel dropped her arm and caught her chin, forcing it upward.

"Did I not promise she is comely?" he demanded of them.

To cover his nervousness, William studied her silently for a moment, astonished. The smell of roses wafted upward as he stared. Comely? Nay, she was more than that—she was prettier than he'd imagined possible. Her hair was more than fair—it was somewhere between silver and gold—and her eyes were a clear, ringed grey, making them the most unusual he'd seen. And she was possessed of fine, straight features set within an oval face. She was not as tall as he had hoped, but neither was she overly short, for her head would come high against his breast.

She was regarding him much as a hare might look at the man who had trapped it, and he knew at that moment that she was far too beautiful for the likes of him. His heart pounded even as he stared.

She wanted to look away from beneath his gaze but her father's fingers held her chin still, and she had no choice but to meet the hazel eyes of the man before her. As big as he'd seemed on the great horse he appeared even larger now, seeming to tower over her as he regarded her intently with those fine hazel eyes. A thin white scar crossed one cheek, ending where his helm must have stopped the blow. The thought crossed her mind that although he would never be mistaken for anything but a fighting man, there was a rugged handsomeness about his face. If only he would smile, if only he would give her some hope . . . but he did not.

This then was the husband her father would give her: this big, silent man. Even as she stared upward into his face she could not entirely hide her panic.

"Well?" Nigel asked impatiently. "What say ye?"

Finally, William of Dunashie nodded. "Aye, she is comely," he answered, in a voice that sounded strange to his ears.

"Do ye take her?"

Arabella sucked in her breath and held it, afraid to breathe as she awaited his answer. The blood pounded in her temples, yet her hands were as ice.

As uneasy as he felt before her, William forced himself to look at her again. Would he take her? Only a fool would refuse such a wife. He exhaled fully, then nodded. "And she is willing, I am satisfied. But I'd hear it of her. What say ye, mistress: Would ye have me also?''

''She is willing,'' Nigel answered for her. He released her chin and grasped her arm again. ''She is well pleased with the marriage.''

''Nay, I'd hear her say it.''

She wanted to cry out that she had no wish to wed him or any, that she was not willing, but even as she hesitated her father's grip tensed. And she knew that if she answered truthfully, Jamie would be lost to her forever. She closed her eyes briefly and swallowed. ''Aye.''

Her answer was barely loud enough to be heard. When she dared to look at him again, William of Dunashie's eyes had narrowed. ''I'd take none as would nae have me,'' he told Nigel.

''Aye,'' she answered again, this time more audibly.

He stepped back, apparently satisfied, and her father eased his hold on her, saying, ''She is as meek and obedient as I can make her, my lord.'' Before she knew what Nigel meant to do his hand had moved to the girdle at her waist, loosening it. Panicked, she wanted to flee.

''Nay, Papa . . .''

''Would you see that she is whole, my lords? The women tell me she's as slender as a girl half her age.''

Will saw the blood drain from her face, and he felt sorry for her. He shook his head. ''Nay, I accept she is whole and unblemished, for there is a child, I am told.''

''She gave Elias of Woolford one son.''

''It doesna matter then, for she isna barren. D'ye have the boy here, or is he at Woolford?'' Even as he asked he turned to pick up his empty cup, holding it out with shaking hand to the lad who still held the pitcher of mead.

It was then that she found her voice. ''I pray you, my lord—I'd take my son to Blackleith also. I'd not be parted from him.'' Ignoring Nigel's frown, she blurted out, ''He's but a wee boy, and—''

Will swung around. "How old is he?"

She bit her lip, afraid that he would deny her, afraid that he would say Jamie ought to be sent away. "He has but six years, my lord, and is small." Behind her, Nigel snorted. "But he is possessed of a sweet nature, and he'll not trouble you, I swear. I pray you—"

The desperation in her voice was not lost on Will. Nodding, he interrupted her. "And his sire's family doesna wish to have him, he is welcome in mine house, Lady Arabella."

She lowered her gaze, staring at the heavy boots he wore. "Elias had other sons, and they've no love for Jamie, my lord. They've not seen him since I returned to my father's keep while he was yet a small babe."

"Fie on them, then. A good man doesna turn away from his blood."

When she dared to look up she thought she saw kindness in his eyes but then it passed. He turned to his brother, saying, "And the dowry satisfies ye, 'tis settled." Then, thinking he ought to say something beyond that, he looked to her again. "Aye, mistress, and ye can stomach me, 'tis pleased enough I am with ye."

"Two hundred silver pennies," Nigel promised. "There isna land. . . ."

" 'Tis enough," Giles answered. "He'll have the greater need of the money."

She looked from one to the other of them, aware that her life had been settled between them. She was going to Blackleith with this giant of a man. She would lie with him, she would bear his children, and she would submit to his will in all things. Despite the air of unreality, something in her chest tightened until she could scarce breathe.

It was done. The lovely woman before him was going to be his to take. Never again would he have to pay a whore for what he would have of a woman. William's eyes traveled from her face to the swell of her breasts, then to her slender waist, and his mouth went

dry with the realization that Arabella of Byrum, a lady
born, would come to him, would lie in his bed. But
even as he looked at her, he thought she flinched beneath his all-too-hungry gaze. Reminding himself that
she was no free-favored whore, he forced himself to
answer, "And it pleases ye, mistress. I'd thought as
ye be a widow we'd wed without the banns, but if ye're
not of that mind I'd share betrothal vows now and
come back fer ye. Otherwise, I'd take ye with me on
the morrow."

It did not matter, and she knew it. Whether it was
now or whether it was next month or even next year,
it would happen. And yet she would stall, if she dared.

When she did not answer, Will smiled wryly. "I'd
thought to be wed while my brother is here for witness, mistress. Aye, I'd hoped to take ye to Blackleith
with me."

"The Lady Elizabeth . . ." she began helplessly.
"Would you not have her come also?"

"My wife awaits childbed and does not travel now,"
Giles responded, disappointing Nigel, who'd hoped to
see Rivaux's daughter at the wedding. "But she has
hopes Arabella will come to Dunashie when the babe
is born." He turned to the woman Will would wed.
"She is eager for your acquaintance, lady."

Arabella did not mistake her father's frown. He
wanted the alliance with the Butcher, and he wanted
it now. She sucked in her breath, then exhaled slowly.
"As you wish, Lord William—it matters not to me."
She held out a hand so cold it was numb.

"Then I'd hear ye bound by yer oath," Nigel insisted.

Lord William. The words were so new to his mind
that it was as though she spoke to another. Nonetheless, knowing now that she did not reject him, Will
reached to clasp her fingers between his, nodding as
he did so. He cleared his throat.

His voice stronger than he felt, he pledged, "I, William of Dunashie, lord to Blackleith, promise to wed

you, Arabella of Byrum, on the morrow, as God, Nigel of Byrum, and Giles of Moray witness.''

It was her turn. Her throat felt almost too tight for speech as she responded low, ''And I, Arabella of Byrum, promise to take you, William of Dunashie, for husband on the morrow, before God and witnesses.''

She was betrothed to the Bastard of Dunashie, and there was naught left to be said now. Pulling her hand from his, she managed a quick bob of obeisance. ''I pray you will pardon me, but there is much to be done ere you sup, and . . .'' Her eyes darted to Giles of Moray. ''Your leave, my lord. Papa.''

''Aye.''

Will followed her into the stairwell, waiting until they were beyond the hearing of the others to speak. ''Mistress . . . Lady Arabella . . .'' He hesitated, wanting her to know he was no great oaf come to take her from her home, even if it meant speaking the stiff Norman tongue.

She stopped, afraid he meant to touch her. ''Aye?''

''My brother and I would have a bath ere we sup.'' It was not what he'd wanted to say, but the look in her eyes did not encourage him. ''If you would order the tub . . .'' His voice trailed off, for want of anything else he could think of to tell her.

''Aye, my lord.'' She started again down the stairs, then stopped once more, this time to look back up at him from a safe distance. ''My thanks, my lord.''

''For what?''

''For accepting I am whole.''

A smile of understanding warmed his face, and he nodded. ''I did not want any other looking on you,'' he said simply. '' 'Tis not meet that they do.''

''I will order the tub for you.''

Once again she was going, and still he would speak with her. ''Mistress . . .'' He reddened slightly as she turned around again, then blurted out the first thing that came to mind. ''You are as lovely as the rosewater you wear, you know. 'Tis pleased I am with the match.''

"My father is pleased also."

Feeling a clumsy fool, he let her go then and returned to Nigel's mead. For once in his life he wished he'd paid more attention to Lang Gib, for there was a man who knew how to flatter a woman. Lang Gib would not have stood there like a great foolish bear, prating of rosewater, he was certain.

It was not until she'd reached the bottom of the dark, winding stairs that she realized he could, when he wanted to, speak like a Norman. But that too did not matter: If he'd carried himself like a belted earl, he could not change the fact that he'd been born a border lord's bastard, nor could he change his size. For a brief moment she recalled his smile, then she forced herself to remember that there had been a time when Elias also had pretended kindness, a time before she'd been delivered into his power. And with that memory she clasped her arms tightly about her, hugging them against her shivering body.

Chapter Four

Her heart pounding, she carried the soap and towels up the stairs to the second-story chamber directly below her father's. She was being foolish, and she knew it, but she had no wish to bathe either the Butcher or the Bastard. Soon enough she would have to endure William of Dunashie's giant body over hers, and she would postpone seeing it as long as possible.

The door was slightly ajar. Balancing the drying sheets on one arm, she pushed the heavy iron bar. At the same time someone on the other side pulled, and she nearly lost her balance, stumbling into William of Dunashie. He caught her arms to steady her, then released her and stepped back, seemingly surprised to see her. His hazel eyes took in the folded towels on her arm, and his mouth twisted into a wry smile.

"Fer me, mistress? Nay, but ye are too late, fer I've bathed." She would have babbled out an apology but he stopped her, and the smile broadened into a grin. " 'Tis daft ye must think me, but I've nae been a lord lang enow to expect ye ter do it fer me." To demonstrate that he had indeed been washed, he combed his wet hair with one hand, spotting the linen undertunic that clung to his still damp body. "And 'tis drapping on ye I am."

His accent was thicker than before, making her wonder if he'd been drinking. He followed her gaze to the table by the bedstead. "Aye, but nae more than a wee bit o' mead frae th' jug." His hazel eyes twinkled at the lift of her brow. "Well, mayhap more than a drap," he conceded, "but nae enough to make me a danger to ye."

The tub still sat before the brazier, its water covered with a waxy film. "Lord Giles?" she asked, backing away from him.

"Och, but I was second in the water, mistress. Lord Giles is below with yer sire."

"Oh."

The sun filtered through the oiled parchment that had been stretched over the arched window, giving the small room a strange, yellowish glow. He watched the light catch her braids, making them nearly gold where they fell forward over her breasts. Comely? Nay, she was beautiful, and she was going to be his. Never again would he have to press a coin into Berta's hand to get what he would have of a woman. As he looked on Arabella of Byrum desire raced unbidden through his veins, heating his body, making his mouth dry. He dared to move closer. And once again the scent of roses floated before him, enticing him.

She'd seen that expression in the eyes of other men before, and it had always unsettled her, but in this instance she felt an even greater panic. On the morrow this hulking, ill-bred man would lie with her. Involuntarily, she took another step backward. The soap slipped from her hands, thunking against the planked floor.

"Ye think me nae but an uncouth lout, don't ye?" he asked.

"Nay," she lied, running her tongue over her lips nervously. "Uh . . . as you are bathed, there is naught left to be done. I will see you at supper, my lord."

But he was loath to see her go. Telling himself that

he did but wish to gain her acquaintance ere they were wed, he gestured to the benches that had been drawn close to the tub. "And ye can spare the time, I'd hae ye stay fer speech, mistress. . . . I'd know of ye." Again he ran his fingers through his dripping hair. "Aye—and I'd take a towel of ye also." When she continued to stare as though she would run, he reached for the drying sheet, lifting it from her arm. "Sit a wee bit. I'd nae ask ye to dry my head."

If she refused she'd anger him, and yet she was afraid to stay. Her heart thudded painfully, and her fingers were icy as she clasped them before her. Finally, she nodded.

"I'd nae devour ye, mistress." As he spoke he shook out the woolen sheet and began to rub his head vigorously, leaning to keep from spotting the linen undertunic further. Out of the corner of his eye he watched her take a seat on the furthest bench, and, suddenly remembering Giles' advice, he tried to keep the border dialect from his speech. "Tell me," he asked her in carefully measured tones, "how is it that you have remained so long unwed?"

As though she could hold her fear of him in check, she clasped her hands more tightly in her lap. "There was none to ask for me."

"Your father gave you the choice?" He finished rubbing the water from his hair, then dropped the towel onto the closer bench. He smoothed his hair with the palms of his hands, pressing it to lie against his head. "Nay, but I'd not believe none asked."

"If any did, Papa did not tell me." She looked up briefly, meeting his gaze, then dropped her eyes to stare at the water spots on the floor. " 'Twas to his comfort to keep me here, I think," she lied.

"And now?"

"And now he would ally himself with one who rises in King David's favor. He has hopes the Bu—that Lord Giles—will bring him to Scotland's notice."

" 'Tis not Giles he gives you to, mistress," he reminded her. Then, for want of anything else to say to her, he blurted out, "Does my bastardy weigh with you? Does it touch your pride? Is that why you do not speak overmuch to me?" Moving closer to stand above her, he willed her to look at him. "For all your words before your father, you do not appear eager for the morrow, Arabella of Byrum." Ere she could answer he added, "I'd have naught but truth between us."

"I have accepted Papa's will in this, my lord." Her chin came up, and once more she met his eyes. "He did not give me the choice." Then, realizing again that she risked angering him, she hastened to add, "And the morrow is but sudden to me, for I do not know you."

"Then why said you 'twas your will to wed with me? Again I'd ask ye: Does my bastardy weigh with you?" he repeated. "I'd have you answer both, and you do not mind it. How is it that you pledged to me?"

She wanted to cry out that she'd done it to save her son, but there was no use saying it now, not now that they were irrevocably tied by the betrothal vows. Instead she sought to placate him. "Because Papa willed it—and your bastardy matters not to me," she answered simply. Sucking in her breath she held it for a moment, then exhaled fully. "I'd have your kindness, my lord. And you give me that, I will try to be a good wife to you."

She spoke low, but there was an appeal in the grey eyes that was more eloquent than her words. "Art afraid of me, mistress?" he dared to ask. "I'd nae harm ye."

She started to deny her fear, then looked again to the floor. "Aye."

He shifted his weight uneasily, groping for the words to reassure her, trying to bridge the awkwardness between them. "For all that I look otherwise, if I am not overgentle I am not an overharsh man either, Arabella," he said quietly. "I have hope there will be love between us."

She sat very still. "As have I, my lord."

He felt unbearably clumsy before her, and yet he wanted very much to touch her. His hand reached out to brush against one of her plaints. "Art bonny," he murmured, "aye—comelier than I expected."

"Papa says I am overtall and far too thin."

"Mayhap 'tis because he is short and heavy. Nay, I'd find no fault with your size or your countenance, mistress." Even as he said it it sounded foolish to his ears, and he wished he were as Lang Gib. "You please me well."

His voice was soft, easing her apprehension a little. Her hands relaxed slightly, and she forced a smile. " 'Tis kind of you to say, my lord."

"Arabella . . ." Again he felt a great ox, and yet he wanted more than a weak smile from her. "And I swear I'll nae touch you wrongly, would ye give me a kiss fer the betrothal?" he asked, lapsing once again into more familiar speech.

She had not the right to refuse him. Yet she sat there, every fiber of her being crying *nay*. "Aye—if 'tis your will," she managed finally. Then, realizing that he probably could not bend that low, she stood, letting the remaining towel slip from her arm unheeded to the floor. Wiping suddenly damp palms against the skirt of her gown, she tried not to flinch as he moved still closer. When his hands clasped her shoulders, then slid lightly down her arms, she closed her eyes and swallowed.

She held herself as stiff as one of the wooden quintains used in battle practice. And as his hands skimmed over her arms, she shuddered.

" 'Tis trembling ye are, mistress," he murmured. Nonetheless, after the first tentative touch, he was emboldened to embrace her with the awkwardness of an untried youth. He bent his head to hers, seeking her lips. They were cold and unresponsive beneath his. She felt like stone.

" 'Twas your kiss I asked—nae mine. But one fer

the morrow," he coaxed, tightening his arms about
her. "I'd nae hurt ye, I swear it."

Despite his nearly overwhelming size, his breath
against her face was soft, almost caressing. And there
was no violence in his embrace. Very slowly, she
stretched to hold him also, smelling the strong fragrance of the lye soap he'd used. Obediently she
pressed her lips against his, tasting the lingering
sweetness of her father's mead. Halfhearted or no, it
was all the encouragement he needed.

She was slender in his arms, and when she reached
to place her hands around his neck, her breasts enticed
his body through the linen of his undertunic, sending
a rush of fire through him. His hands moved over her
back and upward to her shoulders, holding her as his
mouth teased hers the way Berta had liked, urging her
response.

There was a moment's hesitation, then her lips
parted, yielding, and he took possession, sliding his
tongue between her teeth. His arms crushed her to
him, blotting from his mind all but the feel of her body
against his.

He was as warm as she was cold, and despite her
fear of him she was drawn to that warmth. Her hands
clasped his neck, holding him, feeling the muscle and
sinew there, marveling at the strength and power of
the man.

Her response this time chased his promise from his
mind. Telling himself that this was no unknowing virgin, that the betrothal made her his to take, he gave
over to his rising desire. His pulse pounded and the
blood raced, coursing through him, flooding his body
with liquid fire.

She was drowning, overwhelmed by the force and
suddenness of his desire. It was as though her whole
being had been enveloped by the big man who held
her, until she felt his hands slide possessively over her
hips. His fingers gathered the soft material of her
gown, lifting her skirt, baring the backs of her legs.
Frantic to escape before he lost his senses completely,

she struggled, pushing at his arms, twisting her body away from the heat, tearing her mouth from his. "Mother Mary, I beg of you—nay!" she gasped. "You said you would not touch me wrongly!"

Disappointed, he released her and stepped back. "Nay, mistress, I'd nae meant to give ye a fright of me." Yet even as he spoke his breathing was ragged, his eyes darkened with his desire. "I can wait fer the morrow. 'Twill be enough that ye come to me then."

Drawing a deep breath, he turned away to pick up the discarded towels, taking the time to master himself. Swinging back around, he could see she still regarded him like a hare ready to run, and he felt shame. "Ye behold before ye but a flesh-and-blood man, Arabella of Byrum, and I'd give ye nae cause to fear me. And ye keep my household in order and give me fine sons, ye'll nae find me a hard husband." He held out the towels, but she made no move. "I did but mean to show ye I was pleased with ye," he added quietly.

He could see her swallow again as he took a step toward her, and his own words, *Ye think me nae but an uncouth lout, don't ye?* echoed in his ears. And again it was important that he have standing in her eyes. He breathed deeply. And when he spoke, he tried once more to speak as he'd learned to at King Henry's court. He lifted his hand so that the new signet ring that marked him for Blackleith's lord flashed in the yellow light.

" 'Twas too sudden, and I beg pardon for my eagerness," he told her as he laid the towels across her arm. "I'd but meant to learn of you. I'd know where I wed, and I'd have you know of me." She backed away, nearly stumbling over the bench. "Is there aught you would ask of me?"

The wooden bench turned over heavily, unnerving her further. "Nay," he managed, stepping around it. From the safety of distance she faced him, saying quickly, "And you'd eat, I'd best go, my lord. There is much to be done ere we sup."

He reached toward her, not so much to touch her

but rather in a helpless gesture of contrition, and then he let his hand fall. He'd bungled the matter badly already, and he knew it.

"Aye. Until we sup, mistress."

Clutching the towels to her, she started toward the door. "Until we sup, my lord."

Still, he'd not have her leave like that. He'd not have her still afraid of him. His eyes caught the soap on the floor where she'd dropped it, and he stopped to pick it up. "Wait."

She stopped, acutely aware that he moved behind her. Even the flesh on her neck prickled as he again came closer. For a moment, she considered fleeing headlong down the stairs. Instead, she waited warily.

"You forgot this," he said, reaching around her to press the chunk into her hand.

"My thanks," she murmured, eager to be gone from him.

He could think of naught more to say to her, and yet he felt the need to show her he was more than the rutting boar she'd seen. He had to touch her again. "How old are you, Arabella?" he blurted out, for want of anything better to ask.

"Four and twenty—'twill be five and twenty come April, my lord. And—"

Before she knew what he meant to do, he turned her around. And this time his lips brushed hers lightly, scarce touching her ere she could duck away. Then he dropped his hands. "Be off with you now, else I'll not want to wait for the morrow."

"Aye," she whispered. "Aye." She fled then, leaving him alone. It was not until she'd reached the bottom of the dark, dank stairwell that she stopped to lean against the rough stone wall. She stood there, holding the chiseled stone for balance, shaking uncontrollably. Sweet Mary, but she would be at his mercy on the morrow.

He listened to the quickness of her steps on the stairs until he could hear no more. Turning back to where his new, richly embroidered tunic hung from a peg, he considered whether he should finish dressing and join Giles below. Instead, he moved slowly to the rope-hung bed and lay down upon it. For a long time he stared upward into the canopy, seeing not the faded silk but rather a face framed in braids of gold so pale 'twas almost silver, smelling not the musty stone walls but rather the fragrance of roses. "Och," he murmured aloud, "ye've but seen her and already you are besotted, fool that ye are. At two and thirty, ye ought to have more sense to ye."

Supper at Byrum was an early and sparse affair, owing to Nigel's parsimony. He'd not burn the tallow late and waste it, he'd told Arabella again and again when she had complained. But this night his guests did not appear to note the lack of variety in the fare, despite the fact that the single stag was supplemented only by coney and salmon, both boiled, and the other dishes were pitifully few.

Embarrassed by her father's perceived poverty, Arabella watched silently as William of Dunashie carved a rabbit's leg and laid it on her end of their shared trencher. Then, making no comment about the poorness of the meal, he spooned boiled barley over it. One of the two serving boys held out a bowl of stewed onions, and her betrothed added some of those also.

"Would you have some of this?" he asked politely, his hand moving to the dish of oatmeal and prunes.

"Nay."

He placed a dollop on his end of the trencher, then pushed both bowls aside. Unlike her father, who always fell upon his food with unseemly eagerness, William of Dunashie waited for her to pick up her spoon.

"I dinna cut it verra fine," he murmured apologetically, lapsing once again into the common tongue.

"'Tis all right." She forced herself to take a bite. "There is not overmuch to cut."

"Och, but I've ridden to war with far less in my stomach, mistress." As he spoke, he deftly cut into his own hunk of the coney. Carrying it to his mouth, he once again forced himself to speak carefully: "There have been times when I did not even ask what we ate, for fear I'd not wish to know, so 'tis a feast you have laid before me."

"Papa fears to deplete his larder when there is plenty," she responded dryly. "I doubt if King David, were he to come here, would fare any better."

"Well, I've hopes that there's stores for the winter at Blackleith. I sent word I'd hae enow meat—" He paused to correct himself. "Enough meat put into the brine to feed twice the number as serve there." Taking another bite, he washed it down with more of her father's mead. For the first time in his life he found himself all too conscious of what he was, of the graces he lacked, of his rough speech. And he sought to make amends for what she was getting in a husband. "But if there's aught else ye'll be needin'—" Once again he stopped himself and started anew in the tongue he hated. "If there be aught else you have need of, Lady Arabella, I will send to Dunashie. The Lady Elizabeth would be generous to you."

The Lady Elizabeth. The great Guy of Rivaux's daughter. Even at Byrum, Giles of Moray's marriage to the highborn widow had occasioned much comment and envy. For once, Arabella's curiosity overcame her aversion to her betrothed. " 'Tis true that she sits above him at his own table? That she carries herself as a royal princess?" she wanted to know.

"She isna meek," he admitted in understatement, "but the babe she carries has softened her a wee bit. Now she sits beside him in a chair wide enough for both of them." His hazel eyes met hers, and she was surprised by the amusement in them. "Ye'd nae be a female and ye dinna ask of her, I suppose." Cursing inwardly, he tried to remember to speak the Norman tongue.

"Is she as beautiful as 'tis said?"

"Aye. Aye, there's none to dispute she is that. Her eyes are as green as pieces of glass in a chapel window, and her hair is as black as Giles', but for all that

she's as fair to the eye as any I've seen''—his eyes
warmed appreciatively—''save ye, mistress.'Tis fortunate I count myself.''

She had to look away. ''Count Guy was not
pleased.''

The warmth faded, and he sat back abruptly. ''Nay,
but he would have her happy. Despite the difference in
their birth, Lady Arabella, they are well matched in
temper.''

Perceiving that somehow she had angered him, she
bowed her head and toyed with the meat on her end
of the trencher. ''Then she is greatly to be envied. My
father,'' she added bitterly, ''cares only for his own
protection.''

''Mistress—''

''Nay,'' she cut in quickly, '' 'tis of no matter now,
is it? Count Guy is not as mortal men, after all, and I
did but wish to know of his daughter.'' Taking a determined stab at a chunk of the hare, she changed the
subject. '' 'Tis of Blackleith I'd hear.''

He regarded her as she chewed, knowing she'd been
forced to take him, wondering if she'd weep on the
morrow, and yet he feared to know. In a rare moment
of cowardice, he chose to follow where she led him
instead. ''I've not been there these two years past, but
I know there is a pleasant herb garden for you to tend,
and it please you. 'Tis a pretty place—Blackleith is,
and I've hopes you will come to like it.''

''As do I,'' she murmured doubtfully. Her gaze
dropped to the hand that held his knife, and once again
she was struck by the size of him. A momentary wave
of panic washed over her. ''What is there?'' she asked,
turning her fear aside.

He appeared to consider the matter, wondering what
a woman would want to know of the keep. Finally, he
mused aloud, ''Well, there is a well-stocked stew
where your boy can fish—'tis full of plaice and carp.
And there is one square tower that stands above the
mostly timber walls. But on one side, the curtain is of

stone, crenelated as well as any. I've hopes to replace
the rest of the defenses in stone," he confided.

Then, realizing that 'twas not what she'd asked, he
added, "Blackleith sits high, overlooking the joining of
two burns, mistress, and when the mists roll in over the
distant hills, 'tis as a faery place. Aye, and when the sun
shines and the weather warms, ye can smell the heather
a-mingling with the flowers. Ye'll have roses enough fer
yer hair, I promise ye." He paused, letting her digest his
description, then said soberly, " 'Tis a good place to rear
sons and daughters, Arabella." When she said nothing he
felt the need to add also, "Your son will be as welcome
as ours there."

The panic she felt intensified. He'd not seen Jamie,
and when he did she dared not think what he would
say. And he'd not heard the tale of Aidan of Ayrie
either, she reminded herself. If he ever did she feared
he would be like the others, that he'd not believe her.
Would he beat her then—or worse yet, would he kill
her ere she could protest her innocence to him? With
Jamie there to remind others, there was always the
chance someone would speak of it. . . . But she could
not leave her son behind, not when she was the only
one who loved him. Not when Nigel would be likely to
starve him. She closed her eyes briefly to hide her fear.

"I'd write to Woolford, and ye wished it," William
went on, "saying I'd foster the boy myself." He
waited, but she remained silent. "Would it please ye?"
he asked finally. As he said it, he realized that his
speech had lapsed yet again. Try as he would, he could
not sound like the lord she'd wed before him.

Opening her eyes, she sucked in her breath, then let
it out. "Donald would not care—nor would the others," she responded, betraying more bitterness.

"He is born of the blood of Woolford, and 'tis their
right to decide," he reminded her. "They've a right
to know what I would do for the boy."

"I'd keep my son with me. I'd not send a dog to
Woolford, my lord."

"Aye. I did but wish to do what is right."

* * *

The straw mat beneath Arabella seemed to have grown new lumps, and her last night at Byrum passed in wakefulness. It was also the last night she'd sleep with Jamie for a while, and as the darkness crawled slowly toward the dawn she could not help thinking of that. And it worried her, for she'd always been there to comfort her son through the terror of his dreams.

Aye, in a scant few hours she'd wed the border bastard, giving him the right to do with her as he willed. She sighed heavily, and tried to put that from her mind.

Memories of Elias, long forgotten, crowded her mind, bringing forth images that she'd tried to bury with him. The feel of his body tearing at hers, the feel of his teeth in her flesh, the smell of his rancid breath in her face, and the pain—always the pain. It had mattered not whether she'd seemed willing or not—always he'd punished her. If she pretended ardor, she was wanton; if she lay still beneath him, she was cold to him. No matter what she did, he called her ''witch'' and ''whore'' as he took her.

Sweating from the remembered terror, she forced herself to admit that William of Dunashie was not Elias. He was younger, more comely. And bigger. He was pleasant, appearing almost kindly. And bigger. Finally, after hours of tossing upon her pallet, her mind wandered into the netherworld between wakefulness and sleep, where it was the big Scot's body that covered hers, and Elias' words that echoed in her ears.

''My lady?''

''Unnnnhhhhhhh?''

With an effort Arabella forced her eyes open, only to discover that it was yet dark. She blinked as though she could somehow clear her mind, then the reality came home to her: It was her marriage day. She struggled to sit, as the blanket slipped to her waist.

''Jesu, Ena, but 'tis cold,'' she muttered crossly. ''And 'tis overearly.''

''I asked her to wake ye.''

He moved closer, carrying a smoking pitch brand,

until he stood above her. And from where she sat, he
appeared to fill the room. She shrank back, her body
protecting her son's, as she stared upward. Her eyes
traveled the great length of him, scarce noting the
heavy boots, the cross-gartered chausses, or the bur-
nished mail that reflected the fire. From behind the
torch his face was shadowed in red and black. He was
as Lucifer, come to take her away.

At first he'd been angered to find her on naught but
a pallet, but as he looked down on her his anger faded.
The torchlight played on her face, on her shoulders,
and on her bare breasts. Despite the fear he'd seen in
her eyes, he could not help staring also, comparing
her slenderness with the thickened bodies of the
whores he'd known. His breath caught in his chest.
"Mistress," he said finally, his voice nearly unrec-
ognizable. " 'Tis come to part from ye I am."

It was then that she realized he was booted and
spurred and ready to ride. "What. . . ?" She opened
her mouth, then closed it, unable to comprehend.

"Wycklow is under siege," he explained. "I canna
know when I'll return, but I'll come again as soon as
may be. Until then, I'd have ye wish me Godspeed."

He was not wedding her this day. She pulled the
cover up to her chin, disappointing him. "Godspeed,
my lord," she said quickly, trying to hide the intense
relief she felt.

"Nay." For a moment he was at a loss, feeling again
as ill-at-ease as when he'd been but an overgrown lad.
He shifted his weight uneasily. "I'd take a memory
with me, mistress. I'd hae a kiss of farewell."

Though he asked, there was no choice. With an effort she stood, turning to pull the blanket around her.
He gestured to Ena to hand her her undertunic, then
he laid his torch upon the small, cold brazier. As he
looked away Arabella stood and hastily struggled into
the garment, releasing her blanket only as the shift fell
below her hips, covering her nakedness. Her duty
done, Ena fled, leaving them alone.

His mouth dry from what he'd seen of Arabella, he

swung again to face her. "Aye, I'd have a kiss of peace between us—and yer blessing ere I go," he managed almost gruffly.

For a big man, he made almost no noise as he moved toward her. She could feel the strength of his hands as he clasped her shoulders. His hazel eyes seemed to devour her face as his voice softened. "I'd remember ye thus."

"Sweet Mary, but I—" Her feeble protest died in his kiss. This time he went more slowly, brushing her lips, tasting lightly of what he would possess. His warm breath caressed her cold cheek, sending an involuntary shiver through her. As his mouth grew more eager, his arms closed about her. The cold metal links of the chain mail pressed her linen shift into her flesh. And yet there was no violence in his embrace. In her grateful relief that he would leave, she returned his kiss tentatively. His arms tightened as he took possession of her mouth. For a brief moment her fear of him was lost in the intensity of his kiss.

"Will! Art ready to ride?" Giles shouted. "I'd make haste!"

Reluctantly, William released her and stepped back, his desire in his eyes. " 'Tis not a horse I'd ride, and I had the choice," he managed. "Sweet Jesu, Arabella of Byrum, but I'd not leave ye like this." He watched the blood rush to her face before she turned away. "There is nae a man anywhere in Christendom more blessed than I, and ye come to me thus." Moving behind her, he leaned to whisper against her ear, " 'Tis a fond memory ye give me, mistress."

"Godspeed you, my lord."

"Aye. And may he keep you also," he answered solemnly. He brushed his palm lightly over the crown of her hair, then dropped his hand. "And ye dinna mind it, I'd take a favor to remind me of ye, Arabella."

"I . . . I have naught of value that—"

"God's bones, Will!" Giles called out from the

stairs, " 'Tis two days' hard ride for Dunashie, and four days beyond that!"

"Aye!" William shouted back. Turning his attention again to Arabella, he lowered his voice. "One day, mistress, ye'll have all that ye deserve."

She drew one plait over her shoulder and pulled at the golden cord that secured the ends, tugging until it gave way, freeing her hair. " 'Tis poor, but 'tis all—"

Heavy bootsteps sounded closer, prompting William to hastily wrap the cord around his thumb. "I'll wear it until we are met again, Arabella," he said softly. " 'Twill remind me of the pledge between us." He fumbled at the leather pouch that hung from his belt, drawing forth a delicately wrought chain and holding it out to her. "I'd meant to give ye this for yer bridal gift." When she did not take it, he pressed it into her hand. "I'd have ye wear it for me. And when I am come again to Byrum, I will bring ye a jewel to hang on it for your wedding day," he promised.

She looked from the glittering chain to him. " 'Tis pretty, my lord, and I thank you for it."

The firelight warmed his hazel eyes as a smile lightened his face. "Aye, 'tis pleased I am to wed ye, Arabella of Byrum, and I'd have the world know it." Lifting the hand that held the chain, he pressed his lips into her palm. "God keep ye while I am gone from ye."

"Are you ready to ride, Will?" Giles asked from the doorway. Despite the impatience in his voice, he was grinning.

"Aye." Embarrassed, William dropped her hand. "I did but come to bid my lady farewell," he explained defensively. "I couldna leave her expecting to be wed, now could I?"

She stood staring into the semidarkness long after their footsteps had receded down the stairs. It was not until she heard the horses clatter noisily across the drawbridge that she sank down onto a small bench. Her hand crept to her mouth as though she were in a trance, and then her gaze dropped to the golden chain in her hand. For these few days at least, God had granted her a reprieve.

"Mama?" Jamie sat up, rubbing at his eyes. "Mama?" he repeated more plaintively.

She dropped down to the pallet and leaned to smooth his rumpled hair. " 'Twas nothing, sweeting." Then, suppressing the surge of renewed elation, she gathered him close. " 'Twas that the lord of Blackleith rides to fight in England, and we do not go from here yet."

"Will he come again?"

"Aye—but not soon."

He buried his head between her breasts and clung tightly to her. "I would that I had seen him," he murmured wistfully. "Wee Tom says he is a giant."

Her arms tightened protectively around the small, weak child. "Wee Tom speaks nonsense, for he is but overlarge, and I'd not have you worry for it. He is gone for now."

"Wee Tom says the Bastard butchers men."

"He's gone, Jamie. Be still and go back to sleep."

"Wee Tom—"

"Hush."

"But he will come back, Mama."

She settled against the lumpy straw and stared upward, listening to the drawbridge creak upward once more. Aye, he would come back, but she'd not think of that. For now she and her son were safe, and 'twas all that mattered.

Chapter Five

Walter FitzHamon sat alone in his small, dank cell, pondering yet again the future he'd not have. "Seek God's counsel," the abbot had urged him. God's counsel? Nay, but God had forsaken him long ago, leaving him to rot in this place, leaving him to yearn for a far different life.

For nearly eleven years he'd endured the preaching, the contemplation, the seemingly endless study of God's path to Heaven, all the while chafing under the rigorous discipline of a vocation he would not follow. The only thing he had learned in those years was how to dissemble, how to say what it suited others to hear, how to pray using words he did not believe. God's counsel? 'Twas a jest.

Eleven years it had been and still he waited, biding his time whilst the Butcher gained King David's favor. When word had come a month earlier that the flower of Scotland's nobility had perished in battle outside York, he'd dared to hope that Giles of Moray had fallen also. Instead he'd had to listen to those who returned by way of Kelso tell of the Butcher's courage, of how he'd covered his king's retreat back into Scotland. Nay, while Walter rotted, Giles of Moray rose.

God? Nay, if God had cared for Walter FitzHamon, 'twould have been Moray as perished at Dunashie, not Hamon. Walter looked down, seeing the hands clasped in his lap as though he prayed, seeing the thin blue lines carrying his blood over the bones. Hamon of Blackleith's blood mingled with that of a peasant girl there. Nay, he'd not think of the latter—'twas Hamon's blood he bore.

'Tis the last of yer blood ye are, and I'd nae hae ye fergit it. . . . 'Tis ye as must make Giles of Moray pay for what he does this day. . . . The last words of his mother's brother, ere Moray had hanged him.

But vengeance was no easy task for a boy with naught but monks to succor him, Walter mused to himself. And he had to think of his own future also. Mayhap he ought to accept his lot in life. Mayhap he ought to take his vows of chastity, poverty, and obedience and hope to escape out into the world as a tonsured clerk. He would not be the first to swear to one thing and do another, after all.

And yet he would not give up the dreams that had sustained him those eleven years when he'd lain alone on his cot. He could not give up his dream of killing Moray and all of his blood, of returning to Blackleith to rule. 'Twas but fancy, he knew, but 'twas all the hope he had. And it did not matter to his dreams that bastards did not often rule.

He felt anew the surge of hate for the Butcher. Aye, and for his bastard brother also. They'd taken Hamon from this earth. They'd taken all Walter knew, even his name, for now he dared not be "Walter FitzHamon," but only "Walter." 'Twas as though no blood at all flowed in his veins. Others were "Stigand of Langley," or "Patrick of Roxburgh," or "Edmund of Alton," but not he. He was but "Walter," an orphan dumped at Kelso's door. Aye, he hated them for it—'twould have been kinder had he perished with Hamon.

"Walter?"

He looked up, seeing the brother come to summon him. The abbot would know whether he would accept God's mission or go out into the world alone. For a moment, his gaze moved resentfully to the requisite crucifix on the wall above. God's mission? Nay, but God had abandoned him, giving him no choice at all.

"Aye."

He rose slowly and started to follow the monk into the stone-floored corridor. He would, he decided, promise nigh to anything to get out. Surely freedom was worth the loss of his hair. And once he was gone from Kelso he'd be one of those clerks who kept a concubine, he promised himself, for he was not meant to burn. And someday, somehow, he would kill Giles of Moray—aye, and his brother, and his sons, and his brother's sons—he'd not let any of the hated blood live.

He stopped, brought up short by the realization that if he were tonsured, he'd not rule Blackleith. He bent down to adjust the toe of his shoe, delaying whilst his mind raced. There had to be another answer. And if God would not give it, he'd have to look elsewhere. Aye, he'd even bargain with the Devil if he had to. As he straightened up, he felt a certain elation at having allowed his mind to think the unthinkable. But suddenly it seemed sensible: If God would not countenance vengeance, surely Satan would.

The abbot who ruled Kelso looked up impatiently when he entered the room. "Ah, Walter." As he gestured to a low bench, he turned to the sour man beside him. "What think you, Edmund: Would you go?"

"The place is small, and the Butcher's piety such that I doubt there is the need," Edmund of Alton complained.

"But surely the need there is greater than any," the abbot protested. "Besides, 'tis not Dunashie itself but Blackleith as has lost a priest. And 'tis months since we received the request. Nay, we have delayed overlong as it is."

Walter's flesh prickled at the naming of the Butcher,

and it was as though every pore had turned into an ear when he heard the reverend father speak of Blackleith. His breath in abeyance, he watched warily, waiting for more. But 'twas to Edmund that the abbot spoke again.

"Your lack of joy in the task speaks ill of you," he chided.

"They are not like to welcome an Englishman there," Edmund countered.

"I have been to Blackleith," Walter blurted out finally. Then, when they turned to him, he nodded. "Aye—I was born not far from there."

Edmund rubbed his Saxon beard almost happily. "There is your answer, Father: Send Walter."

"Nay—he is overyoung, and has not taken his vows."

"And you wished, I'd take them," Walter offered eagerly.

But the abbot shook his head. "You are untried, and as Edmund has said, the Butcher's people are not noted for their love of God's Church. Nay, I'd have you clerk elsewhere first."

It was as though the possibility had been dangled but briefly before him, then pulled away beneath his eyes. He appealed to Edmund: "And you take me for your clerk, I'd aid you there. Aye—I know the place. The way is rough and dangerous, for the road is steep and the burns like to overflow when it rains."

"It has been too many years. You were but a boy," the abbot objected.

"One does not forget the land of one's birth, Father. As Edmund has said, there is little love for the English there. Young or no, I remember well enough the mislike between them." When he could see Edmund nodding, he pressed his advantage. "At least I am Scots-born, Father. At least I am of there."

"As Edmund has said, 'tis believed the Butcher is lacking in piety, and I'd have one of greater years for the task. Besides, you speak not as a Scot now."

Again the Saxon rubbed his beard. "I do not know. . . ." His voice trailed off briefly as he considered the possibility. "A clerk, you say?" Then, just as Walter's hopes rose, Edmund of Alton dismissed the possibility. "The place is too small to need a clerk, I'd think."

"There are but two hundred souls withal, for the parish has only Blackleith and the villeins that till the fields and tend the sheep beyond," the abbot said.

"Two hundred is many for one," Walter argued. "Aye, and ye wished it, I'd speak as they," he added, dropping into the rhythmic border cadence.

"There isn't time. I'd thought to have Edmund there ere the weather worsens. And you've not given your vows—nay, I'd think on it." For a long moment he stared at Walter. "Not always have I been certain of your devotion to Holy Church."

"Then send me but as Edmund's clerk, and let service be proof ere I am ordained," Walter pleaded. "Aye, I'd even be tonsured as surety of mine intentions. Father, 'tis the land of mine birth."

" 'Twould seem you believe you have a mission there," the abbot murmured. "Leave me be, and I will think on it," he promised. "Aye—go, both of you, that I may pray over the matter."

Walter walked beside the now silent, still dour Edmund of Alton, his mind seeking the means to convince the man. Had it been another he'd have spoken jovially, turning his easy ways to his advantage, but 'twould be more like to turn Edmund against him. Levity of any kind—aye, enjoyment of anything—was regarded by the grim Saxon as a great sin. Piety was solemnity, and there was no questioning of that basic truth as far as he was concerned. After waiting for him to say something, anything at all, Walter observed gravely, "The task at Blackleith is great, Edmund, and you are a good choice to take up God's cudgel there."

"Humph. 'Tis a den of thieves," the older man snorted. "Nay, I did not come to Scotland for this."

"And we are successful, the bishop will raise you— aye, and it could be said you taught me well enough

to take your place there,'' Walter ventured slyly.
''There would be no need to keep you at Blackleith.''

Edmund stopped walking and fixed Walter with an
almost baleful stare. ''I need no help.''

''You mistake my meaning. We would both advance, Father—I to minister to Blackleith eventually,
and you to a better place.'' Despite the fact that he
knew Edmund did not like familiarity, Walter clapped
him on the arm. ''Whilst he thinks of it, I would that
you did also.''

'' 'Tis a grim place, you say?'' Edmund demanded,
shaking loose.

''Barren—and the road is bad.'' Walter rolled his
eyes expressively. ''But no more so than the people,
for they are not overgiven to heeding God's will.'' He
leaned closer and lowered his voice. ''And then there
is the Butcher.''

''They say he does not often go there.''

''Surely he is there for the hallmotes at least once
each year.''

''I deserve better than this,'' Edmund muttered bitterly.

''Then let me aid you to gain it.''

The older man regarded him suspiciously. ''Why
would any wish to serve in a godless place?''

''I was born there.''

Later, as Walter lay upon his cot, he stared contemptuously at the crucifix where it hung on the whitewashed wall. ''Too long I have begged for aid in the
wrong place,'' he said aloud. ''But no more.''

His hands behind his head, he considered the almost
instant stroke of fortune that had come his way. And
he knew it was the Devil's omen. He was going to
Blackleith to kill the Butcher.

Chapter Six

The soot-blackened stone walls of Wycklow rose above the brackish ditch, bearing testimony to the burning the keep had suffered at the hands of its own lord but a few months before. That burning, coupled with the other more brutal one at Dunashie eleven years earlier, had done much to gain Giles of Moray and his bastard brother their reputation for savage ruthlessness. On this day they both scanned the half-mended defenses, the scaffolding that clung to the old square tower below the new roof. The black-and-green pennon that hung limply in the mist. The body of Saft Launcie suspended above the scorched gate. It was obvious that the siege had not lasted long, and for the second time in five months Wycklow had fallen to Giles' enemies.

Will wiped the condensed moisture that dripped from his conical helmet. "They dinna leave it lang in peace," he muttered. "Poor Launcie," he added sadly, correcting his language as he signed the Cross over his soaked surcoat. "May God punish the miscreants."

"Aye," Giles agreed grimly. "I'd see them in Hell for it."

" 'Tis too wet to burn again," Lang Gib observed behind them. "Without the Greek fire . . ." His voice trailed off. In their hasty march to relieve the keep, they'd brought no siege engines and no pitch.

"We could send to Harlowe. Count Guy would—"

"Nay, Will," Giles cut him short. "I'd not have it said that Giles of Moray must needs hide beneath Guy of Rivaux's mantle." His eyes traveled to the body of Saft Launcie again, and his lips formed a silent prayer for the man he'd left in charge of rebuilding the weakened walls. But there were no words sufficient for the anger he felt. "Jesu! I cannot turn my back ere there is a sword at it. Nay, we take it again, and this time I'd remind the English why I am called Butcher."

"Och, and you fail to do it, they'll move into your bed every time you leave it," Will agreed. He flexed his arm to test his wounded shoulder. "It sorrowed me I could not aid you the last time, but afore God, I can give good account of myself now." As he spoke he swung wide, as though he wielded his heavy battle-axe, then leaned back, satisfied. " 'Tis well healed enough to cleave any Englishman."

"My lord, we are too few," the man Ewan protested, only to be silenced by the looks the others gave him.

"I'd take one Scot o'er five English on any day— aye, and for a Scots borderer, I'd double that," Will retorted.

"For now, we withdraw into the woods," Giles muttered.

"Withdraw!" his brother fairly howled. "Nay, I'd nae do it!" he protested, forgetting the speech he practiced so carefully now.

"Until we are reinforced." Giles turned in his saddle to address Ewan. " 'Tis not overfar to Waleran of Edgemont's keep, I think, and he is sworn to the Empress also. I'd have you ride to ask if he'd make sport of one of Stephen's dogs. Unless I mistake me, 'tis

Ralph de Payes' standard up there, and I am told they are enemies."

"There's nae any English as has any love for ye," Will warned. "Ye canna know that he will not come against ye also."

"Then let us hope he hates Ralph more than me."

For two days they camped in the woods beyond Wycklow, enduring intermittent mist and rain while they waited for Waleran's answer. It came not in the form of a message but rather in men, some thirty of them riding behind the baron himself. And within a matter of hours after the huge-girthed Waleran had exchanged his kiss with Giles, Ralph de Payes sued for peace. It was not a popular offer to the Scots or to the men of Edgemont.

"You cannot forget Saft Launcie," Will reminded his brother. "And you let the thieving Ralph leave unscathed, you'll but invite any English as covets it to take Wycklow again."

But there was no need to protest. Giles nodded, his face grim. "Tell your lord that he does not leave my keep alive," he ordered Ralph's stunned messenger. "I hold his life forfeit for the man he has hanged. Tell him if he would spare those who serve him, he will surrender himself unto me for mine justice. Otherwise, I cannot promise mercy to any."

"My lord will ransom—"

"Nay," Giles interrupted curtly.

"God's bones, my lord, but your bargain is hard," Waleran observed gleefully when Ralph's man had been shown out. "You force them to fight or starve. But a ransom—"

"I do not mean to wait for either, now that you are come. As there is no moon tonight, I will move under darkness to retake what is mine." For a long moment his black eyes met the English lord's. "I cannot afford mercy and I would rule here. There are too many who count it weakness."

There was that in Giles of Moray that sent a chill

down Waleran's spine. " 'Tis not a wonder you are called Butcher," he said finally, looking away.

"Only by his enemies," Will growled. "Those who seek his friendship do not call him thus."

The baron looked from the dark Scot to his giant brother, and seeing no humor in either countenance he resolved silently not to use the word again. "There is no love between Ralph de Payes and myself, my lord," he declared. "No love at all. If you were to put the whole of his mesnie to the sword, I'd not mind it. I did but think of the profit to be had, 'twas all."

"Aye." Giles turned to William. "What say you, Will?"

"I'd spare only those as do not fight you."

"So be it." Once again, the black eyes sought Waleran's. "While we waited for your answer, I ordered the cutting of a timber to be laid across the ditch where 'tis the widest, for they'll not expect any to come in there. But once it is down, there is little time to delay. We have not the diversion of fire this time, so 'twill have to be the weather. They'll think we wait until it ceases raining—or at least until there is light."

The fat man digested this, then shook his head. "But you cannot see. . . . I see not how . . ."

"Will?"

"I'd take Hob with me, and they'll not raise the alarm against you—I swear it. You have but to be in readiness at the gate." He glanced lovingly toward his broadaxe, sighing. "But I'd have you bring the Barber with you, that I may strike a blow for you."

Waleran's brow furrowed momentarily, but Giles smiled. " 'Tis Will's jest, my lord—the Barber gives the last haircut."

"The Infidels made it," William admitted proudly. "And 'tis wielded rightly, 'twill behead an ox."

"Jesu! An ox?" Involuntarily, the fat baron's hand crept to his own neck. "Nay, 'twill not," he managed weakly.

"Aye, it will." Giles' smile broadened. "You've not seen Will swing it."

"As long as 'tis not swung against me," Waleran muttered.

It was agreed then between them that William and the one called Hob would go over the side of the wall, silence the sentries, and lower the drawbridge. The only dispute was whether Waleran would lead his men inside or wait to cut down any who sought to escape. In the end 'twas decided that Waleran's men would be divided, with half following Giles, the other half lying in wait outside. That left only the matter of Ralph de Payes. It cost one hundred silver pennies to gain the promise that he was Giles' to kill, for the English baron had come in the expectation of ransoming for his enemy for more than that.

After the baron had left to carry the plan to his own mesnie, William dug into the pouch that hung from his belt to draw out a winking jewel. "And any ill befalls me, I'd have ye send this to Arabella of Byrum," he said gruffly. "I promised her I'd give her something to hang at her neck."

Giles turned over the polished green stone in his palm, recognizing it for one of Elizabeth's. Will flushed, then looked away. "Aye, I bought it of your lady, as there was no time to seek aught else. There be no merchants between here and Byrum, you know."

"One day in the fair Arabella's company, and you are besotted," Giles teased his brother. "You even speak differently."

" 'Twas you as told me 'twas time I practiced what King Henry's clerks taught me," Will retorted, reddening more. "I do but try to deserve the station you have given me. 'Tis not an easy thing to do, ye know," he muttered, "for full half the time I forget and do not note it."

"Ah, and Arabella has naught to do with the change?"

"Jesu! Aye, I'd not have her think me a poor lout— 'tis enough she thinks me a coarse one. 'Tis little enough she gets when she weds a bastard."

"Byrum was eager for the match."

" 'Tis Byrum—not his daughter.'' William looked again at the stone in Giles' hand. "But I'd please her, and women are given to wanting such things."

"Aye, but I'd have given you whatever you wished to give her."

"Nay, ye give me the land. And it means more to me that 'twas bought with mine own silver. Like you, I'd have my wife look to me rather than to a kinsman for what she would have."

"I am glad you are pleased with the match."

"Aye, I am pleased. Who wouldna be? Me a whore's son, a great lout of a man, and she a lord's daughter," William answered. "A man hasna the right to expect a comely lass like that for his bed, and ye've given her to me." He closed his eyes, remembering her as she'd sat up from her pallet, and even the memory sent a flood of longing through him. "I would that I could please her half so well."

"You will."

"She isna like Rivaux's daughter, ye know. Naught's to say that she will not weep when she sees this great, huge body,'' Will ventured, giving voice to a lurking fear.

"Is that why you did not wait for her to bathe us?"

"Aye."

"She's borne a babe—'tis not likely she will be too small after that." Giles moved to lay a hand on his brother's shoulder. "Nay, Will. When she comes to know you, she will love you e'en as I do."

"I'd hoped for more than that." William forced a grudging smile. "I'd rather ye said she'd come to care for me as Elizabeth for ye." Brushing Giles' hand away, he turned to pick up a wineskin. "If I am unharmed, I'd give the jewel myself. 'Tis all I mean to say on the matter."

"Would you that I sent Lang Gib with Hob?"

"Nay. Ye gave me the right to lead for ye when ye raised me above the others. Och, but I forgot again,

did I not? Nine years in Henry's household, and still
I canna speak like a courtier and I do not think on it.''

The stones were wet and slick beneath his hands and
feet as he struggled for a foothold. The night was so
dark that it enveloped him, so dark that William could
see neither above nor below. Behind him, he could
hear Hob's whispered curse. Several times he slipped,
only to catch his fingers in the uneven crevices between the stones and again pull his heavy weight up
by the strength of his arms. In the silent blackness he
thought he heard Hob pass him. He paused long
enough to whisper a furtive prayer that he would live
to take Arabella of Byrum for wife, then he renewed
his climb.

The rain dripped from his helmet and soaked his
back, but for once he was grateful for it. The cold,
steady beat of it kept the sentries huddled over their
sheltered fire at the other end of the wall. As his fingers sought and found the final dip of stone that told
him he'd reached the top, he heaved his body upward,
swinging a leg over the small rise that usually protected archers. The metal of his mail scraped the stone
as he rolled over the side. For a moment he lay still,
to catch his breath and listen for Hob.

The small Scot grunted in the darkness. They'd both
made it up the treacherous wall. Will's cold hands
fumbled for his dagger, closing over the hilt and drawing the nine-inch blade from its sheath.

Hob stood. ''There isna but two by the fire,'' he
observed.

Will peered through the rain to where Ralph's men
warmed themselves, and for a moment he felt almost
sorry for them. But they'd come with their lord to take
another's land, he reminded himself, hardening his
heart for his task. Reaching upward he dislodged his
heavy helm, then leaned to toss it toward where the
sentries sat. It rolled and bounced loudly, the metallic
sound cutting through the steady beat of the rain. Then

he rocked back on his haunches and waited, his dagger ready.

"Who goes there?" One of the men rose, staring into the blackness directly at Will and Hob.

" 'Tis the wind, Gerbod," the other sentry told him.

"Nay."

"One of the stones dislodged. The place is little better than rubble, and I know not why Ralph would have it." Huddling closer to the fire, he grumbled, "Were it I, I'd not challenge the Butcher for it. Sit you down—you are like an old woman."

"I like it not," the first man muttered, moving closer to investigate. Reluctantly, the other man discarded a blanket from his shoulders and heaved himself up also. "The weather makes us uneasy," he complained. Nonetheless, he followed his companion toward the spot where Will and Rob crouched. "What. . . ?"

The first one stumbled over Will's helmet, sending it clattering, and the other jumped back, muttering an oath. "God's bones, Gerbod, but you'll rouse all." Both dropped down to grope in the blackness for the metal helm, and neither knew what hit him.

Will's knife found its mark so swiftly that there was a gurgle rather than an outcry. And as the body of one slid heavily to lie in a pool of water at his feet, he heard rather than saw Hob strike also. Then there was silence, save for the rain.

As both he and Hob had served Giles at Wycklow, there was no need for words. Stopping only for Will to reclaim and reposition his helmet on his head and to take one of the fallen men's swords, they moved the length of the wall toward the fire. When they reached it, Hob paused to pick up the discarded blanket and wrap it about his shoulders lest any should see him.

It was an unnecessary precaution, for those who held the keep slept soundly, lulled by the foul weather. There were none to stop the Scots ere they'd reached the gate, and it was not until the bridge began to creak downward that a cry was raised. By then it was too late. Despite frantic shouts of, "We are attacked! To Payes! To Payes!" the keep was open, and mounted men were pouring over the bridge.

Will raised the Scots' war cry of his savage ancestors, his voice resounding through the keep with a bloodcurdling intensity that sent shudders through Giles' English allies. Almost immediately the walls rang with a cacophony of intermingled shouts of "For St. Andrew and Dunashie! For Moray of Dunashie! For Edgemont! For God and St. Olaf! For St. Olaf and St. George!"

Men roused thus rudely from pallets and beds scrambled into the open—some still struggling into mail shirts, some less than half-armed against the onslaught—and the melee was joined. Slashing with his borrowed sword, Will managed to cut his way toward Giles, who leaned to pass the great axe to him.

From then it was little more than a bloody rout, with those who sought to escape cut down by those of Waleran's men who waited without. Will swung the axe again and again, scarce hearing the death screams of those around him. The shouting, the clash of steel against steel, the frantic neighing of wounded horses filled the air for a few brief moments, then there were only the cries for mercy as Ralph's men threw their weapons down. It was over as quickly as it had begun.

Lesser members of Waleran's mesnie fell upon the dead, stripping them of arms and mail like crows over carrion. Will walked to a part of the yard where the grass was not slick with blood, pulled up a handful, and wiped the broad head of his axe with it.

"Ralph is not among them!" Giles called to him. "The coward hides!"

Giles had already dismounted and was heading up the single tower stairs. Without hesitation, William followed him. A cornered man was a dangerous foe, and the man at the top always had the advantage of the one who climbed.

From the first landing both men inched their way

upward, keeping close to the other wall lest anyone hurl anything down the stairwell. The silence that permeated the tower was broken now only by the dulled beat of the rain on the thatched roof and the sound of Giles' spurs clinking against the stone steps. Will was strangely conscious of the damp, sooty smell that still lingered from the last time Wycklow had been burned.

As they rounded the last turn, they saw Ralph de Payes. Any bravado he'd possessed was gone, replaced by the bloodless white cast of fear. Before Giles could raise his sword, the other man threw his down. It skidded through the doorway, struck the stairwell wall, and bounced noisily down the hole.

'' 'Tis my right to be ransomed!'' he cried.

"No man who would take what is mine lives," Giles answered coldly, moving into the room. "Defend yourself or hang."

"Nay!"

"You killed my man. You hanged one who defended his lord's land."

"I will pay—fine me for it!"

"Jesu! Is that all a man's life is worth to you?" Giles demanded. "A few pennies?"

"He did not yield!"

"A life for a life, Ralph." Giles swung around to face William. "Hang him."

Giles' body blocked Will's view of the lord of Payes, and it was not until the older man had lunged, dagger drawn, toward Giles' back that Will saw the movement at all. Bringing up one arm he knocked his brother out of the way, and almost by reflex he swung wide with the other, catching Ralph solidly in the side. The axe bit through bone and flesh on its way inward.

There was a sound like air released from a bladder, then Ralph de Payes' face was frozen into a look of stunned disbelief. He sank almost noiselessly to the floor. Pink foam bubbled from his mouth as his sightless eyes stared upward.

William leaned over his brother. "Art all right? I

dinna mean to hurt ye, but there wasna time to warn ye.''

"Aye.'' Giles struggled to his feet and managed a lopsided grin. "I'd say your shoulder is full well healed, Will. God's bones, but 'twas a blow you gave him.''

Heavy steps sounded in the stairwell, followed by the labored breathing of one too fat to climb. As Giles turned around, Waleran lumbered into the room. Looking down contemptuously at the body on the floor, he shook his head.

"Fools ne'er gain wisdom, 'twould seem.''

"Nay.''

"There are but eight as survive, my lord, and with your good grace I'd ransom them.''

It was a fair enough request, and not one worth denying. Not many men would have ridden in such weather to aid one with whom there were no ties of blood. It was as though Waleran knew what he thought, for he added, "Ralph de Payes was an overgreedy man. While yet he lived, I dared not leave one hide of my land undefended, for I had no hope Stephen would punish him.''

"Then we gave ye border justice,'' William said.

"Aye.'' The fat man smiled. "I am not unfamiliar with the borders, sir, having held lands of the honor of Huntington from King David also. Aye, and Milo of Woolford, though he is from the English side, is a border man who serves me well in mine own household.''

"The ransoms are yours,'' Giles agreed readily. "All I would have is the lord of Payes' head above mine gate, lest there be others who think I will not hold Wycklow against them.''

"This Milo of Woolford—is he of the blood of Elias?'' William asked suddenly.

"Aye.'Tis his youngest son.''

Will shook his head. "There is James of Woolford.''

"James? Nay, I've not heard of him.''

* * *

Ere Waleran and his men left Wycklow, William determined to see Milo. Although Arabella had said the Woolfords would not care if he took her son to Blackleith, he'd be certain. Women did not always understand the importance of blood to a man, and he'd have James of Woolford's family know he meant to do what was right. He'd have them know that he did not mean to usurp their authority, but that he was more than willing to stand for the boy. Aye, and if they wished it, he would foster him also.

But as he approached the one who'd been shown him, Will suddenly hesitated. Would Arabella's first husband's family not think him unworthy to care for one of their blood? They were of Norman descent, and they held considerably more than the honor of Blackleith, after all, so they surely must want more for the boy than the guidance of a bastard but lately enfiefed. Still, his sense of what was right demanded he speak.

The man was tightening the saddle bands in preparation for leaving. He did not look up until William had cleared his throat to gain his attention. Then his eyes traveled the length of the uncommonly tall frame before resting on Will's face.

"You seek me?"

"Art Milo, son to Elias of Woolford?"

"Aye."

"I am William of Dunashie, lord to Blackleith," Will found himself saying, as though he had to hold lands to speak, and then he felt a fool.

"I know who you are. Art the Butcher's bastard brother."

"Aye." There was no use denying the truth.

Milo went back to tightening the girth, giving it one last tug for his safety's sake. "We are not so far south that we do not hear how 'tis the lord of Dunashie as wed Rivaux's daughter."

"The Lady Elizabeth is well pleased with the match," William said stiffly.

The other man shrugged. "It matters not to me."

"I would speak on the matter of your younger brother."

Milo did not look up. "I am the youngest of my blood."

"Nay, 'tis of James of Woolford I would speak." Not waiting to be rebuffed further, William plunged ahead. "As I am to wed the mother, I'd have ye know I'd take the boy and none of ye mind it. I'd see he wants for nothing."

"If you would seek permission to rear Arabella's brat, you'd best seek out Aidan of Ayrie." Even as he spoke, the dark, slender man swung up into his saddle. " 'Tis Ayrie's bastard she brings to you."

He would have flicked the reins to urge his horse away, but William caught the bridle and held it. " 'Tis my wife's honor you'd dispute," he said tersely. "She was wed to Elias."

Milo's lip curled. "My sire ne'er got that of her— 'twas Aidan's whelp she bore, and he has the mark of the Devil for her sin." Emboldened by the fact he was astride, he leaned closer to William's face. "Elias of Woolford died in pursuit of Aidan of Ayrie, else he'd have punished the both of them—aye, and the babe also."

"Art a whoreson liar!"

For answer the younger man brought his whip down hard across the hand that held his bridle. "Fool!" he spat. "Ask Arabella how 'twas that Donald allowed her to take the brat to Byrum!'Twas because she played the whore for Aidan!"

Will looked to where the welt oozed blood, and he could not contain his fury. Jerking savagely down on the bridle, he reached with his other hand for Milo of Woolford, catching his mailed arm and wrenching it. As the horse reared Milo lost his balance, pitched sideways as he was pulled, and landed roughly at the bigger man's feet.

"Spew more filth and ye'll have nae tongue!" Before Milo could roll away Will had reached for him again, lifted him roughly by one shoulder, and pushed

him toward the drainage ditch. Giving one last mighty
shove, he sent Arabella's accuser face-first into the foul
water. Milo went under, then came up choking while
Will waited on the bank, his hands clenched. "Tell
your brothers when I wed the mother, I'll not have
James of Woolford denied—d'ye hear me?"

Giles, who'd heard everything, caught his brother's
arm. " 'Tis enough, Will—anything more and you will
have to kill him."

"D'ye tell them?" William shouted at Milo.

Still coughing, the younger man climbed onto the
bank. The others in Waleran's mesnie watched silently. It took no great powers of perception for Milo
to know he'd provoked where he would not fight.
Looking away, he mumbled, "Aye, I will tell them."

"I canna hear ye!"

"I said I will tell them!"

"Och, see that ye do." Will stood back, his anger
under control.

His face red, Milo tried to collect what dignity he
could. Passing by William and Giles, he muttered,
"There's others as know the tale. You cannot kill them
all."

For a full three days William was uncharacteristi-
cally preoccupied and distant during the journey
northward. Each time they camped he walked apart in
the leafless woods, keeping his own counsel, until
Giles could stand it no longer. He knew what ailed
him.

As the dusk came on the third evening, silhouetting
the bare trees against the grey-pink horizon, Will again
sought solitude. His boot steps disturbed the forest
floor, sending up the musty odor of damp, crushed
leaves. He hunched his shoulders against the cold, trying to ignore the brother who came after him.

"Will . . ."

"Leave me be," William growled.

Giles fell in beside him as his stride lengthened.

"You do not have to wed her, you know," he said finally.

"The betrothal is binding," Will answered morosely. " 'Tis wrong to deny it."

"An impediment . . ."

His brother swung around almost angrily. "There is nae impediment! Arabella and I are nae of the same blood, ye know, and I'd nae swear to a falsehood!"

"She was misrepresented to us."

For a long moment the hazel eyes held Giles' black ones. " 'Tisna sufficient cause. D'ye think I'd name her boy a bastard before the world, to deny the mother? Me, as knows the pain of bastardy? Nay, I'd not do it!"

"I ought to have asked more of her," Giles admitted soberly.

"And I ought to have known, when Nigel of Byrum offered his gentle-born daughter to a bastard like me, she wasna all she ought to be."

"Will . . ."

"Nay, I'd hear nae more. I'll wed her, but afore God I'll nae wear the horns for her, I promise ye. The sons she gives me will be mine own!" Turning on his heel he stalked deeper into the woods, leaving his brother at a loss.

Briefly Giles considered going after him, but if William did not choose to repudiate his bride there was little more to be said. Sighing heavily, he retraced his steps to join the others.

Will waited until he could no longer hear his brother, then he dropped down to sit on a rotted log. For a time he picked up small sticks, breaking them aimlessly. Milo's accusations against Woolford's widow still stung too deeply for a dispassionate discussion with anyone. And despite his hot words to Elias' son, Will was not at all sure he could ever accept what Arabella had done. He could almost wish that her husband had killed her for it.

Elias of Woolford died in pursuit of Aidan of Ayrie, else he'd have punished the both of them—aye, and the

*babe also. . . . 'Tis Ayrie's bastard she brings to ye
. . . he has the mark of the Devil for her sin. . . .* Even
now, more than three days later, Milo's words rang in
his ears: *There's others as know the tale. Ye cannot
kill them all. There's others as know the tale.* And
what had Waleran said? *'Tis the youngest son.* And
he'd not meant the babe Arabella had borne. Even her
own words condemned her now: *Elias had other sons,
and they've no love for Jamie. . . .* Aye, they had no
love for him, for he was not of their blood, William
reflected bitterly.

He felt betrayed. He'd dared to think Nigel of Byrum
had given William of Dunashie his daughter because
of Will's rise before the world. Now he knew that for
a bitter jest. 'Twas that Nigel could not find another
fool to take her. He'd needed a poor, foolish bastard
like William to rear her bastard. An ignorant lout unlikely to cavil at the discovery. 'Twas not a wonder that
her father had wished to rush the betrothal, nor was it
a wonder that she'd taken him.

He thought of her again, and his fingers snapped a
thick stick savagely. Her reticence took on new meaning for him: 'Twas not that she was modest, 'twas that
she'd not wanted to wed beneath her. He was the punishment Nigel gave her for her sin.

He ought to repudiate her, and he knew it. But he'd
meant what he said to Giles: No matter how many
called James of Woolford ''bastard,'' William could
not bring himself to do it, not even to escape marriage
to one who'd played the harlot for Aidan of Ayrie. And
as reluctant as he was to admit it, as furious as he felt
every time he realized he'd been taken for a fool, there
was still that within him that wanted Arabella of Byrum. Even if she had played the wanton for Aidan of
Ayrie, he'd still have her.

Giles was right: He was besotted. He had been ever
since first he'd seen her. And even now that he knew
what she'd done, he could not lie upon his pallet without seeing her pale, slender body, without remembering the feel of her lips on his. He had but to think of

her to burn. He could close his eyes now and see again the pale hair, the grey eyes that were like pools of silver, the blush that warmed her skin and made him think of Scottish roses . . . and the almost familiar ache would overwhelm him. Repudiate her? Never.

Nay, he would wed her and take her to Blackleith. He would plant his seed within her, and she would bring forth sons and daughters for Blackleith. And there would be no question of whose blood they were born, for he knew how to guard his own. Arabella of Byrum would lie with him and him alone. And he would make sure she did not dare think otherwise.

He looked up at the now dark sky, seeing the cusp of the new moon rising from behind a bank of rolling clouds. The smoke of the cooking fire permeated the crisp autumn air, reminding him that he was both cold and hungry. With an effort, he heaved himself up to walk back.

Giles looked up as Will's boots crunched on the twigs and pieces of bark that had fallen from the firewood. Moving over, he made a place for his brother by the blazing campfire. "Art all right?' he asked as Will dropped down beside him.

"Aye."

Giles dug into the pouch that hung from his belt, retrieving the green stone. To Will it was as though it winked in the firelight, mocking him.

"I'd forgotten to give this to you," Giles said when he did not take it.

"Nay. Ye can give it back to Elizabeth," Will answered, pushing Giles' palm away. "Anything Arabella of Byrum would have of me, she'll earn.'Tis enough I gave her the chain."

Giles shook his head. "You paid good coin for it, and naught's to say that a time won't come when you can forgive her. And you take Arabella of Byrum, you'll have to try." He dropped the stone into William's hand and pressed his fingers closed over it. "Aye, ere you wed with her, you'd best consider that."

"E'en if I could forgive, I canna forget," Will muttered. "Every time I look on the bastard she bore, I will remember Milo of Woolford's words."

" 'Twill gnaw at your soul," Giles predicted. "And I felt as you do, I'd not wed her."

"Fool that I be, I'd have her still," William acknowledged bitterly. "I am not like to get another as could compare." He stared into the dancing flames of the fire for a long moment, then sat back on his haunches and squared his broad shoulders. "But for now I'd think on something else—I'd think of the manor ye give me. Aye, and when I have supped I mean to write to Blackleith, ordering that all be in readiness." He looked up, and his hazel eyes belied the troubled soul within him. "Did ye mean what ye said before? Would ye in truth part with Lang Gib?" he asked suddenly.

As much as it would pain him to lose both men from his household at the same time, Giles knew that William had the greater need. "Aye," he answered, forcing a smile. "And you do not mind his appetite for the women, you are welcome to have him."

"He has served ye well."

"As well as any, save you."

"I'd make him my captain of guards, and my seneschal as well. I'd see he prospers," Will promised. Then, realizing how he must sound, he shook his head ruefully. "Och, but will ye listen to me? But lately I am enfiefed, and already I would speak as though I were of worth."

"You are, Will—you are. You are lord to Blackleith, and who's to say 'tis all you'll have ere you are done?"

"Nay. 'Tis enough what you have done for me."

Giles reached to clasp his brother's shoulder ere he rose. " 'Tis no more than I should have done long ago."

William watched Giles walk over to speak with Lang Gib, then he looked to the stone still in his hand. Briefly he considered casting it into the fire, but it would have been too great a waste. Instead he tucked it in the leather purse he wore at his waist. And as he did so, 'twas his own words that echoed in his ears: *Every time I look on the bastard she bore, I will remember Milo of Woolford's words.*

Chapter Seven

Outside, the wind blew the cold rain against the oiled parchment that covered the small window, flapping it like the armorer's bellows. Arabella hunched closer to the fire, straining her eyes over her stitches in the poor light. From time to time she held up the gown she worked, watching it catch the glow of the firelight in its shimmering folds. It was the last of her bride clothes, made from a generous length of purple sendal sent as a gift by Elizabeth of Rivaux.

" 'Tis worth a fortune in gold," her father had complained. "Ye've no need fer such finery at Blackleith."

For a moment she'd been afraid he meant to keep the cloth for himself, and she'd dared to venture that perhaps the Lady Elizabeth would wish to see what she had made of it. He was not pleased, but neither would he offend Rivaux's daughter, so he'd grudgingly conceded that Arabella should make her wedding dress of it. She'd been so happy that she'd had Byrum's priest write to the lady, thanking her.

She smoothed the glowing fabric over her lap lovingly. Aye, but 'twas the cloth of dreams. And when

her new lord saw her in it . . . well, he could not help
but admire her, she was certain. Her new lord. How
strange it would seem to acknowledge William of Dunashie as husband. Her hand crept to the gold chain at
her neck, fingering the delicate links, even as she
thought of him. Though it had been more than a fortnight since they'd retaken Wycklow, William had tarried at Dunashie, giving her more time to prepare.
Only now did he come for her.

In truth, the weeks that had passed had effected in
her an almost fatalistic acceptance of the inevitable
marriage between them. Besides, for all that he'd once
been overeager, he'd offered her no violence, and the
more she thought on it the more she began to believe
obedience to him would serve her best. Mayhap if she
pleased him, he would tolerate her son.

She glanced down to where Jamie watched Ena work
a new woolen tunic for him. Aye, for Jamie's sake, she
had to make William content. If William should turn
from her son, there would be no place for him. She
clasped her hands momentarily in her lap and prayed
silently that 'twould not happen. But she knew in her
heart that if God answered prayers, Jamie would be
loved by more than her and Ena.

Somewhere in the distance a horn sounded, its tone
contrasting with the high-pitched shriek of the wind.
And somehow she knew it was he—that William of
Dunashie arrived once again at Byrum. She carefully
folded the precious gown, laying it aside, then rose to
go to the window. Unlatching the wooden frame, she
pulled it inward and leaned into the opening. The chill,
rainy wind rushed into the tiny chamber, swirling the
fire in the small brazier.

"Ye'll spot yer gown," Ena warned her.

The column of mail-clad men came over the hill,
blending into the greyness of the day, but there was
no mistaking the bear standard that hung limply above
them. Giles of Moray accompanied his brother to her
wedding.

Despite her resolve she felt a momentary weakness,

a surge of fear. There was a a faint scraping sound as James of Woolford dragged his twisted leg across the floor to join her. When he'd reached the arrow slit he collapsed against her, exhausted by his effort.

"Nay, but you should have had Ena carry you," Arabella murmured. Her hand crept to stroke his fair hair as together they watched the approaching mesnie. " 'Tis Lord William," she added, pointing out the helm that rose above the rest. "He is the second one."

"I pray he does not mislike me," he muttered low.

"Nay, he will not," she reassured him. But even as she said the words, she knew he did not believe them. Her hand dropped to his shoulder, drawing him close to her skirt. "I have hopes he will be kind to both of us."

"Nay." He shook his head.

Her heart went out to him, for in all of his six years there had been few kindnesses for him. And when her father was present, not even Ena dared to smile on him. She could not blame him for fearing William.

"He will like you, for you are my son," she said bracingly.

"He has not seen me, Mama." He ducked beneath her hand and pulled himself into the slit. "Wee Tom still says he is a giant. Wee Tom says he will grind my bones and eat me with his porridge," he added uneasily. "Wee Tom—"

"Wee Tom speaks nonsense," Arabella retorted shortly. "He does but say such things to vex you."

"He says Lord William will know 'tis the Devil as made me, Mama. And if Lord William is a God-fearing giant, he'll kill me," he went on.

"Jesu, but you will take a fever," she muttered, pulling him back. "And Lord William is not a giant, Jamie. He is—" She looked again to where her betrothed rode beside his brother, seeing the huge destrier beneath him. "He is overtall, 'tis true, but he is not misshapen. There are those who might even call him pleasing."

"I know not who," Ena muttered under her breath

behind Arabella. " 'Twill be a wonder and ye can breathe beneath him. If he isna a giant, I am a dwarf.''

Her anger evident in her face, Arabella spun around to face her woman. Nodding briefly to the serving boy who brought mulled wine, she ordered him, "Wilken, take Jamie below to the kitchens, and ask Daft Bess for a sweet bun for him.''

"The lord willna like it, and he knows,'' the serving boy complained sullenly. "He says we are nae to coddle—'' There was a brief hesitation, then he finished with "him,'' saying the word as though he'd wanted to call Jamie something else. "Nay, but I—''

"You'll not tell him,'' Arabella declared flatly. "Go on—ere I have you beaten for your insolence.''

"But Mama,'' Jamie protested, "I'd see the Bastard when he comes! I'd see what he is—I . . . I would!''

"Nay.'' She ruffled his hair affectionately, then lifted him onto the reluctant Wilkin's shoulders. "You'll meet him on the morrow,'' she promised. And as she spoke the words, she added yet another silent prayer that William would not be filled with loathing when he saw her son. "Now be off with you. I'd have no more speech of giants.''

It was not until she could no longer hear them on the stairs that she turned again to Ena. "What good does it serve to frighten me or my son?'' she asked coldly. "Whether William of Dunashie is bastard, giant, or devil even, he will be my lord husband.''

"I dinna mean—''

"Aye, you did, and I'd not listen.'Tis a better service to say that he is good and kind. Jamie has come to expect the worst of everyone already, and well you know it.''

"The Bastard willna want him,'' Ena declared defensively.

"I have to hope Lord William will come to value us, Ena, else I cannot survive.'' Arabella walked back to the slit and banged the shutter closed over it. Sucking in her breath, she let it out slowly before facing her woman again. "Now—if you would aid me, you will plait my hair ere he sees me. Aye, and I'd have my blue gown brushed also.''

But even as she spoke, she smoothed damp palms over her woolen skirt. And inside her, her heart thudded with fear for her young son. Her new husband had to accept Jamie—he *had* to. 'Twas the only reason she'd agreed to this marriage.

William leaned back in the tub and closed his eyes. Despite the warmth of the fire and the water, he was still so cold and bone-weary from the long ride that he doubted he'd ever again be warm or rested. A body servant moved silently about the small room, gathering his and Giles' mail for cleaning ere it rusted. Just then, Will did not care if he ever wore it again.

''Since you would not have her tend you, would you that Wat washed you?'' Giles asked him.

''Nay. I'd soak the cold from my bones.''

''I spoke to Nigel, and 'tis agreed you wed her on the morrow.'' When William merely grunted, his brother moved closer. ''There is still time to delay, if you'd not take his daughter.''

''I'd nae speak of it—I said I'd wed her.''

In the days since they'd last discussed Arabella of Byrum, William had avoided any further mention of his betrothed, focusing instead on his duties as the new lord to Blackleith. Worried that his brother would have no happiness with Arabella of Byrum now, Giles tried one last time. ''Will . . .''

''Nay.'' The hazel eyes opened to regard him defensively. ''And I had the choice, I'd hae a virtuous woman,'' he admitted, ''but there's nae one as would want a bastard like me. At least the Lady Arabella hasna the choice in the matter.''

''If you cannot accept what she has done, you'd best not take her.''

''She'll nae put horns on me, if 'tis what you are fearing,'' Will retorted. ''I'll nae stand for it. Had I been Elias of Woolford, Aidan of Ayrie'd be naught but a crow-picked skull on a pike.''

"And Arabella?" Giles asked. "What would you have done to her?"

It was a question William had asked himself more than once since Milo had told him, and he had no answer for it. It would, he supposed, depend on whether she had borne babes to him. A man could not kill the mother of his children. Shaking his head, he answered in little more than a growl, "Nay, 'twill nae come to that."

Giles sighed heavily. For whatever reason, Will would take Arabella of Byrum, and there was naught more to be said. He could only hope that somehow they could discover a passion for each other. "Art a grim bridegroom," he chided finally. "I'd not part from you like this."

Suddenly the bigger man grinned. "Ye know what ails ye, Giles? 'Tis that ye'll nae have me with ye after the morrow. Ye'll nae know how to go on without me."

In a way, he spoke the truth. It would be the first time since Giles' birth that they'd been separated for more than a few weeks. When the younger man made no answer, Will sobered. "Ye don't regret giving Blackleith to me, do ye?"

" 'Tis like parting from a mother to let you go," Giles admitted. For a moment his black eyes grew distant with memory, seeing again the small, frightened boy sent to King Henry's hostile court, remembering the brother who'd held him when the loneliness had been overwhelming, who'd fought those who taunted him. The brother who'd aided him in regaining his patrimony from Hamon of Blackleith. The brother who'd served him with no thought of self. Forcing a wry smile, he came back to the present. "Nay, Will— 'tis something I should have done long ago. I could never have taken Hamon without you." He leaned over to clasp a wet, muscular shoulder, gripping it briefly. "Until Elizabeth, 'twas your love as sustained me."

Arabella forgotten momentarily, William blinked back the sudden mist of tears. "Nay, be off with ye,

else I am like to go back to Dunashie to plague ye,"
he muttered gruffly. "Ye've got Rivaux's proud daughter—aye, and a son of your own a-coming. Ye'll do
well without me."

"I'd have you stand godfather to the babe."

The tears spilled over onto the bigger man's cheeks.
"Nay, 'tis not meet. . . . Elizabeth canna wish . . .
Well, it ought to be Count Guy as guides your son."
He choked, unable to go on.

"Elizabeth agrees with me." Giles stepped back,
his own eyes strangely wet. "I'd stand for your son
also, Will."

William wiped his cheek with the back of his hand.
"God's bones, Giles! Ye've got the both of us maun-
dering! One would think we meant to part forever."

"Aye. And if you do not finish your bath, we'll be
late to sup." Moving to the slit that served for window, Giles listened to the steady beat of rain against
parchment. " 'Tis the weather that lowers both our
spirits," he observed finally. Swinging around, he
added, "And you do not mind being left alone, I'd
seek Nigel to tell him I do not stay overlong. I'd return
to Elizabeth as soon as the festivities are done."

"And the feast is no better than the suppers, I am
for Blackleith also. A week here and I'd be naught but
bones." Will frowned. "I'd leave on the morrow and
I could, but Nigel tells me we hunt boar on the day
after, and I canna miss that."

"Any other time I'd welcome it, but not now."

Will waved a wet hand toward Wat. "Ye'd best get
the rust out today, for we stay but three days and nae
more. And while ye are about it I'd hae ye see if there
is any spiced wine to be had here, or if there's naught
but new ale."

As the boy disappeared with the heavy bag of mail,
Giles threw his fur-lined cloak over his shoulder.
" 'Tis to be hoped Byrum's hall is warmer than its
bedchamber. Were I you, I'd not tarry overlong here."

"I am loath to leave the warmth of the water."

For a long time after Giles had left William soaked

his cold body, staring soberly into the flickering flames of the fire. He ought to be feeling as though he had all of Christendom at his feet, but he did not. Aye, he was lord of Blackleith, but he had to leave Giles. He was wedding Arabella of Byrum, but he was getting an unchaste wife. It was as though each happiness were balanced with an opposing sadness.

Despite a certain unwillingness to dwell on Arabella, his thoughts again turned to her. Could he forgive her for lying with Aidan of Ayrie those long years ago? If she'd betrayed Elias of Woolford, would she betray him? The questions nagged at his soul, for they had no answers.

"My lord. . . ?"

Startled by the sound of her voice, he straightened quickly in the tub and thrust the washing cloth over his lap to hide himself. When he glanced up, she was facing him uncertainly. In her hands she held a steaming cup.

"Aye," he growled.

His aspect was so different from when last she'd seen him that she fought the urge to flee. "The boy said you wished some spiced wine. I . . . I mulled it myself, as 'tis so cold outside."

When he did not answer, she turned to set the cup on the small table. "I did not know you were still at your bath," she offered lamely. Her hands shook as she looked at him again. She had to please him—she had to. She had to conquer her fear of him. "Would you that I aided you?"

As his gaze traveled upward, taking in the slenderness of her waist, the swell of still firm breasts, the fairness of her skin, the way her hair hung like two pale golden ropes over her soft woolen gown, he was unprepared for the effect she had on him. Despite all he now knew of her he could still appreciate her beauty, he could still feel the rise of desire when he looked on her.

His mouth was almost too dry for speech. With an

effort he tore his eyes away from her. "Nay. I'd not spoil your gown, mistress," he muttered.

She hesitated, knowing she ought to deny it. Dear God, but she had to broach the matter of Jamie before he saw him. Instead she found herself saying, "You'd best drink the wine ere it cools."

She was leaving, and for all his anger toward her he did not want her to go. "Wait."

She turned back, her face betraying a momentary wariness. "Aye?"

She was wearing the chain he'd given her. It hung nearly to her breasts, reminding him of the last time he'd seen her, the last time before he *knew*. He looked down to where the gold thread still twined about his finger like a ring. For all that he'd cursed her, he'd not removed it. He cleared his throat. "I'd have your company still. Sit you down until I am done." As he said it, he reached for the chunk of tallow soap and began to lather himself.

She had to bridge the chasm between this stranger and herself. On the morrow, he would become master to her and to Jamie. On the morrow, she would be his to do with as he willed. Twisting her hands against the folds of her gown, she forced herself to offer again.

"If you would have the service, I do not mind washing you."

" 'Tis not meet," he muttered, reddening.

"There is little difference between now and the morning, my lord. After that, I shall be expected to attend you." She smiled faintly. "As I am widowed, you are not the first man I have ever washed."

What had Giles said—that she had borne a babe and could not be too small? He looked at the cloth that floated above his lap. And he felt a certain reluctance. He'd never quite forgotten that he'd had to pay Berta more than her other customers did for the privilege of delving between the whore's ample legs. Nor had he forgotten the crude jests he'd endured when the others had discovered what she'd charged him.

When he raised his eyes again, he found himself

staring into the swell of Arabella of Byrum's breasts. Aye, he supposed there was little difference between now and the morrow.

"And you get my head, I can do the rest," he decided. "Then I will have naught but the need of a barber to shave me in the morning."

He handed her the soap, then ducked his head beneath the water. When he came up, he pushed his wet hair back and closed his eyes against the rivulets that coursed down his face. She leaned over him to pick up the cloth, but he held it tightly against his belly.

As mistress of the house Arabella had bathed other men, but this was different. This man would be her husband. She stared at the broad, bare shoulders, the wide expanse of chest, the powerful arms. Sweet Mary, but he was bigger even than she'd remembered.

"You'll have to lean back, else you'll have soap in your eyes."

"Aye," he murmured obediently.

His dark red hair was thick and luxuriant beneath her fingers as she lathered it. Knowing how it must've sweated beneath the leather cap and heavy helmet, she rubbed his scalp with her thumbs, rotating them in circles from the front to the back, then over the ears. She could feel him relax beneath her hands.

All of his life he'd been second, third, or further down into the bathwater, and more often than not he'd chosen to wash himself rather than endure the rough scrubbings meted out by the boys who stood ready to douse him with the buckets after. Thus the gentle, soothing lathering Arabella now gave him was a luxurious experience for him. He closed his eyes and gave himself over to enjoying the feeling of her hands in his hair.

When she looked down again, his face bore a sleepy expression. She'd told Jamie that William's countenance was not unpleasant, she recalled. Nay, she'd done him an injustice, for 'twas more than that. His features were well chiseled: a good, straight nose, well-defined cheekbones, strong chin, almost sensuous lips. His eyes, still closed beneath faintly purpling lids, were fringed by lashes so dark they were almost black against his skin. If there was a flaw, it was the fine scar that crossed his cheek where neither his nasal nor his helm had been able to protect him. And even that was not unhandsome, for it made him look strong. She looked lower, seeing the scar that puckered at his shoulder, and she would have asked of it, but he was so still she thought he drowsed. It was not until she reached for the ewer of rinse water that he spoke.

"I'd nae have ye stop, mistress," he said softly.

Even the burred accent, which she'd thought distinctly uncouth before, sounded warm and inviting. Without thinking, she lapsed into the language of her old nurse. "Ye canna sit aboot all the day, else ye'll nae eat," she murmured.

He thought she mocked him. Opening his eyes, he stared into hers. "I can speak as well as any Norman, and you'd hear it."

"Nay, but I—"

"But I've little liking for the tongue. 'Twas the Normans at Moray as hanged my sire, and 'twas the Normans as kept my brother and me in exile at Henry's court."

"I am sorry."

"For what? For considering me the bastard lout that I am?" he gibed.

"Nay, 'twas sorry I am for you."

It was the wrong thing to say. His hand caught her wrist and held it, pulling her down until she was but inches from him. " 'Tis not pity I'd have from you, Arabella of Byrum." He watched her eyes widen in fright, and his anger faded. He released her hand and ducked his head once again. The soapsuds scummed the surface of the cooling water. When he came up, he pressed his dripping hair against his head.

Baffled by the sudden change in his manner, Arabella tried to make amends for whatever it was that she'd done. "My lord, you mistake me. . . . I—" Her

eyes caught the soap scum that still clung like wet ashes
to his hair. "Nay. You'll not get it clean like that."

Before he knew what she meant to do, she dashed
the ewer of scented water over him. He sputtered and
grasped for her skirt, using it to blot his eyes. "And
you do not try that again, I'd count us even, mistress.
Turn your back that I may get out."

At least his anger was gone. She knew she was supposed to offer to dry him, but she did not. Disconcerted, she turned to stare across the room at the only
bed at Byrum. That her father had given it over to his
guests bespoke the importance he attached to this marriage. On the morrow, she would sleep there with William of Dunashie. Her hands went cold at the thought.
She wanted to run, but dared not. Not until she'd spoken of Jamie.

The bathwater showered the floor, then there was
the hasty rustling of clothes as he dressed, the scraping of the bench when he sat to garter his chausses.
And the soft sound of his feet as he came up behind
her. Startled, she spun around, and the room was suddenly far too small.

"Art still afraid of me, Arabella of Byrum?"

The hazel eyes seemed to bore into hers. She swallowed visibly, then nodded. "Aye," she answered low.

"Give me no cause for anger, and you've naught to
fear of me, mistress." When she would have looked
away, he lifted her chin with his knuckle. "Nay. For
good or ill, we've taken each other, Arabella, and I'd
abide by the bargain between us."

She nodded.

"But I'd hear again why you agreed to wed me,"
he said suddenly, startling her.

What did he want her to answer? Did he want her
to pretend that which she did not feel? She dropped
her eyes to his stockinged feet and once again spoke
the truth. "I told you—'twas for Jamie. I wed for Jamie."

"For Jamie," he repeated. " 'Twas all? 'Twas not
because I was the only man as would— 'Twas not to

hide—'' He started to accuse her, to tell her what he knew, but he could not put it into words.

It was her best chance to explain ere he saw her son. She twisted away, then knotted her skirt in her hands. Facing him from a safe distance of several feet, she blurted out, ''He is not what you think him! And 'tis not God's punishment that he is what he is! But I pray that you will accept him, else I'd not go to Blackleith!''

''Nay, I—''

''I'd not have him scorned anymore, my lord—I'd not!'' Her voice rose almost shrilly, as though she could drown any objection.

''I know what he is, Arabella.''

For a moment she stared blankly. ''You *know?* But you've not seen him. Papa would not—nay, you cannot know!''

For all that he'd asked, he'd not discuss Aidan of Ayrie with her, for he was still too raw inside with the knowledge of what she'd done. He knew not why he'd pulled the scab from his own wound by bringing it up. He shook his head. ''I'd not speak of this, mistress.''

''But can you accept him? Can you find pity in your heart for my son?'' she cried.

There was a long pause as her question hung in the air between them. For all that he'd sworn he could not bear to look on Ayrie's son, he found it difficult to deny a bastard like himself. The boy could not be faulted for the sins of the mother, but William still was not sure he could accept him.

''My lord, I'd know ere I wed,'' she persisted urgently. ''I'd not see my flesh mistreated.''

''Aye,'' he sighed, answering finally. ''A bairn cannot help how it comes into the world. I'd not mistreat him for it.''

Tears streamed down her face. ''You swear it? You swear you will not harm him? Please—I'd hear you say it.''

''Who am I to judge your son for what he is?'' he asked harshly. As bitter as he was, her tears unnerved

him. "Nay, ye've no cause to cry for that, Arabella."
He moved closer and brushed at her wet cheek awkwardly. "I will try to do what is right for him, I swear
it."

She caught his hand and held it, pressing it against
her skin. "And you do, I'd honor you for it," she
whispered. "And you do, I'd be a good wife to you,
William of Dunashie."

It was the best he could hope for, and he knew it.
His free arm closed around her, pulling her close.
"Then there is no quarrel between us."

The scent of the rosewater wafted upward from her
shining hair. He bent to nuzzle the crown, savoring
the sweetness of the roses, forgetting Aidan of Ayrie,
forgetting everything but the warmth of the woman.
She dropped her hand and slid her arms about his
waist, returning his embrace. And the intensity of his
desire nearly overwhelmed him.

"Arabella," he heard himself say in a voice he
scarce recognized, "there is little difference between
now and the morrow. I'd lie with you now, mistress—
I'd not wait."

The brief haven she'd felt in his arms vanished in a
rush of panic. "Supper—"

" 'Twill not take long," he murmured above her
ear. "It has been overlong since I've lain with any."

The memory of Elias, of the cruel couplings he'd
inflicted on her, flashed through her mind, and she
knew a sudden terror. This man was far bigger, far
stronger than the husband who'd taken such pleasure
in her pain.

"Sweet Mary, but I—"

He felt her stiffen. "There's none to know, for you'll
not be expected to bleed in the marriage bed," he
coaxed.

"I'd say the words first, my lord," she pleaded
desperately. "I'd have God's blessing." As she
spoke, she twisted in his arms. "Not yet . . . The
morrow . . ."

His clasp tightened, imprisoning her against him.

"I'd nae be lied to, Arabella—ye canna say one thing
and do another with me. Ye said ye'd be a good wife
to me."

"Aye—on the morrow. Please God—"

"Ye said today was little different from the morrow," he reminded her with her own words. "And I'd
have ye now."

"I'd not lie where I am not wed!" White-faced, she
struggled against him. "I'd say the words first!"

He'd never forced a woman in his life, and despite
what he knew of her he could not do it now. He wanted
to shout back that she'd said no words with Ayrie's
son, but he'd not have that between them. Angered, he
pushed her away, and she stumbled.

"Ye'll have your words, then, mistress! But afore
God, once they are done, ye'll lie with me and none
other, d'ye hear?" His eyes met hers and held, as he
struggled with his temper. "I'll nae take a cold woman
to my bed—d'ye understand that, Arabella of Byrum?"

Her throat constricted. "Aye."

"Then be off with ye, ere I forget I said I'd wait."

The words were scarce out of his mouth ere she'd
fled. He stood there, listening to her shoes tripping
down the stone stairs as though she could not run fast
enough to escape him, and once again he felt a surge
of anger. She'd lain where she was not wed before, but
not for him. When finally he could hear her no more,
he turned to the cup of mulled wine she'd set on the
table. It had cooled as much as his ardor.

He held it up and his distorted reflection mocked
him from its shiny surface. "Och, ye are but the Bastard of Dunashie to her, Fool Will," he muttered.
"For all that ye would have her, she is but what Aidan
of Ayrie left ye."

And instead of drinking, he flung the cup toward the
brazier. For a brief moment the fire flared and the
wine sizzled, while the vessel bounced and rolled
across the floor. Then there was naught but stillness.

Why had she come up to him? Why had she bothered to wash his hair? But even as he asked himself, he could hear again her answer: *Jamie. I wed for Jamie.* And it took no great powers of perception for him to realize that Nigel did not want her bastard there. She'd spoken the truth: She did but want to get her son away from Byrum.

"Ah, Will," he muttered again to himself, "the truth pains when 'tis not what ye'd hear. For all that ye know of her, ye'd still have her want ye. And for all that ye know of her, mayhap 'tis still in Aidan of Ayrie's arms she'd lie, and she had the choice."

For a long moment he stared morosely into the fire, then he straightened his shoulders. She had not the choice. She was his, and his alone. Never again would she see this Aidan. Any babes she bore after the morrow would belong to him, else he would kill her.

Chapter Eight

"By the Blessed Virgin, Walter, but I cannot see anything," Edmund grumbled. "I cannot think why you would have us ride in this."

"Nor can I," the younger man lied. "I'd not expected the weather to be so bad."

The fog swirled around them, shrouding the hills in an eerie mist and isolating the two riders even from the road beneath them, making the way treacherous. It was, Walter reflected grimly, a day suited to his purpose.

"Are you certain of the way?" Edmund asked yet again. Then he muttered, "I know not how you would know where we are."

"I know."

" 'Tis a day only Satan would venture out."

"Aye."

Edmund strained to see anything beyond his mount, and was denied. "This Blackleith sits in a barren place. I began to regret I said I would come."

" 'Tis not so barren in the sun," Walter retorted, tired of the priest's complaints. "There are those who count it a pretty place."

"How many years since last you were there?"

Walter also stared into the dense fog for a moment before answering, "Too many."

"Yet you were born there."

"Aye."

"And you wrote of our coming?"

"Aye."

Actually he'd only mentioned one of them, but it had not served him to say aught besides a priest came from Kelso to replace the one who'd died. Nay, the less said now the easier 'twould be later.

"I cannot think you would ask to accompany, and you'd seen this place," Edmund muttered under his breath. "Jesu, but 'tis as we were before the portals of Hell."

Ah, but you are, Walter thought to himself. Smiling into the oblivion, he said aloud, " 'Tis not nearly so warm as I would expect Hell to be, Father."

The older man looked irritably, trying to fathom his companion's expression, but he could not. "Your jest ill becomes you—'tis no wonder you are scribe rather than priest. Eleven years and more you were at Kelso, and it seems we instilled no piety in you."

"The life did not suit me."

There was that about young Walter that Edmund could not like. Aye, had he to choose again, he'd not have taken the clerk with him. But it had been a matter of expedience, for he had wanted company on the journey to this less-than-welcome duty. But for whatever reason Walter *had* asked, saying he knew the way to this forsaken border keep. Idly, the priest wondered if the Butcher would want to feed a clerk, if he'd be angered to discover that Kelso had sent not one but two to preach to the people of Blackleith. But it was beyond that now, for Walter came with him.

He looked over at the young man, seeing the straight profile of a handsome face beneath his cowl, and he could not help wondering of him. What had Brother Patrick said of Walter? That he'd been left an orphan at Kelso, and for all that he'd grown to manhood there, there was none as truly knew him.

He cleared his throat to ask, "How is it that you speak as a Norman, if you were Scots-born?"

So the priest would pry, would he? Well, no matter, for he'd not speak of it after this day, Walter reasoned to himself. He shrugged, then answered, "Mine future was uncertain, so I once thought to seek my fortune in England." He favored Edmund with a wry smile that did not warm his face at all. "I'd not have any there think me but a Scots fool, for there would be no advancement there. Why do you ask?" he queried bluntly.

"It matters not—'tis what a clerk writes that is heeded."

"I do not mean to be a clerk all of my life."

"Nay, there is no other life for one who has no land," Edmund reminded him. "And you are untrained to be a mercenary."

Walter fell silent at that, but his fingers clenched the reins in his hands more tightly. It was as well that the priest could not see the anger in his eyes. He could not know he'd touched a wound that festered on the soul.

"Think you I cannot live by mine wits?" he muttered.

But Edmund did not respond to that. Instead he changed the subject abruptly. "Mayhap you have some of your blood there—a distant relation?"

"What?"

"At Blackleith. Mayhap 'tis that you have family there still?" the priest repeated.

Walter straightened in his saddle. "Nay," he answered harshly, "I am all of my blood that lives."

"Well, were I you, I'd not return to naught," the other man muttered under his breath. " 'Tis a barren place," he said yet again.

When Walter made no further answer the priest's thoughts turned inward sourly, wondering how he, Edmund of Alton, had come to this pass, how he could have allowed himself to be sent to this awful place. Unlike Walter, he had the right to hope for better.

Born a Saxon, Edmund had gone to Kelso after his ordination to the priesthood, hoping to escape the preponderance of Norman clergy in England and seeing in David of Scotland's support of the abbeys an opportunity to advance. *Advance,* he thought bitterly. The gall rose every time he considered his assignment to Blackleith. There was naught but punishment for his sins to explain it.

His donkey stumbled slightly on the rocky path that passed for a road, unnerving him further. He could only take solace that Walter had been down it before.

"We are nearly there."

"I know not how you can tell."

"I know. For all the years that have passed, this road is still writ on my mind." Walter reined in and listened briefly. "The river is but ahead."

"The river?"

"Aye." The younger man clicked his reins and nudged his horse forward, noting with some satisfaction, "It has rained overmuch, and 'twill be full."

The priest peered intently into the fog after Walter, afraid when he heard the rush of water. "I'd not cross where 'tis flooded—is there a passable ford here?" he asked nervously.

"Aye."

"God's bones, but I cannot see, and neither can I swim. I'd not—"

Walter reached for the other man's reins, tugging them from his hands. "You'd best let me lead you, for the burn is overdeep elsewhere."

But the sound frightened Edmund, and he wanted to draw back. "Jesu, but I'd wait. . . . I'd not go. . . ." The perspiration of fear mingled with the mist on his forehead. "Mother of God, nay! I say we wait!"

But his voice was lost in the fog as Walter led him forward. It was not until the water lapped about his legs, dragging at his cassock, that Edmund realized there was no ford. Terrified, he clung to his donkey's saddle, screaming to Walter, " 'Tis too deep! Sweet Jesu, but—nay! Mother of God, deliver me!''

The younger man caught at his arm, jerking it hard, unbalancing him. The priest gasped desperately, clutching for Walter's stirrup as he fell beneath the cold water. His frantic cries were swallowed in the swirling current.

Spurring his own frightened mount across the swollen river, Walter leaned to grasp the cowl of Edmund's garment, dragging the flailing priest after him. When the man did not cease struggling, Walter kicked his head with a spurred boot and cursed him. At the other bank he pulled Edmund's inert body from the water, then dismounted to lean over it. Thinking he detected breath, he rolled the priest over and pressed his face into the mud with his boot, holding him there until there was no chance for survival.

Finally satisfied, he stripped the body clumsily with his cold hands, taking as much care as he could not to tear the cassock overmuch. Then he undressed in the chill fog and donned it. Shivering, he stood for a moment, listening to the sound of the water and drawing the foggy air into his lungs.

"Farewell, Father," he murmured, as he lifted the dead man and pushed him once again into the river. "May God grant you more contentment there than here," he added, as Edmund's body sank beneath the surface.

Turning back, he walked to where the two mounts, horse and ass, stood waiting. His eyes moved lovingly over the chestnut, then he slapped the animal's rump resolutely. "God give you a better master, Flauvel!" he cried, driving it away. He told himself he'd planned well, for when the naked body and the horse turned up, 'twould be thought Edmund had been but a traveler robbed on the road.

The cassock bagging heavily at his ankles, he swung himself into the donkey's saddle and adjusted the reins.

"Come on, you stupid creature," he urged. " 'Tis not far to Blackleith.''

But as he rode in the chill fog he began to think 'twas further than he'd remembered, for the keep of his childhood memory had been close by the burn. He leaned forward, huddling his wet, cold body over the donkey's rude saddle.'Twould be a wonder if he did not take a sickness in the lungs from this day. Nay, he told himself fiercely, the Devil would not claim him ere he was done with Giles of Moray.

His teeth chattered, and his fingers were almost too cold to grasp the reins. Surely . . . He stared intently into the swirling mist and thought he saw something lurking within. Spurring the donkey to a faster gait, he hastened on.

It was not a tower, but rather a peasant hut that clung to a hill. Disappointed, he nonetheless would seek refuge there. The smell of burning peat promised a fire at least. When he reached it, he dismounted and pounded on the rough-hewn door.

A dirty woman came, opening it but enough to peer suspiciously out. " 'Bod!'' she bawled out when she saw him, "ye'll nae believe it, but there be a priest without!''

"Good woman, I'd have your aid," Walter told her, shivering whilst he waited for her husband. " 'Tis nigh to freezing I am. The fog was so heavy I could not see where I rode, and I have nearly drowned.''

Her eyes moved over his torn and muddy cassock and his sodden cloak. "Aye. Ye look as though ye've been in the water.'' She opened the door wider as a stoop-shouldered man came up behind her. " 'Bod, ye'd best run ter the castle wi' word he is come.''

"A blessing on your house, woman, and you share your fire,'' Walter promised through blue lips.

"Aye.''

They stepped back to let him in. He moved to stand over the center fire, holding his numb hands over the flames. She followed him into the single room asking, "Hae ye met with trouble on the road?''

"Aye. The water was too high to cross, and I nearly perished."

"Bod!"

"I be gaing," her husband protested, drawing on a thin, worn cloak. He squinted at Walter. "And what would ye I told 'em at Blackleith?"

"Tell them Father Edmund comes to tend Giles of Moray's soul."

They exchanged glances. "Nay, he isna laird here now."

For a moment Walter thought he'd come too late, that he'd been cheated on his revenge. "Moray is dead?" he asked with disbelief.

"Nay, but 'tis the Bastard of Dunashie who holds Blackleith of him, Father."

A fleeting memory of the redhaired giant passed through Walter's mind. "The Bastard of Dunashie," he repeated slowly. "The Bastard holds Blackleith of Moray?"

"Aye, but he hasna come yet."

It was an unexpected blow to his *plans*. For a moment he stared nonplussed into the peat fire. Moray was not lord to Dunashie. 'Twas his bastard brother, the one who'd taken him to Kelso. He allowed himself to recall the kindness, then his heart hardened. Nay, but they were like, for they were both born of the same blood. And if aught ill befell the Bastard, the Butcher would come.

"Ye be all right?" the woman asked him.

"Aye. I am but cold and tired from the ride." He turned back to the man. "Tell them to make haste also, for I'd sleep within the walls of Blackleith this night."

" 'Tis Father Edmund, I'm ter say?"

"Aye."

" 'Tisna a Scots name," the woman murmured. Then, she noted, "And ye dinna speak Scots."

"I am Saxon-born," Walter lied.

"English!" She fairly spat the word out.

"Nay, I've no more love for them than you—those you would call 'English' are but Norman louts."

There was some truth to that, she supposed. "Aye," she acknowledged grudgingly. "And ye be a man of God, arter all, and 'tis needed ye are, here."

Chapter Nine

It was the morrow. She lay awake, listening to the heavy, even breathing of Ena and the occasional whimper of Jamie. Tossing restlessly, the boy fought nightmares again, but who could blame him for it? Each time he cried, she held him close and patted his thin body until he was still. Finally she turned over in the darkness to peer toward the cold brazier, knowing that ere long one of the scullery boys would carry coals up to start the fire.

It was the morrow. There were no more days, and few hours, in which she could deny William of Dunashie. This day she would wed him, this night she would share his bed. And when the sun came up the second time, she would leave Byrum for Blackleith with him. For good or ill, until one of them died, she would belong to him.

For hours she had lain in the darkness, reliving all she knew of him, all that had ever passed between them. He was so unlike her father or Elias, for he mixed kindness with the anger. He was as a great bear, a huge man who towered above all others, and his body bore the marks of battles fought and won. There

was that fine scar on his face, and the terrible one that
puckered beneath his shoulder. She'd meant to ask of
that, but the moment had passed ere she dared. He
had come back different, harsher than when he'd left
for Wycklow those weeks ago, and she knew not why.
But it did not matter now.

She'd dwell on the kindness, taking hope from that.
Her hand crept to touch the chain that lay between her
breasts, and she recalled how he'd pressed it into her
palm with his lips. He would bring her a stone to hang
on it, he'd said, but he'd not given it to her yet. A
jewel of her own to wear, the first she'd ever had. Elias
had frowned on such things, saying he'd not have his
wife preening herself like a strumpet. Today, she
would have a jewel of her own.

Temper and kindness were strangely mixed within
William of Dunashie. He'd been angered over small
things, and yet he'd accepted what Jamie was without
reservation. How had he known? Despite Nigel's at-
tempts to hide the boy, had there been someone to tell
that James of Woolford was not whole? It did not matter. He would not recoil when he saw her son, and that
was the important thing. Unlike so many others, he
would not sign the Cross over his breast when he
looked on her child.

*I know what he is, Arabella. . . . A bairn cannot
help how it comes into the world. . . . Who am I to
judge your son for what he is? . . . I'd not mistreat
him for it. . . . I'd do what is right by him. . . .* For
all that he'd hesitated in saying it, he'd said it, and she
had to believe him.

But if his acceptance of Jamie calmed her, his passion frightened. It took no more than a look, a gesture, a smile, much less a single kiss to rouse him,
and he was so big. . . . She tore her thoughts away
from that. She did not want to think of lying with him.

It was enough remembering the aging Elias. As his
ability had begun to wane his jealousy had soared, and
with it came the beatings. In his household she'd
learned to fear and loathe a husband's touch. Nay, but

she'd had no kindness of Elias. Nor from any other there—save Aidan of Ayrie.

Aye, and in the deepest, most secret place in her heart, she knew that if Aidan had ever claimed to love her, she gladly would have fled with him. Aidan. It had been years since she'd forced him from her mind. And yet she still felt damned for the sinful thoughts she'd cherished so long ago for Ayrie's son. Perhaps it was not actual adultery, but the desires of her mind that had marked Jamie. Mayhap God had seen the foolish yearning she'd hidden within.

But Aidan, for all his smiles and his kindnesses, had never touched her. And now he'd become no more than a near forgotten memory, much like the stick dolls of her childhood. Why did her thoughts turn again to him on this, her second wedding day? For that she had no answer. It was not that she still longed for him, for she could scarce recall his face.

It was the morrow. And 'twas William of Dunashie that claimed her. "Mother Mary," she whispered into the darkness, "grant that we will please each other. Grant that there will be happiness between us."

"My lady. . . ?" Ena sat up. "Art all right?"

"Aye," Arabella lied. "Go back to sleep."

"I think 'tis time to rise."

As the woman spoke, Arabella heard footsteps in the stairwell and smelled the smoke from the kitchen fires. Throwing aside the warmth of her covers, she groped in the darkness for her discarded gown, then rose to pull it on quickly. As the boys from below carried in the glowing coals, she opened the wood-and-parchment shutter, then half climbed into the window slit to look outside.

Although the waning moon was still shrouded with mist, the rain had finally stopped, and along the distant horizon the faint, warm glow of dawn promised a better day. Leafless trees stood eerily silhouetted, a black-limbed army above the purple-grey hills. She stared long, scarce aware of the chill air that rushed

in around her, thinking 'twas but hours ere she was to
be wed.

"Would you have me wake the boy?" Ena asked
behind her. "They have laid the fire."

"Nay. He did not sleep well." Reluctantly, Arabella
withdrew from the slit and rubbed her cold arms.
Walking to stand over her son, she looked down on
his now peaceful face. Even in the orange light of the
flames he was pale and bloodless. "Nay," she repeated
softly, bending over to tuck the thick blanket about his
small shoulders. "I'd let him sleep whilst he can."

He scarce moved when she touched him. For a long
moment she stared at the nearly helpless child she'd
borne. *Sweet Jamie, with the saft gold hair.* Her mouth
formed the words silently. No matter what any thought,
God had given him to her to love, and she'd not betray
his trust. As she looked down on him, he sighed in
his sleep and snuggled deeper within the warmth of
the covers.

"What will Lord William say when he sees him?"
Ena wondered aloud.

Arabella straightened up. "He already knows."

"Ye told him?"

"It does not matter. He has said he accepts Jamie
as he is."

"And he does, his heart is as big as his body," the
woman muttered, her tone indicating that she doubted
it. "He hasna seen him."

But Arabella's thoughts were once again on William
of Dunashie. If she would have him love Jamie she'd
have to win him herself, and she knew not if she could
do it. She feared she was too afraid of him for the
task.

She smoothed the shimmering sendal over her hips,
straightening the folds beneath the chain girdle, then
turned before the fire, watching the gold and silver
threads in the purple cloth catch the orange of the
flames. It swished stiffly over the bleached linen un-

dergown. She wondered what William would think when he saw her in her wedding robe.

She sat for Ena to plait her hair, working threads that had been raveled from the fabric of the gown through the braids. When the woman was done, they hung like golden ropes past her breasts. Arabella fished beneath the neck of her gown to draw out the chain William had given her, letting it fall over her gown. She'd have him see she valued it. Hopefully the jewel would match her gown. She stooped for Ena to place the baudekin veil over her head, arranging it to fall like a mantle of shimmering mist about her.

"Mama, I'd go down with ye!" Jamie pleaded, his eyes shining with the reflection of the grand gown. "I'd see ye wed!"

Nigel had said he did not want them to see the boy, that he'd not have the Butcher or the Bastard draw back. But they could not—not after the betrothal. And William had said he knew about her child, and from this day forward Nigel would rule her no more. Impulsively, she knelt down.

"And so you shall, lovey."

"But the master . . ." Ena protested.

"What harm can it do when they already know?" Arabella pulled the bottom of his new blue tunic straight, then smoothed his hair with her hands. Smiling into his upturned face, she whispered encouragingly, "Ah, Jamie, 'tis a fine man you'll be when you are grown." But even as she said it, she knew he did not believe her. "We are going to Blackleith with Lord William, and you will never have to hide from your grandsire again."

"Mama, what if Lord William mislikes me?" he asked once more. His eyes dropped to where his leg twisted within the folds of his hose. His foot turned inward so that no one even expected him to try to walk on it. "He hasna seen me, Mama."

"He will be as a papa to you," she promised, drawing him close for a quick embrace. "And you are good, he cannot help liking you, Jamie of Woolford."

"Your sire says Lord William awaits!" someone called through the heavy door.

She rose and dried her suddenly wet palms against her skirt. Dipping her hands into a bowl of dried rose petals, she crushed the fragrant bits against her palms, rubbing them together for the scent. Brushing the petals away, she smoothed her palms over the ends of her braids. Then, licking dry lips, she reached for her son.

"Ye canna carry him. Filben or one of the others—"

"There is not time to call him." Shouldering her son resolutely, Arabella opened the thick wooden door. When the man who had come for her appeared startled, she gave him a look that dared comment. "Hold me, Jamie, else we'll lose our footing," she murmured as she started down.

The wedding party awaited her at the foot of the tower. Nigel looked up, saw she had the boy, and cursed loudly. But William could only stare at her. Despite the chill the sun had come out, and its rays reflected off the metallic threads of the sendal, seeming to bathe her in a brilliant purple light. The wind gusted, catching the sheer baudekin and blowing it back from her head. Her pale braids fell over her shoulders nearly to her waist. He moved forward to meet her.

At the bottom of the steps she lowered the boy, holding his hand to balance him. He swayed on the one good leg and clutched the skirt of her gown. Smiling tentatively at her bridegroom, she made her obeisance. "I give you James of Woolford, my lord."

"Aye." He looked down, prepared to be pleasant to the child, but instead he stared, shocked by what he saw. James of Whatever she chose to call him could not stand unaided on a foot that turned nearly over. William's eyes took in the short, twisted leg, then moved upward to note the thin, frail body and the blue eyes that were too large for the pinched, pale face. The boy cringed beneath his gaze and clung more tightly to the shining fabric, creasing it.

So this was Arabella's bastard brat. As used as he was to those maimed in battle, William wanted to look away. Milo of Woolford was right: She brought him the Devil's changeling, a boy God had marked for her sin. From the looks of his deformity, this child had been cursed in the womb.

Arabella ran her tongue over her lips nervously and waited. It was as though she dared not breathe, for William said nothing. Her father moved forward, his face thunderous, ready to wrest Jamie from her. She held on, and tried not to betray her fear before her betrothed.

The child saw his grandsire and cringed. As Nigel reached angrily for the boy, Will was moved to pity. "Nay, there is no need," he muttered curtly. Leaning down, his face grave, he forced himself to address Arabella's son, " 'Tis a fine new tunic ye wear to your mother's wedding, young James."

James of Woolford managed to nod, his eyes still wary.

"My lord . . . ." Nigel began, frowning.

"Nay. It doesna matter." Will laid a tentative hand on Jamie's head. "Ye are coming to Blackleith with me, ye know."

The boy bowed his head. "My sire's people dinna want me," he mumbled.

Arabella's eyes filled with unshed tears as she appealed mutely to William of Dunashie. And as much as he considered James of Woolford's disfigurement to be God's punishment, William knew he could not deny the child if he would wed her. Hiding the revulsion he felt, he ruffled his pale hair lightly ere he drew away. "Well, for your mother's sake I'd welcome ye, James," he said.

Arabella's throat ached from the tension within her. "My thanks for your kindness, my lord," she whispered painfully. "Ena, I'd have you take him now."

The tiring woman hurried forward to disengage Jamie's hand from the gown, then she lifted him away.

"And ye'd watch, ye'll come with me," she murmured to him.

"But I've nae seen the Butcher," Jamie whimpered as his arms circled her neck.

"Hush," Ena admonished. "Ye've no need to see him."

William stared after them, then turned to his betrothed. " 'Tisna the child I'd fault, mistress," he said shortly. His eyes dropped from her face to the chain at her neck, and he forced a smile. "And I'd still wed the mother."

If he did not appear enthusiastic over her child, at least he had not turned away like so many others. And she knew that was the best she could have hoped. "Aye," she managed, trying to still the misgiving she still felt.

As this was her second wedding, and as it was the Bastard rather than his brother that she wed, there were to be few of the customary festivities to celebrate the marriage. Aye, instead of days of feasting there would be but the ceremony, one banquet, and a boar hunt to mark it. And she suspected the latter was more for her father's own gratification than for his guests'.

Showing how little importance she had for him, Nigel had dispensed with the customary procession to the chapel, leaving William to lead Arabella there himself. She walked beside him in the cold sunlight, her stiff silk gown rustling over the linen beneath, her leather slippers sinking slightly in the still damp turf. Her father, Lord Giles, and nearly everyone else in the keep followed silently. Absent were the horses, the viols, the flutes that she'd had ten years before when 'twas Elias who'd wed her.

William's hand was warm, his clasp strong. Shivering in the chill wind she hurried to match his long strides, scarce daring to look at him. When they reached the chapel door, the priest was there to greet them. William changed hands, taking her right in his. She looked up then, seeing that his face was sober, almost grim.

"Who comes forth to be wed?" the priest demanded, looking to Nigel.

"Arabella of Byrum and William of Dunashie," her father answered loudly.

"And who gives this woman into a husband's keeping?"

"I do." Nigel cleared his throat, then added, "As I am her sire."

The old priest's gaze traveled over those who shivered behind William and Arabella. "And is there any to object—any impediment to this marriage?" There was a chorus of impatient "nays." Turning again to the couple before him, he slipped a small jeweled casket beneath their clasped hands, asking, "Do you, William, lord to Blackleith, take this woman for wife, to have her, to hold for her, to honor her in your house, so long as ye both may live?"

William cleared his throat. "Aye."

"And you, Arabella, born of Byrum, do you take this man for husband, promising to obey him in all things, to be true and faithful to him, to honor him in his house, so long as ye both may live?"

Despite the panic that rose in her breast, despite the finality of what she did, Arabella nodded. The priest looked up, frowning. "I'd hear you say it," he reminded her.

"Aye." Her eyes on the hand that held hers, she repeated more loudly, "Aye."

"Then may God, who is just and merciful, from whom all things come, bless this union between you and make you fruitful, that you may bring forth sons and daughters to praise His Name."

"So be it," William murmured.

"So be it," she repeated.

The old man held up the box containing a saint's bone, announcing loudly, "As William and Arabella have sworn before God and witnesses upon this sacred relic, they are henceforward man and wife." Without further delay he turned to throw open the chapel for the celebratory Mass, and the chilled crowd pressed to get inside.

William released her hand to catch the door before it banged in the wind. Shivering, she ducked beneath his arm into Byrum's chapel. The rest was but ceremony—by her own words, she was already bound forever to Dunashie's bastard. As he sat beside her on the hard, carved bench, she bent her head in prayer to plead of God for a kind husband, for a man who would be tolerant of Jamie. If He could but give her that, she'd do all she could to please William of Dunashie.

Chapter Ten

The smoke from the fire in the great hearth permeated the hall, mingling with the smells of the wedding feast. For once, Nigel's parsimony had been supplanted by his wish to appear generous at his daughter's wedding. The meal was served with as much ceremony as the dishes deserved, for there were not only the customary stag and hare, but also a roasted boar, a stew made of lampreys, several well-presented fowl, and a large pigeon pie. Accompanying the meats were no fewer than ten other dishes, as well as a crudely made marzipan castle, from which flew small silk pennons painted with Dunashie's bear and Byrum's crossed spears.

That her father had chosen the Butcher's symbol rather than the Bastard's was scarce noted. It was accepted that the alliance was with Dunashie. Briefly Arabella wondered if William rode to battle behind a plain shield, or if he used the bear also. It did not matter now, she supposed.

Unused as they were to such meals, Nigel's household fell upon the food, washing it down with large quantities of sour wine, mead, and ale. And long ere the tables had been cleared there were drunken fights, which spilled outside the hall and into the cold courtyard. That they disputed over nothing was unimportant—they were borderers, after all, and therefore inclined to brawl. But if 'twas unseemly behavior, neither William nor his brother seemed to note it, prompting Arabella to wonder further if Dunashie and Blackleith were even rougher than Byrum.

Throughout the lengthy meal Giles conversed with his host politely, while William sat back, toying with his food and watching Arabella silently. Disconcerted, she tried to keep her eyes on the trencher they shared. Sweet Mary, but did he have to look at her constantly? Did he not know she was half out of her wits with fright as it was?

The firelight from the pitch torch above them played upon the shimmering sheerness of the baudekin veil whenever she moved. Will drained the mead from their cup and leaned back, savoring the almost ethereal loveliness of his bride, forgetting for the moment what she'd been to Aidan of Ayrie. She was his. Those three words reverberated with the rhythm of the jongleurs' castanets. *She was his.*

The lazy movement of his gaze belied the eagerness he felt as he drank in the pale gold hair, the fine profile of her face, the slender, graceful neck. Nay, but the bards who still sang of Saxon Harold's Edith had not seen Arabella of Byrum. The woman beside him must surely be the Helen of Scotland. His eyes moved lower, over her shoulders to where the golden chain dipped between her breasts, and his mouth was again dry with desire. The rose fragrance that floated about her was almost as intoxicating as the wine.

Absently he lifted his refilled cup, his thoughts on later. Jesu, but he'd not sit listening to a jongleur's song, not when he had the right to lie with Arabella of Byrum. Not when he had a comely wife to slake his desire and to warm his bones.

She looked up almost furtively, and unwilling to have her see his naked thoughts, he dropped his gaze to the cup, swirling the sweet liquid within. "Would you drink?" he asked, his voice hoarse. " 'Tis little enough you have eaten."

"I am unused to so much."

Nonetheless she took the cup with unsteady hands, and for a moment she simply held it. Then, reddening as he watched expectantly, she turned it to where his lips had been and sipped.

His hand brushed over the silk veil, drawing it off, exposing the pale gold braids that fell forward over her shoulders. " 'Tis lovely hair you have," he said low.

His hand slid downward, and his fingertips traced the shoulder seam of her gown lightly, sending a shudder through her. Turning to set the cup before him, she was acutely aware of how big he was. His velvet-covered shoulder was more than a handbreadth higher than hers, and the hand that rested on the table was strong, powerful enough to snap her bones. He leaned closer, so close that his warm breath rushed against her ear when he spoke. "And they dance, I'd not stay," he whispered.

" 'Tis the custom to lead the round," she reminded him. "And you do not mind it I'd not flaunt tradition, for I'd have good fortune." She hoped he could not hear the fear in her voice.

He was a warrior, not a courtier, and he'd not have her see him for the clumsy fool he was. His fingers moved from the stiff silk to the softness of her hair, stroking it. "I'd nae hae ye laugh at me, Arabella," he murmured, lapsing into the familiar speech.

It was as though the sand were running from the glass, and she was desperate to delay. "I swear I will not laugh, my lord, and you honor me with the round."

Nigel heard her and rose to clap, signaling the beginning of the dance music. Those who'd not drunk themselves into a stupor joined in, while sturdy boys hastened to move the tables out of the way. The jongleurs regrouped, forming a line, and wended their way around the hall as they played their flutes, viols, and castanets to the accompaniment of a portable organ. Inebriated household knights fell into line behind them, gathering the maids as they passed, until a circle had been formed in the center of the room.

"And you do not take your bride out, Will, the task will fall to me," Giles chided, grinning.

There was no help for it, then. Despite the love he had for his brother, William felt at an acute disadvantage now: 'Twas Giles who was handsome, Giles who was rich and powerful, Giles who had won Rivaux's daughter. "Nay," he growled. "And any leads her, I'd do it myself." He rose, feeling more awkward than he ever remembered. Bowing to Arabella, he tried to sound gallant.

" 'Tis ye as honors me."

As the clapping intensified, Arabella took his hand and followed him into the center of the circle. There was an expectant pause, then the jongleurs began anew, this time playing the dance of the chaplet. Will glanced helplessly at his bride, hoping that he would not disgrace himself before her. There was no sound now but the music.

"Bend low," she whispered as she dropped a deep curtsy before him.

"Aye," he muttered, doing as she said. "I'd rather slay dragons for ye than this."

Lifting his hand, he raised her, then stepped back. Coming forward again, he linked arms with her and circled first one way, then the other. Turning aside, they exchanged arms and repeated the measure. The circle around them broke up into half a dozen smaller ones, with the pairs copying what they had done.

He felt stiff and wooden, his face frozen into a grimace, but he managed to keep time to the music, all the while following her lead. He had been, he was to reflect later, much like a bear trying to dance with a cat. Mercifully the song was not a long one, and as the flutes and viols held their last notes William clasped her waist, pulled her forward, lifted her, and kissed her full on the mouth. Her eyes widened as shouts of approval spread through the crowd.

"Ye dinna think I'd take toll?" he murmured wickedly when at last he'd released her.

Once again she was intensely aware of his size. She was not a small woman, and yet he'd lifted her as effortlessly as if she were a babe. He smiled crookedly at her, his hazel eyes watching hers.

"Ye did not disgrace either of us," she managed through suddenly parched lips. "Sweet Mary, but I . . ."

To him, it was as though there were no others there. But the musicians, heeding the call for more, began anew, this time playing a vigorous round, so called for the continuous twirling of pairs in a moving circle. It was a matter of dance, or be felled by those who did. Still afraid of the warmth in her new husband's gaze, Arabella caught at his hand, tugging him into the group. "Come on—they play for us," she dared to urge him.

A melee could scarce have been wilder than the whirling madness about him as William gave over. Grasping both her hands, he stomped out the beat until he felt it, then he twirled her round and round, keeping up with the music. The veil, which had been at her shoulders, fell to the floor beneath their feet. Her braids swung outward like swinging ropes of gold, and her grey eyes sparkled with the abandon of the moment. He forgot his fear of playing the fool as he watched her obvious pleasure in the dance. The circle moved faster and faster, until she could scarce catch her breath, and still she kept the pace, her smile urging him on. The beat reverberated in his head as his body sought to match it. He had no sense of anything but the music and the woman.

The orange-gold flames of the torches could be seen in the ever-moving iridescence of her magnificent gown. She was some faery creature from another world, too beautiful almost to touch, and yet it was his hands that held hers. Even the faint sheen of perspiration that damped her brow beguiled him. Finally the castanets ceased, the flutes held the last high notes, and it was over.

They stood there, catching their breath for a moment, as the circle dissolved around them. "Nae more," he gasped.

"Aye."

She was panting. Freeing one hand, she pushed at escaping strands of hair. Gone was the faery creature, replaced by a flesh-and-blood woman. His eyes dropped to her still heaving bosom.

"I'd retire ere the music starts again." Then, realizing how eager he must sound, he added, "I'd nae be overtired for the hunt in the morning."

Her eyes widened and her breath caught. Despite the heat, she suddenly felt cold. "I—I'd go up first, my lord," she managed. "I'd move Jamie ere you come. He usually sleeps with me, for he has ill dreams."

"And would ye unplait your hair?" His big hand reached to touch it lightly, stroking it back from her temple. "Aye. I'd feel the silk of it, Arabella." Even as he spoke he leaned closer, drawing in the scent of the golden plaits. "I'd smell the roses."

Despite the fact that it would tangle later, 'twould give her more time. "Aye."

It was as though he knew her thoughts, for he nodded. "I'd nae give ye long."

She swallowed visibly. "Aye." Unable to meet the desire in his gaze, she turned to look for Ena. Motioning for the woman to go with her, she started back to the high table. "Papa, with your leave I'd retire," she said simply.

Nigel, more than a little flushed from drink, waved her out. At his side, Giles of Moray rose and lifted a cup of mead to her. "And I do not see you ere I go, Lady Arabella, I'd wish you health and happiness now. May God smile on you and my brother."

"Amen," she wished fervently.

" 'Tis a good man you have taken for husband," he added.

"And ye canna say he doesna pant fer ye!" her father brayed at her. "Ye'll nae need a fire this night!" As William took the bench beside him again, Nigel clapped him hard on the shoulder. "Aye, 'tis a fine stallion my silver buys for the mare!"

Ribald shouts followed her as she hurried from the hall, with one of her father's retainers wondering loudly if the groom's nether parts matched the rest of him. Others joined in, proposing to strip the Bastard ere they sent him up to her. She glanced back nervously to see William of Dunashie lift an overflowing cup to his lips. Mayhap he would be too drunk to bed her.

But as Ena went ahead, lighting the darkened stairway with a sputtering torch, Arabella climbed silently, knowing that it did not matter. If not this night, then on the morrow, and on as many morrows after as he would choose.

Jamie was asleep within the feather mattress, an unheard of treat for the boy denied so much. Parting the heavy curtains, Arabella leaned over to lift him from the warmth. He whimpered slightly as she shifted him into the tiring woman's arms. For a long moment Arabella looked into his face, then she bent to brush a kiss against his brow.

"I'll take him ter my pallet, mistress," Ena offered.

"Aye." It would not do for him to hear William of Dunashie bed her. "Aye," Arabella repeated. With nearly numb fingers, she fumbled at the lacings beneath her arms. "Go on—I can tend to the rest. I'd be abed ere he comes."

"Yer hair . . ."

" 'Twill be no hard task to undo it. Please—I'd have Jamie gone ere he comes."

"God aid ye, mistress," Ena murmured. "May the Bastard prove a better husband than the last."

The woman had scarce left ere there were loud shouts on the stairs. Panicked, Arabella pulled the threads from her braids and combed the ripples with her fingers. For a moment she considered whether to scramble between the sheets or to await her new lord as she was, unlaced but still clothed. The door burst open, taking the choice from her, and half a dozen men thrust her husband into the room. Gone were his shoes, his velvet tunic, and his fine linen undershert, all apparently pulled off by others. The ties of his chausses were hanging half-undone, as though he'd put up more of a fight over them.

"God's bones, but ye'll have ter school her!" someone shouted from behind him. "She isna abed!"

William turned on them, growling, "I'd nae hae ye see her—off with ye." When a Byrum man reached around him to tug at the chausses, he pushed him toward the door. "I'd nae want to crack heads tonight, but afore God, I will," he warned the rest of them. "Off, I said—there's still ale aplenty below."

Amid much grumbling they backed down, and as soon as the last one was on the stairs William threw the heavy bar over the latch. Turning back to her, he could see she was as pale as her hair. And he did not blame her for it.

For all his eagerness, he was unsure now. She was not Berta, ready to lie beneath him for King David's pennies. She was Arabella of Byrum, the wife who'd bear the sons of his body, a gentle-born woman. And by the looks of it he'd have no easy task, for she wore again the expression of a cornered animal. Afraid his perceived roughness would frighten her more, he willed himself to speak again like the gentle-born.

" 'Tis cold," he observed finally. "You ought to be abed ere you take a chill."

"There was no time," she answered simply.

"Your woman . . ."

"I sent her with Jamie."

Jamie. The bastard she'd borne Aidan of Ayrie. He'd not wanted to think of that, not now when she came to him. But she'd spoken the words, and he could not help it. When she lay with him, would her thoughts be of Duncan's son? Would she remember another, mayhap better lover? He had to delay, to put that from his mind.

"While you ready yourself, I will build up the fire," he decided. "I'd not have you sicken."

At least he was not going to throw himself on her forthwith. "I could warm some wine for you," she offered. "Papa keeps a honey pot and spices here that he would not share, but surely this night . . ." Her voice trailed off uncertainly.

He'd had enough already, but it would give him time to gain her acceptance. "Nay," he demurred, "but I'd not stop you, and you wanted some for yourself."

She opened the small cabinet and drew out the precious spices Nigel reserved for himself. Taking out a cup, she dared to pour into it her father's best wine, that which had come from faraway Aquitaine. After liberally sprinkling powdered cloves, ginger, and shaved cinnamon over the dark liquid, she stirred a spoon of honey into the mixture. Dipping her finger into it, she tasted for sweetness, then added a little more, taking care not to get any of the waxy comb. She carried her cup to where he readjusted the burning logs.

"Is it hot?" she asked, waiting for him to hand her the poker.

"Aye. Be careful that you do not mark yourself."

She blew the ashes from the metal rod, then thrust the end into the wine. The liquid hissed, and the aroma of the spices floated into the air. "Art certain you'd have none?" she asked.

"Nay. I'd not be a sot for you this night."

She sipped, then moved away gracefully, her gown swishing stiffly. It, the sizzling poker, and the popping fire were the only sounds in the room. "To your health, my lord," she said quietly, lifting her cup.

"And yours also," he answered soberly.

For William, the minutes seemed to be measured by the beat of his heart. She was his—he had the right to take her. He waited for her to drain the cup, then his hands shook as he reached to take it from her. " 'Tis time we were abed,'' he decided finally.

"I'll warrant 'tis,'' she agreed, looking away. Sweet Jesu, she thought desperately, I'd not do this. But it mattered not now, for she had not the right to refuse him.

He felt like an awkward boy who faced the spinning quintains for the first time, not knowing whether he would hit them or make a fool of himself. Nonetheless, he set the empty vessel down and moved behind her. His fingertips traced the line of her shoulder where her hair fell away. "Would you that I aided you?"

She stood very still, feeling as though she would break if she moved. The big man behind her was a stranger. And now he would bed her. Her whole body went cold.

"Nay.''

He was aware she feared him, and yet he knew not how to ease her. He tried with words. "Arabella, I know I am not what you would have, but 'tis done,'' he said. "And as we are bound by the oaths we have given, 'tis our task to give each other whatever happiness there is.''

"Aye,'' she whispered.

Very gently, he turned her around. She stared into the dark red hair that curled against his bared chest. "You were wounded,'' she murmured foolishly, grasping at anything to say, daring to touch the puckered scar. "I'd meant to ask . . . but I . . .''

Her hands were like ice against him. "It has nearly healed.'Twas my folly—I had it when Reyner of Eury captured Wycklow last summer.''

She forced herself to look up. He was watching her, his hazel eyes warm, his mouth curved into a crooked smile. His auburn hair was tousled from where they'd pulled his clothes over his head. Despite his thirty-two years, he looked more the overgrown boy than the man, she told herself.

"And your face? How had you that, my lord?''

He felt the thin scar, rubbing at it. "I cannot remember taking this one—I did not note it until after the battle was done. For all the skirmishes I've fought, I've not taken many marks.''

''Oh.''

There was an awkward silence between them, until he could stand it no longer. ''Arabella,'' he said softly, ''I am no ogre, I swear to you. I'd have your kiss again now.''

The sand was running from the glass, and she knew it. This time, no matter what he did to her, 'twas his right. Telling herself she had to please him for Jamie, she stepped closer. Obediently, she reached for his neck, pulling his head to meet hers. His skin was hot and alive beneath her fingers. His arms went around her, holding her close, as she tentatively pressed her lips against his.

It was all the encouragement he needed. His mouth sought hers hungrily, taking what she offered and more. His tongue tested, then plundered, possessing her mouth with an eagerness that overwhelmed. And despite the sendal gown, despite the linen undershift beneath, she could feel the rising of his body against hers. Panic rose in her breast, stifling her breath, and yet she dared not push him away.

His hands moved over her shoulders, her back, her hips, exploring, pressing, molding her to him, urging her to respond to him. His fingers gathered the stiff skirt of her wedding gown, drawing it upward, baring her legs as he'd done before. She twisted her head, tearing her mouth from his.

''Nay,'' she protested, desperate for time, ''I'd not ruin my gown.''

His breath rushed past her ear, sending new shivers coursing down her neck and spine. ''I'd hae ye take it off,'' he whispered hotly, when his hands found the bare flesh beneath.

''Aye,'' she croaked, closing her eyes as his palm cupped her hip, while his other hand slid between their bodies to touch her. She held her breath, afraid to move, until he found the scant wetness there. A sob rose in her throat. There was no more time. The sand was gone from the glass.

Abruptly he released her, and her gown fell again about her legs. "I'd nae wait, Arabella."

Her eyes flew open as he reached under her arms for her loosened laces. "Nay, I'd do it," she managed, backing away. Before he could touch her again she'd turned and lifted the hem of the heavy gown, pulling it quickly over her head. Aware that he watched her, she folded it and carried it to the chest beyond the bed. There, in the red and black shadows, she moved the undershift. "Bed me then, and be done," she said, whirling around to face him again. "I'd not deny you." Her gaze dropped from the naked desire in his eyes. He'd removed his chausses. "Sweet Mary," she breathed.

Her eyes were dilated, much like those of a filly about to be ridden the first time. For all his misgivings, he'd not expected her to be like this. "You have borne a babe," was all he could think of to say as he approached her. "I'd nae hurt you."

This time, there were no clothes between them when he embraced her. Her whole body trembled. "Come to bed ere you freeze," he murmured against her ear. His hands twined in her hair, holding her face between them, as his mouth possessed hers more gently than before. When he raised his head, his eyes were dark with passion. "I'd lie with you now, Arabella of Byrum," he whispered.

When she did not answer he reached for her hand, pulling her with him toward the curtained bed. She scrambled between the sheets as he eased down next to her. For a long moment he stared into her shadowed face, thinking she was the most beautiful creature of his memory.

"I've nae had any but whores, but I'd try to please you."

"And you do not hurt me, 'tis enough," she croaked.

"It has been too long for me. But if I hurt you, you

have but to tell me, and I will stop,'' he promised,
bending his head to hers.

She could only make it worse by delaying and risk-
ing his anger. She forced herself to touch his face, to
feel the reassuring warmth of his breath. He was, she
told herself, no Elias, but rather a younger, more virile
man who would please her if she'd let him. ''And for
me also,'' she answered finally, her voice scarce above
a whisper. ''It has been long for me also.''

''Hold me,'' he murmured against her lips.

This time, when he kissed her, her hands clasped
his bare back, holding him, and she could not help
marveling at the strength of him. Telling herself that
it would soon be over, she kissed him also.

Her touch sent fire coursing through his veins, heating his body beneath her hands. Having thought of
little else for hours, he was ready. His hand moved
over her hip inward to slip between her thighs, touching the softness there. Her body tensed, and she gasped
at the suddenness of what he did. Telling himself that
she was wet enough, that she was ready, he waited no
longer. He rolled her onto her back, stifled her startled
protest with his mouth, and sought her body with his
own.

She cried out as he held her hips and thrust within,
then lay trembling beneath him. He tried to gentle her
as he would a horse, speaking softly, '' 'Tis all right,
Arabella . . . 'tis all right,'' holding himself still until
she slackened to accommodate him. Then he began to
move, tentatively at first, trying not to hurt her. When
she did not cry again he thrust harder and deeper,
moving rhythmically until he lost all rational thought
of her. He was drowning in the exquisite pleasure her
body gave him.

She'd been unprepared for the feel of him within
her, but as he moved her body tried to respond. Her
hands clenched and unclenched, holding him, raking
his back. Moving and twisting beneath him, she
strained to match him, until she felt the hunger also.
But she was too late: As the first primordial cries

welled within her, she felt the flood of his seed, and
he collapsed over her. He lay spent, while her body
screamed silently for what it had been denied. It was
over.

Finally, thinking he crushed her, he rolled away. "I
did not mean to pain you," he said after a time.

"You did not."

Her voice was flat and toneless, shaming him. He'd
been but a clumsy dolt again, and he knew it. She was
no whore who had to pretend for money that he had
pleased her when he had not. He raised himself
slightly, easing her tangled hair from beneath his
shoulder, then turned to face her. His hand stroked the
soft hair, smoothing it over her skin. " 'Twill be better on the morrow," he promised. "You were overtired, and I did not want to use you roughly." She lay
there, scarce breathing, saying nothing. "Nay," he
admitted, sighing heavily, "mayhap I know not how
to please you. I am more used to swinging my battle-
axe than lying with a woman."

" 'Tis all right," she managed, trying to hide her
disappointment, telling herself it was enough that he'd
not hurt her. For all his size, he'd not hurt her.

Her hair was like silk beneath his palm. He continued smoothing it, savoring the feel of it, stroking
it where it fell over her breast. Her breath caught,
and he could hear her swallow as the nipple hardened
beneath his hand. A shiver he could feel rippled
through her. Mistaking the reason, he started to draw
away.

"I'd cover you ere you chill."

"I pray you will not." Even though he could scarce
see her in the faint light, she closed her eyes to hide
from him ere she dared to speak. "Nay," she said,
swallowing again.

"I wanted more between us," he murmured lamely.

" 'Twas good."

He knew she lied, for when 'twas good with Berta
the whore had panted and cried, begging for more,
and he could tell the difference. Mayhap he'd expected

overmuch from this first coupling, mayhap 'twas different for a gentlewoman. Then he thought of Giles and Elizabeth, and the sounds of passion he'd heard between them. Nay, there was no higher-born woman than Elizabeth of Rivaux. If there was any fault in his marriage bed, 'twas his. And he'd not sleep if she lay beside him like this.

He stared into the shadowed darkness of the curtained bed, trying to study Arabella's face. Very gently, he pushed her hair back from brow, and leaned over her.

"And ye do not mind it, I'd not wait until the morrow to mend the matter," he said softly. "I'd try to do better by ye, I swear."

His breath caressed her skin, sending a rush of unexpected desire through her. His hand sought her breast, cupping it, and his thumb rubbed her taut nipple. And this time, it was as though her whole body quickened beneath his touch.

"I do not mind it." As she said the words, she closed her eyes to hide her embarrassment.

Marveling that she could still want him, he eased closer and bent his head to hers, murmuring, "Aye, there is no need to wait for the morrow."

For answer her arms embraced him, pulling him down to her. This time, he was in no hurry. He tasted and teased her lips, her earlobes, the hollow of her throat, her shoulders, and finally each breast, exploring slowly, tasting, enjoying fully her response to him until she thought she could stand it no longer. Forgetting her earlier fear of him, she twisted beneath him, tormenting him wantonly, demanding more as his desire rose again. And to him, knowing she wanted him was far headier, far more intoxicating than the spiced wine he tasted on her lips.

This time, when he entered her, she gave herself wholeheartedly, moving with abandon, moaning as though she could not wait for him. This time, her response told him he did not need to fear hurting her. He drove harder and harder, urged on by the heat of her body, until all thought deserted him, until her moans became cries. Her hands raked his back, her nails dug into his skin, and still she would have more of him. There was no other time, no other place for either of them until the mindless rhythm carried them home.

This time, she knew peace as she floated back to reality, her arms and legs still wrapped tightly around him. She held him, listening contentedly to his ragged breathing against her ear. He lay over her, making no move to leave her.

"God's bones, Arabella, but I've had an easier ride breaking a horse," he panted, when at last he'd found his voice.

Mortified, she turned her head away. "Sweet Mary, but what you must think me," she choked. " 'Twas but—"

"Nay." His finger stilled her lips. "I'd think you pleased me well." Knowing he was too heavy for her he finally rolled away, then propped himself on an elbow to face her. Brushing her damp face with the back of his hand, he added softly, "I've never had the like."

She swallowed as the blood rushed to her face. " 'Twas never . . . Elias . . ."

"Nay, I'd not think of any other. 'Tis us—William and Arabella—now," he murmured, silencing her again.

But later, as he listened to the even rhythm of her breathing, he lay awake. And for all that he would not think of that, he could not help wondering if she'd lain so for Aidan of Ayrie. It did not matter, he told himself resolutely, for only he had the right to have her from this night forward. Wrapping his arms around her, he forced Duncan's son from his mind by reliving the feel of her beneath him.

Chapter Eleven

William wanted to linger abed, savoring the warmth of the woman beside him, but already the hunting horn sounded in the courtyard below. She slept soundly still, and he'd not waken her, not after the night she'd given him. He rolled over and lifted the curtain slightly, letting in the grey morning light.

Jesu, but she was lovely. Her tangled hair was like a mass of pale, spun gold, the spiral pattern of her braids still visible where the strands fell across his pillow. His fingers stroked it lightly, feeling again the softness of it. And the faint fragrance of rosewater seemed to rise from beneath his hand. From this day forward, whenever he saw or smelled a rose, he'd think of her.

For all that she'd lain beneath him the night before, she gave the appearance in sleep of utter innocence, and the thought crossed his mind that she looked as the priests described angels. He eased the covers from her bare shoulder to look on her again, and his mouth went dry with remembered desire. Unlike the whores he'd known, she was as fair of form as of face. But more than that, she was now his and his alone.

The horn sounded again, and he could hear the shouts of men and the baying of Nigel's prized alaunts. Reluctantly, he drew the covers up again, and rolled to sit on the side of the bed. The chill, damp air hit his legs, making him regret that he'd told Nigel he'd go. A man belonged abed after the first night of his marriage, not out chasing wild boars over the hills. The only rutting boar he'd meet, and he had the choice, was himself.

Heaving himself up, he searched for his chausses and garters, then pulled the leggings on and sat again to wrap the leather bands, smoothing the knitted wool over his calves. He rose to rummage within the boxes that Arabella's woman had already packed for his warmest tunic, for he suspected 'twould be damp and cold, if not actually rainy outside. He found it and pulled it on quickly. Curious, he unlatched the shutters and looked into the yard below. He'd been right: The early morning sky was overcast, and the mists mingled with the dew, leaving beads of moisture on the stone sill. The steam of his breath blew back in his face.

The chill wind gusted across the room, blowing the opened bed curtains. Arabella stirred within, at first only dimly aware of the loss of warmth from the bed, then she knew she was alone. She stretched limbs still stiff from sleep and turned over, peering out into the faint grey light, seeing him silhouetted against the open window. Merciful Mary, but she'd survived her first night with him.

Nay, 'twas more than that, she admitted, for not only had he not harmed her, but she'd been nearly as pleased as he to discover the passion between them. It had been far different this marriage night, for she bore no bruises. Unlike Elias, William of Dunashie had not beaten her for what she was afraid to do. Unlike Elias, he had wanted to please her also.

He swung around and saw that she'd wakened. "Your pardon—I'd not meant to disturb you." Leaving the window unshuttered, he walked back to the bed, smiling. " 'Tis little enough sleep I gave ye, Arabella of Byrum," he murmured softly, lapsing into the soft burr of the border. When she said nothing, he teased her lightly, " 'Tis the morrow, and ye still live."

The warmth in his hazel eyes brought a hot rush of blood to her face, reddening it. He sank to sit on the edge of the mattress, his weight bowing the ropes beneath, then he leaned over her. His smile broadened into an almost boyish grin.

"Ye canna know how loath I am to leave ye for the company of men and hounds." As her blush deepened even further, he added wickedly, "Aye, I can think of a dozen other things I'd rather do with ye—and all of them right here."

"A dozen?" she croaked weakly.

"Aye." He bent low enough to brush his lips against her skin, and the warmth of his breath sent shivers coursing through her. "We have but begun, Arabella of Byrum," he whispered against her ear. Abruptly, he straightened up and sighed. "But they wait below, and I doubt me they'd tarry enough for me to do right by ye." He forced himself to rise, then walked to shutter the window. "Would ye that I laid a fire for ye ere I left?"

"Nay. Ena or one of the scullery boys will do it."

She swung her legs over the side to sit, and when he turned back to face her she was acutely conscious of her nakedness. She grasped the bed curtain and pulled it to cover her, but not before she'd seen the desire in his eyes.

"Bella, ye are as beautiful as God could make ye."

"I look a frightful creature, my lord," she contradicted, blushing anew.

He grinned again, and once more she was struck by how young he looked for his years. "Ah, but 'tis how I'd remember ye," he teased her. Turning to the packed boxes, he found a plain blue wool gown for her. Holding it up, he asked, "Would ye wear this— or would ye that I called the woman for ye?" Then, before she could answer, he added, "And ye nae mind it, I'd hae your kiss ere she comes up."

"Aye."

His brow lifted, but his grin remained. " 'Aye'? Which is it: aye, ye'd wear this, or aye, ye'd hae the woman?"

He was so big standing there before her that she could scarce imagine what they'd done in the night, she could scarce believe she'd lain unharmed beneath this huge stranger. That she had actually coupled with him not only once, but twice. She hesitated, but she knew what he'd have her say.

"The gown."

He held it out, but made no move to bring it to her. For a long moment, he waited for her. "A kiss for the gown," he offered. "And I'd even put it on ye." When she still sat, he took one step closer. "I'd seen ye again, Arabella of Byrum—I'd see ye again ere I leave ye."

Despite the fact he'd looked on her before, despite what they'd done in the night, she felt suddenly inadequate. "I am too thin!" she blurted out. "Elias said I was naught but bones!"

"Then he was blind."

There was no help for it: She had not the right to refuse William of Dunashie anything now, for he was her husband in fact as well as words. Reluctantly she let the curtain drop, and she stood before him. As his eyes traveled over her body, lingering on her breasts, then on her waist and her bared belly, she felt flooded with heat.

"Come here."

His grin was gone, and what she saw in his face was hunger. Her heart pounding, she forced herself to walk to him. For want of anything else to say, she managed to mumble, "For your good fortune on the hunt," as she raised herself on tiptoe to touch his lips lightly with hers.

He dropped the gown and his arms closed around her, holding her tightly, molding her body into his, while his mouth possessed hers eagerly, tasting deeply. One hand reached to cradle her head, while the other moved over the bare skin of her back and hip. Somewhere in the distance the horn blew insistently, but she scarce heard it as she gave herself over to what he did to her.

"Will! Will! God's bones, but you are abed overlong! Tarry any longer and Nigel himself will come up for you!" As Giles' voice carried through the thick, wood-planked door, he pounded on it loudly. "And you'd eat, come on!"

Reluctantly, William released her and stepped back. As he bent over to retrieve her gown she stood there, her body shaking from the intensity of her own desire. He straightened up and hung the garment over her neck awkwardly. His hazel eyes were almost gold as they met hers. "God knows I'd not hunt just now, but there's no help for it."

She breathed deeply, then managed to nod. "Aye."

" 'Twill be as good between us tonight as now," he promised. For a brief moment he favored her with a crooked smile. "Until then I'd have you prepare the pits for roasting, for 'tis a big one I mean to bring you."

She waited until he was nearly to the door, then she called after him, "Have a care that you are not hurt, my lord!"

He stopped and turned back momentarily, grinning. "Och, but ye behold one who can hunt with a lance as well as with an arrow, Arabella of Byrum."

After he'd left she pulled the heavy gown down over her body, then hastened to unlatch the shutter to watch. When he emerged into the yard she saw him bend down to scratch behind the head of her father's favorite alaunt, a fierce dog not often tolerant of strangers. But this day the beast wagged his tail and rolled over, as though he would offer his belly as well. When William straightened up Malmet would have followed him, but for Nigel's vicious jerk on the studded collar. The one called "Lang Gib" said something she could not hear,

but she could see the others laugh. Then someone
handed William a hunk of cheese and half a loaf of
dark bread as he heaved his great body into his saddle.

As they rode out over the lowered bridge, she drew
back in and closed the shutters. Walking back across
the room, she sat on the edge of the bed and reached
for her stockings. She paused long enough to offer a
quick prayer for her new husband's safety. For all that
she'd not wanted to wed him, she would not complain
of him now. She was, after all, still whole, and he was
well pleased with her.

The morning mists swirled over the road, obscuring
visibility, and yet the boar hounds lunged before the
huntsman who struggled to hold them. Nigel reined in
and waited for the others to stop also. Pointing into
the fog, he told Giles, "A large one was sighted over
that hill but last week, and there's been none to hunt
him since. I told my men to save him for ye, my lord."

"Aye," a man corroborated for him, "this one is
possessed of tusks so great he could slit a man from
knee to breastbone with 'em."

" 'Twill be no easy task to find him in this," Giles
murmured, "but I am willing to attempt it. What say
you, Will?"

His thoughts still on Arabella of Byrum, William
roused himself guiltily. "Eh? Oh—aye, and ye lead me
to the beast, I'd take him."

Nigel leaned forward in his saddle to survey the hills
to either side of the road. Of all that he hunted he
counted the boar the greatest challenge, for it was far
more cunning and far more deadly than the stag. He
drew deeply of the chill air, savoring the dampness of
it, then exhaled the steam. It was, he considered, the
right weather. Raising his hand, he signaled to the
huntsmen to loose the dogs.

Flushing the boar was never easy, for it was a cau-
tious beast, not overgiven to venturing from cover
without first sniffing, listening, and peering from its
narrow den. And if it became suspicious, it could not

be lured from the lair. Unlike the stag, neither notes
blown on the ivory oliphants nor shouts from the hunters would flush a boar out. Unless one was discovered
in the open, it would take the dogs to corner the fe-
rocious animal, and more than one alaunt would be
ripped open in the process. A cornered boar was always vicious, and determined to fight to the end.

As the leashes were removed the pack of dogs surged
forward, running nearly to the crest of the hill ere they
stopped to sniff. Malmet raised his long, pointed muz-
zle into the air, taking measure of the boar's scent
from all directions, then he broke again into a full run
toward the brush, and the others raced after him. 'Twas
what Nigel liked best about the powerful dog: It knew
how to lead. Had he been offered the equivalent of
Arabella's dowry for the beast, he'd have refused it.
He murmured a quick prayer to St. Martin for the dog's
safety, then he spurred his horse to follow the yelping
pack.

The terrain was rugged, the tangle of brush thick
where an irregular gully sliced between the hills. As
the horses stumbled down the rough incline, the fog
hovered in the low places, enveloping everything.
Ahead of William a beater lost his footing on the dead,
slippery grass and fell into a narrow stream that snaked
along the gully's path. And William himself was nearly
unseated when Malmet stopped directly in front of his
horse to smell of fresh spoor.

Nigel's huntsman knelt to study the freshly disturbed mud, then pronounced, ''Aye—'tis where he
has dug for worms, my lord.''

''When?''

''This morning.''

Once again the powerful dog took off before them,
barking even more loudly than before. And the pack
followed. Nigel rose in his saddle, but could see little
for the fog.

''We are not far, my lords!'' he chortled gleefully.
''Malmet's call grows insistent!''

The gully widened and the floor flattened, revealing

the source of the stream in a small spring. And directly ahead, the pack of dogs jumped and yipped eagerly at their quarry. The sound of the pig mingled with their barking.

It was cornered at its lair, a narrow place dug between the bared, twining roots of two trees. And Nigel's man had been right: 'Twas a goodly-sized beast that stood, its feet spread, its huge tusks thrust upward in defiance, daring the hounds to come closer. One of the younger dogs rushed forward to attack, but his bark turned to a high-pitched yelp as he fell, cut open.

Fearing the loss of his best hound, Nigel shouted, "Malmet! Malmet! Draw off!" as William, Giles, and the others grasped spears. The beaters raised their stout staffs, poised to direct the boar toward the lords. As the big alaunt pulled back reluctantly, another dog challenged the wild pig and died.

"Stand ready, my lords!" Nigel called out, brandishing his sword.

The beast feinted at the nearest hound, then bolted into the mists. The dead brush rustled and crackled beneath him as it ran. Nigel cursed loudly and rode over the dead dogs in pursuit. And once again Malmet surged ahead, leading them into the fog.

They rode some distance before there was a pause in the barking. Giles pulled up and listened, wondering aloud if they'd lost the trail, but Nigel would not have it. "Nay. Malmet willna let him escape," he promised.

The big dog circled several times then headed over the hill, and once again the others joined him eagerly. As tired as he was, William felt his own anticipation rise as he applied the spurs to his horse. He'd promised Arabella a big boar, and afore God, he'd bring this one to her.

It was a wily creature, he'd give it that, for it led them on a rigorous chase, taking them through gullies, bramble-filled ravines, and over rough hills, crossing back and forth, stopping to kill dogs that closed the distance, then taking off again and again. 'Twas not a wonder it had grown to such size, for it knew how to elude both men and dogs.

Finally exhausted, the old boar stopped in front of a patch of heavy underbrush and drank from the stream. Snorting defiantly, he watched the hunters dismount and close in for the kill. "Go on!" Nigel urged Giles, "he is yours to take!"

But Giles drew back. "Nay—'tis the bridegroom as should carry home the tusks! Will!"

"Aye—I am ready!"

"But 'twas for ye we saved him!" Arabella's father protested to Giles. "Nay, 'tis yours—and I'd hae ye take him! My lord, 'tis more meet . . ."

His words were drowned out in the noise of the barking, lunging hounds, as they taunted their prey. The boar attacked another one that had dared too far, felling it, then turned on the closest beater, ripping at him and tearing his arm. As blood spurted from the man's wound, William circled to draw the beast away. But it wheeled and charged Nigel of Byrum instead, and as Nigel backed up to brace his spear he tripped over an exposed root. One of the animal's tusks gored his shoulder as he fell, and for a moment William thought Nigel's arm had been torn from its socket. To save the older man, he poked the beast in the rump.

It whirled to charge him, leaping over Nigel's leg, its head lowered to a point just beneath William's abdomen, ready to disembowel him. There was scarce time for the big man to fall to his knees and raise the lance. Thrusting forward with all the force he could muster, he caught the boar solidly in the center of its chest. There was a high-pitched squeal as the shaft shattered, then the boar swerved, ran a few feet, and dropped dead.

"Well done!" Giles shouted. " 'Twas a solid hit!"

But William knelt to attend Nigel. For all that he could not like him, there was now the marriage bond between them. "Get me something to staunch the blood," he ordered those who stood around him. "Jesu, but he bleeds more than the pig!" Pulling off

his own tunic, he tied the sleeves tightly together over
Nigel's shoulder, making a knot above the wound.
"Roll something that I may put it beneath. Aye, and
look to the beater."

Someone thrust a hastily cut piece of cloth at him
and he folded it, forcing it beneath the knot. When he
sat back on his haunches, he could tell that his father-
in-law's color was still good. Nigel's hand reached to
the strange bandage, and when he drew it away his
fingers were bloody.

"How bad is it?" he asked, looking up at Giles.

For answer, William gently lifted Nigel's arm above
his head and lowered it several times. " 'Tis but the
flesh—the bone is intact."

"Aye."

Lang Gib filled his pot helmet from the stream and
carried it to the lord of Byrum. Nigel drank deeply,
then leaned back against William.

"Jesu," he breathed.

"My lord . . ." The man called Ewan, William's
newly named master of his horse, moved forward to
hold out his linen undershert. " 'Twill be better than
the wool."

"I'd see the bleeding stops ere I change the cloth,"
Will muttered. But even as he said it, he could see that
the wool was too bulky to be effective. Sighing, he
untied it, then poured the rest of the cold water over
the shoulder, noting for the first time that the wound,
although deep, was a puncture rather than a tear. "Ye
are fortunate," he told Nigel. "And he'd raised his
head, ye'd hae lost the arm."

"Aye."

This time William drew his dagger and separated the
sleeves from the undershert, rolled the body into a
tight ball, and then used the sleeves separately to tie
it to Arabella's father's shoulder. There was no question it was a better arrangement. He picked up his
bloodied tunic and pulled it on again.

"Can ye ride—or would ye that we made a litter?"
he asked Nigel.

As the awareness that he'd survive took root, whatever small amount of gratitude Nigel possessed turned to chagrin. "I'd ride," he muttered through clenched teeth. "I am nae a helpless hinny." With an effort he lurched to his feet, then stumbled to where one of his men held his horse. "Get me up," he ordered.

"Would ye that I took the tusks fer ye?" Ewan asked William.

"Nay. Carry it back—I promised my lady a big one, and I'd have her see it whole."

One of Byrum's beaters tapped Will on the shoulder, and as he swung around the man gave voice to his admiration. " 'Twas a strong blow, my lord—as good and clean as ever I have seen." He looked to where Nigel sat his horse, then back to Will. " 'Twas a brave thing ye did, for all that he doesna thank ye for it."

They rode back in subdued silence, some of them mourning the loss of good dogs, others concerned for the beater who stood to lose the use of his arm. Every now and again Will twisted in his saddle to look back at the boar suspended between two poles. It was the biggest he'd ever seen.

" 'Twas a stroke of luck," Nigel said finally. "Ye got him from behind." He turned to Giles of Moray, shaking his head, "I'd hoped 'twould be ye as took him, for ye hae the greater skill."

Giles' black eyes went cold for a moment. "Nay," he contradicted, " 'twas a blow as saved your life— and probably the best I have ever witnessed."

"Well, and I'd known ye dinna want it, I'd hae taken it myself," Nigel grumbled.

There was no mistaking the older man's meaning: He considered William too insignificant to gain such a prize. 'Twas the gentle-born as had the right to such things, not a "Will o' Dunashie." And for all that he'd given his daughter in marriage to the bastard, 'twas only for the bond of blood he'd share with Giles. And again, William could not help wondering if 'twas because of Arabella's disgrace that Nigel had deigned to give her to him at all.

As soon as they'd crossed the bridge into Byrum, nearly everyone in the keep gathered 'round to admire the boar Will had taken. As scullery lads elbowed with stable boys to look on the beast, William started across the yard. Arabella was coming down the outside steps of the tower, but she stopped momentarily when she saw him, and her eyes widened in horror at the bloodied tunic he wore.

"Sweet Mary!" she gasped. "Art all right?"

"Aye—'tis your father as took the wound."

But 'twas to him that she came, making certain first that he was whole ere she turned her attention to her father, and that gratified him. Nigel might think him worthless, but at least his daughter realized where her loyalty lay.

Behind him they lifted the lord of Byrum from his saddle, easing him to the ground. In obvious pain now from his wound, he looked up at Giles rather than Will.

"Do you stay to feast on the boar, my lord?" he asked.

"Nay. I have tarried overlong as it is." Giles turned to William. "And you?"

"Nay," Will muttered. "I'd leave on the morrow also."

Chapter Twelve

Whether 'twas because of the festivities or because of the passion he'd shared during the night, William came awake slowly. His mind wanted to linger in the netherworld where fancy clouded thought.

He'd been in battle, and his arm ached from wielding his axe. Smoke and flames had surrounded him, and yet he'd shivered from the cold. Above, bodies had hung on gibbets while a boy cried beneath. Giles, his face sooty, his cheeks streaked with tears, knelt to pray for forgiveness. And Arabella of Byrum brought a wreath of roses for the victors, while Elizabeth of Rivaux sat astride a great white horse, clad as a nun.

Gradually he became aware that his arm was numb beneath him, and he rolled over to ease it, facing the brazier. Even the coals had died, leaving the room cold. As he focused bleary eyes on the ashes, he remembered he was at Byrum. And his wild dreams were replaced by a flood of memories of the day and night just passed, memories of the boar hunt, of Nigel's seeming coldness, of Arabella's fear when she'd seen the bloody tunic he wore, of the pride she'd taken in his boar. And he remembered also the whispered

words, the scent of roses, and the warm, yielding body
of his wife. *His wife.* The words seemed almost too
new to be said, but there was no doubting she belonged to him now. "The fairest rose on the border,"
he'd called her sometime in the night. The phrase stuck
in his mind. His *belle rose.* His desire rose anew as
he thought of her.

He yawned and stretched muscles cramped from being folded into the short bed, aware that he ought to
rise and relieve himself ere he wakened her. Yet he
was loath to leave the warmth of feather mattresses
above and below. He straightened his knees, letting
his feet stick out from the bottom of the bed, testing
the temperature. It was too cold. He rolled over to
warm himself against Arabella, and came fully awake
with a start. He was alone.

Surprised, he parted the curtains and rolled to sit
on the edge of the rope-hung bed, nearly overturning
it. The air hit his bare skin like a wave of cold water.
"Jesu, but are there none at Byrum to light the fires
at morning?" he muttered to himself. Despite the
darkness he could hear the sounds that came from the
kitchens, and he knew much of the keep was already
stirring. Again he wondered that she'd left him so
early: Where would she have gone, and for what reason? Then he recalled they left for Blackleith this day.
Mayhap she already prepared for the journey.

Shivering, he groped for the pouch that held his tinder and flint. He was tired from the night, and his arm
ached still, either from sleeping on it or from the force
of the blow that had felled the boar. It did not matter—
for whatever reason, he felt out of temper. He could
see his breath as he worked to spark a fire, and finally
woolen lint caught. Adding dry, broken sticks to the
brazier, he blew on the small flame, taking care not
to extinguish it. After a time his patience was rewarded, and the bits of wood began to burn.

While he waited for her to return he yet had business
to attend to, business he'd meant to take care of ere
now but had been loath to do. Freezing in the cold

chamber, he dressed quickly, pulling on his cloak over his clothes, then he searched among the box he'd brought for his writing supplies.

When he'd found them he carried them to a small, crude table, then sat down to compose what he would say to his new people at Blackleith. How should he couch what he would say? 'Twas the reason he'd not done it earlier, he admitted, for he knew not how to sound like the ruler rather than the ruled. And he'd not have them think him weak or ignorant because of his birth.

He'd thought about the matter of ruling almost from the moment Giles had told him he would have Blackleith. Aye, and now that the exhilaration of his elevation had passed, he was faced with the task of ordering his new household to his liking. And like Giles, he would surround himself with those he trusted most, those who'd served beside him ere he was raised, men he'd stood shield-to-shield with in battle.

Well, he'd delayed long enough in telling Giles' seneschal at Blackleith that he'd have his own man in his place. 'Twould be better to let Robert of Carnan tell the others as he would, for William would spare him his pride. As long as Giles had held Hamon's fiefs of King David, Robert had administered Blackleith for him—and done it well, Will conceded. But serving Giles of Moray was not the same as serving one whose birth was lower than Robert's own, and William was not at all certain the seneschal would not resent him. Nay, 'twas better to set Lang Gib above Blackleith, for he knew him almost as well as he knew himself.

He drew in a deep breath and unrolled the parchment he'd brought for the purpose. Stretching the sheepskin flat, he held it in place with his elbow while he unstoppered his ink. Taking up his quill, he dipped it and began to write carefully, trying to sound as formal as he thought he ought. As his pen scratched over the surface, the words appeared stilted, cold even. He paused to dip his pen again, reading what he'd written ere he went on. It was not very satisfactory, and yet he'd make it plain to any that he was lord now, that it was his wishes that would be served.

When at last he'd finished he scanned it, and for a moment he considered discarding it and starting anew. But the parchment was precious, and for all that he held Blackleith 'twas a small fief, and he could ill afford the waste. It would have to do. Besides, when he arrived at his keep he'd see that Robert of Carnan knew 'twas not a lack of regard that caused his replacement, but rather 'twas that William knew Gilbert of Kilburnie better.

There was, however, one more small matter to attend to, he decided. After years of sleeping on pallets too short for his feet, he'd have a bed long enough for him. He took up his quill again and added instructions that one be made big enough for him and Arabella to lie together in comfort.

That done, he pared a small piece of wax into his traveling spoon and carried it to the fire, where he held it until it melted. Then he returned to the table and poured the liquid blob onto the bottom of the page and waited for it to congeal. Just before it hardened, he pressed the iron ring Giles had given him into the wax, making a poor but nonetheless legal seal. Reading the whole again he felt it was unsatisfactory, and his sense of inadequacy for the task he faced nearly overwhelmed him. He was less a lord than many he would rule.

Reluctantly, he rolled it up and inserted it into the cylindrical case. As soon as they left Byrum he'd send Wat ahead with it. The unpleasant task finally done, he put away his writing materials carefully.

Behind him the heavy door creaked inward, sending a new rush of cold, damp air across the room. "Jesu, but you are overlate," he complained, "for I have already started the fire." He swung around to tell the scullery boys to take their pan away, but 'twas Arabella. And she had the boy with her. Disappointed, he could scarce hide that he'd have her alone.

"I did not think you'd waken," she announced

cheerfully, coming into the room. She stopped to balance Jamie on her shoulder and the ember pan in her hand. "I brought coals from the kitchen fire." She favored him with a shy, almost tentative smile. "I knew you were overtired, my lord, for you scarce moved once you slept."

His eyes traveled from the coal pan to the clinging child. "Hand me my tunic," he muttered. Then, realizing she had both hands full, he crossed the room to get it for himself.

The little boy stared wide-eyed at him. It was as though he'd not seen a naked man before, and Will wondered irritably if he had been kept only in the company of women. Rummaging in his box, he found a reasonably clean linen *shert* and a serviceable woolen tunic. "I thought he was with the woman Ena," he grumbled, pulling the garment over his head, muffling his words.

"He had bad dreams, and I heard him crying," she answered, carrying the boy to the bed. "I'd meant to bring him to lie between us."

She was bringing her changeling to his bed. Still chagrined that she'd left him at all, Will shook his head. " 'Tis not meet—he is overold for that. 'Tis unseemly."

Jamie's hands clasped her neck more tightly. "I do not sleep naked before him," she managed stiffly. "And he was afraid."

"You sleep naked before me," Will retorted, bending to retrieve his chausses. "And we are but newly wed," he added pointedly.

The color drained from her face with the realization that he meant to rebuff her son. "I did not think . . . That is, after the night . . ."

"It matters not what you thought—he belongs not in my bed." He smoothed the leggings over his calves and thighs, banding them with his garters, ere he straightened to tie them at his waist. When he looked up again, he could see the tears coursing down the boy's cheeks. "Jesu! Why does he cry now?" he demanded impatiently. Dropping to a bench, he pulled on his boots.

Her own eyes hot with unshed tears, Arabella held Jamie closer. "Mayhap 'tis that he has had little kindness of men, and he'd dared to hope 'twould be different with you," she answered evenly. "Mayhap he dared to expect his lot to better when I wed."

He rose to walk to where she stood, and, unable to look on the misshappen leg, he kept his eyes on the child's face. "And ye'd ever be a man, James, ye'll stop this. I am nae ogre, ye know," he told him, lapsing into the soft, burred accent of the border.

Jamie turned his head into Arabella's neck and whimpered, "Mama . . ."

"Nay. I'd have ye speak to me."

"Please, my lord . . ."

"And he lives with me, he speaks to me."

"You said you would not—" She stopped, afraid to say more.

"I said I'd not mistreat him," he muttered curtly. "But if you would have me do what is right by him, ye'll not expect me to treat him like a babe." When the little boy kept his head hidden, Will moved behind Arabella to speak over her shoulder. "How old are ye, James?"

"I told you he was six," Arabella answered.

"Nay, I didna speak to ye, did I? 'Twas him I asked. Jamie . . ."

"Mama . . ."

Aware that he could yet refuse to take her son with them, Arabella loosened Jamie's grip on her shoulder and forced him to face her husband. "Answer him," she urged the reluctant child.

"He doesna need your aid. How many years d'ye have, James?" Will repeated.

The boy's eyes were huge in his pale face as he shrank against his mother. But this time she could not help him. He looked from the big man to the floor. "Six, my lord," he mumbled finally.

"Six is it? Then ye are overold to hang on your mother, don't ye think?"

"My lord . . ."

"I didna ask ye!" he snapped at her. "James. . . ?"

Big tears rolled down the child's cheeks. "But I canna walk!" he cried. "I canna walk!" Turning his head again into his mother's shoulder, he wailed, "God gave me a useless leg!"

Will had resented the boy ever since he'd found out about Aidan of Ayrie, and yet he was again unprepared for the rush of pity he felt. His anger faded abruptly, replaced by guilt over his harshness to a child. "God shame ye for such words, Jamie," he chided almost gently. "If 'tis your lot—"

" 'Tis enough, my lord," Arabella whispered. "I pray you. . . ."

But Will kept his eyes on the boy. "James, ye canna help how ye were born no more than I can help my size, but—"

"My lord, I beg you. . . ." She ran her tongue over her lips nervously. "And you have a care—"

"But God expects each of us to be what we can, ye know," he continued. "Like ye, I—"

" 'Tis enough, my lord!" she cried. " 'Tis enough! I will take him back to Ena!"

"Nay. He is too big for ye to carry."

Before she knew what he meant to do, he'd reached to lift Jamie over her shoulder. "Come on, ye wee brat."

"He cannot walk—he will fall on the steps!"

"Did I set him down?" he countered.

She tried to keep her voice calm as he started for the door. "Where are you taking him?" When he made no answer she followed him, forgetting her fear. "Where do you take him?" she demanded more loudly. "Let me call for Ena, I pray you!"

"Nay. I'd have you pack your things that we may leave, for I smell more rain. In truth, I'd travel ere the roads turn to mire."

Panicked, she caught at his arm. "And Jamie—you

said you'd take my son to Blackleith! My lord, I pray you do not forget you said he could come with me!''

"Jesu, woman," he muttered, pulling away. Then, aware of the desperation in her voice, he relented. "Aye, I take him to Blackleith. I have never promised that which I do not mean to keep. But I'd have you know you have no more gratitude for what I do than your father."

"Mamaaaaa!!!!" The boy twisted in Will's arms, leaning for her. "Mamaaaaaaaa!!!!"

She hesitated, afraid again to interfere as her son cried out. Her throat tightened painfully. "You will not harm him, will you?" she asked in little more than a whisper.

"I said I was no ogre! But you try my patience, the both of you! Jesu, but 'tis not a wonder he is fearful, Bella, for 'tis you as makes him so!"

"Mamaaaaa!!!!"

"Please, my lord . . ."

"Nay," he interrupted tersely. "Get you ready to leave."

She dropped her hand and let him go, stifling an urge to tell him to have a care on the steps. He was so tall she feared he'd knock Jamie' head. After he'd left she stood rooted, listening to his footsteps on the stairs. And when she heard the door close below, she moved to throw open the shutter to watch apprehensively.

Will hoisted the boy onto his shoulder, and as his hand grasped the twisted leg he felt revulsion. But if James of Whatever was to live in his household, he'd have to overcome that, as well as his anger and his resentment, ere they ate at his soul. Telling himself yet again that the child could not be held accountable for the sins of the parents, he tried to reassure Arabella's frightened son by lapsing into the familiar tongue.

"Och, but 'tis time ye saw the world from a higher place, ye know. The women, for all that they are kind, canna carry a great lad like ye forever."

As they moved across the open courtyard Jamie looked down, and his fear of falling warred with his fear of the man who carried him. And when the big man bobbed low to avoid a gnarled branch, the boy grabbed frantically for his head, twining his fingers tightly in the auburn hair.

"Ouch, ye misbegotten heathen!" Will muttered. "Have a care, else ye'll have me bald!"

The way the big man said it, there was no real anger. The little boy looked again to the ground. " 'Tis too far," he whimpered pitifully.

"And ye promise ye'll nae do that again, ye can ride my neck," Will offered. Then, without waiting for an answer, he shifted the boy, settling him astraddle his shoulders. The child squealed and clutched convulsively at his head, again pulling his hair. "Enough, I said! I dinna let you fall, did I?" Will demanded impatiently. "God's bones, but I'd nae drop ye, I tell ye. Now cease the wailing, that we may search for the woman Ena."

"She is in the kitchens," Jamie volunteered tearfully, his hands still tightly grasping Will's head. "Mama sent her there."

"Aye," William muttered. "Ye might hold my neck, ye know."

As he started across the courtyard to the building that housed Byrum's kitchen, he wished he'd not been so quick to take the boy, for Jamie continued to weep as though he expected Will to cast him into the pits of Hell.

"My lord!"

They stopped and waited for Ewan to approach. William acknowledged his greeting with a nod.

"Do we still ride today?"

"Aye. As soon as I give over the boy, I'd seek Lang Gib."

"He tarries on the steps with a serving maid, my lord," the grizzled one answered, grinning. "Ye know how 'tis with Gib: There's nae a woman born as he thinks he canna bed."

"Tell him 'tis a captain's duty to gather his men. I'd leave as soon as the night's fast is broken. Aye, and tell him there's nae time for leaving another bastard." Then, aware that Ewan stared at the boy on his shoulder, Will frowned. " 'Tis James—of Woolford." He said the last two words almost defiantly. "My lady's son."

His eyes still spilling tears, Jamie cringed as the older man's gaze settled on him. Ewan nodded. "Young James," he noted, smiling as he slapped the boy's good foot. "Is this the best mount he'd give ye?" he teased. "Tell him ye'd hae one with four legs, will ye?"

"Ewan . . ." Will growled. "There'll be nae speech of legs before him."

But Jamie had stopped crying to regard the rough Scot suspiciously. Perceiving that William's frown had deepened, Ewan hesitated, then explained, "I dinna mean harm, my lord. My sire was one-legged, ye know, and I dinna think, fer I'd grown used to it. Yer pardon, young James."

"Was . . . was he borned like me?" Jamie asked curiously, forgetting his fear for the moment.

"Nay, 'twas a wound, and it festered until 'twas him or the limb. But when the priest came to shrive him, he'd nae hear o' it. 'Send fer the saw,' he said, 'fer I am needful of more time to mend my soul.' " Ewan smiled, revealing a mouthful of crooked teeth. "I can still remember the smell when they burned the stump, but he lived. Learned to walk and ride like that."

The boy stared round-eyed at him. "I canna walk." Then, thinking the man somehow lied, he wanted to know more. "Does he yet live?"

Ewan spat onto the wet grass. "Nay—his horse threw him. Broke his neck." He spat again. "But 'twas not fer the leg that he perished—his beast bolted in battle."

"I canna sit a horse also," Jamie admitted wistfully.

Ewan looked from William to the boy. "Aye, ye can, and the saddle's right fer ye."

Not even the priests, who were supposed to love all, had been able to look on him, but the rough-looking man before him did not seem to recoil. Jamie's curiosity outweighed his fear. "If he had but one leg, how did he do it—walk, I mean?"

Will had heard enough, and he'd not have Ewan put impossible ideas into the boy's head. "Ye can ask him later," he muttered. "There isna time now."

"Do you go to Blackleith?' Jamie asked hopefully.

"Aye. And ye?"

"Aye."

"Ewan is master of my horse," Will explained shortly.

"But ye nae hunt much, do ye?" Ewan complained good-naturedly. " 'Tis little enough ye give me ter do. Until yesterday, I'd given up on ye."

" 'Tis little enough time I've had for sport since ye've come to serve me." William glanced up at the rolling clouds, shaking his head. "Jesu. By the looks of that, we tarry overlong here." His eyes traveled over the courtyard to the kitchen. "D'ye see my lady's woman?"

"Nay, but and ye gie him o'er, I'll find her fer ye. Lang Gib'll nae grumble when 'tis ye as tells him we ride."

Relieved, William lifted James of Woolford from his shoulders and handed him to Ewan. "Tell her I'd have all in readiness to leave within the hour. And then I'd have ye tell Lang Gib we ride."

"Ye want him sent ter ye?"

Will's gaze lifted to the empty arrow slit, and he felt guilt for the way he'd left Arabella. "Nay. 'Tis enough that all is made ready to go."

As Will turned to walk back toward the tower, he heard Ewan ask the boy, "Have ye got good seat? My sire was used to do this, ye know, when I was a wee lad like yerself."

"My sire is dead," Jamie volunteered.

Jesu, but she'd not even told the boy of Ayrie. It did not matter, Will supposed, for it was unlikely that Duncan's son would claim a cripple. And 'twas as well that he did not: Too many already probably knew of Arabella's shame. He paused briefly and looked upward again. Aye, he wished he'd never heard the tale from Milo of Woolford.

The cold, dank wind cut through his tunic like a knife, reminding him 'twas folly to tarry. Hunching his shoulders against it, he considered that the weather would make for a miserable journey to Blackleith.

She was waiting when he came up the stairs. "Where is he—what did you with my son?" she demanded anxiously. "Who was the man who took him?"

She'd been watching him. He felt a surge of resentment that she considered her brat before him. "Have done," he muttered. "I did but give him to Ewan." He pushed past her into the room. "God's bones, woman, but I'd nae hear this!"

"I know not this Ewan!"

"He'll nae harm him," he snapped. But as his eyes met hers he could see she was still so fearful she trembled, and again he relented. "He takes the boy to your woman, Bella." Moving closer, he reached to push a strand of pale gold hair back from her face, and any anger that lingered was forgotten in the rush of renewed desire. "I did not think to quarrel with you so soon after the bedding," he said more softly.

She stared upward, scarce able to comprehend the sudden change in his manner. "Nay, I . . ." She would have stepped back, but there was a bench in the way.

His hand cupped her chin. "If I am angered, 'tis that I did not find you beside me when I wakened," he murmured, bending his head to hers.

"Sweet Mary, there is no time. . . ." she whispered weakly.

" 'Twill not take overlong," he promised against her lips. "And 'twill improve my temper."

She slid her arms about his waist and raised her face

Chapter Thirteen

Shivering so hard that her teeth chattered, Arabella pulled her cloak closer and leaned forward in her saddle to shelter her son. Beside her William rode silently, his shoulders hunched against the cold also. She glanced over to him, wondering that he did not complain, for he was encased in steel and must surely be chilled to the bone.

For all that they'd shared in the night he was still a stranger to her, this giant of Dunashie. To take her mind from the bitter weather she studied him covertly, seeing the mail that glistened with condensed mist, the heavy leather gloves over the strong hands, the woolen surcoat that fell away from thighs that were as thick as the trunk of a young tree. Sweet Mary, but she'd not known any his size before, and was not like to again.

Did he not know 'twas cold? Did he not feel the chill that gnawed at her bones? She dared to look upward to his face, wondering what he thought. But it was set, impassive, unreadable beneath the polished nasal of his helm. Had she not lain with him the night before, she'd have been afraid just to look on him.

God's bones, but how could any want to face him in battle?

She knew there were those who yet pitied her for the husband she'd been given, for 'twas not only Ena as had eyed her curiously when she'd come down to break her fast. It was as though they were surprised she was unharmed. Ah, Ena. Arabella had to smile at how the woman had stared when she'd admitted she was content enough with him. "I canna see how ye can sit," she'd muttered, when Arabella had come for Jamie.

"At least he did not beat me," she'd retorted to the woman.

"The boy tires you. 'Tis a wonder your arm has feeling in it." It was the first he'd spoken in what seemed to have been hours. His eyes met hers, and his expression softened. "I'd have you give him to Ena."

"Nay. 'Tis b-but that I am c-cold."

"Arabella . . ."

"Her c-cloak is th-thinner th-than mine." She tried to clench her teeth to still their chattering. "Besides, he s-sleeps."

Once more he felt an unreasoning stab of jealousy for her child, and he wondered again why he'd said he would take a boy he could scarce look on. As long as she had her Jamie she had neither eyes nor ears for anyone else, or so it seemed to him. And every time they stopped, every time he watched her carry the boy, he could not but think of Aidan of Ayrie and feel cheated. Elias of Woolford he could understand, for she'd been wed to him. But 'twas Ayrie's son she'd borne. 'Twas Ayrie's son she guarded so ferociously. Already William could not bear to see her with the boy, and the journey had but begun. He had years ahead in which to watch and know he had taken an unchaste wife.

That it was wrong of him to dislike the child for the mother's sin weighed on him, but he could not help himself. And yet he could not send her boy away, for

had he not promised to take him? But he'd never be
free of this reminder of Ayrie, not when the boy could
not even stand unaided. 'Twas not as though he could
be sent to foster in another house, and even the Church
would not want him. There was no use to James of
Whatever, no use at all, and yet Arabella shielded him
like a mother wolf over her cub. It was, William reflected resentfully, the only time she completely lost
her fear of him.

Nay, 'twas not so, he had to own in truth. For all
that he saw fear in her eyes otherwise, she forgot it
when she lay beneath him, when she had no thought
of her son. Had she not brought the boy with her,
William could have hoped she would learn to love him.
As it was, he did not think there was room for any in
her heart but the Devil's changeling she'd borne. He
could not forget she'd left his bed for her Jamie.

He looked again to where she sat hovered over the
boy. " 'Tis more meet that another carry him," he said
finally.

"He is all r-right," she protested, holding the sleeping boy closer.

"Nay. Lang Gib!"

"Aye, my lord?"

"Take the boy to his nurse."

Arabella shook her head. "Ena's cloak is th-thinner
than m-mine."

"You cannot even pull your mantle about you for
him," Will observed curtly. "Gib!"

"Nay!" Even as she said it Arabella reddened,
aware that her husband's eyebrow had disappeared beneath his helm. "Nay," she said more meekly. "He
will not g-go to a st-stranger, and Ena cannot k-keep
him warm. I am all right, I swear.'

William had no wish to quarrel with her, but neither
would he have her dispute his word before men who
had but lately been his equals. It was as he'd told Giles:
A man who could not rule his wife could not rule
men.

"Then give him over to me," he muttered tersely.

"Naught's wrong with my mantle—'tis heavier than any."

Arabella looked down to where Jamie clung to her breast, and she shook her head. "I'd n-not w-waken him."

"God's bones, woman!" William snapped. "I dinna ask ye, did I? 'Tis ye as makes him scared and saft! Give him o'er, I said!" He edged his horse closer and leaned for the boy. "Come on, James—up with ye."

Thus awakened, the child stared up at the big man, his pale eyes round with fright. "N-nay," he whimpered, clutching at Arabella's neck. "Mama—nay!"

"Jesu!" Will's gloved hand grasped the boy's arm. " 'Tis enough, James," he growled. "Ye canna wish for your mama to freeze for ye."

"Mamaaaaaa! Mamaaaaaa!" the child cried, pulling away and clinging frantically to Arabella.

"My lord . . ."

"Gie him o'er, I said," Will repeated.

"He is but six, and too little . . ."

"Aye, and had he been whole, he'd have been sent away ere now." As soon as the words had left his mouth he was sorry for them, for she blenched. In an attempt to master his rising temper he drew in his breath, then let it out slowly. The puff of steam hung in the air. "Hand him to me, Arabella," he said yet again, this time in measured tones.

"My lord . . ."

He'd raised his hand, and she thought he meant to hit them, and she was afraid for Jamie. She shrank against the high wooden cantle of her saddle as though she could absorb the blow. "Have done!" she cried. "I will give him over!" As she spoke, she loosened her mantle from around her son almost frantically.

The fear in her eyes angered him even more than her defiance, for it made him think of Giles' cringing first wife. "Art daft, woman," he growled, leaning again to lift the boy. "I've nae harmed him yet."

Jamie twisted in his hands, struggling to escape him, wailing, "Mama—mamaaaaaaa! Mamaaaaaaaa!"

shrilly. For a brief moment the boy hung with his good leg kicking, then Will sat him between his body and the high pommel.

"Get two blankets from the pack, Gib," he ordered, ignoring the child's cries. "Give my lady one that she does not sicken, and I'll have the other."

"Aye, my lord."

The mounted column waited until he'd wrapped both his cloak and the stiff woolen blanket about himself and the boy, then William gave the signal to move again. In front of him James of Whatever sat stiffly, his small pinched face turned toward his mother. He'd quit crying openly and now merely sniffled, while she bore the anxious expression of a mare separated from its colt.

"Lay back," Will ordered gruffly as he held the child with his mailed arm. " 'Tis warm enough ye are now." He spurred his huge horse forward on the sodden road, reestablishing the hard, steady trot.

But the boy sat forward, until he could stand the punishing gait no longer. After scarce half a league the pain forced him to lie against the man. Still unable to bear the weight on his hip, he was finally forced to turn sideways and rest his head against the Bastard of Dunashie's broad, hard chest. The smell of wet wool, leather, and oiled mail intermingled beneath his nose. Despite his fear and his distrust of the man who held him, James of Woolford closed his eyes after a time, and dared to wonder what it would be like to be a warrior.

None of them spoke. Will again was silent, still seething with the knowledge that only fear had mastered his wife's defiance. Between Arabella and the boy they'd made him feel like a great beast, and he did not like it. And yet he'd rule in his own house. He had to. When a man had not the legitimacy of birth he ruled by his strength, and there was no room for any perceived weakness.

It was not until the fine mist had turned into a steady

drizzle dripping from his helmet that he thought to look down again. Despite the water that fell on him, the boy did not move. Will lifted his cloak to cover the pale hair, and was surprised to discover that Jamie's thin arms clung to his surcoat while he slept. In sleep, his small face held a trace of his mother's beauty. For a moment Will forgot his dislike in a surge of protectiveness. It was wrong of him to resent a helpless child. Without thinking, his arm tightened around the boy.

"Is he all right?" Arabella asked, speaking the first strained words since he'd taken James from her.

Will looked down again. "Aye, he is warm enough that he sleeps." An almost rueful smile lightened his face. "I would that I were half so eased as he."

She hesitated, wondering whether she should say more, then could not forbear explaining, "He has had so little kindness, my lord, for most turn away at the sight of him. Even my own sire cannot bear his company, and ever have I had to hide him from Nigel's eyes." When William said nothing, she sighed, "You cannot know what 'tis like when your own grandsire begrudges the food to keep you alive."

"I grew to manhood with neither grandsire nor sire," he reminded her. "There was none to care whether I lived or died."

"Then surely you must understand . . . surely you must know. . . . Sweet Mary, but—"

"Nay. There was Giles, and I had to survive for him. 'Twas the oath I gave my sire ere he died."

"But you could tell yourself he would have loved you had he lived! But Elias—"

He did not want her to lie to him. "Nay," he cut in curtly, "what is past is past, Arabella, and I'd not hear of it."

There seemed to be no way to reach him, no way to make him understand about Jamie. She lifted her hand as in supplication, then let it drop to her side. It would have to be enough for now that he did not harm her son.

"I am all he has," she said finally.

"At Blackleith he will have a place." Once again he looked down on the sleeping child. "He has greater need of food and sun than of your coddling, if he is to grow."

"He is my son."

"God willing, you will have others also."

"You cannot expect me to deny him."

"Nay, I do not ask that." But even as he said the words, he knew he lied. Had he the choice, he'd have no reminder that she'd lain with Aidan of Ayrie.

Once again there was a strained silence between them, but William chose to ignore it. The sooner he weaned her from the boy, the better for all of them. When they reached Blackleith he'd take steps to provide separate quarters for James of—Jesu, but even in his thoughts, he choked on "Woolford." And yet to call the child anything else would have been to brand Arabella a whore.

Somewhere beyond the cloud-darkened horizon bells sounded, calling monks to prayer. William looked upward into the drizzle, frowning. Within the hour, he was certain the skies would pour. " 'Tis but nones," he murmured, "and I'd hoped to travel further this day." Had he had only men with him he'd have ridden on, but now he had a wife to consider. "You are soaked and chilled to the bone," he observed tiredly. "And we do not stop, you are like to sicken."

"I am all right. The blanket—"

"Nay. 'Tis too far to the next chapter house, and I'd not have you take a fever from this." Shifting the boy's body slightly, he turned to call out to his captain, "Lang Gib!"

"Aye?"

"We stop, and hope it clears ere the morrow."

In all the years Gib had served beside William, he'd thought him inured to the discomfort and pain of heat and cold, sun and rain. Aye, they'd ridden day and night in snow and ice, and never once had he heard so much as a complaint of any of it. Now he looked to the horizon, measuring the height of the sun behind the clouds.

'' 'Tis overearly, my lord.''

"Jesu! You also, Gib? Do you dispute with me also?''

It was not like William to be out of temper either. For a moment his captain considered chiding him about it, but then thought better of it. He was not the bastard's equal anymore, and it was hard having to remember it.

"Nay,'' he answered, wheeling to ride back along the small mesnie, giving the word they stopped.

There were times when Will wished for the security of serving his brother again, for the companionship rather than the leadership of his men. But that time had passed when he'd put his hands between Giles and taken the oath that had enfiefed him. Now he could ill afford any questioning of his right to lead. He twisted in his saddle to survey those who followed him. Lang Gib. Young Wat. Ewan. Fairlie. Nib o' Kinmurrie. Black Jock. And a dozen more who were little more than grey shadows in the mist. Every one of them had served Giles with him. Every one of them probably questioned his right to lead them now.

And once again his own words haunted him: *A man who doesna rule his wife canna rule men.* Though he'd said it when Elizabeth insisted on sitting above his brother, he believed it still. And Arabella was not Rivaux's daughter, after all, so he dared not tolerate any dispute from her. Nay, but ere they reached Blackleith, he would have authority over her and her son.

Father Sampson surveyed the small, bedraggled mesnie almost sourly, saying that it had been a poor growing season and he had scarce enough food for the brothers. But William, not wanting to appear weak before Arabella or his men, would not be turned away.

"I have silver,'' he declared tersely, "and so I'd tell the bishop. 'Tis your Christian duty to provide a bed for sojourners.''

"There is an inn at—"

"Nay," Will cut in, " 'tis here I'd stay. My lady and the boy can go no further."

The abbot shook his head. "I regret—"

"Fool!" Lang Gib spat. "My lord of Dunashie willna understand how 'tis ye deny his brother!"

Sampson paled. "Dunashie?" he asked faintly. "The Butcher of Dunashie?"

"Aye," Will growled, embarrassed by Gib's blatant use of Giles' reputation.

"The one as wed Rivaux's daughter?"

"Is there another?" Gib demanded derisively. "Jesu!"

The churchman's eyes traveled the full length of the giant before him, taking in the sodden cloak, the wet blanket that covered the child. Nay, but if this man were indeed the Butcher's brother, he'd not tempt him to anger. He glanced at Arabella curiously.

"Nay. Ask me, and you would know."

The way the big man said the words sent a chill down Sampson's spine, and every awful tale told of the Butcher and his men came to mind. He looked into hazel eyes that had gone cold, and found he did not care to ask anything.

"You are welcome to share what little we have, of course," he lied. " 'Tis not overmuch."

Angered to be treated thus before Arabella, William unhooked the leather pouch that hung from his belt and carefully counted out five of his precious silver pennies. Flinging them to the ground at the abbot's feet, he muttered, "St. Benedict taught humility and service, and well you know it. Mayhap when you are on your knees counting my money, you might remember his rule." Shifting the silent, wide-eyed Jamie onto his other shoulder, he turned to Lang Gib. "See that the pallets be clean, for I'd not be cheated."

As they followed the stiff-necked Sampson through the narrow, stone-arched corridor toward the guest house, Arabella reached for her son. "I'd carry him, and you do not mind it."

"Nay." He stopped to set the boy down. "I'd have him walk." Jamie teetered precariously, then caught hold of William's soaked surcoat, looking to his mother. One shoulder went down as the foot on his shorter leg turned nearly over.

"But he cannot!" Arabella protested. "Sweet Mary, but he cannot!"

"And you cannot carry him forever," William countered, balancing the child with his hand. "I'd not have you lose one bairn for the other."

For a moment, she was at a loss. "But I am not with child."

"And God wills it, you will be."

She stared. "But he cannot walk," she repeated, as though she explained the obvious to a child.

The abbot swung around impatiently, then saw the boy's badly twisted leg. The open revulsion in his face made Jamie shrink against William's knee.

"Mama," he whimpered pitifully.

" 'Tis the Devil's mark he bears, and I'd not have him—"

William cut him off quickly. "And you'd breathe until the morrow, you'll not say it," he growled. Reaching down, he caught Jamie beneath his arm. " 'Tis a man you'll be from this day, James."

"But he cannot!"

"Jesu! You've got to cease saying that, woman!" His eyes on the boy, he insisted, "Aye, you can. I care not how you do it, James, but afore God, you'll walk."

"Mama!"

"Nay—look to me. She cannot aid you."

Arabella licked dry lips and smoothed her palms against her gown. "My lord . . ."

"Nay."

"Holy Jesu," Lang Gib muttered under his breath. "If he canna walk then—" He caught the set of William's jaw and stopped. The man Ewan stepped forward, hesitated, then stepped back. It was as though the silence reverberated through the narrow, stone-walled walkway. Will lifted Jamie's shoulder higher, taking his weight from the useless leg. Hot tears welled and stung Arabella's eyes, but she did not dare say more. She swallowed back words that threatened to choke her.

The child's large eyes moved from the huge man who held him up to his mother's stricken face, then back again. "I . . . I canna . . . I canna do it, my lord. My leg . . . my foot . . . when I try, I fall, and . . ." He faltered, bowing his head in humiliation, and new tears rolled down his cheeks, as Arabella looked away.

"James."

"I canna!" the boy cried. "I canna!"

It was too much for Arabella. She dropped to her knees before her husband. "My lord, I beg you. . . . You can see . . ."

William nudged her out of the way with his leg. "Nay. You would give him into mine keeping, and 'tis for me to decide."

"God's mercy, my lord!"

"Get up, woman." Looking down on the small bent head, he spoke more kindly in his familiar speech. "Ye canna do anything and ye willna try, James. I'd nae let ye fall."

" 'Tis God's punishment that he is as he is," the abbot muttered. "I'd not tarry for this."

There was such contempt in his voice that William's hand tightened beneath the boy's armpit. It was the same contempt that James of Woolford had known all his young life, and it stung beyond the words. Gritting his teeth, Jamie grasped the big man's chausses between the quarters, twisting the knitted wool tightly in his hands, holding on for balance. He'd struggled often enough to know the leg would not support him, and he was loath to have them laugh at him when he fell. He looked upward at William of Dunashie fearfully. " 'Tisna far," Will encouraged him.

Jamie reached down to lift his nearly useless leg, setting it beneath him. As his weight bore down, his foot turned over again from the ankle. Gritting his teeth, he started forward with the other foot, and he stumbled as his leg gave way. To his surprise his step-father did not let him fall, nor did he laugh at the pitiful attempt. Emboldened by this, Jamie swallowed hard and then hurtled his body forward, stumbling again, and still the big man held him up. Instead of the laughter that had dogged him much of his life, now there was only the uneasy silence of those who watched him struggle. He rested, bit his lip against the pain that shot from his ankle upward through the useless leg, and tried again.

Finally, after watching him move several feet forward, each awful, faltering step agonizingly slow, Arabella could stand no more. Moving again in front of her husband, she stretched out her hands. "No more— 'tis enough, I pray you! God's mercy, my lord—he is but one small, helpless boy!"

"Nae so helpless as ye'd have him," William retorted. "But aye, 'tis enough this day." He turned to the man who shadowed him. "Ewan, I'd have ye take the boy."

"But I would carry him—he knows not this Ewan!" As William's expression darkened she lowered her eyes, amending hastily, "I'd have Ena, and you do not mind it."

He shook his head. "He is too much in the company of women. Ewan . . ."

The borderer stepped forward to lift James of Woolford, swinging him easily onto his shoulder. For a moment there was terror, as the child grasped his head. Forgetting this was the man who'd found Ena for him earlier, Jamie looked to his mother.

"Here now—ye'll blind me!" Ewan protested. He then turned to his lord, asking, "And where would ye that I took him?"

"I am giving him to your keeping. Until we reach Blackleith, I'd have you tend him."

Arabella was stunned. "But he needs me!" Reaching to touch William's sleeve, she implored him, "I pray you: He is but one small boy amongst strangers! He cannot—''

''I tire of hearing what he canna do!'' William snapped. ''And ye have yer way, he'll nae grow to a man.''

''He is my son!''

He did not want to quarrel with her before his men, but neither would he back down. ''Ye make him a pitiful creature, Arabella, and I'll nae have it. He will pallet with Ewan.''

''Nay!''

They faced each other, she losing her fear of him for her child, and he seeing naught but defiance. And the charity he'd but lately felt for her bastard vanished. ''You forget yourself, madam,'' he said coldly, taking care to speak properly. ''In mine household, 'tis I who rules. Now—lest you'd be beaten for your tongue— you'll stand aside.''

Afraid now that her anger would cost her son, she looked away. And when she spoke again, she schooled meekness into her voice. '' 'Tis as you would wish, of course, but—''

''Nay. I'd not have you agree in part, then argue under the guise of obedience, Arabella. I'd have you correct your error, and I'd hear no more of this.''

There were so many things she wanted to say, so many bitter words, but when she raised her head again she saw only hardness in his eyes. ''Aye,'' she whispered.

Ewan, who'd been about to protest that he was no nurse, thought better of it. Instead he patted the boy's bony hip awkwardly. ''Here now, ye canna snore— d'ye hear me?''

''Mama!''

For answer, Arabella had to look away. ''Go with this . . . this Ewan, Jamie.''

William reached for her arm, holding her beneath the elbow. When he spoke again, 'twas to Sampson. ''My lady is cold and overtired—I'd have hot wine to warm her blood. Aye, and dry blankets also.''

Chapter Fourteen

Arabella watched her husband nervously across the narrow chamber, trying not to hear the pitiful wails that came from the pilgrims' common room. When it had come home to him that he would in truth sleep in a room filled with strangers, Jamie had screamed until they could scarce hear the monks sing Compline. And if he did not stop soon, she feared William would beat him for it.

But so far he'd ignored the boy's cries, and now, while he waited for her to ready herself for bed, he pulled a low bench closer to the fire. Taking great care with them, he drew out pieces of parchment from his pouch and held them to the flickering light. His lips moved soundlessly as his eyes traveled over the Latin words.

Thinking to broach the matter of Ena's taking James once more, she walked behind him and laid a timid hand on his huge shoulder. "My lord . . ." But as she peered over his shoulder, she was curious. "What is it you do?" she dared to ask.

He finished the page, then made the sign of the Cross over his breast. " 'Tis the Hours," he answered. "I did not say them the last two nights." The soft scent of rosewater wafted up, reminding him of why. His hand moved to cover hers. "A man can be forgiven forgetting when he is first wed, don't you think?"

"You can read!" she observed, astonished.

"Aye." He looked up, and a smile curved his mouth. "It surprises you."

"Aye. Not even Papa—"

"Alas, but I cannot take credit for it: There were none in Beauclerc's household as did not learn. At the time I was angered, but now I am heartily glad—'tis all I thank King Henry for."

There was so much she did not know of this man. "Can you cipher also?" she wondered aloud.

"Aye." His fingers massaged hers, as the rosewater kindled his desire. "Does it please you to know we will not be cheated?"

"You were taught to be a clerk." She would have pulled her fingers away, but his hand had tightened.

"Aye, but 'tis not letters and figures I'd speak of now," he murmured. With his free hand he laid the precious scraps of parchment aside, then he half turned to pull her down onto his lap. "I'd think of bed, madam wife."

"My lord . . ." She sat stiffly before him, trying to gain the courage to plead for her son. "I beg you will reconsider," she began haltingly, "for Jamie is but one small boy, away from all he knows."

William's hand worked clumsily at the laces beneath her arms. "Arabella," he said softly, "I'd not sleep with mine own babe between us."

"Ena—"

"Nay." As the laces came loose, he leaned forward to nuzzle the crown of her hair, smelling the roses again. "I'd hear no more of the boy." His hands slid around her to cup her breasts. "I'd feel the fire between us again, Bella."

She closed her eyes and swallowed hard, telling herself that she lay with him for Jamie, that later she'd ask again for Jamie. And as his hands moved over her body possessively, she tried not to hear the cries of her child.

He still marveled at how different she was from the whore Berta, how smooth and firm she was, yet how soft and yielding she'd been beneath him the night before. His mouth went dry at the memory. Abruptly, he eased her off his lap and stood.

"I'd see you again, Arabella."

She stood still for a moment, then reached to unhook the heavy chain that girded her hips. It slid to clink noisily onto the flagged stone floor. Her cold hands lifted the skirt of her still damp woolen gown, pulling it upward over her head. It joined the girdle in a heap at her feet. Edging closer to the warmth of the fire, she leaned over to untie the garters that held her hose and push them down, removing both with her slippers. When she straightened and looked again to William, he was watching her hungrily.

"And the other."

She felt too stiff to move, but she forced herself to lift the linen and draw it upward, revealing her body for him. As the undertunic covered her head, she could hear his sharp intake of breath. And as it dropped there was no sound beyond the beating of her heart. She swallowed again and waited.

Her pale skin glowed in the firelight as he stared at her. He moved between her and the brazier, shadowing her with his body. "Art more beautiful every time I look on you, Arabella of Byrum," he said hoarsely as his hand brushed a bared breast.

A shudder went through her at his touch. He bent his head to hers, tasting her unresponsive lips, and then his arms closed about her. She felt as stone within his embrace. Telling herself she still chilled, he let her go.

"Get ye into bed, that I may warm ye."

This night there was no feather mattress, only a straw-filled pallet placed on the floor of a guest house cell. As she sank down to it, William blew out the smelly tallow candles and stepped into the darkness beyond the fire. She heard rather than saw him undress. And when he padded toward the pallet on bare feet, she tried to will herself to feign passion and to ignore the wails that reverberated off the stone walls.

He dropped down beside her, easing beneath the blanket and raising the cover over them both, and then he reached for her. "Art cold," he murmured, pulling her back against the heat of his body. His hand smoothed one of her braids against her bare shoulder as she shivered, then slid around her arm to caress her breast again. "One day, Arabella, I will be able to command better for you, and 'tis a bed we'll have when we stop," he whispered. As he nuzzled her neck, she could feel the rise of his manhood against her back. "Turn over, and I will warm you."

Sweet Mary, but she did not want this, not while her son wept loudly but a room away. And yet his fingers moved downward, brushing over her rib cage, skimming her belly, dipping to the thatch below. She clenched her teeth to still the denial that welled in her throat. Did he not know—could he not tell—that her body rebelled at what he did to her? Did it not matter that she could not stand listening to her son cry for her? As his fingers stroked within her, she screamed silently.

She was not nearly so wet as she'd been the night before, and Will knew she was not ready. Thinking he went too fast, he stopped. "I'd lie with you," he whispered.

"I am too tired," she lied.

The flat, toneless quality of her voice angered him. A woman had not the right to refuse her husband, and well she knew it. "Nay, but 'tis my right to have ye, Arabella, and ye'll lie willing fer me." He caught her shoulder, turning her onto her back. In the darkness, he could see only the faint glimmer of her eyes as she stared up at him. "I'd have ye, Bella."

There was that about him that frightened her, that reminded her of Elias. "I—I cannot, my lord," she managed to choke out. "Not while Jamie . . . Merciful Mary, not now . . ."

"Jesu!" He rolled to sit, staring into the coals that glowed in the brazier. "Can ye think of naught but him?" he demanded furiously. "Ye make him into a puling weakling!" Lurching from the bed, he groped for his discarded chausses, muttering, "I'll have peace in mine house—afore God, I will!"

"He is but a small, helpless boy!"

He pulled the hose on and tied them at his waist, then started for the door. Cold terror struck at her heart: He was going to harm her son.

"Nay! Sweet Mary, but where do you go?" she cried, scrambling after him. "Nay! I pray you—come back! And you want, I will lie willing for you! I—I swear it!" she babbled, catching at his arms. "My lord, I will do as you ask!"

He turned around, caught her by her shoulders, and shook her hard. "Art daft, woman!" he roared. Shoving her back toward the pallet, he started again for the door. "Get ye to bed ere ye ail."

"I said I would lie willing for you! I do not deny you! Do not go—do not harm my son!" The words tumbled almost incoherently from her. "Please . . ."

"I will be back," he muttered tersely. "And ye love him, ye'll nae interfere between us."

He threatened Jamie. She sank to her knees on the pallet and prayed frantically as he left her. "Blessed Mary, Holy Virgin, as one mother to another, I beseech you—do not let him harm my son. Sweet Mary, I'd have them learn to love each other ere 'tis too late! Mother of Heaven . . ." She knew not how long she prayed nor what words she used, only that she begged for intercession with her angry husband. She prayed so intently she knew not when the crying ceased.

"Lie down ere you are ill," William told her from the doorway. Moving to stand over her, he untied his chausses and pushed them down. " 'Tis too cold for that."

She looked up, aware now of the silence. "Is . . . is my son all right?"

"Aye." He stepped out of the footed stockings. "You did not have to ask it." Once again, he eased his body down next to hers. "And now I'd have you keep the promise you made ere I left."

"But what. . . ?"

"It matters not—'tis done." He pulled her down. "Now I'd have you willing."

She lay stiff and unyielding beside him. "You did not beat him?"

Once again he felt a surge of anger that she placed the boy above him. "I did not touch him." He turned her to face him and bent his head to hers. "I'd hear no more of the boy this night, I tell you."

As much as he tried to make her want him, she barely responded to his touch. Finally, telling himself 'twas his right, he rolled her onto her back and possessed her body eagerly. And when she did not cry out he began to move, losing himself in his desire for her, scarce aware that she did not writhe and moan and buck beneath him. He drove himself until he exploded within her, then as he floated back to reality he rested above her. His hand brushed against her cheek, feeling the wetness there, and he was ashamed. He rolled away and lay staring at the ceiling of the cell.

"I dinna mean to hurt ye," he said finally.

"I am all right."

He felt like a great beast. He smoothed errant strands of hair back from her face and groped for the means to make amends. "Arabella . . ."

" 'Twas your right, my lord."

"Not like that—I'd nay have ye like that."

They lay there, both silent, both awake far into the night. For Will there was an inexplicable sense of loss, that somehow it was not enough to possess her body when her mind was unwilling. And yet beyond what he'd already said to her, he knew not what he could do to bridge the chasm between them. For a time he considered that he ought to have refused to take her son, but then he had to own that it was wrong of him to blame the boy for what he himself had done. Finally, thinking she slept, he turned away, letting his mind wander in a troubled netherworld until it reached oblivion.

Arabella stared into the darkness, straining for some sound of her son, afraid to ask further and yet unable to sleep. Then, as William's breathing evened into the steady rhythm of sleep, she dared to creep from the warmth of the pallet. Shivering, she pulled on her overgown and slipped into the deserted corridor. There she lifted a smoking torch from its ring and made her way into the common room to search for Jamie.

"God's bones, have a care," someone mumbled sleepily as she trod on his arm. She would have passed, but he sat up and caught the skirt of her gown, nearly tripping her. "What the—Jesu, lady!" he whispered loudly. " 'Tisna the place—"

"I am come to see my son is safe," she hissed low. "Where is he?"

"And yer lord finds ye here, I am a dead man," he muttered, pulling his blanket up to hide his nakedness. "The boy is there." He jerked his head toward the row of sleeping men.

Holding the smoking torch before her, she moved carefully among them until she found Jamie, and what she saw astounded her. The man Ewan lay, his greying head barely visible above the blanket, his arm circling her son, holding him close, while Ena's body curved the other way, warming him. Jamie was as snug as a pea in a pod between them. Not daring to wake them, Arabella tiptoed back to where Lang Gib still sat watching her.

"Does my lord know?" she asked.

"Aye." His handsome face broke into a smile. " 'Twas he as brought her here, though she dinna want to come. She disputed with him, saying 'twas not meet, but he told her that Ewan would nae get a babe on her if she kept the boy between them." He followed her gaze as she looked again to her son. "And we dinna make any jests for it, for she quieted the wee one that we could sleep.''

"He did not beat him?''

"Nay, for all that we wanted him to, he dinna.''

"But he was angered with him.''

"Aye, but he brought the woman.'' His eyes traveled the length of her appreciatively, then he sighed regretfully. "Ye'd best get back, mistress, fer I'd keep my head, and ye don't mind it.''

"Aye.''

She rehung the torch in the narrow passageway, then felt her way back to where her husband slept, thinking all the while that she'd wronged him. Shedding her gown quickly, she rolled into the pallet beside him and snuggled against the great warmth of him. He roused and turned to face her.

"Jesu, but art cold,'' he muttered, pulling her closer. His hands rubbed her chilled arms. "You were up.''

"Aye. I went to the garderobe,'' she lied.

"Ought to have used the chamber pot—'tis too cold to go so far.''

"Nay, I'd not make the noise.''

Despite the chill-roughened flesh, her body seemed less stiff where it touched his. He lifted his hand from beneath the covers to brush at the hairs that strayed from her braids.

The memory of how it had been between them earlier washed over him, leaving him aching. He'd wanted more than that, he'd have given more than that. She was his wife, the gentle-born woman given to him for life, and he'd have her turn to him for all she would have in this world. And he could he'd forget Ayrie, he'd forget the boy, he'd forget the day just past.

"I'd nae have minded it,'' he said softly.

Gone was the man who'd been so angered, who'd demanded his due of her. She thought of Jamie, who lay now so peacefully between Ena and Ewan, and she felt guilt for what she'd denied him. She reached to rub the thick hair at the back of his head, then touched lightly the roughness of his two days' growth of beard. Grateful that he could not see her face in the darkness, she whispered, "And you willed it, I'd lie willing enough now."

For a moment he thought he'd misheard her, that he but dreamed she said it. He tried to make out her features, and thought he could see her smile at him. He felt the surge of an overwhelming desire.

"Aye?" he rasped, through lips nearly too dry for speech.

"Aye."

She was willing to give him what he wanted of her. His own face broke into a grin as he rolled her onto her back into the straw. "Ye'll move a wee bit this time?"

"Aye."

He kissed her then, lingering long and leisurely over her mouth as though he would test her promise. Her arms went around his neck, holding him, as her body enticed him from beneath. When at last he raised his head he added wickedly, "And would ye pant and moan a bit also?" As he asked his hand cupped her breast, rubbing the nipple between his thumb and forefinger, hardening it. And then he eased his body lower to taste of it.

She squirmed as his mouth teased, and her whole body came alive beneath his touch. Her fingers caressed the thick waves of his sleep-disordered hair as her desire rose to match his own. "The task is yours to make," she gasped.

His hand moved lower, feeling the flood of wetness there, and he knew that this time 'twould be good. Still he tarried, exploring her with his mouth and his hands, savoring her response to him, until she moaned and writhed, telling him what she would have of him.

Her body arched beneath his hand and her hands tugged at his hair, drawing his head back to hers. He grasped her hips and took possession of her mouth and her body at the same time.

This time she gave herself wholeheartedly to the

union of their bodies, panting, moaning, thrashing, urging him on almost frantically with her words and her hands. Her nails dug into his back, holding him until her breath came in great gasps, until her cries intensified with the waves of ecstasy that spread through her body. And still he drove relentlessly, riding those waves harder and faster. He cried out as the seed spilled within her, then collapsed to lie still above her.

For a time there was no sound beyond the exhausted panting they shared. Finally he became aware of his great weight over her, and reluctantly he rolled away. As he eased back against the lumpy, straw-filled bag, he pulled her into the crook of his arm.

"Well," he observed, still gulping for air, "I doubt me even the monks slept through that." His fingertips grazed her bare arms lightly, tracing her flesh along the bone. "I canna claim ever having the like." He craned his neck to look downward, trying to see what he could of her face in the darkness. "I would I knew what changed ye, for I'd see ye had more of it," he teased.

"I saw that you got Ena for Jamie," she said simply.

He stiffened for a moment, then sighed heavily, falling silent. "Och, ye went there, did ye?" he said finally.

"Aye."

And as good as it had been between them, he now felt cheated. He lay there, still cradling her against him, thinking she'd not done it for him—'twas for Aidan of Ayrie's bastard she'd done it. After a time he eased her head off his arm, sighing again.

"Ye'd best sleep, for we've a long ride on the morrow."

She knew she'd made a mistake, for she sensed the change in him, yet she was uncertain what to do about it. Was it that, despite his words, he could not tolerate Jamie? Or did she but imagine he disliked her son? The image of how he'd held the sleeping boy, sheltering him from the cold, came to mind, then faded to the memory of his cruelty in the corridor. Nay, he was no better than everyone else: For all his earlier words of understanding, William of Dunashie could scarce bear the sight of her crippled child.

But if he were as all the rest, why had he said he'd take Jamie? And if he believed her child was truly cursed, why had he wed her? She shifted her weight slightly against the lumpy straw, felt the lingering stickiness of his seed—and had her answer. 'Twas for that, and that alone. He was as any other: He'd taken her in hopes she would breed. He would have sons of his body to rule Blackleith after him. Like Elias, he would believe he would get whole babes of her.

But at least he was not as bad as Elias, she had to own finally. Even in his anger William had not beaten her, nor had he beaten Jamie, and for that at least she'd praise God. Had Jamie screamed so in Elias' presence he'd not have survived, no matter what blood Elias thought he bore. At Woolford, even his older sons had been ruled by fear. Nay, this husband was not like that. She had but to see the affection of his men to know it. Woolford had had no Lang Gibs, no Wats, no Ewans there. If only he could show some small measure of tolerance for her son . . .

Outside there was the muffled sound of slippers on stone-floored passages, followed by the haunting beauty of chanted prayers in the chapel as the monks sang Matins, marking the hour of midnight. She listened in the darkness, and knew William did not sleep.

"My lord . . . ." she whispered tentatively.

"What?"

"If I have offended you, I'd offer amends for it."

There was a long pause ere he answered. "Nay," he said finally, " 'tis wrong of me to fault you for what you cannot help." He rolled closer and put his arm around her. "We are both overtired, and 'tis yet far to Blackleith." He drew in the musty rose fragrance from her braids, then exhaled. "I had hopes of making the

journey in two days, but with you and the boy—and
the weather—'twill be three or more.''

''I am sorry.''

''You cannot command the rain to cease.'' With his
free arm he pulled the covers yet higher, exposing his
feet even more. He was silent a moment, then muttered. ''Jesu, but 'tis cold on this floor.'' Abruptly, he
sat up and groped for his chausses to warm his legs.
''When we reach Blackleith, we shall have a bed as
fits me. For at least twenty of my thirty-two years I
have had cold feet in winter.'' He managed to pull
them on without rising, then lay again against
her.''Ah, Bella,'' he murmured, ''you cannot know
how much I've wanted a woman to warm my bones.
For that alone, I'd prize you.''

For all that she could not understand him, for all
that she'd not wanted to wed him, she had to admit
there was a certain security in lying next to his big,
warm body. She snuggled beneath the strength of the
arm that held her, thinking that on the morrow everything would be better. When he grew used to Jamie,
when he truly understood how it was for the boy,
surely he would be moved to greater pity. Despite his
gruffness she'd glimpsed some kindness in William of
Dunashie, and on that she would build her hope.

His arm hugged her more tightly, pulling her even
closer as he curved his big body around hers. ''I have
always loved roses,'' he murmured sleepily against her
hair. ''Better than gillyflowers even, I love the roses.''

Chapter Fifteen

There was little formality at Blackleith, and few paid any attention as Robert of Carnan listened to the young priest read William of Dunashie's letter. It was not until he swore furiously, blaspheming God and cursing the Bastard and the Butcher at the same time, that those around him stopped to watch the seneschal's display of temper.

The priest, who still held the offending letter, seemed more amused than offended by Robert of Carnan's outburst. While the castle's chief officer raged he merely studied the parchment again, smiling faintly as his eyes traveled over the page. Let Robert seek the sympathy of the garrison, he thought, for 'twould serve his greater purpose if the man were provoked into rebellion.

He regarded the offending letter as the Hebrews must have looked on the manna sent from heaven. And he had used it well, reading arrogance into words that bore none, adding an inflection of condescension where it did not exist. And to good effect. Had he not chosen this path, Walter was certain he could have earned his bread as a trouvère of some invention. Aye,

his interpretation of William of Dunashie's words had
inflamed far beyond their intention.

He waited until Robert of Carnan had in his fury
flung himself from the small hall, then he enlightened
the rest of the household, reading provocatively:

> To Robert of Carnan, at Blackleith, seneschal
> by writ of Giles of Moray, I give greetings this
> 15th day of November, in the year of our Lord,
> 1138.
>
> Be advised that I am delayed and do not reach
> you until Thursday at the earliest. Nonetheless, I
> would have the ordering of a welcome as befits
> the lord and lady of the keep and manor of Black-
> leith.

Jesu, for but a lowly bastard of Dunashie, this William wrote like a royal clerk. Walter cleared his throat
and continued:

> Moreover, though it is late to ask it, I would
> have the making of a new bed, seven English feet
> in length, with at least two mattresses of fresh
> feathers in clean ticking, hung upon the stoutest
> ropes to be had. Further, despite the weather, I
> would have you make haste to see the garderobes
> are sweetened and the hall freshly limed ere you
> are greeted by your new lady, Arabella, born of
> Byrum, wed to me but two days past.

They watched, perplexed that such words had angered Robert so, until Walter went on,

> Though I am decided to pass the keys of your
> office to a man of my choosing, Gilbert of Kil-
> burnie, without ceremony, if it be your will to
> serve me you are most welcome to remain at
> Blackleith. And to determine whosoever else will
> hold office of me, I'd have an assemblage upon
> my arrival. Until then I'd suspend all hallmotes

held in my name, that I may mete out mine own justice and issue all writs of Blackleith in mine own name. And ere you are relieved, I'd have all accounts readied and all taxes, duties, and fees held listed that I may determine my rights and obligations as lord.

Subscribed by me and in mine own hand, I am William, born of Dunashie, vassal to Lord Giles, holder of Blackleith, as witnessed by my seal.

Having read the latter portions with veiled sarcasm, Walter hoped he'd succeeded in promoting unease. Murmurs of " 'whosoever else will hold office of me'?'' and " 'all taxes, duties, and fees held listed'?'' mingled with muttered comments that this bastard patterned himself after the Old Conqueror and his Domesday book. And there was a groundswell of resentment. Had the Butcher ever complained he had not his due? Had any failed in his duty to the overlord of Dunashie? Nay, but if they'd given him any cause for concern he'd not shown it, for he had seldom even come to Blackleith in the years he'd held it. Like Hamon before him, the Butcher had preferred his larger keeps. But now the Bastard would come, demanding what they had always freely given.

Walter looked contemptuously to the seal. It was naught but the imperfect impression of a carved ring in cheap wax. He smiled again. The Bastard, for all his desire to act as befitted a lord, had given Walter the means to his revenge. He rerolled the letter carefully and tucked it into the neck of his tunic, then he sought Robert of Carnan.

At the top of the circular tower steps the wind whistled over the wall, flapping the pennon above loudly, but Robert seemed impervious to the biting cold. He leaned against the newly crenelated battlement, the pride of his tenure as seneschal to Blackleith, and looked to the river below. Walter watched silently, thinking he could read the older man's thoughts. Aye,

Robert's pride was stung at the thought of giving over his authority to one probably lesser-born than himself.

Moreover, he was bitter to learn that after twenty and more years' service here he was unneeded. What had Robert boasted to him? That not even when Hamon had been killed by Moray had he been asked to give up his keys. And now he would have to surrender these symbols of his authority, becoming but another knight in service. And the man who asked it had no blood claim either, for William of Dunashie was but Moray's bastard brother.

But a few nights earlier, when Robert had been more than a little drunk before the fire, he'd told Walter that the best years of his life had been at Blackleith. He'd boasted of how he'd husbanded the demesne's resources, thwarting the bailiff's tendency to squander, that he might build the keep's defenses. How he'd struggled with the bailiff to see that every penny, every bushel, every bag of wool had been paid, in good times and in bad. He'd served his absent lords so well that there had been times he'd nearly thought of Blackleith as his, he'd confessed. But that was before the Bastard had come to claim it.

The older man's shoulders shook as he leaned over the wall, and Walter was suddenly afraid he meant to jump. Not to be thwarted thus, he gathered the skirt of his cassock and hastened onto the wall.

" 'Tis overcold to walk this day, sir. By the looks of yon sky, God gives us more rain."

"Or snow," Robert muttered. He pushed back from the battlement and swung around angrily. "Ye'll have to look to other souls, Father Edmund, for I'd nae speak of God this day."

"You are troubled, my son."

The older man snorted. "Yer son? Jesu, but I wore mail ere ye were swaddled! Nay, get ye down where your words are needed, and leave me in peace." When Walter made no move to leave, Robert clenched his fists. "God's bones, but are ye deaf also? I said I'd be alone!"

"I am come to tend your troubled soul."

"Tend the Bastard's!" Robert shouted at him, his voice rising into the howling wind. "Aye, ye saw what he wrote, dinna ye? Ye read it yerself! And ye would feed ye, ye'll look to him rather than me!"

Walter considered the angry man before him, then gambled. "Mayhap all is not lost, my son."

"Jesu! Give me peace, Father! What would a priest know of loss?" Robert sneered. "Ye have but to prate yer prayers, and ye are fed. There's none to care that ye canna wield a sword or axe! There's none to care that ye dinna ride forth again and again to other men's battles!"

"God asks different things of us," Walter observed, meeting the other man's angry eyes. "And God helps those who are willing to act," he added significantly.

His meaning went past Robert. "Were ye not in cassock, I'd throw ye from this wall that ye would cease prattling to me," he muttered sourly. Very deliberately, he turned his back on Walter and again leaned on the battlement.

But Walter had not yet sown enough seeds to bear fruit. Despite Robert's hostility, he moved to lean beside him. "You know not of me, Robert of Carnan," he said almost softly. "I too have been displaced by Moray and his brother."

"From one living to another?" Robert gibed. "What care they for a priest?"

" 'Twas more than that."

"And ye'd tell me God provided, would ye? Ye waste yer words on me, Father Edmund."

"In a manner, He did."

"Well, He doesna provide for me. He gives me but the choice of serving beneath this Gilbert or starving! Twenty years' service I have given this keep, and what thanks have I for it? Gilbert of Kilburnie comes to take my keys from me!"

"Twenty years is a long time," Walter agreed.

"Long? I came here when I was but a boy, and 'twas Hamon as ruled here. Aye, 'twas before he had Dun-

ashie or any of the other. I grew to manhood serving
Hamon, and when King David gave Blackleith to Moray, I served him also! Nay, 'tis poor thanks I have
had for it, Father! Now 'tis Moray who gives rule over
this keep to one who did not sit at his own table a year
ago! And the bastard he raises chooses one even lower
than himself to put above me!''

"Aye." Walter said no more, hoping the older man's
musings would fuel his bitterness beyond bearing.

"What would ye know of it?" Robert demanded
viciously. "Blackleith means naught to ye—ye are but
lately come!''

"I know, Robert of Carnan—I *know.*''

"Nay, ye canna." Robert pushed away from the wall
again and swept the air with his hand. "Look about
ye, Father: Every stone on this wall I ordered. I have
done everything here: I have husbanded and built, I
have watched the old priest keep honest accounts, I
have held counts in the lord's absence and meted out
even justice, I have tended to rents, services, cus-
toms—nay, I have tended Giles of Moray's lands well,
I tell you! I have ridden every hide of them!''

"Aye.''

Robert turned again to stare out over the demesne's
lands, and his gaze grew distant as his voice lowered.
"After he had Blackleith, Hamon cared not for this
place, but I did. And so it was with the Butcher also:
He left me to rule here in his name. I have never
wanted to live anywhere else, ye know. But there is
nae hope for it now: William of Dunashie comes to
take away all I have strived for.''

"'Twould seem 'tis poor reward for your service,"
Walter agreed slyly.

"And now I canna stay," Robert admitted slowly.
"There isna a place for me here.''

But Walter shook his head. "Nay, you must not go,
for there are too many here who have need of you still.
No more than you, will they wish to serve this bastard.''

"What good am I to them now? Jesu, but I can only answer to this Gilbert—and I'd nae do it!''

''Your right is older than his—or the Bastard's.'' Walter leaned in front of Robert, meeting his eyes soberly. ''There are those here who would choose to serve you, there are those who would say your right is as great as his.''

''He holds it of Moray,'' the older man reminded him.

''There are those who will remember Moray was not born here. There are yet those who remember he murdered Hamon for it.''

Robert eyed him suspiciously, wondering where the young priest meant to lead him. ''Father Edmund, you behold one who is nae a fool. There's none as has stood against the Butcher and lived.''

''William of Dunashie has less claim than his brother. King David cannot like it that Moray raises a baseborn knave into the barony. And 'tis to be wondered why 'twas done: Was it that Moray feared to have the Bastard at Dunashie?''

''Yer thoughts are overaddled by yer prayers.'' Hunching his shoulders against the cold, the seneschal leaned forward on the crenelated wall. ''Heard ye nae of Wycklow? Art so cloistered in yer church, you dinna know of that? Ralph de Payes would have usurped Wycklow, and he died fer it!''

''The Bastard is not the Butcher,'' Walter reminded him again. ''And if Moray had no greater care for Blackleith than to give it to one of no worth, mayhap he does but wish this William away.'' Pausing to let his words effect doubt, he then added softly, ''Were it I, I should rather ask who followed me.''

''E'en the Butcher wouldna hang a priest,'' Robert retorted, turning again to face Walter. ''Why do ye urge me to rebellion?'' he asked, his eyes narrowing. ''What matters it to ye who rules here?''

''They are godless men.''

There was none to doubt that, Robert conceded silently. Did the priest really think he could wrest Blackleith from them? The idea was an impossible one. "Ye forget 'tis King David as consented," he muttered, suddenly afraid of where his thoughts carried him. "Whether he likes the Bastard or no, he consented."

"Aye, as he consented to Hamon and to Moray before him. David is nothing if not a practical man." Aware that he'd now prodded Robert of Carnan far enough to give him the thoughts he wanted, Walter pushed back from the wall and shrugged.

"Ye guide me wrongly, Father."

"Did I say you should rebel? Nay, you mistake me: I did but agree 'tis an injustice they do you. Mayhap this Gilbert will falter, and once again you will lead Blackleith for the lord." As he spoke, he pulled the ends of his sleeves down over his hands to warm them. "I did but mean that God would have you hope. He would have you look to yourself." He clasped his arms tightly before him, trying to shut out the cold. "The only meek who inherit are the meek who are born to what they have."

"Ye speak in riddles, Edmund. For all the words ye give me, I'll nae ferget yer youth makes ye overbold with yer counsel."

Yet after the priest had gone Robert paced the wall, letting the raw wind cool his mind. Blackleith was not Wycklow, after all, and Giles of Moray seldom put forth the effort to come there. And had not King David given the Butcher lands far greater than these? But 'twas the Bastard who came, he argued within himself. Aye, he conceded, but who could say whether Moray would fight for one who shared but half his blood and none of his name? Mayhap he wanted William of Dunashie away from his own patrimony. Bastard kinsmen sometimes were troublesome, after all. If only he could be certain he'd not incur the Butcher's wrath . . .

Walter paused at the bottom of the stairs to savor what he hoped his wits would win him. And a slow smile of satisfaction crossed his face. If he could but get Robert to kill the Bastard, he knew the Butcher would come. No matter what he'd told the fool, he still

Chapter Sixteen

The morning fog had lifted and the sun was almost visible, brightening the clouds from behind. It no longer rained. For three days the steady downpour had hampered their progress, soaking them, freezing them in the late autumn cold, until Arabella had almost yearned for the warmth of Byrum's fires. But this day gave only the promise that she would not arrive a sodden, bedraggled hag before Blackleith. She leaned forward in her saddle, shifting her aching body to look at the muddy road ahead.

"We are nearly there," William encouraged her. "And we reach the second hill, you will see it: 'Tis but beyond the bend in the burn."

"We have to cross water?" She looked skyward, then back to the mud that mired their horses, slowing their pace. "Sweet Jesu, but—"

He shook his head. "And you came from the east, aye, but we do not approach that way. It sits on this side." He stretched also before he added, " 'Tis as well, for the burn will be flooded. Robert of Carnan wrote Giles often, saying that it should be dammed above, but if 'twas done I've not heard it." His gaze met hers and warmed. "Art weary?"

"Aye."

"Well, 'twill be no rude pallet tonight for ye. When I wrote, I asked a new bed and mattress be made." He watched the blood rise to her face as she blushed, and he grinned, shaking his head. "Nay, this night I'd not plague ye. 'Tis overfar we have ridden, and once yer bones are warmed and yer stomach filled, I'd see ye take to the bed." His hazel eyes twinkled as he added, "But when the sun comes up on the morrow . . ." His voice trailed off, but there was no mistaking his meaning.

Her blush deepening, she looked down to where her oft-soaked gown hung limply over her legs. "I'd have a bath ere I had aught else, I think."

"Aye." He said nothing for a moment, then blurted out, "I have hopes ye'll be pleased wi' Blackleith, Arabella."

How could she be pleased there? she wondered, as the resentment returned. How could she be pleased when he'd removed Jamie from her care? And yet it did no good to quarrel with him, for that would but set him further against her son. She glanced back down the column to where Ewan held the little boy, seeing the reproach in Jamie's pinched white face. And yet William would have her answer.

"As 'tis not Byrum, I have hopes of it also," she murmured finally.

" 'Tisna nearly so fine as Woolford."

"I would not go again to Woolford if Donald, Hugh, and Milo all perished, and 'twas given to Jamie," she declared emphatically, her voice betraying her bitterness. "I had no happiness in Elias' keep."

He wished he'd not mentioned the place, for 'twas but a reminder of things he'd not think on. And the fault was his this time. Cursing his own foolish tongue, he fell silent.

For a time she stared at the sodden road that lay ahead, not wanting to think of Elias or Woolford or anything past. For whatever reason, God had given her to William of Dunashie now, and from this time forward 'twas to William and Blackleith she belonged. Had she the chance she'd carve her life and Jamie's again from clean stone, and forget what had passed before. But the task was almost too great, for she could think of no way to make William value her son.

She stole a sidewise glance at her new husband. It had been easy at first to think of him as naught but "the Bastard," an overgrown oaf with naught but his brother's fearsome reputation to recommend him. But now she knew not what to make of him. Where she had expected pain he'd given her passion, showing small kindnesses even, and yet always there was that about him that seemed unable to bear Jamie's company. Mayhap 'twas but that he was unused to seeing one so lame, mayhap 'twas that he was like so many others, fearing what he did not know. But there seemed to be more to it than that. Nay, he had denied her the right to provide company and comfort to her son, she recalled, feeling anew the loss.

But for all that he'd separated her and Jamie from each other, she had to admit he'd not actually offered either of them any violence. And for all that he was stern and unyielding, he'd not been truly unkind to Jamie. And unlike her father, he'd neither taunted nor cursed the boy for his misshapen leg. Nor had he quarreled with her before her son since that first day. But then neither had she defied him since.

Aye, now 'twas Ewan who carried Jamie, Ewan who tended him, Ewan who slept with him. And since Jamie's wellspring of tears had finally run dry, her son no longer screamed and cried for her. It was as though he recognized the futility of his anguish. But now every time she met his eyes, they reproached her silently.

What William would not understand was that he deprived her as well. For every day and night of her son's six years they had clung to each other, drawing mutual comfort against a cruel and unjust world. Her need for Jamie was nearly as great as his for her. 'Twas wrong of William to expect he could supplant her son in her thoughts from the moment he'd wed her.

And yet he rode beside her, seemingly unaware of the turmoil in her heart. He did not know and probably did not care that she wept inwardly. Or that she struggled to accept what he had done. Nay, but he behaved as though there were naught but happiness between them.

But if she had anything to be grateful to William for, 'twas that he'd not forced Jamie to walk since that first night. Mayhap seeing how painfully Jamie had stumbled on his short, twisted leg had touched him more than he betrayed. And if 'twas so, then mayhap all hope was not lost for love to grow between William and her son. And mayhap if he could not learn to love, he could be moved to pity.

She stole another glance at her husband, reminding herself again that, for all she faulted him, he was far kinder than Elias or her father. Aye, were it not for Jamie, she could almost count herself content with this huge man who reminded her much of his brother's bear standard.

As she watched him covertly, her thoughts turned from Jamie to him. And she had to smile at the way he seemed to struggle with his speech, trying to sound as Norman as his brother. Yet in unguarded moments of emotion, 'twas the language of his ancestors that came to his lips.

"And you look to the second hill, you can see Blackleith now," he told her proudly, cutting into her reverie.

She roused to look, but saw nothing. He leaned so close that his mailed arm brushed against hers as he pointed. "There."

Her gaze followed his arm, and found it. " 'Tis stone," she murmured in surprise. "I thought 'twas timber."

"Robert of Carnan counts himself a builder, and with Giles' permission he has raised a new wall on this side. The one that faces the river is still wood, as there's not many who would be foolish enough to mount an attack from there.''

''Robert of Carnan?''

''Giles' seneschal here.'' He paused, frowning. ''A good man, by all accounts, but I'd bring one as serves me now.''

''Lang Gib.''

''Aye. 'Tis 'Gilbert of Kilburnie' when he takes the keys. 'Twill sound strange to mine ears to call him thus.'' He sighed, then favored her with a rueful smile. ''But if he can manage to call me 'William' after years of 'Wee Willie,' I can say 'Gilbert' also.''

''You were called 'wee'?'' she asked, lifting a brow.

''Aye.'' His smile broadened. ''When I was a small lad I was undersized, but then I grew until 'twas a jest.''

''And grew.''

''And grew,'' he agreed. ''And then I grew more yet, becoming this great fellow ye behold. 'Moray's bear,' the clerks at Winchester taunted, bringing Giles a bell to hang upon my neck.'' His expression changed and his eyes were distant, as though they looked backward to years long past. ''I lay upon my pallet at night, planning for the day I'd go back with axe instead of pen to still their laughter.'' He stopped, then settled his shoulders. ''But who could blame them? I ask ye, for I grew far too fast for grace, making me a clumsy fellow. 'Tis nae a wonder they laughed at one whose gown came halfway to his knees, is it?''

''But it pained you,'' she decided.

''Aye. Words are like arrows, ye know: Ill-loosed they wound, leaving scars behind. I once stabbed a fellow with my pen knife, wishing it were a dagger, for the words he'd fired at me.''

''Twas wrong of them to make you a clerk, when 'tis plain you were destined for a warrior.''

''Nay, I do not fault them for that, for I learned much from copying my lessons.'' He shrugged, resettling his broad shoulders. ''Though King Henry gave me no thought, 'twas his gift that I learned to read, and 'tis all I thank him for.''

She felt a stab of envy that she, who was better-born than he, could make naught but a mark for her name. It was easier to think on the pain he'd revealed, for in that they were equal. She reached to touch the cold steel links that covered his arm.

'' 'Twould seem you and Jamie have shared more than you would admit, my lord, for he also is taunted for what he cannot help,'' she said softly.

Sweet Jesu, but why did every thought come back to the boy? She could not even give him freely of her sympathy without speaking of James of Whatever. In the guise of adjusting his reins, he moved his arm away.

''Nay, 'tis more the reason he must learn strength also. The more ye coddle him, the greater target ye make of him.''

''Unlike you, he cannot grow beyond the taunts,'' she reminded him. ''He—''

''And he doesna learn to look to himself, ye make him prisoner to ye.'' He lifted his hand as though he would silence her, then stood in his saddle to study the keep ahead. ''And ye look now, ye can see the tower is goodly size,'' he told her proudly, directing her thoughts away from the boy. ''Aye, Old Robert has even roofed it with slate rather than thatch, so 'twill not be so easily burned.''

'' 'Tis fine.''

Aware by her change in manner that he'd been too critical about the boy, he sought to make amends. ''When we are settled within, I'd have ye determine what ye'd have for yer comfort. Elizabeth said to send to her for aught ye need, and I told her ye would.'' When she made no answer he went on conversationally, ''Ye'll find the walls are not damp, despite the clime. And beyond the tower''—he stopped to point along the line of the wall—''the garden is at the end. I am told 'tis filled with enough herbs and flowers for yer simples.'' Twisting in his saddle to look at her, he smiled. "Aye, and though I canna claim any great knowledge of them, I can tell ye there's roses and gillyflowers as blooms in plenty come summer." His arm made a circling motion, encompassing the area around them. "And out here, the heather blooms until the hillsides are purple with it."

He reined in and leaned forward, bracing himself against the high pommel, drinking in the sight of his keep. *His keep.* Never in all the years of Giles' exile, never in all the years since, had he ever expected to rule anything. "Och, but I would that my dam had lived t' see this," he murmured. "She'd nae ha believed it else she touched it, I expect."

It was the first time Arabella had considered that he'd had a mother. "She is long dead?" she asked gently.

"Aye. When the Moray came to Dunashie for Giles' mother, they killed mine, saying she was naught but my father's whore," he recalled bitterly. "I'd hae counted it justice when Judith of Moray died, but she'd just birthed Giles then, and 'twas a hard thing for him. She left him to be despised with me."

"She was wed to your father—Judith of Moray, I mean?"

"Aye. He looked high, my sire, when he looked to the Moray, and when they said nay, he took her away. By the time they came to claim her back 'twas overlate, for she was filled with Iain of Dunashie's child." He exhaled. "My sire was but a Scots-born borderer of low repute, ye see, and they took pride in being Normans of the lineage of de Maurais. 'Twas an insult not to be suffered, they said when they came for her. But in the end Lady Judith died in childbed, and they hanged my sire for it." His mouth twisted wryly. "My dam was a stout lass, while Lady Judith was small and pretty. 'Tis nae a wonder that he wed her instead. That, and it gave him pride to wed a Moray," he added, forcing a smile. "Though he dinna live, he passed his pride to Giles, ye know, for Giles wouldna hae any but the daughter of Rivaux."

"But you were reared by the Moray?"

"Reared?" he snorted derisively. "Nay. When Henry of England would have hostages of Scotland against the raiding, they gave us both into his keeping. And had we been blinded, 'twould have been as naught to them, I can tell ye." His eyes met hers soberly. "Reared me? Nay, 'twas the lowest of Henry's court as reared me, Arabella—and 'twas I as reared Giles."

"But if he was of Moray's blood . . ."

"The blood they saw in him was Dunashie's, and there was none as wanted to be reminded of it. While he languished in England's household, the Moray did not even stand for Giles when King Alexander of Scotland declared Dunashie forfeit and gave it to Hamon of Blackleith."

"But surely—"

"And do not think to defend the Moray, Arabella, for they had nae cause for what they did to Giles. They wouldna even support him when he came to reclaim his patrimony. His own grandsire swore before Alexander's brother David that Giles was born at, but not of, the blood of Moray. But even King David had to acknowledge his birth, for the marriage was recorded in the parish register." He dropped his eyes, focusing on the muddy road below. " 'Twas thus that we came to burn Dunashie, and with Hamon's family in it, no matter what ye may have heard."

It was the most he'd spoken of his family or of whence he'd come. "Well, it does not matter now," she consoled him, "for Lord Giles has Dunashie again, and we are before Blackleith. You have been rewarded for your loyalty, my lord."

"Aye. And there's none of Hamon's family left to dispute it," he agreed grimly. He clicked his reins, urging his huge destrier forward again. "Blackleith is mine now, and I'd go inside."

To the last instant Robert of Carnan paced the wall, his thoughts torn between honor and ambition. It was mad what he did, and he knew it, and yet he'd not go from Blackleith tamely. Below, the archers tightened the springs on their crossbows and nocked their arrows in readiness, and still he waited to give the signal.

The shrouded November sun managed to illuminate the distant helmets, making them look like bobbing silver pennies. There were not many: William of Dunashie brought less than twenty men with him. There was no mistaking the Bastard, for even at two furlongs and more his head was visible above the others. Beside him rode a woman.

Robert frowned, recalling the Bastard's message: *Your new lady, Arabella, born of Byrum, wed to me but two days past* . . . 'Twould have been four days now. Not that the time mattered. But there was the matter of Nigel of Byrum: Would he avenge his daughter's husband? More to the point, would the Butcher avenge his half-brother? He looked down uneasily, wavering in his resolve, for he had not the answers.

His memory hearkened back to the two times Giles of Moray had come to Blackleith, and he strained to recollect how it had been between the Butcher and his brother. Jesu, but then he'd given the giant no notice beyond his size, for he was but another bastard. Nay, but Giles had not even brought him to table with him, as Robert recalled. William of Dunashie had sat amongst the mesnie—'twas why he scarce remembered him. He'd not been overvalued then, and 'twas yet a wonder that Moray had seen fit to raise him now.

He tortured his brain for something to tilt the balance one way or the other. What had Father Edmund said but moments before? That 'twas clear as yon pike that the lord of Dunashie wanted rid of his bastard half-brother, for did Elizabeth of Rivaux not breed? And where there were legitimate heirs, there was no room for bastards.

And still he hesitated to give the order. What about Nigel of Byrum? Once the deed was done, would he demand satisfaction? And if he did, would it be more than a few marks of silver?

Mayhap Robert could claim 'twas an accident. Nay,

not unless all perished along with William, and then what accident was that? E'en if 'twas claimed they'd drowned in the flooded burn, not all would have died so.

The horn sounded their approach and still he watched, thinking there was no way he could justify to any what he would do. Jesu, but there was no justice in this world. He'd have to let them enter—he'd have to submit and give up the keys to Blackleith. But he'd wait until they were inside ere he went down to them. 'Twas enough that he had to swallow the bitter draught that was his pride.

For the first time in his forty-one years, he felt a coward before his men. After urging them to rebellion, he could not bring himself to give the order.

Below him Walter watched from a narrow window, every nerve tautening as the mesnie moved closer. God's bones, but they were in range now. Even he could hit them. He squeezed further into the opening and craned his neck upward. For what did Robert of Carnan wait?

The horn sounded again across the flooded ditch, and when Walter looked down they were almost below him. To his left and right the archers were lying in the slits, poised to take William of Dunashie down, and still there was no signal from above. To Walter's dismay, the bridge began to creak downward. Did Robert think 'twould be easier to let them inside? Mayhap he wanted to be certain none lived to tell the tale. But if he waited overlong, 'twould be too late. As many years as had passed between, Walter could still remember how the Bastard had fought in the taking of Dunashie.

Gathering his cassock up with one hand and a bow with the other, Walter ran for the tower steps. He'd not let a fool like Robert of Carnan cheat him, not now. It did not serve his plan to let the Bastard live.

"God's bones, my lord, but they come inside!" he cried in protest, ere he'd reached the wall.

Robert turned around, his bitterness in his eyes.

"Aye. 'Twas folly to think the Butcher and Byrum would let me rule."

"Nay, all is not lost: You have but to say 'twas an accident. The guards confused the order, 'twas all."

But Robert shook his head. "I'd have to kill them all. And for all that I'd have Blackleith, I'd not murder a woman for it."

"Jesu!"

"What is it to ye that I rule here, Father?" Robert asked suddenly. " 'Tis yer priestly duty to counsel love and reason, not murder."

In that moment, Walter knew the older man had not the stomach to kill the Bastard of Dunashie. Turning away, he nocked a quarrel into the string, then pulled the spring taut with his foot, keeping the bow pointed down. Aiming over the side, he loosed the arrow. And as it swooshed through the air the archers below fired also, sending a hail of arrows down on the incoming men below.

"What the—nay! God's blood, but you will kill us all!" Robert yelled, grabbing for Walter's bow. "Art mad, Father?" he demanded, wresting it from him.

As Walter gave up the weapon, he ducked beneath the older man's arm and pushed. Robert lost his balance and fell, still clutching the bow, over the side. His cry of surprise died with him on the rocks beneath.

As the first arrow struck the horse behind him, William flung his body across Arabella's, carrying them both to the bridge. Horses neighed and reared, pawing the air in fright, as William pushed her into the narrow portcullis slit, holding her there.

Lang Gib charged past them, his battle-axe drawn, shouting, "For St. Andrew and Dunashie! Whoreson cowards! Fight ye like men!"

Seeing that Robert had fallen, everyone inside rushed to throw down their weapons, emerging almost sheepishly from the arrow slits. " 'Twas a mistake— aye, a mistake!" someone yelled. "God's mercy, sirs!"

William stood and reached a hand to Arabella. "Art all right?" he asked anxiously.

"Naught but my gown suffered, and 'twas ruined before," she answered, turning to look behind him. "But Jamie . . . Sweet Mary, but where is Jamie?" she cried. "Jamie!" She broke into a run when she saw Ewan's horse. "Mother of God, is he all right?"

For answer, the man leaned from his saddle and handed the boy down to her. "Naught's harmed, my lady—we turned to flee at the first arrow."

The little boy clutched at her convulsively, burying his head in her breast, as she held him and wept. "Shhhh, lovey . . . shhhh . . ." she babbled against his hair, nuzzling it. "Mama has you safe, sweeting."

As relieved as he too was to see the boy safe, William had to stifle a pang of resentment. He'd had no gratitude from her, for she could spare no thought for any but the boy. Picking up his helm where it had come dislodged, he jammed it onto his head again and walked to them.

"He is all right," he muttered, reaching for Jamie. " 'Tis not meet that ye carry him."

"He is my son!"

"Aye, and I do not deny it," he countered, lifting the boy to his shoulder. "But he is overheavy for ye."

"Ena . . ."

"And for her also. Ewan!"

"Aye, my lord?"

"I'd have ye take the boy until 'tis determined how safe we are."

"Aye."

"But—"

"But nay," William cut in brusquely. Turning his attention to the sullen silence within the courtyard, he left her to cross to where Lang Gib interrogated the gatekeeper. "Jesu, is this how ye greet yer lord?" he demanded angrily.

" 'Twas . . . 'twas a mistake, my lord—I swear it!"

"He says 'twas Robert of Carnan as ordered 'em ter take ye down," Gib explained.

"Why?"

Perceiving that a wrong answer could cost him his head, the hapless fellow appealed mutely to the others. There was an uneasy shifting of weight, but none answered. Gib was just about to tickle his neck with the sharp side of his dagger when a young priest hurried forward breathlessly.

"Thanks be to God you are spared, my lord!" He stopped to gulp air. "I tried to stop him, but could not!" Then, seeing the knife Gib held to the gatekeeper's throat, he hastened to intervene. "Nay, the fault is not theirs, my lord—'twas Carnan as had them loose the arrows."

"Robert of Carnan served my brother well—aye, and Hamon of Blackleith before him," William told him curtly.

As vexed as he was that the Bastard had survived, Walter managed to shake his head sorrowfully. "Alas, but the sin of envy weighed heavily on him, my lord."

"Envy? God's bones, but what nonsense do ye speak?" Gib snorted. "He was seneschal here!"

"Aye, but when 'twas made known to him that he would lose his office, his reason left him." Walter glanced slyly up at William, then added, "He would have it that one who is bastard-born and bears no blood of Hamon had less right than he to rule Blackleith, my lord."

Lang Gib shook his head in disbelief. "Nay, Carnan had nae right at all: My lord holds the fief of his brother."

But William was watching the priest. " 'Twas ye as stopped him?"

"Nay, but I could not—'twas not until he let fly the arrow that I disputed with him for the bow, my lord." Walter paused again for breath. "God forgive me, but he slipped and fell." He looked skyward for a moment. "And may God forgive him also, and give rest to his soul," he added piously. "And you do not mind it, I'd shrive him, for there was good in him also."

William's gaze traveled from the soiled hem of the

priest's cassock upward to his face. God's bones, he thought, but they ordain fellows too young for spurs now. Aloud he merely muttered, "I thought 'twas an old man who served as chaplain here."

"Alas, but he died, and when word came to Kelso of your need, I was glad to serve." Perceiving that William's eyes had narrowed, Walter smiled. "And I am not so young as you would think, my lord—for long years have I studied God's lessons."

"Ye come from Kelso?" Will asked abruptly.

"Aye. You have been there?"

"Nae lately."

Briefly, William considered inquiring of the child he'd taken to Kelso so long ago, then he recalled that he had not even a name for the boy. No doubt there were dozens like him who'd been sent there since. And he had more pressing matters at hand.

The attack was over. For a moment William was inclined to mete out stern punishment, but the man most responsible was already dead. And he still had to rule those who remained. Taking note of the fact that the others had surrendered swiftly, he nodded and turned his attention back to the priest.

"How are ye called, Father?"

"Edmund—Edmund of Alton, my lord."

"And ye are Saxon-born?"

Walter's smile broadened. "Aye—as the English Church is overrun with Normans, there seemed greater opportunity here."

"It is that," Will agreed. "How many are lost, Gib?"

"But three wounded, and none like to die."

"Aye, see to Robert of Carnan's soul, Father," Will decided finally.

"Aye, my lord."

"And as for ye others"—Will turned to address the chastened defenders—"I'd hae ye know William of Dunashie brooks no further rebellion—ye ken?" There was a collective nod of assent. Satisfied, he pulled off his gloves and dislodged his helmet. Tossing them to

Wat, he held out his bare hands. "Ere ye'd forget it, I'd have the oaths due me now. And ere the morrow is out, I'd have all archers learn better competence with their bows—God's teeth, but ye dinna wound but three!"

Walter paused to look back, watching the first man of Blackleith kneel to place his hands between the Bastard's, and the rage within him welled anew. And then he noted that while most gave their attention to William of Dunashie, the one called "Muckle Mou' Tom" for his wide, drooping mouth stared back at him. And for a moment his blood ran cold with the fear that mayhap the fellow knew. There was reproach in the great gaping face, and Walter recalled suddenly that Tom had been on the other side, on the timbered wall. But if he knew, he'd held his tongue. Still . . .

Walter thrust his arms into the warmth of his sleeves and moved on to the task of saying words over Robert of Carnan's broken body. There was, he reflected bitterly, none but he who had the courage to kill the Bastard or his brother. He'd been a fool to hope otherwise.

Chapter Seventeen

Her first night at Blackleith she could not sleep,
fearing first that 'twas a hostile place, then that 'twas
a new world for which she was unprepared. Finally,
when William's breathing had evened out, she dressed
and stole from the small solar to seek her son, where
he slept with Ewan in the common room at the one
end of the hall. Somehow, as she crossed the open
yard in the faint moonlight, she found it less frightening outside than in. It was, she supposed, that she
was awake to confront her fears.

There'd been no need to worry for Jamie, for she
found him sleeping peacefully, his small body snuggled against the back of the grizzled man-at-arms, beneath the smoking light of a pitch torch that hung in
the iron ring above. It was not right, she reasoned
resentfully, for soon he would come to rely more on
Ewan than on her. Already 'twas the man as fed him,
bathed him, dressed him, and carried him about. And
as far as she could tell, though he made no open complaint, Ewan was as uncomfortable with his orders as
she was. She longed to lean down and smooth the
small, tousled head of hair, but she did not, for she'd

not waken the snoring men. She'd not have any tell
William she'd been there.

Satisfied at least that Jamie was all right, she clasped
her cloak tightly about her and made her way back out
into the cold night air. Again there was naught but the
glow of the half-moon above to illuminate the eerily
silent courtyard as she crossed it. Then she heard the
soft, stealthy movements of someone ahead of her.
She stopped suddenly, and her heart rose to her throat
at the fear of discovery. She was too late.

" 'Tis not safe to go about unattended, even in your
own castle, lady."

A figure emerged from deep shadows to confront
her, and she jumped, then relaxed with relief. 'Twas
but the priest. "Sweet Mary, but you have given me a
fright!" she admitted, exhaling to still the rapid beating of her heart.

" 'Tis too soon, for there are still those here who
would strike first, then look," he chided. "Until the
men of Blackleith and the men of Dunashie learn of
each other, there is little trust or liking, gentle lady."
His eyes gleamed blackly in the moonlight. "Nay, but
were I you, I'd not be out alone."

"Aye, but we are safe enough: Two men of Dunashie sleep upon pallets in the solar, and the door is
barred."

"Nay, 'tis not, for you are down here."

She thought she detected a faint smile. "I did but
come to see how my son fared," she explained defensively.

"The lame boy is yours?"

"Aye." She looked down as he came closer. "And
you, Father: I could ask also how 'tis that you are
about."

"I am but come from the chapel. 'Tis just past Matins."

'But 'tis not Kelso here. There are no monks to join
you."

"Nay, 'tis not," he agreed readily. "But the habits
of nigh a dozen years are slow to depart." He moved

to where he could see her face more clearly. "At least I have the better excuse, I think."

"I could not sleep until I saw my son was all right."

"And your soul is sorely troubled this night. You fear for the boy," he guessed.

She started to deny it, then nodded. "Aye. I am all he has, but my husband will not accept him as he is," she answered low.

"Why?"

Priest or no, she had no business standing there in the dark with him, for what if William should wake and find her gone? "I know not the reason, Father," she replied, glancing toward the darkened door. "And I must return."

"Ask God for the answer, my daughter."

How often had she heard such words from those who did not know? It was as though she could not let them pass yet again, not when this priest knew not of what he spoke. "Think you I have not? Think you I have not begged to know why God marks Jamie so? Think you I have not prayed that my husband will love my son?" she demanded angrily. Then, not wanting to say more, she started to pass him. "Your pardon, Father, but God gives me no answers." ·

He waited until she was nearly to the steep stone stairs. "Is it that your lord believes the boy damned?" he asked almost softly. "If so, he is wrong."

She stopped. "I know not what he believes, Father, for he will not tell me. And he had his wishes, he'd not speak of Jamie."

"And if I tell you God takes pity on the lame?"

"Pity!" She spun around to face him, hurling the word at him. "Is it pity that He marks my son that people turn away in fear? Is it pity that He lets them spit on him? Nay, 'tis not pity He gives James of Woolford—'tis a curse!"

"Ere you ask of God, daughter, look to yourself."

" 'Tis not right that Jamie must atone for any sins I have committed!"

"Have you confessed these sins?" he asked gently.

Once again, he moved closer. "Would you that I prayed with you?"

"Prayers cannot heal my son!"

"God works His wonders in ways we cannot understand, daughter," he murmured.

She closed her eyes and swallowed, that he would not see the rawness of the wound within. "Not for me, Father—not for me."

"Are you such a sinner that you fear to ask?"

"God gave me Elias of Woolford for husband when I was scarce more than a child, and I was beaten sorely for all that I said and did. And then He let Jamie come forth too lame to walk," she answered low. "Do not speak to me of God's mercy, Father."

"And now He gives you the Bastard for husband, and you think yourself well and truly cursed."

"Nay. Not for that." She opened her eyes and met his, seeing only apparent sympathy there. "Nay, if my husband could be brought to care for my son, I would be content."

He reached out to touch her arm. "Then let us pray for that, Lady Arabella. 'Tis a small enough thing to ask."

"Now? Sweet Mary, but I—"

"The time to seek God is when you have need of Him, daughter, and 'twould seem that time is now."

"Ay, but . . ." Her gaze darted anxiously to the stairs behind her. For all that she was drawn to his kindness, he seemed far too young to confess her.

"If William of Dunashie would fault you for praying, then he is a godless man."

"Nay, he is not godless," she protested, remembering the way William pored over his paper prayers. " 'Tis but I would he understood my son. He asks overmuch of one small, nearly helpless boy. Were it not that, I'd have no complaint of the lord I am given."

Her hair was pale, her eyes luminous in the soft moonlight, making her even lovelier than when he'd seen her earlier. As Walter looked upon her, he felt yet another reason to envy Dunashie's bastard.

"Then we will ask God to remedy that also."

"Father Edmund! Father Edmund! Praise God ye are still awake! 'Tis needed ye are in the gatehouse!" The sentry who ran toward them stopped when he saw her. "Yer pardon," he mumbled, looking down.

" 'Tis all right. I did but come out for air, and Father Edmund chides me for being about so late."

Too overset to realize that the air was too cold to be healthy, he turned again to Walter. " 'Tis Muckle Mou' Tom, Father!" he blurted out. "I know not what ails him, but Sim would hae it he dies. When he found him, poor Tom couldna speak!"

For a moment Walter stood quite still, then he dared to ask, "He cannot speak at all? He said naught to Sim?"

"Nay. Sim says he was lying upon the floor, his whole body a-tremble, and when Sim would know what happened he couldna answer."

"Then 'twould seem he has suffered a fit."

"Would ye shrive him, Father?"

"Aye." Walter hesitated, delaying. "Go on—I will come as soon as I can get the water I have brought from Kelso."

There was the sound of stumbling feet, as those roused by the guard's shouts emerged from the common room. "God's bones, but ye wake the saints!" someone carrying a torch complained.

" 'Tis Tom—Sim says he is dying!"

"Dying? Nay, at supper he was all right, I can tell ye."

"He canna speak now!"

"He was as hale as ye or me," another protested.

"My son," Walter reminded them solemnly, "we know not whence God will send for us—'tis why our souls must be constantly mended in readiness."

Arabella looked around her and made up her mind. "We tarry overlong when haste will serve best. Whilst Father Edmund fetches the holy water, I will see to this man."

"You, lady?"

When they turned to stare suspiciously at her, she nodded. "At Byrum, 'twas I who was skilled at simples."

"Nay, lady, but he is beyond that," the fellow who'd come for Walter protested. " 'Tis a priest he needs."

"Where is he?"

"In the gatehouse—'twas his watch."

Not waiting for further protest, she pulled her cloak closer and started back across the yard. "Wake my lord," she called over her shoulder. "He would know of this." When none moved toward the tower she snapped, "Now!"

" 'Tis an ill omen," someone muttered direly. "First there was the old man as washed up from the river, then 'twas Robert of Carnan, and now 'tis poor Tom. By the Blessed Virgin, but I know not what to make of it."

"Be content 'tis the third one now, for the Devil chooses them in threes," his companion whispered, making the sign of the Cross over his breast.

"Nay, the Devil'd nae take Tom, I tell ye. He was a goodly fellow."

Walter hurried to the small room behind the chapel, where he picked up the vial of water. Stopping briefly, he swept the dried black berries off the table into his hand, then tossed them into the fire. They popped loudly for a moment, and the flames brightened. Then it was as before. And so 'twas with life, Walter observed pithily ere he passed from the room.

"Nay, Father, but ye be too late," Sim murmured sorrowfully when he reached the tiny, crowded room.

Walter knelt beside the dead man, and dipping his fingers into the holy water, he made the sign of the Cross on Muckle Mou' Tom's forehead. "In the name of the Father, the Son, and the Holy Spirit, I commend your soul to God, whence it was given. May He from whom all things good and glorious come grant you the peace of heaven. Amen." As he pronounced the last word, he closed the sightless eyes.

A chorus of "amens" followed.

"Here now—what goes?" His hair rumpled from sleep, his chausses bagging ungartered, William pushed his way into the tiny guardroom. He stopped when he saw the body. "Who found him?"

" 'Twas I, my lord," the one called Sim spoke up. " 'Twas my time to take his place, and when I came he was lying there, and his limbs was twitching. I knelt down to speak with him, but he couldna make a sound." He looked up at Will. "I thought he'd been struck a blow, but there wasna a mark I could see."

" 'Twould seem he was taken by a fit, my lord," Walter observed, rising.

"In the end, he couldna move or speak," Sim offered yet again.

"Did you shrive him?" Will asked Walter.

"I could not confess him, but I commended his soul to God, my lord."

"Aye." Will's gaze moved to Arabella, but if he was surprised or angered to see her there he gave no sign. " 'Tis late, and naught more's to be done ere morning, then. On the morrow Father Edmund will say Mass for this man's soul, and I'd have all attend." As he spoke, he possessed her elbow. "And you, mistress . . . 'tis overlate for you to be in the night air, for 'tis unhealthy."

She'd been about to admit she'd gone to see Jamie, when the priest spoke up. "The place is yet new to her, my lord, and she lost her way in the dark."

It was not until they were alone on the stairs that William spoke again. "And you have the need, Arabella, I'd hae you use the chamber pot. For all that they swore to me this day, I'd not forget 'twas also these men who fired on me."

"Aye."

"And if you'd know how the boy fares, you have but to ask. I'd have told you he slept, for I saw with mine own eyes ere I came up to bed."

"I could not sleep else I knew," she said simply.

"Ewan shows him great kindness."

"Ewan is a man."

He stopped on the stairs and turned to tower over her. His eyes reflected the red of the torch that lit the door above, and his aspect would have been frightening had he not been smiling crookedly down on her.

"Och, and ye think 'tis the women who have the only hearts, do ye, Arabella of Byrum?" he asked softly.

"My son needs a mother's love, my lord."

"Nay. He has the greater need of a man's example. He needs to be dared to try." He turned back and climbed again.

"Why do you hate him, my lord?" she whispered to his back. "Is it that he is lame? Are you like the rest?"

It was not until the heavy door had swung inward, and he had stepped aside to let her pass inside, that he answered. "God makes everything, Arabella—even James. I do but what I think is best for the both of ye."

The two men who palleted within the door were awake. Will nodded to the first. "Och, but a man suffered a fit and died—'twas all. Nay, but I'd have ye take your beds and join the others, for I see no danger now."

He waited until they had left, then turned to lift the mantle from her shoulders. "I'd thought to spare you this night, for you were overtired from the journey," he murmured, nuzzling the crown of her hair. "But if ye've the strength to be wandering about . . ." His voice trailed off as his lips traced the line of her neck upward to her ear, sending shivers coursing down her spine. "Come to bed, Bella, and let me warm ye."

It was not until later, until he slept seated beside her, that she wondered how two so very different men had spoken of God this night. And as she drifted toward sleep herself, she puzzled why it was that the priest had lied for her.

Chapter Eighteen

There was so much to be done in the keep. For the first month, Arabella spent her days seeing to the ordering of a place that had been far too long without a chatelaine. Despite what William had said of it, she considered it nearly a pigsty on the inside. It was, she supposed, that men had different requirements than women. They looked to defense and a few amenities as being all as was needed, whilst 'twas the woman who longed for comfort.

But he'd been right: Aside from the filth, 'twas a pretty place. And filth was one thing that could easily be remedied. Ignoring their grumbling, she ordered every man not otherwise occupied to clean, starting with the hall. The stinking, half-rotted rushes were removed, the wooden floor covered first with sand, to blot up the grease from spilled food, and then scrubbed with a strong solution of limewater to kill the odors. From there she moved upward to the walls, supervising the scouring with stout brushes, the replastering, and finally the laying on of three coats of whitewash to cover the smoke-blackened areas above the torch rings. In a few places the greasy soot still shone

through, but overall the result was clean and pleasant.
Not finished yet, she then drew a design of leaves and
roses and went about the household offering a full set
of new clothes to any who could execute it on the
whitewashed walls.

"I wouldna know," Lang Gib murmured, scratch-
ing his head as he looked at the stylized flowers.
"What are they?"

"Roses." She could see him comparing her crude
sketch with his memory. "Not the man-petaled ones,"
she hastened to explain. "The single ones that grow
wild on the hills."

He stared again, then smiled. "Aye—but ye've got
the petal too even, lady."

" 'Tis a design," she retorted peevishly. "And I
would have a border painted of them. I'd have you find
one who can do this."

"Ye'll hae to ask, but I canna think any here . . ."
His voice trailed off doubtfully.

In the end she'd stood on the scaffold herself and
taken pieces of charred wood to outline her idea, while
the men looked on skeptically. Finally it was Father
Edmund who came to her assistance, saying that he'd
watched the monks paint upon their manuscripts and
that a wall could not be so very different, only larger.
There were those who grumbled that their young priest
deserted his duties to stand and paint beside her, but
Walter told them they'd celebrate with a feast when
'twas done.

And as the chain of leaves took shape the heads
stopped shaking, and soon those who had doubted
stood back to advise critically when a stem strayed too
low upon the wall. In fact when the weather worsened
at the beginning of December, some of the more ven-
turesome offered their aid, volunteering to fill in the
stylized, squarish petals on her roses.

Eventually she directed them, marveling with them
as her vision took colored shape.

On one particular dreary day Ewan brought Jamie
to watch, laying a pallet in a corner where the boy

could sit and admire. When William said nothing against it the man began bringing the boy for several hours every day, and he and Ena tended him by turns. Jamie watched eagerly, telling any who would grudgingly listen when the flowers did not match. And Arabella took the opportunity to sit with him, fussing over him, plying him with sweetmeats, making a game of their time together.

For the first time in years, she was almost content. It was as close as she'd ever come to that idealized dream she'd cherished before she'd wed Elias. She had a household of her own, she had a husband who did not beat her, and for all that she resented her husband's interference with Jamie, her son seemed to prosper. Ewan reported that he was eating better than at first, and she could see that he was. Already his thin body was taking on meat, and Ewan jested that soon 'twould have to be a younger, stouter man as carried him about. But for all the kindness the rough borderer showed Jamie, William still scarce noted him. It was as though he wished her son did not exist. And that alone marred her happiness.

There was no question that William took great pride in her. And he took great pride in what she did, for he too stopped several times each day to check the progress of her wall. And when finally the last flower had been painted over the twining leaves, he stood back, smiling his approval.

"Aye—'tis fine," he assured her. "Ye've given me a garden of roses to admire all winter. I'll warrant there's none in Christendom with another like it. Winter roses," he declared, looking around him. Clasping her shoulders he bent over her, drawing in the scent of her hair. "Aye, now I can see as well as smell them."

"And you do not mind it, I'd make new hangings also," she murmured, leaning back against him for a better view. As she spoke, she rubbed the side of her nose. "They *are* pretty," she decided.

"And I could, I'd pluck one for you."

He moved his hands possessively over her shoulder, feeling the chain he'd given her. For a moment he considered that he ought to give her the green stone to wear on it. These days past had been the best of his life, he reflected, as he breathed again of the rosewater she wore. Sometimes he feared to wake up and discover 'twas but a dream that he was lord to his own land, that he had a wife such as this one. Whole days and nights went by when he never gave a thought to his bastard birth or his unworthiness. None of that mattered as much now: He had Blackleith, and he had her. His fingertip slipped beneath the gold chain, lifting it. Aye, come Christmas, he would give her the stone he'd promised before.

He'd not answered about the hangings. She twisted to look up at him. "If we cannot afford the cloth . . ."

"Nay. I'd have you get what you would, Bella," he answered. " 'Tis but that I think you have the greater need yourself. I'd see you make gowns ere you make aught else for Blackleith."

"I have my brideclothes," she reminded him.

"Two woolen overtunics and plain undergowns, 'tis all. I'd see you had better."

"There is my bridal gown—you forget the cloth Rivaux's daughter sent me."

" 'Tis too fine for here. You'll have to wear it when we go to Dunashie." He reached to rub the smudge of paint from her nose. "Aye—we go there when Elizabeth is delivered, that I may stand godfather to the babe." His smile broadened. " 'Tis her will, ye know," he murmured, lapsing into his familiar tongue. "I dinna expect it."

She would see Count Guy's daughter. She would look as naught beside Elizabeth of Rivaux, and she knew it. "When do we go?" she asked aloud.

"Not until after Christmas. I doubt her babe comes ere Epiphany." Then, as though he knew her thoughts, he added, "Lest you worry over it, there's more men there to envy me for you."

"The bards say she is as fair as Helen."

His arms tightened around her, pulling her back against him again. "Aye, but there's barbs aplenty with her beauty, I can tell you. Unlike you, she is a rose with so many thorns 'tis better to admire her from afar."

"You speak as though you do not like her," she chided.

"Nay, I like her well enough. For all her airs and tempers she suits her husband, and 'tis all that matters."

"Well, what think you, my lord?" Walter asked, coming up behind them. "Art pleased?"

"Aye. 'Tis a fine hall you have painted for me, Father."

" 'Twas your lady's design. I did but find the means to aid her." As Walter spoke, he smiled.

There was that about the priest William did not like, and yet he had no reason. 'Twas, he supposed, that there was a growing familiarity between the young, comely man and Arabella. Chiding himself that jealousy in any form was a sin, he told himself that it was natural for a woman to seek a confessor. Besides, he already had his knowledge of Aidan of Ayrie to plague his peace, and 'twas enough. At least Edmund, for all his looks and graces, had taken his vows of chastity, obedience, and poverty at Kelso along with the rest. But still it bothered him that no matter how often Edmund of Alton smiled, the warmth never seemed to reach his eyes.

"Aye," he said abruptly, aware that both watched him curiously. "Aye, Father. And you think it meet, I'd have you bless this hall ere Christmas."

"I think it fitting, my lord." Walter looked upward at the bright roses. "And 'tis not overdear, I'd see blessed candles burned for then."

"I can afford it. When would you have them?"

"On the eve of our Savior's birth. On Christmas vigil."

"So be it."

As pleased as Arabella was at this recognition of her

efforts, she'd not cost him so much. " 'Tis enough to bless it, my lord.''

"Nay, 'tis not,'' Will told her. "Were it not so close to Elizabeth's time, I'd have Giles come to see what you have done to my hall.''

Walter felt the prickles travel down his neck. "Surely he could come without her,'' he murmured, trying not to betray his hope. " 'Tis not overfar.''

"He does not leave her, else he must. 'Tis her first lying in, and he'd not forget 'tis how he lost his mother, I think. Besides, we go there after Epiphany.'' William squeezed his wife's shoulder again, then released her. " 'Twill serve both purposes: Dunashie's heir is christened, and I am properly invested before his other vassals.''

Arabella looked to where her son sat playing at dice with Ewan. "My lord, I'd take Jamie—I'd have him see it,'' she said impulsively. "I'd have him see the christening.''

Her words hung there, waiting for his answer. He inhaled sharply then shook his head, knowing he could not do it. The boy would surely remind Giles of her shame. "Nay,'' he said finally. "The journey would tire him greatly.'' As soon as he'd spoken he could see her stiffen. "Bella, I'd not have the boy sicken,'' he added defensively. " 'Tis better for him here.''

And suddenly it was as though all she'd done at Blackleith had been for naught. "My lord, I'd not go without him. E'en though 'tis Ewan who tends him now, I'd not leave him.''

Unwilling to argue before the priest, William shrugged as though it were no great matter, saying, "As 'tis a month and more, I'd not dispute it this day. Aye, mayhap you can persuade me later, but I think it a foolish risk. Besides, look at him: He is content enough with Ewan.''

That there was a measure of truth in his words rankled. "He has little choice in that, my lord,'' she reminded him bitterly.

Grasping for more reasons not to take James of

Woolford with them, he remembered also, " 'Tis time Father Edmund began his lessons, and I'd not have them interrupted." When they both turned to stare at him, Will nodded. "Aye, I'd see him learn something of use to him. 'Tis wrong to let him sit with naught to do."

For all his words of comfort to Arabella, Walter could scarce stand the sight of her crippled son. "What would you that I taught him?" he asked carefully. "He appears to know his prayers."

"As 'tis not likely he will inherit anything of Woolford, I'd have you teach him to read and cipher. And he cannot use his body, I'd see his mind employed."

A dozen excuses came to Walter's mind, but he'd spent too much time and effort ingratiating himself with Arabella of Byrum. To deny her brat would not serve him, not when he had hopes of using her trust. "I suppose 'twould do no harm. . . ." he began slowly. "He seems overyoung, but . . ."

"My lord, he is too young," Arabella protested, agreeing with Walter. "Surely—"

"Nay. Giles was but five when we went into King Henry's household, and he learned more quickly than I. The longer the wait, the harder the task." William looked again to his young priest. "As you yourself have surely seen, Father Edmund, there is a need for clerks, and 'tis a goodly occupation," he reasoned.

"Aye."

"I'd at least know if he has a mind for it."

It did no good to argue over Jamie with him, and well she knew it. Every quarrel she'd forced, she'd lost. Telling herself that at least now she saw her son, she bit back bitter words. For all that she wanted to rail at William, for all that she wanted to accuse him of hating the boy, she said nothing.

" 'Twill be as you ask, my lord," Walter promised smoothly. "When would you that we began?"

"The morrow is soon enough." William turned to leave, then stopped, his gaze taking in the painted walls of his hall once more. "Aye—'tis fine, Bella," he murmured. "You give me pride in it."

After he'd left, Walter sighed. "I'd have him come to me when morning prayers are done, I think."

"Nay," she responded slowly. Looking up at him, she managed a weak smile. "After midday would be better, Father, for I would come also."

"You?"

Despite the fact that the blood rushed to her face, she met his eyes steadily. "Aye. I cannot read, Father, and mayhap when I watch, I will learn."

"You would have me teach you to read?"

"Aye. That—and I would see my son."

Bowing slightly, he kept his face grave despite the hope that rose in his breast. "Lady Arabella, you would honor me with the task."

"And I'd not have my lord know of it."

He bowed again, and this time he smiled. "As in all else, 'twill be as you wish."

As she wished? Nay, for all that they prayed together, this priest could not give her William's love for her son. She looked to where her husband left the hall, then turned her gaze once more to the brightly painted walls.

"At least he is pleased with what we have done." Her eyes took in the large blossoms that hovered above William's chair. "Winter roses," she repeated softly.

"And he is displeased with anything about you, he is a fool," Walter murmured behind her.

Surprised by the tone of his voice she turned quickly, and for a moment she saw the warmth in his blue eyes. Then just as quickly they cooled, robbing his face of its handsomeness. Telling herself she must be mistaken, she looked down to the clean rushes beneath her slippers.

"I have prayed he will love me first, then my son," she said low. Her toe lifted the thin reeds, revealing the crushed herbs and flowers she'd had strewn beneath. " 'Tis all I'd ask, Father Edmund." As the sweet fragrance floated upward, she dared to meet his eyes again. "For all that I would have greater kindness for Jamie, I'd still honor my husband."

"Lady, I did not think else," he hastened to assure her. " 'Tis a wife's duty to be obedient to her husband."

"And no matter how sorely it pains me, I will try."

He would not let his thoughts betray him, not now, not yet, but neither could he accept that she could love her giant of a husband. He glanced to where James of Woolford bent over his game. "Mayhap you mistake how he thinks of the boy, you know," he said slyly. "As the child cannot be fostered, mayhap Lord William would send him to the Church. And the boy can read, there will be a place for him there. Mayhap he looks to your son's future."

For an awful moment she stood very still, not wanting to hear him. "Nay, you are mistaken, for he has promised to let me keep Jamie with me." But even as she said it the words rang hollow in her ears. "He cannot send him away—he cannot. Jamie requires too much care."

"It would not surprise me and he did," Walter said gently. "He does not seem to like the boy."

"Your words carry little comfort this day, Father." She started toward Jamie. "Until supper . . ."

"Wait—you do not come to prayers first?"

She shook her head. "Too long have I neglected my sewing for the wall, and Christmas draws near."

"Leave it to your woman," he advised, "and we will pray for James of Woolford once more."

"Ena cannot make my husband's tunic for me. I'd have it be the best I can sew, ere I speak again of Jamie to him. And I can make him love me, mayhap he'll not deny me."

Cursing himself for having misplayed a pawn, Walter watched as she stopped to hug her son ere she left. Jesu, but she was far too lovely and graceful for that great bear she'd wed, and now he, Walter FitzHamon, in a moment of foolishness, had only pushed her back into William of Dunashie's arms. And all because of her brat. Jesu, but if she could be brought to stay with him after the Bastard was gone from this earth, he'd send the boy away also. 'Twas one thing he could not fault her lord for.

He stared after her, the thought crossing his mind that if he waited overlong she was like to conceive, complicating things for him. Nay, but for all that he would have her, he dared not let any born of William's or Giles of Moray's blood live. It was the first time that he'd considered the Devil had made him a cruel bargain.

Chapter Nineteen

She'd been so very occupied with running her household that it did not seem as though she'd been at Blackleith a full month and a fortnight. And yet Christmas was upon them, and now the keep bustled with preparations for the second greatest feast day in Christendom. Still, despite the endless sewing and the hundreds of small tasks to be done, she managed to slip away for a time every afternoon, leaving Ena to prod and bully the women over their needles whilst she struggled with her letters and with a son who did not want to learn them.

But not today. On this, the eve of the celebration of Christ's birth, Arabella bent low over the precious velvet she'd begged and cajoled out of the cloth merchant, getting him to disguise the purchase as part of the "stout cloth" she'd bought for the household's Christmas robes. When William had pored over the accounts, he'd merely grunted that the cost of wool must have gone up. She suffered pangs of conscience at the deception, then told herself 'twas worth it, for would he not forgive her when he saw what she'd made him? Besides, when she'd confessed the sin to Father Ed-

mund, he had merely shrugged and absolved her, saying if 'twas the worst she'd done, the Kingdom of
Heaven surely awaited her.

Her fingers worked nimbly, plying the needle
through the small pearls—a purchase that had been
listed as "wax candles"—fixing them within the embroidered design. Aye, when they went to Dunashie,
her husband would be dressed as fine as Giles of Moray. She bent to bite the gold thread, then knotted it
carefully.

Holding up the tunic she viewed it critically, wishing she'd been able to make it of crimson rather than
blue, but the red came even more dearly. It was, she
decided with satisfaction, as fine a thing as she'd ever
fashioned with her needle. Laying it across her lap,
she traced the delicate golden flowers that circled the
neck, then rubbed at the shining pearls that were sewn
in the center of each, making certain they were secure.
Like her wall below the design was of her own making, filled with the roses he admired so much. Her
hands moved lovingly over the broad width of the garment, seeing it as it would look when it lay over powerful shoulders. And she blushed with the thoughts
that came to mind.

She folded it carefully, smoothing the soft nap with
her palm until it nearly had the sheen of satin. The
firelight from the small brazier played upon the richness of the fabric and warmed the pearls. If William
of Dunashie did not like this, then surely he could not
be pleased.

Reluctantly, she laid it aside and picked up the
scraps of parchment on which Father Edmund had
written her lesson. William had been right about this:
'Twas no easy thing to learn that which ought to have
been taught to a child. For all that Jamie did not want
to do it, he was the better pupil.

Tracing over the bold characters, she spelled B . . .
E . . . L   F . . . I . . . L . . . S. *Pretty son . . . handsome son* . . . Aloud, she spelled each letter, then repeated the words: *"Bel fils."*

And she could not help thinking of Jamie. What hopes she'd had for the babe she'd carried, in what seemed an age ago! She'd been like any other, wanting a tall, fine son. But it had not happened. 'Twas Jamie she'd brought forth, and for all that she regretted his lameness, she could not regret him. No matter what Elias, her father—or William—had thought, her small son could not be considered a curse. But none of them understood.

Sighing, she moved resolutely to the next words, saying them several times each, committing the letters to memory. She'd wanted to learn more than this—she'd wanted to learn something useful ere William discovered what she did. When she showed him, she wanted to surprise him with what she knew—not with a few words. But Father Edmund had said 'twas how it was done. First the letters, then the words, then the thoughts, he'd said. It would be years ere she could read enough French to matter, years ere she could equal the skill of William. As she'd struggled her pride in her husband had grown, for 'twas not only French but also Latin that he knew as well as any clerk.

"What is it that you do so much away from the others?"

She jumped, startled, and would have thrust the parchment beneath her cushion had not he towered over her. "You ought to warn rather than creep," she muttered crossly. "Were I a guard, I'd have swung round with mine dagger."

"Were you a guard, I'd have disarmed you." Before she could hide her lesson he'd reached to pick it up. " 'Comely son'," he murmured. "Or 'sweet son'."

"Comely. Sweet is *douce*," she retorted, snatching it back. "And I was but looking at what it is that Edmund teaches Jamie."

"The rose has thorns this day," he teased, dropping down to the bench beside her. " 'Tis that you spend too much time alone. Ena says you labor long after you send her away."

"Sweet Mary, but there is not time enough for what

must be done, my lord. There are the candles for the chapel, the cloths for the hall, the alms to be divided for the morrow, the robes to be finished for Lang Gib and the others, the food for a feast, and—''

'' 'Tis Christmas,'' he said softly.

'' 'Tis Christmas, and I am unready for it. I—'' She started to rise but he caught her arm gently, pulling her onto his lap. ''Sweet Mary, but I have not the time,'' she finished weakly as his hands touched the laces beneath her arm. ''There are the gifts . . .''

''Ena tells me the robes are nearly done,'' he whispered against the crown of her hair. His fingers tangled in the cords, loosening them and freeing her gown. Nuzzling the top of her head, he savored the smell of dried roses. ''*Douce* . . . sweet . . .'' he murmured, as his hand found the opening to the wide sleeve and slipped within, moving to the drawstring neck of her undergown. ''Nay, Bella, but the only gift I'd have of ye,'' he said softly, ''is that ye lie willing for me.''

His warm palm brushed over her breast lightly, then cupped it, and his fingers massaged her nipple. As it hardened beneath his touch, the rest of her body came instantly alive to his desire. She held herself very still, despite the overwhelming sense of him that surrounded her. The rush of his breath, the heat of his body . . . the strength of the man, the sheer power of him flooded her with an anticipation so intense she felt brittle, ready to shatter. She turned into him, hiding her face in the soft wool of his tunic, lest he see what he did to her. But she could not hide the heat that rose beneath his hand. Nor could she still the wild beating of her heart that accompanied the sharp intake of her breath.

''And ye dinna mind it, I'd nae wait for the night,'' he whispered hotly against her ear.

Still she would not go mindlessly, tamely to him yet again. She'd savor what he did to her. Her hands crept between their bodies, catching his through the gown.

''The door—''

'' 'Tis barred.''

"Ena—"

"She will not come up."

He shifted her slightly on his lap, turning her for better access, all the while tracing the line of her neck with his lips. Shaking free of her protesting hands, he explored her body beneath her loosened gown, tracing the smooth, bare flesh over her ribs, down to her belly, and below. And everywhere he touched, he could feel the heat rising under his palm.

It was going to be good between them, and both knew it. For all the times he'd lain with her before, there was yet an urgency that was as great as that first time she'd come to him. Only now he knew how to please her.

His hand moved over her, playing her with the new-found skill of a troubadour lately proficient on his lute, touching, tantalizing, eliciting the low moan of her response, until she forgot her resolve to hold back. She leaned back in his arms and closed her eyes, savoring the ecstasy of his touch. His free hand eased her gown and undershift upward, baring her legs to the chill air, revealing flesh pebbled by heat rather than cold.

The firelight played on the planes of her face, illuminating the purple of closed eyelids, the thick fringe of lashes. Jesu, but she was as beautiful as any he'd ever seen. And she was his, his alone to have.

Her low moan rose to a sob when his fingers slid between the fold to discover the familiar wetness within, and she turned in his arms to cling to him. She was as ready as he was.

He ought to have taken her to bed, and he knew it, and yet he would not break the bond of heat that was between them. Kissing her, possessing her mouth fully, he worked her clothes up further, tugging them until there was naught but her bare skin against his chausses. His hand delved beneath her to untie them, freeing himself and pushing her gown and shifts out of the way. And then he sought her again.

She'd wait no longer. She was too hot to breathe,

and still the fire raged within her. She twisted against him, feeling his aroused body under hers.

"The bed," she gasped, tearing her mouth from his.

For answer he lifted her, turned her. "I'd hae ye ride me here," he told her thickly. "Now." He withdrew his hand and guided her over him, filling her body.

"Sweet Mary!" she breathed in shock. For an awkward moment they teetered on the bench, then she managed to bring up her legs, resting her knees at either side of him. Afraid of falling, she grasped his head, holding it against her breast.

"Ye can move," he urged her, leaning forward to bury his face against her breasts. "I'd hae ye show me."

It was as though 'twas she who took him. She moved tentatively at first, savoring the sense of power. He pushed her gown over her shoulder while his mouth sought a nipple, drawing on it. His tongue curved around the hardened button as every fiber of her being tautened anew. Twisting her hips against his, she moved greedily, rocking and sliding, feeling like a primal goddess granting her favor, while he worshiped her with his mouth, his hands, and his body. Her thoughts urged her on, chanting rhythmically in her ears, "He is yours to take—yours to take!"

For Will it had been a matter of expediency, of the urgency of the moment, but as she rode, her body twisting and grinding against his with such abandon, he stroked her damp skin restlessly, losing himself in what she did to him. The bench rocked, knocking upon the wooden floor of the solar, and still she did not stop. He bucked and thrust beneath her, trying to capture the elusive woman who rode him, until he thought he'd burst. He grasped her hips, holding her, crying out loudly as he released his seed. She gave one last long moan as her body quivered almost convulsively, then she too was quiet.

She leaned forward, spent, and waited for the peace

to descend. His arms still encircled her waist, holding her hips in that most ancient of embraces, as her head rested on his shoulder. For a time she gasped for air, and waited for the blood that pounded in her temples to slow. There was no sound beyond the labor of their breathing. Finally, there was the calm. And still she was loath to leave him.

Running feet were heard on the stairs outside, then someone shouted, "Is all all right, my lord?"

William's hand smoothed the thick braid over her disordered gown, whispering, "Aye." Then, still holding her, he raised his head to answer loudly, "Aye! All's well!"

Blood flooded her face, heating it, and she did not dare look at him for the sudden embarrassment she felt. She closed her eyes, this time to hide from him.

"Art beautiful, Arabella of Byrum," he muttered against her hair. "I have never seen your like." He shifted her slightly, pulled down her gown and undergown to cover her backside.

"You must think me little better than a whore," she whispered, betraying her mortification. " 'Twas the most wanton thing I have ever done."

"There is no shame in loving where you are wed, Bella," he countered gently, lifting her chin. "Aye—it pleases me to have you want me also." There was such warmth in his hazel eyes that they seemed nearly gold. He grinned crookedly, then nodded. "I'd hae ye know, Arabella of Byrum," he added, lapsing into the familiar Scots tongue, "I'd hae ye and none other, I swear to ye."

"And I you, my lord," she answered softly.

"I'd hae no more anger between us."

"Aye."

He lifted her slightly, and she separated from him. Edging from the bench, she stood, and her gown fell about her ankles once more. She felt the trickle down her leg and turned to search for a cloth.

" 'Tis a messy business when 'tis done," he observed as he retied his chausses. "Would you that I aided you?"

"Nay." She could see that he'd spied the blue velvet tunic, and she was afraid he would pick it up before she could give it to him. She moved between him and the folded garment. "I'd thought to wait to give you this until the chairing," she said, smiling almost shyly as she lifted it. "But as you have seen it already, I'd give it now."

"Nay, but I did not expect anything, Bella."

She swung around, holding it up before him proudly. "I'd not have you go again to Dunashie in less, my lord," she said softly. When he said nothing, she moved closer to fit it at his shoulders. Smoothing the soft fabric over his broad chest, she dared to look up at him. " 'Tis the finest I have ever made, William."

He looked down, seeing the richness of the gold thread, the luster of the pearls against the shimmering blue of the velvet, and he was overwhelmed that she'd fashioned it for him. The time it must have taken, the care she'd lavished on the intricate embroidery, the money she'd spent—'twas beyond any expectation. His eyes burned with unshed tears. " 'Tis the finest I have ever had—I swear it." His voice broke for a moment, then he managed to clear his throat. "Aye—I'd wear it to Mass tonight." While she still held it against him, he lifted his hand to touch the softness. "Ye gie me more than my station warrants, Bella."

"Nay. You are the lord of Blackleith, William of Dunashie. I'd have you wear it for the blessing of the hall, and you do not mind it."

He touched the embroidered flowers lightly, feeling the pearls against the metallic thread. "Aye. Ye surround me with roses, don't ye?"

"You said you liked them," she reminded him.

"More than any other—better than the gillyflowers or the heather in the spring. Aye, better than the bluebells on the hills." His smile again warmed his eyes, lightening them. "And ye—would ye wear your wedding gown then also?"

She knew then that she'd truly pleased him. "And you wished it," she answered lightly.

"Well, I'd nae be a fancy fellow alone," he countered, his smile broadening even more. "Aye—I'd like it."

She nodded. "I'd rather wear it here than at Dunashie."

He took the tunic from her hands. "Whilst ye tend to the other, I'd try it for the fit."

She moved away to clean herself. Pouring a small amount of water into the basin, she dipped a cloth into it. Out of the corner of her eyes, she could see him remove his plain woolen shert and lay it aside. Then, with as much care as if he handled Christ's altar cloth, he eased the blue velvet over his head. Still watching him, she lifted her skirt and thrust the wet cloth between her legs to wash. He was tugging the tunic down to his knees. He straightened, then wiped his hands on his discarded shert before he smoothed them over the soft fabric. Aye, he was more pleased than she'd ever seen him.

She dropped the cloth into the basin and let her skirt fall. It was now, if at all, she told herself, sucking in her breath for courage. Surely after what had passed between them, after the gift she'd given him, he could not deny her.

"My lord . . ."

He looked across at her. " 'Tis a good fit."

"My lord, 'tis Christmas and I . . . I'd have your kindness for my son."

The warmth in his eyes faded to wariness. "I have not forgotten him," he muttered defensively, recalling an earlier confrontation with Ewan. He'd disputed it then, but now mayhap his man was right. "Aye—I have spoken to Ewan, and 'tis decided he will teach the boy to ride. I'd give James a small horse."

For a moment, her purpose was forgotten. "A horse? A horse?" Her voice rose incredulously. "But he cannot ride!"

"Ewan says if a new cantle and pommel are seated on a saddle, he can."

"Ewan!" She fairly spat the word. "Jesu! And what does Ewan know of it? He'll fall!"

"And the boy cannot learn, there is the cart. The horse is but a small beast, after all, and can pull a cart."

She stared, realizing he meant it. "You cannot give a child who cannot even walk a horse," she said evenly.

"He canna sit forever!" he retorted, stung by her rejection of his generosity. "And he canna be carried forever!"

"He is but six!"

"And next year he will be seven! And the year after, eight! Aye, and ten years from now, sixteen! God's bones, Bella, but what would you he did?"

She took a deep breath, then let it out slowly. It would do no good to dispute with him, and well she knew it. "My lord," she began again, measuring her words carefully. "I am James of Woolford's mother. Yet you would deny me the right to care for him, to succor him." She held out her hands, palms up in supplication. "I accept that he sleeps with this Ewan, but I'd have him about me by day. I'd have him about me whilst I work with the women." She licked her lips nervously when he did not answer, then she blurted out, "Aye, and I'd not leave him when we go to Dunashie, my lord."

"Bella . . ."

"If 'tis that you mislike him for what he cannot help, 'tis wrong of you, my lord. Are you as hard of heart as the rest? Can you not see him for what he is? One small boy whose need for love is greater than any other's?"

"Whether he goes to Dunashie or no has naught to do with misliking. There is no reason for him to go."

"Is it not reason enough that I ask it?" she demanded, her voice again rising. "Why will you not even look on him? What is there about him that you

would not see? Is it his leg? 'Tis a shame on you if so,
for he is blameless!''

" 'Tis not his leg! Have done, Bella—I'd not speak
of this!''

"Then what? You said you would accept him, but
you have not!''

"I am giving him a horse!''

"A horse! Why? So he can fall and die? So he can
ride when you send him away?''

"You speak nonsense, woman!''

"You cannot deny you despise my son!''

"I deny it!''

"Then give him back to me! My lord, you promised
I could bring him here! You promised to welcome
him!''

"He is below. He eats of my bread and wears the
clothes my money has bought him. You have no right
to charge me thus, Bella!'' He turned away and tried
to speak more calmly. "I'd not quarrel with you over
the boy—not at Christmas.''

"Then let him come with us to Dunashie, my lord.
Give him proof that you accept him! Do not be as the
others, William, I pray you.''

"Jesu, woman, but you know not what you ask—I
have said he does not go! D'ye hear me this last time?
He does not go, Bella!''

For all that she would try, he was as unyielding as
the thick stone wall behind him. Her anger rose, making her reckless. Walking up to him, she caught at his
velvet sleeve, pulling it. "Why? What is it about my
son that you hate so much that you cannot bear to have
him in my company? William, I have done all that I
know to please you: I have lain whenever, however
you would have me, I have cleaned your hall, I have
sewed for you—and still you would deny me! I would
that I had not made this for you, for you do not deserve
it!''

He wanted to shout back that he was more than she
deserved, that he knew about Aidan of Ayrie—but he
could not bring himself to say the words. For all that

he was angered with her now, he'd still not have that
between them. As much as his knowledge of Aidan
ate at his soul, he did not want to hear the other man's
name on her lips. He shook free, and started to leave.

"I will come back when you are calm, Bella," he
muttered.

"Am I nothing to you? Is there naught between us
but the bedding?" she cried, moving in front of him.

"There would be more and you'd let it, but there is
room for none but your Jamie in your heart, and well
you know it! Never is it William, is it? 'Tis always
Jamie—everything you have done for me has been for
him! Nay, do not deny it—I'd nae have ye lie to me,
Bella!"

She stared after him through scalding tears. "All I
ask is your kindness for my son," she managed,
speaking in little more than a whisper.

"Kindness has naught to do with this!"

"Giles of Moray has seen Jamie, my lord. He knows
what he is, and he did not turn from him." When he
said nothing she charged bitterly, "You are like my
father, William. You would hide my son that he can
be forgotten, wouldn't you? Sweet Mary, but do you
think that Elizabeth of Rivaux will think less of me
for him? If 'tis so, I'd not know her—I'd not go to
Dunashie with you."

She was so close to the truth that it shamed him,
but he shook his head. " 'Tis that I'd nae take him to
Dunashie, 'tis all," he answered defensively. "The
ride would be too difficult for him, Bella. Anything
beyond that is your fancy and nothing more."

"You cannot love me and hate my son!"

He raised his arm as though he'd strike her, then
dropped it. "I'd not listen to this! Get out of my way,
woman!"

She'd lost, and she knew it. She stepped back to let
him go. For all that she'd done to please him, he still
thought she asked too much. As he threw the bar so
savagely that it cracked against the stone wall, she
crossed the chamber to put away her sewing box, then

sank upon the bench. For all that she'd tried, she'd failed. For all that she would love him, he did not want anything of her but her body, and he was willing to give her nothing in return. Her fingers crept to the empty chain that hung around her neck, feeling of it. Despite all the sweet words he'd spoken in passion, he'd not even given her the stone he'd promised ere they were wed.

Tears of self-pity, mingled with those of anger and despair, now coursed unchecked down her cheeks. Once it would have been enough that he did not beat her, but now she'd have him love her and her small son. But for all that she had tried, she could not make him do that. Her body, her labor, her care for him, all were as naught when she would ask but one favor of him.

"Gentle lady . . ."

She looked up, seeing the priest through her tears, and thought she could not bear his company. She swallowed hard, then spoke in little more than a whisper. "I would that you went away, Father, for I am sorely tried."

He'd come up to inquire whether they would have the hall blessed now or later, but when he'd encountered William on the stairs the big man had growled "Ask her" ere he'd brushed past him. Obviously, all was not well between the Bastard and Arabella of Byrum. Instead of leaving, Walter moved closer.

"I'd aid you, lady, and you'd let me," he said gently, reaching to touch her hair. It was like silk beneath his fingers. "I'd share your burden, lightening it, and you'd let me."

"There's naught any can do, Father. For all that I have prayed for it, William has no love for me or for my son!"

"Nay, daughter—so long as I am with you, God is with you also." His fingertips traced the curves of her braids lightly, then rested on her crown. "Come—tell me how it is that you are troubled," he coaxed. "And then we will pray for God's deliverance."

"Is it wrong to want to be loved, Father? Is it wrong to hope for that which I have never had?" Before he could answer, she burst into tears anew. "Sweet Jesu, but I am the most miserable of women, Father!"

As she leaned forward Walter pressed her head into his heavy winter cassock, holding her and stroking her braids against her back. It was as close as he'd ever been to a woman, and he savored the feel, the warmth, the scent of her until he ached. As she cried against him, he dared to think of what it would be like to take her.

"Nay, Arabella," he whispered softly, "William of Dunashie is not worth the grief he gives you. When he is gone, there will be another to love you." As he spoke, his hands dropped to caress her shoulders. "Arabella . . ."

She became aware that his manner had changed, that his touch was more lover-like, and she straightened, sitting back upon the bench, disappointing him. Wiping her wet face with her hand, she managed shakily, "I thank you for your kindness, Father, for there are days when I should perish without it." Looking upward, she caught the warmth in his eyes ere it faded. Telling herself it was but her fancy, she managed a weak smile. " 'Twas foolish of me to think a new tunic would change his mind, after all."

He forced himself to step back. "So you have quarreled with him over the boy," he decided.

"Aye."

"Does he send him away?"

"Nay, but still he does not take him to Dunashie with us. He is as ashamed of Jamie as Papa was." Unwilling to tell him more of her dispute with William, she inhaled deeply, then sighed. " 'Tis poor Christmas cheer I give you, Father Edmund. Tell me: Is all in readiness below?"

The moment of intimacy between them had passed, Walter realized with more than a trace of regret. Telling himself he'd at least made a beginning, he assured her, " 'Tis ready whenever you choose to come down, gentle lady. Your winter roses bloom above a hundred waxen candles. Do you come down to see them with me?''

"Nay." She looked down to where her hands twisted the wool of her gown. "Not yet, Father. I'd change my gown first."

Heedless of those who would seek speech with him, William crossed the courtyard, hunching his shoulders against the bitter, howling wind. Tiny ice crystals hit his face like sand, but he was too angered to notice. The villeins who'd crowded into Blackleith huddled about small fires as they waited for festivities to begin. Most looked up, saw his scowl, and turned back to the fire. Only a fool would try to gain the notice of the Bastard in high temper, they murmured in agreement amongst themselves.

He'd not wanted this quarrel—he'd even been prepared to give her the green stone. But not now. Not when he now realized that no matter what she did, it was not really for him at all. All of it—the hall, the tunic, mayhap the very passion she gave him—was but a means to her: a means to make him accept her brat. She had no right to expect him to like Aidan's son, to welcome this living proof of her sin, this constant reminder that she'd lain for another outside her marriage bed.

Jesu, but did she take him for a fool? Did she think him so dull-witted that he did not know what she did? Did she think she could lead him by his nether parts? Well, she could not. Whether she gave him peace or no, he'd rule in his own house.

But as his stride lengthened, her words echoed in his ears: *I'd have your kindness for my son. Why will you not even look on him? Why will you not even look on him? Why will you not even look on him? You are like my father. . . . You are like my father. . . .*

He was not like Nigel of Byrum, and he resented that she would accuse him of it. If he did not look on the boy willingly, 'twas not for the reasons she believed. He could not see James without wondering about Aidan of Ayrie, about the passion that had conceived the lame child. He could not see James and still love Arabella, for then he would have to remember she'd lain with Aidan of Ayrie. When he spared no thought to the boy he could hold Arabella in his arms and believe she was what he would have her, a chaste wife who would lie with no other.

She'd been unjust in her accusations, for he'd not been unkind. For all that she was bitter over it he'd done well, aye, better than most would have, for Arabella's pitiful son. He'd given him the company of a man who did not turn away in disgust, who did not complain overmuch about him. And if the truth be told Ewan was good for young James, for he did not coddle him. 'Twas Ewan who'd said he believed the boy could learn to ride, and 'twas Ewan who would teach him. Left to Arabella, James of Woolford or Whatever would be naught but a helpless, useless creature.

Nay, she wronged him. He was not unkind to the boy. Unkindness required discourse, after all, and between him and James there was nearly none. Not once had he raised his hand to the child, not once had he shouted at him. Instead he'd spent money for new robes and shoes for him, he recalled with growing resentment. Nor had he complained when she'd ordered expensive dates to tempt the frail boy's appetite, though he supposed she did not know he knew. There was much she bought for her precious Jamie that he could have refused her, that he could have quarreled over, but he had not. And he'd paid Father Edmund an extra two shillings to teach the boy. Had he been truly unkind he'd have sent the child away, he'd have hidden James in some distant monastery where he did not have to look on him.

But he could not deny that the boy was sickly and frail, a child greatly to be pitied, and when he was out of sight William did not truly mind the expense of him. Separate from Arabella he would have touched William's heart, but there was no separating the boy from her. Not knowing that her husband knew, she would flaunt the living proof of her sin before him.

His thoughts seething on the injustice she'd done him, he scarce realized he'd reached Blackleith's chapel until he was at the door. He let himself in the door and stood in the dim, musty greyness, blinking his eyes to adjust to the lack of light. The small nave was empty, deserted as of yet for the greater warmth of Blackleith's hall. In front, at either side of the altar rail, candles flickered, carrying prayers heavenward on tiny curls of smoke. Above, the sleet rattled the tin roof against the rough-hewn beams supporting it, and the wind banged the shutters over the high-placed windows. Some day, and God willed it, he'd have glass for his chapel, glass like the thick green panes at Dunashie. But for now it was enough that he was alone within the narrow nave.

Despite the crudeness of the room, despite the rows of crude benches that faced the rail, despite the musty dampness, there was a sense of sanctity here. There was an odor of holiness to the place. Mayhap it was the silence, mayhap it was the smell of freshly hung boughs of fir, but there was an odor of holiness here.

His footsteps echoed through the silence as he walked toward the altar rail. The scent of wax and incense mingled with the steam of his breath. He knelt, looking upward to the crudely carved statue of the Blessed Virgin holding an infant Christ. Seeking refuge from his anger he began whispering his prayers, beginning with the Pater Noster and then continuing with his customary appeals to Sts. Andrew and Columba, and finally to the Virgin herself.

"Blessed Mother, I'd have your aid. I'd have peace in mine house . . . aye, and I'd have peace within myself," he began, groping for the words to explain that which he was not certain he understood himself. "When I took Arabella of Byrum I knew she came not pure to me, but still I would have her for her beauty. For all that, my pride cannot accept what she has done, and every time I look upon her son I am reminded of

it. Every time I see him, I think that I must appear the
great fool to all. Still, I'd ask that ye grant me the will
to accept what she has done, that I may forgive her,
else I will have no peace in mine heart either.''

He stared at the painted face intently, adding, ''I'd
not be unkind to the boy, but I know not how to conquer what I feel within me. Mother Mary, I'd have
your aid,'' he repeated. ''I'd know what God would
have of me.''

He paused, hearing only the sound of the wind
against the roof and shutters. Before him, the flame of
one of the candles was caught in a gusting draft. It
bent over, flickering valiantly, then went out. 'Twas
an ill omen for someone's prayer. With hands nearly
too cold for the task he found the striker and the flint,
and using his body to shield it against the wind, relit
the candle. Once more it joined the others in illuminating Mary's carved feet. He sank back on his
haunches to look upward again.

As his eyes traveled to the babe bundled in the Virgin's arms, his thoughts went back to that Christmas
in Bethlehem a millennium and more ago. What had
Joseph thought when Mary came to him carrying a
child not his own? Did he wonder, when she claimed
it was God's son she bore? For a time, had he doubted
her? Was it that he believed her, or was it that he
forgave her? Nay, 'twas blasphemy to ask such a thing.
But had Joseph turned away from her, William did not
doubt that she'd have been branded unchaste. 'Twas
Joseph who'd learned to love the child she brought him.

He looked to the other side of the altar, seeing the
rude figure of Mary's husband. Despite the deep lines
and the flattened planes made by adze and chisel, there
was a kindliness in the wooden face. It seemed to say
to William, ''I did but what was right and good in
God's eyes.''

But Ayrie's son was not the same. If anything, God
showed his displeasure in Arabella's poor crippled son.
If anything, the boy should not have lived. His mouth
formed silent words, saying only to himself, ''But I

am no Joseph, Lord. I am not a saint, but only flesh-and-blood man.'' Yet even as he thought them his conscience answered, '' 'Tis wrong to deny a child for its birth, William of Dunashie. James of Woolford suffers enough for his mother's sin.''

Did the Holy Family give him this sign he'd sought? When he looked again to the painted, carved image of Mary, her face was serene, her eyes focused on some distant thought. Nay, he supposed not: In his heart he already knew what was right.

No longer angry, he heaved himself up, aware now that he was cold to the bone. Rubbing his arms through the velvet, he started back. The cold wind hit his face again, biting into it. Despite it, he felt better.

''My lord!''

He stopped, waiting for Wat to catch up to him. Already the young man's face was flushed, either from the extra measure of ale allotted him or from the raw wind. ''Och, but ye be celebrating early, eh?'' Will teased him.

Wat reddened further, then nodded. ''Aye. Lang Gib sent me to find ye, for we'd know when ye'd hae Father Edmund bless the hall.'' He sniffled, then wiped his nose on his sleeve. ''When ye couldna be discovered I asked of Lady Arabella, but she dinna answer. The woman Ena said she was there, but she dinna answer.''

She was still angered, then. Will drew in a deep breath, then let it out slowly. ''Tell him, when 'tis dark. I'd see the candles in darkness, I think.''

''Aye.''

William climbed the stairs slowly, wondering how best to make his peace with her. He'd do anything but take James to Dunashie, he decided. The door creaked inward on its heavy iron hinges. There was no sign of Ena or the others. He stepped inside and sucked in his breath, hesitating. On the other side of the center brazier Arabella sat, her face pale above the brilliance of the gown she wore. Mayhap 'twas the reflection from the fire that made her eyes seem reddened, and mayhap 'twas not. Mayhap she'd cried ever since he'd left her.

"Bella . . ."

She jumped, startled, as he crossed the room to her. Moving around to face her, he stared down, his expression solemn. She swallowed and waited.

" 'Tis still Christmas," he said softly, "and I'd have no quarrel between us." His hand touched the part on her crown, smoothing the hairs that strayed from her braids. With an effort he added, "Bella, would it please you to have the boy attend Mass with us this night? I'd let him sit with you rather than with Ewan."

"Aye." It was not all she wanted, but she could gain no more by quarreling with him, and she knew it. " 'Twill please him, my lord."

"And you? Will it please you?"

"Aye."

He knew she was not satisfied, but he could offer no more. Telling himself he did not take the boy to Dunashie as much for her honor as for his, he straightened his shoulders and tried to speak more lightly.

" 'Tis settled then. Come on—else we are late for the blessing of your hall." As she rose slowly, he offered his arm. "Art beautiful this night, Arabella of Byrum," he told her.

Chapter Twenty

For all that Blackleith was a small keep of but forty men and eleven women within and three-score peasant families without, all the hillsides around it seemed to be ablaze with small fires set to commemorate the star that had shone over Bethlehem more than a thousand years before. And despite the cold, the open yard was crowded with those who came to keep the Christmas vigil with their lord. Some held battered cups in rag-wrapped hands, waiting for Blackleith's alewife to mete out heated mead to warm them.

"God aid yer lor'ship! God aid yer good lady!" they cried out as William and Arabella entered the courtyard. "Peace and health to ye both!"

"And to you also!" Will called back. "What say you: Do you join us in our hall this Christmas Eve?"

There were cheers as the crowd surged to follow them. Arabella breathed deeply of the cold air, smelling the smoke from the fires, as she walked beside her husband, holding his arm. Beneath her soft shoes the ground glistened with crackling ice, which reflected the light of the torches above. 'Twas a fitting night to be reminded of the miracle of Christ's birth.

Inside, the hall was lit with a hundred fine wax candles instead of the usual pitch-dipped torches, and
above Arabella's painted roses the walls were hung
with garlands of holm, ivy, and bay. Below, the rushes
had been sprinkled with a mixture of herbs and dried
roses, and the mingled scents wafted upward to blend
with the smoke from the main hearth.

Though none would eat during the vigil, the tables
were covered with bleached linen cloths, and on each
one a polished cresset lamp burned. Already, in preparation for the morrow, precious silver platters bore
an impressive array of sweetened oatcakes drizzled
with honey, sugared dates, and marzipan candies
shaped into stars. Peasant women used to naught but
dried peas, salt meat, and thin porridge the rest of the
year eyed them eagerly. On the morrow, God willing,
the lady would see that each got one of the rare sweets
with the customary loaf of white bread, a hen, and
one gallon of the lord's ale.

But this night they'd wait as the angels had waited
for Mary to bring forth her child. The heavy double
doors swung outward once more, letting in a gust of
cold air that bent the floating wicks on the lamps, admitting six sturdy men carrying a section of a huge
tree. Amid huzzahs from the rest, they struggled to
settle it onto the fire. It went into the fire pit with
scarce an English inch to spare.

Unlike much of the wood they burned it was fresh-
cut, so that it would be consumed slowly, for it had to
last the full twelve nights if the manor were to prosper.
Those within the hall joined hands, forming circles
within circles, as they danced an ancient carol. The
last priest had frowned on such things, saying 'twas a
pagan practice, but Father Edmund had not forbidden
them this year. And as they danced they crushed the
dried herbs and petals further, releasing the sweet
smell into the air. It was not until a man shouted,
"The log catches!" that they ceased.

As all eyes turned expectantly to him, Walter raised
his hands in blessing, wishing them to be of peace and

good cheer this night above all others. Silence descended when he cleared his throat and began to speak
of Blackleith's hall, telling of how the Lady Arabella
had, out of love for her new people, caused to be made
a garden that would bloom even in winter upon the
walls. As he looked up at the painted border, serving
boys hastened to douse the lamps so that only the candles illuminated the line of red roses. A low murmur
of approval spread around the room.

Raising his hands again, Walter intoned, "Almighty
God, Father in Heaven, Divine Maker of all things
seen and unseen, bless this hall and all the people
herein, that one may serve the other throughout the
years to come, and grant us Thy mercy and Thy grace,
now and forever. These things we ask in the name of
He who was born this night those many years ago in
the city of David. Amen."

The congregation echoed him. "Amen."

Lang Gib leaned over to whisper to William, "Ye
canna say we havena a proper priest, for all that he is
young, can ye?"

"He speaks well enough," Will agreed. Changing
the subject abruptly, he observed, " 'Tis so crowded
I canna see Ewan."

"He is over there," Arabella hastened to tell him.
"By the doors."

The grizzled borderer leaned against the door frame,
the little boy perched on his shoulder. The light from
one of the expensive candles showed the excitement
on James of Woolford's small, pinched face. And for
a moment William chose to forget his resentment,
thinking again of St. Joseph instead. He started for the
boy.

Arabella hurried after him, then stopped. For all
that she was eager to see her son, she sensed 'twould
be better if William went to him. And so she watched
as the big man reached for the little boy, lifting him
and settling him astraddle his broad neck. Sweet Mary,
but they were an odd pair for the eyes, the red-haired
giant and the pale, thin child. There was so much noise

that she knew not what one said to the other, but she could tell that Jamie smiled.

Balancing the boy on his shoulders, William threaded his way through the throng of well-wishers back to her. Over the din Jamie called out, "Come on, Mama: We are for the Church to see the animals! Aye, and ye dinna mind it, I am to listen to the viols after!"

Her throat felt oddly tight, but she managed to nod and smile through a mist of tears. Never once in six years at Byrum had her father carried her son. Never once in those years had he offered Jamie anything but anger or coldness. And she chided herself for thinking of the stone that William had not brought her, for this Christmas his kindness, however small, was the greater gift.

"Aye," she said finally. "Aye."

Blackleith's bellringer banged the iron bell enthusiastically, summoning all to Vigil Mass. With one hand on Jamie's good leg to steady him, William reached the other out to her.

"Make haste, ere the place is filled."

They crowded into the small chapel that served as parish church also, sitting close that Lang Gib and the other household officers might share the bench, for even those amongst the villeins that shirked on other days came now. There was even less room for them, for several benches had been removed to make space for the traditional reminder of the circumstances of Christ's birth. The spot where they had been was now strewn with straw, and sturdy boys herded a sheep, a cow, a donkey, and an ox to stand over an empty manger.

The bell clanged more loudly, calling the last who would press within. Then a young villein's wife, clad in a new robe of blue wool, moved forward to lay her own babe in the manger ere she knelt over it. A hushed silence, broken only by the shuffling of those chosen to represent Joseph, the shepherds, and two angels, ensued. Then two small boys preceded Father

Edmund to the front, each carrying a pure white candle with which to light those at the altar.

William eased Jamie from his shoulders and settled him between Arabella and himself, only to discover that there was no place left at the end for Wat. He shifted the boy back onto his lap and moved closer to his wife.

The Mass was brief, for Father Edmund, eloquent as he could often be, chose not to speak at length, a circumstance perhaps caused by the ox's having relieved itself nearly at the altar rail. The homily was shortened and the prayers hurried, until Will could scarce follow them. Instead he looked down on the boy's head, then up to the statue of St. Joseph, and he realized then that he would have to accept Arabella's son ere he could forget what she had done. And it would be no easy task, for much of his life he'd had naught but his pride and his honor to succor him.

The bells were rung, the steaming incense waved, and the host administered with unseemly haste. But as the smells of a hundred mouths and bodies mingled with those of incense and animal excrement, there was none to complain when Blackleith's priest merely held his hands above them and said, ''May Almighty God bless all herein. The Mass is ended: Go forth in peace.''

When Arabella rose after the shortened benediction, she looked to her husband, seeing that Jamie slept against his shoulder, his pale hair like flax against the rich blue velvet of William's new tunic, and she added her own silent prayer of thanks for this small beginning. Ena approached to take him, but William shook his head.

''Nay. I have promised he shall hear the viols, and for all that ye may hear of me, there'll be none to say Will 'o Dunashie dinna keep his word.''

Arabella touched the chain that hung over her rich gown, and for all that she told herself again that it did not matter, she wondered if he had forgotten her promised stone. But with this gesture of kindness he gave her son, she dared not ask. She ought to be content with that and cease yearning for more.

Outside, despite the fact that the wind spat fine sleet at them, the revelers danced and slid around small fires to the crude beat of drums made of overturned tubs and castanets, while two men piped on wooden flutes. And already the alewife came out to fill their cups. As the cold air touched the boy's face he roused, murmuring against Will's neck, "I dinna miss the viols, did I?"

"Nay. D'ye come up with us, Gib?" Will called out.

"Nay—I'd see they do not start a fire!" Lang Gib shouted back.

"And ye, Ewan?"

The older man looked to the boy on William's shoulder, then to Ena, before nodding. "Aye—ye honor me. What say ye, woman—d'ye share a cup wi' me?"

"And ye dinna drink more than your share."

Even the bower had been decorated for the season with bits of holm hung in clusters, and bowls of dried rose petals floating on a mixture of perfumed oils, symbols of the gifts the wise men carried to the holy infant. As they entered the room a young maid lit these bowls, sending the scent into the air. Over the brazier hung a pot filled with heated wine, spices, and even a rare Spanish orange that had been cut, peel and all, into it.

It seemed that all of Dunashie celebrated, with the villeins dancing in the yard, the household servants singing ancient carols in the hall, and all with any claim to gentle birth whatsoever gathered in Arabella's small bower. For this one night she'd spent a precious shilling to hire a traveling trouvère, who would spin tales for them as the viol players played softly behind him.

There were not enough benches, so most made places for themselves on the floor near the fire, and even Arabella dropped down to sit among the sweetened rushes and listen. Above her Will sat on a stool,

his big arm encircling the small boy as his foot tapped
out the beat of the music. From time to time Jamie
stole a glance upward, as though he half expected his
stepfather to change his mind. Arabella watched him
covertly, thinking how little kindness he'd had in his
short life, how little reason he'd had to trust any but
her and Ena. And Ewan. She glanced over to where
the older man sat, his greying head bent close to
Ena's, listening to the woman. For this night at least, it
was as though there were a bond between all of them.

The spiced wine warmed her empty stomach, making her feel dreamily secure as she heard the trouvère
weave a fantastic story of trolls and giants, fanciful
beasts from another land, and the brave knights who
dared to ride through walls of fire to challenge them.
She looked up again to see her son leaning forward,
his face betraying his eagerness to hear more, and she
felt a surge of gratitude toward William. Whether he
could love Jamie or not, this night he'd given the child
something worth remembering.

The wine made her sleepy and she leaned back,
resting her head against her husband's knee. William's
hand crept to stroke her crown, watching how the light
from the perfumed bowls made her hair look as though
it were as gold as the chain she wore about her neck.
Nay, even the Saxon Edith of the songs could not have
been lovelier than Arabella of Byrum this night. She
was worth even what it cost him in pride to hold her
son. For a moment his eyes moved over the others,
and he wondered how many thought him a fool for
her. Then he told himself that in his own house it did
not matter. As long as they followed him as lord in
Blackleith, they'd say nothing.

On his lap Jamie twisted, then blurted out, "I'd go
to the garderobe."

Ena rose hastily and took him, but Ewan stopped
her. "Nay—'tis more meet that I go with him." Looking over her shoulder to William, he added, "And it
dinna displease ye, I'd take him to bed."

He'd done his duty—he'd kept his word to Arabella

and to the boy, and he'd assuaged his conscience in the bargain. Relieved, William nodded. "Aye—'tis overlate for him."

"But I . . ." As sleepy as he was, Jamie's lower lip trembled, betraying his disappointment. "I'd hear if Sir Launfel slays the two-headed monster!" he blurted out.

"Ena can tell ye on the morrow," William said. "Besides, I'd hae ye aid Ewan to choose a pony for ye then."

The boy blinked back the tears that had welled in his pale eyes, and for a moment he stared. "A pony!" he breathed. "Nae a stick one?"

"Well, I'd have him see as if there was one as suits ye," Will answered, grinning.

The thin face was transformed as it broke into an excited smile. Jamie wiped at his eyes with a closed fist, blotting the wetness. "Ye'd gie me a pony?"

"Aye."

And then the boy's face fell, and he looked away. "But I canna ride—I canna ride!"

"Ye have to try first to know it, James. Ye have to try first ere ye say ye canna," Will told him. "God willing, Ewan will find ye a horse as ye can master."

"Come on, ye wee pest—I'd go, ere ye ruin my new tunic when ye canna hold it longer." To Ena Ewan added, "And ye—ye can come with me an ye want, but I'd hae ye stand outside."

Arabella rose with difficulty, for the room spun, and went to her son. Leaning to kiss him, she murmured, "God keep you safe through the night, sweet son, for you are dear to me." More than a little overwhelmed by the wine, she crooned softly, "Sweet Jamie, so saft and fair . . . sweet Jamie with the golden hair . . ."

"I'd nae be saft, Mama. I am a boy."

" 'Tis enough, good people," Will said, coming up behind her to hold her shoulders. "Until the morrow, James. Ewan, take him to bed."

It was the signal for all to go, and as they filed out more than one stumbled or lurched from the effects of

too much wine. Waiting until William had barred the
door after them, Arabella reached to loosen the laces
beneath her arms. But her fingers were suddenly
clumsy, and the room was strangely atilt. She swayed
slightly. A wave of nausea washed over her, making
her whole body seem wet. She should have stayed
seated.

"Sweet Mary, but I . . ."

" 'Twould seem ye had too much of the wine also,
mistress." But as he walked toward her, William was
smiling.

"Ena . . ." She covered her mouth and swallowed
valiantly.

"Nay, ye dinna need her, sweeting."

"My lord, I think I am going to be heartily sick!"
The words were scarce out ere she began to retch violently. He caught her at her waist and pushed her
toward the empty washing basin. As he watched helplessly, she emptied the liquid from her stomach. With
one arm still around her, bracing her, he reached with
the other for a cloth.

As the sickness subsided she looked down to where
she'd soiled the hem of her wedding gown, and she
began to wail, "I've ruined it, and I'll never have
another like it! Sweet Mary, I've ruined my gown!"

"Shhhhhh." Still holding her, he managed to pour
from the drinking pitcher, wetting the cloth. As he
wiped her sweaty face, he tried to soothe her. "Ena
can remove the spots, Bella, else we'll get ye another."

" 'Tis the finest I have ever had!" she cried.

"And 'tis but the first of many," he promised.
"Come on—I'd get ye to bed ere ye are chilled.
Come," he coaxed, " 'tis the drink as oversets ye."

" 'Tis Christmas!" she sobbed, clutching at his tunic. "And I've ruined my gown!"

"Ye'll be all right on the morrow, Bella—'tis but
that your stomach was too empty for the wine." He
spoke softly, gently, as his fingers worked her laces,
loosening them. Leaning her forward over his arm, he

pulled the iridescent gown upward and over her head, then down over her arms, turning it inside out ere it fell in a heap at their feet. "There is but the under-tunic, Bella—can you hold your head down that I may take it also?"

"Aye." Her voice was muffled as the undershift covered her head. "I feel unwell, my lord."

"Would ye that I got the basin again?"

"Nay."

He lifted her effortlessly and carried her to bed. Turning back the coverlet and the top feather mattress he thrust her beneath them, then pulled them over her. She rolled over and drew up her knees. The room still seemed to move around her.

He doused the oil lamps, then opened the shutters to look into the yard below. It was quiet now, aban-doned by those who'd dance there earlier, and the blazes had become naught but piles of glowing ashes, bits of red against a faery world of shining ice. His gaze traveled to the hills beyond the keep itself and there he saw the many fires that burned still, dotting the crests where they met the sky, appearing like doz-ens of the stars they were meant to represent. The beauty of it was almost too great.

Briefly he considered saying his prayers ere he re-tired, then he discarded the notion. Tonight 'twas deeds rather than words that had mattered. He'd held Arabella's son with little more than a passing thought to the boy's father, and it had made him feel good. He reshuttered the windows and turned to undress by the waning fire. Then, shivering from the cold air he'd let into the room, he crawled beneath the cover and rolled to warm himself against Arabella's back.

"I am not much good to you tonight," she mum-bled miserably, "but—"

His hand smoothed a braid that hung over her shoul-der. "Nay, Bella—this night 'tis enough that I hold you."

Chapter Twenty-One

Despite the bitter cold, Arabella followed William into the yard as Young Wat led the pony from the stable. She eyed the beast with great misgiving, biting back words of fear. But she dared not speak openly against what they did, for William had told Ewan to bring Jamie to her every afternoon after Father Edmund's lessons. The rest of the time he was to be under Ewan's guidance still. The Christmas dispute had been settled thus, and she had to count it a victory, however small.

Across the open area she watched Ewan hand her son to Nib, then turn to lift the saddle onto the pony's back. It was a strange wooden affair, padded with wool and covered withal in stout cloth, with scarce room to sit between a high pommel in front and an even higher cantle behind. On one side hung a stirrup, on the other something that looked like a wide cloth sheath.

There was no mistaking the excitement in the child's eyes as he watched Ewan seat the saddle and tighten the girth. But as Ewan turned again to him, Jamie's expression changed to one of fear.

"Come on, ye wee heathen—nay, there'll be none

o' that now,'' the grizzled man chided, lifting him.
''Show yer mother as ye are strong, else she'll think
'tis a wee lass ye be rather than a man.''

''Mama!''

She started forward, but William caught her arm in
warning. ''Ewan'll nae let him fall,'' he growled.

''Mamaaaaa!''

Even as Jamie screamed the man settled him into
the strange saddle, while Nib held the pony's reins.
''Hold the pommel,'' Ewan advised, as he adjusted
the single stirrup over the boy's good foot. Satisfied,
he shifted the small body back a little against the cantle. ''Aye, 'tis a good enough fit fer ye.'' Moving to
the other side, he lifted Jamie's useless leg and eased
it into the sheath, telling the boy, ''See now—'tis secure ye are.''

The boy looked down uneasily. ''I'll fall,'' he
whimpered.

''Nay, ye willna and ye hold on—there isna anywhere fer ye to go.'' Ewan looked to where Arabella
and William stood, flashing them a grin. ''I'd tie him
on and ye want, but I'd nae think he needs it.''

''Tie him on,'' Arabella managed hoarsely. ''Sweet
Mary, but what if. . . ?''

''Nay, leave him be,'' William ordered. ''He has to
learn he willna fall.''

''Mama!''

''Och, and ye think I'd nae catch ye?'' Ewan asked.
''Fer shame, Jamie of Woolford! Would ye hae yer
mama think ye a bigger bairn than ye are? Go on,
Nib—lead him.''

Arabella stood on tiptoe, leaning forward anxiously.
''I would you were careful, Ewan!''

Nib o' Kinmurrie walked slowly, and the pony followed the reins. Beside Jamie the grey-haired man
steadied the saddle, then kept a comforting hand on
the boy's leg. At first the child sat still as stone, his
face frozen with fright, but as they walked the length
of the yard and back his fear gave way to pleasure. By

the third time around the courtyard he had raised one of his hands from the pommel to wave at Arabella.

"Mama, I dinna fall!"

"Aye." She managed to smile, despite the tenseness of her jaw. "Aye, 'tis proud of you I am." She turned quickly to William. "My lord, 'tis too cold to tarry without."

He looked down. "Then ye'd best get inside."

"But 'tis too cold for Jamie."

"Nay. He wears a sturdy cloak."

"Father Edmund awaits him."

"Mama! Watch me!"

"And you are chilled, go on," William urged her. "Ewan will take him to the priest when he is done. You have seen he is safe enough."

"Mama! Look!"

"Aye." She walked forward, signaling for Nib to stop. Reaching up, she smoothed the loose chausses over the twisted leg. "Aye, Jamie, 'tis well you have done this day, but I'd not have you forget your lessons."

His small face fell. "But Mama . . ."

"Now that you have a horse of your own, I am sure Ewan will bring you out often."

"Bella . . ."

"Look at you, Jamie—'tis chilled you are," she insisted.

"Nay, I am not cold at all."

"Walk him around again, Nib." Will came up behind her and laid a hand on her shoulder. "Come inside, Bella. You worry overmuch, and I'll not have it." He leaned past her to slap the pony's rump, and it lunged forward. The boy squealed as Nib broke into a trot to keep up with the animal. "God willing, he'll like it enough to try again."

"And if he falls?"

"If he falls, Ewan will put him up again. But he won't fall from that."

"You cannot know it."

" 'Tis time you had another babe. You've swaddled

this one overlong.'' She looked up to dispute it, then caught the warmth in his eyes. ''Ye canna say I am unwilling to try, can ye?'' he added softly.

''I thank you for your kindness to Jamie this day,'' she murmured, mistaking his meaning.

'' 'Twas not what I meant, and well you know it.'' He lifted an errant strand of her hair and tucked it beneath her veil. ''Aye, I'd make a son of mine own, Bella.''

Despite the cold, the now familiar heat coursed through her. ''Now?'' she asked weakly. ''Ena—''

''I'd have you send her away.''

Father Edmund waited for her already, but there was that in William's eyes that promised far more than letters. For a moment she looked to where Nib had started yet another circle around the yard, then she raised her gaze to her husband's once more.

'' 'Tis too cold to send her to aid Ewan.''

''Let her get sweetcakes and spiced wine for them.''

''She'll know what we do,'' she protested, prolonging the moment.

''Do you care?'' he countered, tracing the line of her jaw lightly with a fingertip. ''What say ye, Bella?''

''Aye.''

''Will!'' There was a hesitation, then, ''My lord!'' Lang Gib's voice carried through the heavy door. '' 'Tis Burwell—the murdering English have raided Burwell!''

''Jesu!'' William rolled from between the feather mattresses to sit on the edge of the rope-hung bed. Groping in the darkness for his chausses, he shouted back, ''When?''

''Scarce hours ago—it burns still! Kenneth comes sorely wounded, asking for aid. They fired the door to his tower, smoking the garrison there, then cut them down as they fled, leaving him for dead and taking those as survived to ransom! Aye, and they have driven off his sheep and cows as well!''

''Jesu, but they are a lawless lot,'' Will muttered,

pulling on the stockings and tying them. "'Tis not even Epiphany yet! This time 'tis Burwell, but who's to say it won't be Blackleith the next? God's bones, but I'd stop them ere they think to come again."

Arabella scrambled from the bed and pulled on her gown to cover her nakedness. "I'll arm you," she offered quickly, moving to light a straw from the coals in the brazier.

"Aye. Gather up ten others, making six of them archers," he ordered Gib, unbarring the door. "I'd take no more, for I'd not leave Blackleith undefended."

Turning around, Arabella touched the small flame to the floating wicks in the cresset lamps. The waxed strings caught, flaring briefly, then flickered, chasing shadows over her face. Without looking up, she addressed Lang Gib.

"And you have need of the fresh loaves from the bakehouse, take them, for we can fire the ovens anew come morning."

"Aye." Gib hesitated, then blurted out to William, "I'd take Ewan, my lord, for he knows both sides of the border."

"Tell him to give the boy over to Ena." Leaning down to find his garters and boots, William looked over at Arabella. "He can pallet with her this night."

"Aye."

"We'll await ye in the yard, my lord," Gib promised. "I have but to arm myself."

While William finished dressing, Arabella hastened to pull his padded gambeson from one of the wooden boxes that lined a wall. As soon as he'd straightened his linen undertunic at the hips, she hung the gambeson over his neck and waited for him to thrust his arms upward. He smoothed it over his body while she searched again for his *cuir bouilli*, and finding the boiled leather garment she carried it back to him. He sat while she laced it for him, tightening it until it fit like a hard leather case over his back and chest.

A boy ran up the stairs to watch, and Arabella ordered him curtly, "Fetch my lord's mail—'tis in the farthest box." Dropping to her knees, she wrapped the leather garters over William's chausses, tying the ends and tucking them under. Then she waited for him to pull on his heavy boots.

Taking the heavy hauberk from the boy, she managed to lift it over her husband's head and work the kinks from the metal links as it fell downward over his chest. He stood for her to pull it over his hips while he adjusted the sleeves. The boy waited with the leather cap and coif. William forced the cap over his thick hair and fastened it beneath his chin, then ducked so that Arabella might slip the mail coif onto his head, smoothing the cold links and hooking it to the hauberk at the shoulders. That done, she held out his woolen overtunic to him. He pulled it over all the rest and waited for her to lace the neck.

"You'll freeze," she muttered, as her fingers worked deftly.

"Aye," he agreed grimly. "War is a cold business in winter."

There was a moment of awkwardness, a moment when she could scarce conceal her fear for him. "How far do you pursue them?"

"Until they are punished."

Then, perceiving she regarded him anxiously, he caught her hand and held it against his beard-roughened cheek. " 'Twill nae take overlong, I promise ye, for they canna flee fast with animals and prisoners."

"But you are not many," she cautioned him. "And knowing those who came to Woolford, I can say the English are as treacherous as any. They are like to lie in wait for those who pursue."

" 'Tis I who mean to wait for them, Bella. The surprise is theirs, for 'tis faster I can travel than they." Though his face was grim, his eyes warmed briefly when they met hers. "Aye—they'll nae cross the Cheviots before me."

"You cannot know how they will go."

" 'Tis Burwell they have raided, and they'll nae want to tarry this side of the border. Unless they'd do leagues beyond their way, they'll keep to the road southward.'' He rubbed his cheek against the palm of her hand. "I, on the other hand, am not impeded by booty like they. And as Burwell lies eastward, I'd cross the river ere I cut south. By the time they are come, mine archers will lie in wait.''

It sounded so simple, and yet she knew the risks. "And Kenneth of Burwell? What of him?''

"I'd hae ye tend him.'' He rose and took his helmet from the serving boy. Jamming it on his head, he adjusted the nasal to cover his nose, then reached to take his heavy gloves. "And after, I'd hae ye get back to bed, for ye need the rest and 'tis still dark outside.'' He started for the door. "God willing, I'll be back shortly after the next nightfall.''

"Wait—do you send for aid to your brother at Dunashie?''

He hesitated, then shook his head. "Nay—'tis too close to Elizabeth's lying-in, and I'd not have it said that I could not ride without him.''

She moved to look up at him. In his helm and mail he was huge, towering like the giant he was called, but for all that she knew he was as mortal as any other. And men fell in border skirmishes as often as in battle.

"My lord . . .''

"Aye?''

"God aid and keep you, William.''

"Aye.''

Unshed tears sparkled in her eyes and her lower lip trembled, but somehow she managed to smile. For a long moment he stared into her upturned face, seeing not the tangled hair or the face still imprinted with wrinkled bed covers, but rather the fear her eyes held for him. And he knew if he lived another score of years he'd not forget the way she looked at him, for it was the first time he had dared to think she might love him.

"Bella, I do not kill easily,'' he said softly, taking

her into his arms. "You behold a man who has faced
the English a hundred times and more."

She leaned into him, clutching his tunic, smelling
the oiled steel and leather beneath, savoring the
strength of his arms about her. "Still, I would you
took care for me," she whispered against his chest.

"Aye."

"My lord. . . ?"

" 'Twas Lang Gib come for him. Heedless of what
the man would think, Arabella rose on tiptoe to brush
her lips against William's, and then she broke away.

"Godspeed, my lord."

"Lady, Father Edmund is with Kenneth of Burwell
now, for he bleeds heavily," Gib told her. "He asks
that you bring your needle with ye when ye come
down."

"Sweet Mary—aye."

"You'd best tend Kenneth ere he is a dead man,"
Will advised. "And dinna be worrying for me," he
added, his mouth twisting into a crooked smile. "Have
a care for yourself, ye hear?"

She nodded. Turning to look for her sewing box,
she heard him ask Gib if all was ready, but Gib's answer was lost in the sound of their footsteps on the
stone stairs. "Mother Mary, grant him a safe return
to me," she prayed under her breath, as she bent to
retrieve the box from beneath a bench.

William met Ewan carrying a sleepy Jamie up from
below. "Ena gathers food, my lord," he told him,
"and I'd take the boy to Lady Arabella, unless ye mind
it. There's been nae time to arm myself."

There was no time to wait. "Nay, she comes down
to tend Kenneth." Reluctantly, Will reached to take
the boy. " 'Tis all right—I'll take him to the kitchen
to the woman myself."

As he crossed the courtyard past the milling men
and horses, William shifted Jamie against his shoulder. The child clutched his tunic tightly and twisted to
watch the small mesnie mount up.

"Ewan says ye ride to kill the English—I would that I could see it."

" 'Tisna anything for a wee one's eyes," Will retorted gruffly. "Besides, the Woolfords are English," he reminded him.

"I hate the Woolfords," Jamie responded bitterly. "Nay, ye'll kill all the raiders—I know it. Ye'll make them rue the day they crossed the border, won't ye?"

"Aye."

"Ewan says there isna another like ye. He says ye can cleave a horse's neck with an axe," the boy continued, betraying his excitement. "He says—"

" 'Twould seem Ewan talks overmuch," William muttered, crossing the threshold into the kitchen.

"He says there isna any as can stand against the Barber."

" 'Tis but an axe like any other." It wasn't true, and William knew it, but the boy's admiration made him uncomfortable.

"Aye. Ewan says 'tis the swing as matters, and there's none as can wield it like ye."

" 'Tis my size," Will admitted tersely. "Ena!" he called out. "Come take the boy, that I may ride!"

For all that William had tried, he still had difficulty accepting Jamie, and he felt great guilt for it. As soon as Ena reached for the boy Will shifted him onto her shoulder. But as he looked downward he could not miss the wistful expression on the small face. He found himself needing to say something.

"Here now—have a care for your mother and Ena, James. The women worry when the men ride out, ye know."

"I would I went with ye. I'd see ye hang 'em."

Will started to say he was too little, then thought better of it. Instead, he tweaked the boy's good foot. "Nae this time." His eyes met Ena's. "After ye get the boy to bed, I'd hae ye aid Arabella with Kenneth. Lang Gib says he is sorely wounded."

"Aye, my lord."

It was not until he was nearly out of the kitchen that he heard Jamie call out, ''God aid ye and the Barber!''

Will swung around and raised his hand in acknowledgment. ''I'll bring back an English dagger for ye,'' he promised.

It wasn't until he'd heaved himself into his saddle and given the order to lower the bridge that he wondered why he'd said it. It showed, he supposed, that even he was not proof against the boy's words. Besides, it was not much to offer—and God aided him, he'd bring back more than that, anyway. And God aided him, the men of Dunashie would wear English mail when he was done.

Chapter Twenty-Two

Dawn broke through the cold mists that covered the desolate, treeless hilltops and dipped to the lonely gullies below. William reined in and took stock of the endless ridges of rock and dead, rough grass ahead. There stretched the craggy, stony mountains, the lean wasteland he knew as the Cheviot Hills. Even the place names bore grim, macabre testimony to the savage barrenness: Bloody Bush, Foul Bog, Hungry Hill, Wolf Rig, Foul Play. This was No Man's Land, the oft-disputed, blood-soaked ground that lay between belligerent neighbors.

"They dinna come this way," Lang Gib observed, leaning over his horse's neck to study the rutted road. "There isna any new sheep dung."

"Aye." Will rubbed his cold, nearly numb arms and rose to stretch in his saddle. "I expect they follow the Tyne southward." His eyes scanned the bleak horizon, then he sat back, shrugging his shoulders to ease them. "We've followed long enough to know where they are headed. We'll cross into Tynedale and await them."

"The Devil will take us and we are caught."

"The English are saft, Gib—there's naught out but
raiders in this. The warden'll be hovering o'er his fire,
and well ye know it." Despite the cold, William managed to grin. "But I'd gie him summat to complain of
at the next border meeting."

"The sun comes up," Ewan observed uneasily.

"Aye. We leave the road when we cross into England. Ye said ye knew the land," Will reminded him.

The older man nodded.

"Och, then we'll fall in behind ye there."

There was not much more to be said. For hours
they'd ridden the night-shrouded road almost eagerly,
every man ready to avenge with an equal savagery the
burning of Burwell's small wooden stockade and
tower. And despite Gib's warning, they knew they had
two advantages: They traveled unencumbered by bag-
gage, and they were unexpected. The grim jest among
them was that when the English watched for pursuit
over their shoulders, they would look the wrong way.

They proceeded southward also, keeping to the
steeper hills, threading their way through moors and
gullies until they reached the keeps that faced each
other across the arbitrary line England and Scotland
currently called "The Border." With each successive
sovereign aggression the castles changed hands, moving from Scotland to England and back again so often
that the disputed villeins had little allegiance to either.
Whichever way they leaned, they were likely to be
burned and murdered by the other side.

Across the way on the English side, church bells
rang, pealing out the last day of Christmas on this, the
sixth of January, 1139. The sun shone coldly over the
sheep-dotted hills, giving the deceptive impression of
peace. For all the barren cragginess that surrounded
them, William had to own there was a certain beauty
to the land.

Signaling a halt with his hand he waited for the others to draw up also, then decided, "We wait until they
are at Mass to cross. When 'tis seen we are few and

do not stop, I doubt we will be pursued. Whilst we tarry here, I'd eat.''

"We should reach the Rede some five or six leagues eastward, my lord," Ewan told him, "and 'tis not likely the English will be there before us.''

"Aye." William's eyes took in the seemingly unending hills. "I'd choose a place where we are covered."

Lang Gib leaned forward, resting his weary body against his pommel. "Ewan?"

"When we are beyond the border keeps, there will not be many traveled roads. 'Tis not as the way to Wycklow." Ewan appeared to ponder what he remembered of the area, then he nodded. "Aye, there are a dozen and more places we could lie in wait."

"I'd take the first—I'd nae tarry on English soil any more than I must," Will murmured. "There's nae an Englishman as would hae any love for the Butcher's bastard brother, and we are too few to fight our way all the way back to the border. Besides, I'd nae wait long for the thieves. I'd sleep abed tonight."

There was none as disagreed with that, for to a man they were cold and wearied from the sleepless night. But it was a grim business, the meting out of punishment to those who reived across the border, and it was one that they all regarded as justice. An eye for an eye, a keep for a keep, else the English would think them weak.

As Nib o' Kinmurrie divided the loaves of bread between them, the church bells fell silent. Tearing off a chunk of his loaf, Will ordered Ewan, "We eat as we ride, then."

The sun waxed high ere they'd reached the first place Will considered suitable to an ambush: a long, narrow stretch of road that wended between rocky hills. They took more than a small measure of satisfaction when Ewan announced 'twas between places called "Whip Snag" and "Dead Heath," for even the names were auspicious for their business. They staked out the high

ground and waited, whilst Nib was sent back up the
road to watch.

Despite the rocky, tortuous way they'd come, they
had a considerable respite of hours ere Nib returned
with word that a band of "murderin' English" could
be seen driving sheep and men before them.

"How many?"

"Twenty or more."

"How soon?"

Nib looked skyward, seeing the winter sun lowering
behind clouds that hovered along the western horizon.
"Ere dark," he predicted. "The animals slow them
still, for the sheep are falling by the way, but I'd say
they come within the hour."

Will placed his archers at the narrowest point in the
road, ordering them to tighten the springs to their bows
and lie down until the prisoners and animals had
passed. Only then were they to rise and fire upon the
raiders. In the ensuing confusion Lang Gib was to
charge from the front, driving animals and men back
into another hail of arrows, while William and the others fell upon their rear. There was no consideration
that they were outnumbered, for it was the accepted
opinion that one good Scots borderer was worth any
ten Englishmen when surprised. Besides, if all went
as planned, 'twould be like slaughtering beasts for the
table.

The raiders came down the road, still herding tired
prisoners and bleating, sore-footed sheep. Many were
confident enough that they'd escaped pursuit that their
helmets dangled from their saddles. Above the road
William's few archers nocked their arrows and chose
their targets carefully, taking aim at those who least
expected trouble.

It was not until the sheep and prisoners were nearly
through the narrowest part that William shouted the
eerie battle cry of his ancestors. As the reivers looked
ahead in surprise, the first arrows flew in their faces.
Their apparent leader slumped forward in his saddle,
his eye pierced by a steel-tipped shaft. The sheep and

cows, frightened by Lang Gib's shouts as he charged
them, stumbled back, effectively blocking escape.

As the English wheeled to flee William hit them
from behind, riding into them, swinging his battle-
axe, calling out, "Fight, ye whoreson curs!" As one
man hastily jammed on his helmet the Barber caught
him below his arm, caving in his ribs and spraying
William's shield. He rose in his saddle, then toppled
to the ground, where he was trampled by his own
horse.

Panicked, the English discovered they had nowhere
to turn. Those Scots prisoners who could get to them
grappled for their weapons, pulling several of the hated
enemy down. Horses reared among squalling sheep
beneath a new hail of arrows. Men and beasts fell in
the fury of the Scots' onslaught until the first Englishman cried, "Have done! Have done!" as he threw
down his mace and shield. It was a futile gesture, for
an archer had already marked him, and he too was hit.
The arrow struck his throat, cutting short his surrender.

Those caught in the middle of the dying lost their
will to fight and began calling out for mercy. As weapons were dropped and hands raised, the brief but
bloody battle ended. And those who had been prisoners but minutes before waded through the tangle of
horses and sheep and bodies to wreak their vengeance.
Lang Gib threaded his way between them, shouting,
"Save them to ransom!" but for a time his words fell
on deaf ears. One man, tears streaming down his face,
cried back that the murdering English had burned his
wife and son. Before any could stop him he swung
viciously, nearly decapitating an erstwhile captor with
his own discarded weapon. Will rode over to him,
wresting the axe from him.

"Enough! 'Tis enough!"

Finally there was a sullen calm, marred only by the
bleating of the animals and the groans of the dying.
Nib and the archers descended to begin stripping the
precious mail from the bodies, as Lang Gib counted

the cost on both sides. William dismounted to wipe hair, blood, and shattered bone from the Barber's blade with dead grass. When he looked down, his woolen overtunic clung wetly to his mail where the blood had soaked it. It was then that he realized his shield arm ached.

"My lord, ye are wounded," Ewan told him.

"Aye."

Th sleeve of his mail hauberk was rent above his left elbow, and congealing blood still oozed there. In the heat of the melee he'd not even felt the blow. With his right hand he caught at the hem of his tunic and wiped at the wound, revealing a gash of several inches in the flesh.

"The bone's intact, so 'twill heal," he muttered. "I'll wash it in the river ere we leave." His gaze traveled to Lang Gib. "How many as survive?"

"We lost but one dead and two wounded, my lord, and of the men of Burwell, two perished and two are hurt. As to the English, there are but nine as survive. Eight died unshriven, and four I blessed ere they breathed their last," he reported. "The men of Burwell would that we hanged the rest," he added.

"Nay. Tell them I'd ransom them, that Kenneth may rebuild his keep."

"They willna like it—most lost someone there."

William considered for a moment, then nodded grimly. "Ask them how many died there, then."

Gib was gone for a moment to confer with the man Will had disarmed. When he returned he answered, "They say 'twas at least fourteen, mayhap more, as were lost at Burwell to the English. They say they had nae chance, my lord."

It was not an easy choice, but William understood the ancient animosity well. He looked to where the prisoners watched, their faces sullen.

"Then 'twas sixteen in all. Aye. Sixteen in turn is fair enough. Choose the man of Burwell with greatest rank and let him pick four to hang. But tell him to have a care how he does it, for I'd hae him choose those who inflicted the greatest harm. The rest I'd take to Kenneth that he may ask a ransom. And he dies, one more will hang for it.''

''Aye. And the other dead?''

''Strip them and leave them for carrion. I'd hae the English know the price we charge for Burwell.''

He reached to dislodge his helmet, but his injured arm felt weak. Ewan hastened to remove it for him. ''My thanks,'' he murmured. ''Now I'd seek the river. I'd nae go home like this.'' He started for his horse, then stopped. ''While ye take the clothes and arms, I'd hae ye find a dagger for the boy.''

The older man's face broke into a grin. '' 'Tis glad I am ye do it, my lord. 'Tis little enough the puir wee little thing has had, ye know.''

William shrugged. ''It cost me nothing.''

Ewan watched his master swing up onto his huge horse, and his grin broadened. ''Och, and ye think so, do ye?'' he asked softly under his breath. ''Nay, but he cost ye the thought, and 'tis a beginning, Will o' Dunashie.''

Chapter Twenty-Three

The letters blurred before her eyes. She could not think on Father Edmund's words as he spoke and spelled out Jamie's lesson. Beside her, her son stared not at the parchment but rather toward the shuttered window, the mulish set of his jaw evident. And every time the priest addressed him he answered reluctantly, unwilling to recite aloud as Edmund had told him to do. Usually she'd take him to task for his manners, but this day she scarce heard the exchange between them. Somewhere her husband traded blows with English raiders, and she knew not if he were injured—or worse. Too many times at Byrum she'd seen men carried home from border skirmishes. Too many times she'd heard Mass for the repose of their souls.

She'd not returned to her bed after she'd tended Kenneth of Burwell, and already she'd seen to far more than usual. In the absence of her husband she'd meted out the customary Twelfth Day gifts of a gallon of ale and one good loaf of bread to every villein's hut, and she'd received the good wishes of Blackleith's people on this, the last day of Christmas. Beyond that there'd been no celebration, the raid at Burwell and the sub-

sequent pursuit having ended any of the planned festivities. Instead, they'd prayed for Kenneth's recovery
at Mass.

But for all that she'd been busy her thoughts would
dwell on William, making the rest seem distant and
unreal. Briefly, she bowed her head for possibly the
hundredth time since he'd left, praying silently. *In the
name of Mary and all the saints you hold holy, Father
in Heaven, I ask that you keep mine husband safe.*

"For the last time, James, I'd have you read what I
have shown you," Walter spoke impatiently. "And you
do it right, you may go."

The boy flashed him a look of dislike, then lowered
his eyes to the scrap of parchment on which the priest
had written. "I dinna want this," he muttered rebel-
liously, casting a sidewise glance at his mother. When
she said nothing he sighed, then began to read the
memorized words haltingly, tracing them with his finger, "James of Woolford . . . born in . . . England
. . . on April . . . nine . . . nineteenth . . . in the year
of our Lord . . . eleven . . . hundred and thirty-two."

"Which says 'England'?"

"This one," the boy grumbled, pointing to it.

"Aye. I'd have you copy the whole five times, James,
and then I'd see you write your name yet another ten
as I have shown you."

Again the boy looked to his mother, and then, seeing she did not attend him, he shook his head. "I
dinna want this," he repeated more loudly. "I dinna."

Though he could scarce stand Arabella's hellborn
brat, Walter did not want to risk alienating her by
striking the child. Swallowing his rising anger at the
boy's obvious sullenness, he reminded him sternly,
" 'Tis six years you have, James, and 'tis time you
learned both your letters and your manners."

"Nearly seven," Jamie countered. "And I'd nae be
a clerk!"

Startled from her detached reverie, Arabella turned
her attention to her son. "Jamie!"

"I'd nae do it, Mama!"

"Your pardon, Father, but he did not sleep enough," she murmured, embarrassed by the boy's outburst. "I will see he does the lesson."

"Mama!" Jamie's voice rose indignantly. "I'd nae be a clerk nor a priest!"

"There's naught else for you," Walter snapped, betraying his contempt. Then, lest he offended Arabella, he forced himself to add more kindly, " 'Tis a waste not to use the good mind God gave you, James." There. He'd managed to praise the brat somewhat before her.

"Lord William reads and writes—and ciphers, Jamie," Arabella said soothingly. Perceiving that he did not believe her, she sought the means to convince him. "He says it means he will not be cheated by the clerks. He says 'tis all he would thank King Henry for—I swear it."

Though they'd worked far less than the hour allotted, Walter could not wait to be rid of the boy. And yet he'd not forgo his time with the mother, for he counted it the best part of his day. Setting aside his pen and bits of precious paper, he rose to unshutter the window. Leaning into the cold blast of air, he called to a boy passing below, "Come take James of Woolford to his nurse!"

"Nay, Father, but I would take him," Arabella protested behind him.

He turned around, holding the wide sleeves of his cassock over his arms for warmth. "Daughter, you are sorely troubled, and I'd hear of it. Confess to me, and I will give you ease," he promised. "Let God share the burden you bear," he added unctuously.

" 'Tis not a sin to worry for my husband, Father."

It was not what he would hear, for it did not serve him. And yet he'd still not have her leave him. He banged the shutter into place with unwarranted force and fastened it securely, then came back to the fire. Stretching his hands over it, he tried not to betray his need for her company.

"And you wished it, I'd pray with you for his safety, daughter."

Though he addressed Arabella often thus, and she called him "Father" also, it seemed awkward. For all that he'd told William his looks belied his age, she'd warrant he was not any older than she was. And the warmth she often saw in his eyes seemed to be for her alone. Nay, she must be mistaken—'twas the years of Elias' blind jealousy over her that still made her wary of men, she supposed. There was naught but kindness for her in Edmund of Alton. Still, she hesitated.

"I ought to tend to my packing, that I may be ready when word of Elizabeth of Rivaux's safe delivery comes from Dunashie."

"Do I go, Mama?" Jamie's hand tugged at her skirt for attention. "I'd go to Dunashie, Mama—I'd see the Butcher."

As much as she'd disputed with William over it, she found herself lamely giving her husband's excuses. "Nay—'tis overfar, and the weather uncertain." Seeing the disappointment in his eyes, she ruffled his fair hair affectionately. "Besides, 'twould pain you to ride so far."

His face fell and his eyes filled with tears. "I could ride Minette—I know I could!"

"Nay, Jamie."

"But why? I'd nae ask any to hold me—I'd not!"

"Jamie . . ."

"Art ashamed of me, Mama?" he cried. "Art like all the rest?"

"James!" Walter reached to cuff him, but Arabella's arms closed protectively about her son. "Nay, James, but you must not say such to your lady mother," he scolded, dropping his hand. "You must ask her pardon for your insolence."

The boy's lower lip quivered as his eyes spilled over. "Nay, Mama, I did not mean it."

She wanted to cry with him, but dared not. Instead she swallowed to regain her composure and then, stroking his hair gently, tried to ease the coming sep-

aration for him. "I know you did not," she murmured
soothingly. " 'Twill be crowded there, as Dunashie's
vassals will come also, and William—and we," she
corrected herself, "do not believe you would like the
journey. 'Twill be better that you stay here with
Ewan."

"My lady . . ."

She looked up, seeing the boy who'd come up for
her son. Resolutely, she set Jamie from her and forced
a smile. "And you are good, I'd get Minette for you
later—we could walk the yard together," she coaxed.
"Until then, I'd have you practice your letters for Father Edmund."

"Where would you that I took him, lady?" the boy
asked.

"I'd have you carry him to Ena."

"Aye. Hold on, Woolford," he said, reaching back
to catch the smaller child's legs.

"I'm not Woolford!"

"Nay? Then what are ye?"

"James! I hate the Woolfords!"

"Have a care on the stairs!" Arabella called after
them. Bending over, she retrieved the quill pen and
the papers he'd dropped. She knew she'd not convinced her son, and even to her own ears her words
had sounded foolish. Straightening up, she faced the
priest. "I would that I believed in miracles, Father,
for if I did I'd ask that one might heal him."

"We will pray for that also."

"Nay. And words could do it, he'd have walked long
ere now. Think you I have not said them?" she cried.
"God listens not to me in that!" Her hand clenched
tightly over the quill, breaking it, as she sought to
compose herself. Her voice dropped low. "From the
moment of his birth—nay, before then even—I have
prayed for my son, Father. I have prayed for his leg.
I have prayed that others will love him. I have prayed
that William will understand. . . ."

His hand closed over hers, holding it. "Sweet lady,

I would aid you. I'd have you know you are not alone in your prayers, Arabella of Byrum.''

"And what if aught should befall William?" she cried, giving vent to her fear. "Then Jamie and I will go again to Byrum to a sire who has little love for me—and none at all for my poor Jamie! My only hope is William!"

"And God gave you to a harsh husband," he murmured, massaging her fingers with his own. Emboldened when she did not pull away, he dared to lay a comforting arm around her shoulder. For a moment he savored the smell of roses that wafted upward from her hair. "William of Dunashie does not deserve what he is given," he said softly.

The intensity of his gaze discomfitted her. Had he been another, she'd have thought he meant to kiss her. She drew back from his embrace and turned away. "Nay, you have mistaken my words, Father. And he can be brought to care for my son, I am well content with my husband."

"And if he cannot . . ?"

"Then I must make him."

"My poor child. God would succor you, and you asked Him."

She dug within the small leather pouch she carried at her girdle and drew out a single silver penny. Wheeling again to face him, she held it out. " 'Tis not overmuch, Father, but I'd give it for your prayers."

"You have them already, gentle lady."

"Here—mayhap God will listen if I give it for alms." When he made no move to take her money, she pressed it into his hand. "Two things I'd ask, Father Edmund: I'd have my husband safely returned, and I'd have his love for Jamie."

"I will set a wax candle for each," he promised, laying it aside. "And you would kneel, I would bless you, daughter."

"Aye."

She dropped to her knees before him and bowed her

head. For a long moment he looked down on her pale, golden braids, thinking she was as lovely as any he'd ever seen. Slowly, he placed his hand on her crown, then intoned, "May God grant that which you ask of him, Arabella of Byrum, and may He keep you always safe."

"And may He bless William of Dunashie and James of Woolford, keeping them safe and well also," she added.

Rather than repeat her words, he merely murmured, "In the name of the Father, the Son, and the Holy Spirit, Amen."

"My thanks, Father," she said, rising. "For all that I would tarry, I must look again to Kenneth. And I can help it, I'd not have him perish in mine house."

"Aye."

Later, after she'd left, he leaned into the cold slit that passed for his window and watched her cross the yard below. Aye, he'd have her if he could, but he'd have to be more careful: He could ill afford to let his nether parts cost him his revenge on the Butcher and the Bastard. And when 'twas done, there would be time for Arabella of Byrum.

Reluctantly, he turned back to the table strewn with his paper, his quills, and his ink. Seeing the penny where he'd placed it, he felt a surge of anger that she would ask him to pray for William of Dunashie. Light candles for the Bastard and her brat? Nay, when he lit them, he'd look downward, to ask that all of Giles of Moray's blood should perish.

Chapter Twenty-Four

"My lady, ye must sleep," Ena murmured, bringing her a cup of hot spiced wine. " 'Tis angered yer lord will be, and I let ye sicken."

"Jesu, but I cannot. Night has come again, and still there is no word of him."

" 'Tis the lot of women to wait," the tiring woman reminded her.

"Aye, but 'tis no easy thing to do." She sipped of the steaming cup, looking over the brim. "Did you not worry ere you were widowed?"

The older woman looked away. "Aye, but 'twas not in mine hands, my lady. When Fair Thomas dinna come back, 'twas the will o' God, ye know."

They'd scarce spoken of Ena's husband since he'd fallen in one of King David's incursions into England some twelve years before. Yet for all that had been unsaid between them, Arabella could still remember the woman's tears. For a month and more she'd been inconsolable, weeping and rending her clothes. And even later she could not bring herself to say his name without pain. Nigel had said she would wed again, but Ena had professed herself content to go with Arabella

to Woolford instead. It had been so long ago that it
had been easy to forget that Ena had been born daughter to a landless knight.

For a moment the woman's eyes misted, then she
seemed to recover. But her mouth twisted hideously
as she whispered, "I canna remember much of
Thomas now—'twas so lang ago."

"Ena . . ."

"Nay." She dabbed self-consciously at her eyes, and
tried to smile. " 'Twas nae his fault he left me to
wither, was it?"

"Of course not," Arabella consoled her gently.
"Ena, would you that I asked William to find another
husband for you?"

"Nay."

"How many years have you?" Arabella asked suddenly. "I have forgotten, but you cannot be so very
old."

"Five and thirty, my lady—'tis ten years more than
ye."

"You are yet young enough to breed, and you
wanted."

The woman colored, then shook her head. "I
couldna bring him anything." She gathered up the
wineskin and the spices and moved to put them away,
avoiding further comment. "And ye hae need of me,
ye can waken me," she said from behind the cupboard
door.

"Let me ask William."

"Nay."

Arabella looked to where Jamie slept on the pallet
near the fire. William had said only that he could sleep
with Ena, after all, and he'd be vexed enough if he
returned to find the boy there. "I'd have you pallet
here until my husband returns," she decided. "And
the news is not good, I'd have you with me."

"Let the wine ease ye, fer he'll come back wi'out
a hair harmed."

"I would that I knew it."

"God aids the Scots in this."

Later, as she lay within the great curtained bed, Arabella still could not sleep. She wished she shared the blind faith of the others, but she did not. She wished she could be as Jamie, who had been as insistent as Ena, saying the men of Blackleith would return to a man, for were they not Scots? Aye, for who could stand against William of Dunashie? he had demanded, thinking she disputed it.

She was alone with naught but her thought for company now, listening to the noises of a keep nearly silenced by night. Across the room, on a pallet pulled close to the brazier fire, Ena lay beside Jamie. She had begun to snore, but the boy made no sound. For a moment Arabella was tempted to rise and look on him, but then she decided he was safe enough. Sweet Mary, it had been difficult enough to get him to bed, for he too had wanted to stay awake for the return of the men. Nay, she'd not risk waking him now.

The night crept slowly, as though the sands must have clogged the glass, and still there was no word. She stared upward into the darkness of the closed hangings, asking herself what she'd do if he did not come home. Without a child to inherit of him she'd be returned to Byrum, something that did not bear thinking. Again she'd be a widow in her father's house, again she and Jamie would be at Nigel's mercy. Nay, she could not bear it.

For all that she could fault William where Jamie was concerned, he'd proven far kinder to her than she'd expected. In another week 'twould be two months since they'd wed, and not once had he beaten her. And she could not deny there had been times she'd angered him greatly.

He was a strange man, her William. When she'd first heard of him she knew him only as the Butcher's bastard brother, and like so many others she'd heard of the blood they'd let at Dunashie. And when she'd first seen him she'd been so very afraid of him. Sweet Mary, but all she could think of was his size. She remembered how she'd hoped he would find her unpleasing, but he had not.

She smiled in the darkness, hearing again the words he'd spoken of and to her: *Aye, she is comely. And she is willing, I am satisfied. But I'd hear it of her: What say ye, mistress—would ye have me also? I'd take none as would nae have me.* It had actually mattered to him what she wanted, what she thought of him. Unlike Elias, he wanted her willing.

Ye think me naught but an uncouth lout, don't ye? Aye, she had, but 'twas before she knew he could speak as a Norman also, 'twas before she knew he could read more than his name. *I'd have naught but truth between us.* Nigel would have beaten her senseless had she spoken the truth. And yet for all that she'd feared him, there had been a certain fascination also. She could still remember the almost diffident way he'd asked to kiss her. *And I swear I'll nae touch ye wrongly. . . .* 'Twas the first of many, each better than the last.

Her body went hot with remembered passion. For all that he'd been awkward at first, he'd taught her the pleasure of coupling that Elias had denied her. Now the very body that had once frightened her enticed her, drawing forth such a wanton hunger that the memory of it made her blush. Once she'd lain in his arms only in the hope that his pleasure in her would buy her son tolerance. Now she lay with him for herself.

When he lay over her she still marveled at the size, the physical strength, the power of him. But he was more than some great brute, for he was also possessed of a certain gentleness she'd not expected, a love of God that made him say his prayers ere he retired.

And she would that those prayers aided him now, wherever he was, for if he did not come back to her she did not think she could bear it. Nay, she'd not lie abed thinking such thoughts. She'd force her attention to Jamie, for he troubled her also. She had to think of how she could aid her son. She had to think how she could ease his lot.

But every thought that came to mind strayed back

to her husband. Jamie's fate no less than hers was
tied to William. Her happiness was tied to William.
Her life was tied to William. And if William did not
return . . .

She could stand it no longer. Rolling from the
warmth of her feather bed, she groped for her gown
and pulled it over her head. Jesu, but 'twas cold, and
he was out there somewhere, his body encased in icy
steel. 'Twould be a wonder if he did not sicken.

Drawing close to the warmth of the waning fire, she
managed to light the cresset lamp and place it on the
low table. The small flame floated, illuminating the oil
beneath it. Taking out the scraps of parchment Father
Edmund had given her, she laid them beside the lamp
and bent her head low to study them.

*Arabella, born at Byrum, on the tenth of May, in
the year of Our Lord eleven hundred and thirteen. Arabella of Byrum.* A—R—A—B—E—L—L—A. The
next time she witnessed something, she would write
more than her mark. And one day she would read the
prayers with William. Already she could compare the
written letters with the memorized words of the Pater
Noster.

On the other side of the fire Ena paused in her
snoring, to sigh heavily in her sleep. Then she turned
over, so that her back was to the dim, flickering light,
her body curled around Jamie. Satisfied that she'd not
wakened them, Arabella returned her attention to the
papers.

She could write her name. She could write Jamie's.
On impulse, she dug into her basket for her sharpened
quill and her pot of ink. Opening the pot and setting
it next to the lamp bowl, she dipped her pen and la-
boriously wrote a G, then a U and an I, followed
slowly by L—L—A—U—M—E. *Guillaume.* William.
Did he spell it that way? she wondered. Nay, even if
he did he wrote it better than that, for her letters were
crooked and uneven. Someday, when she had learned
to read and write better, she'd be able to send mes-

sages to him when he was away from Blackleith. And
he would write her also, for she could read.

The wind howled, jarring the shutters and bending
the flame that floated on the lamp. Arabella's fingers
were so stiff from the cold that her letters grew worse,
looking as poor as Jamie's grudging efforts. Reluctantly, she put away her lessons and her ink and rose
to stretch tired shoulders. Nay, she had to sleep.

Without William to make a warm place for her,
'twould be cold there again. Shivering, she blew out
the lamp and sought her bed again. Without undressing in the chilly air, she rolled into the rope-hung bed,
slipping between the feather mattresses and closing the
curtains, then pulled her pillow over her head to blot
out the noise of the wind. Finally she drifted into a
dream-tossed netherworld, where Jamie wept and William came to her.

"My lady . . ." Ena's voice seemed to float from a
distance.

"Nay, let her sleep."

"My lord, ye are wounded," the woman protested.

Arabella came awake with a start, uncertain whether
she'd heard him or whether she'd but dreamed it. But
between the gap in the draft-blown bed curtains she
could see the faint light of a lamp. *Wounded?*

"William . . ?" she asked tentatively, thrusting her
head out.

"Aye. Stay abed, for 'tis too cold for you until the
fire is rekindled."

He might as well have spoken to the wind, for her
feet hit the floor on the instant. Her eyes sought his
face eagerly, then moved over him, seeking reassurance that he was whole. They stopped when she saw
the blood on his tunic and the rent in his mail. Her
face paled in the flickering orange light.

"Sweet Jesu—nay!"

" 'Tis but the arm—'twill heal."

"Ena, fetch the basin and heat some water."

"Nay—I am all right."

But she was already working the torn mail from

above his wound, trying to see how bad it was. "Sit you down that I may soak the cloth away," she muttered. " 'Tis stuck to the blood."

"I am too tired," he protested. "In the morning—"

" 'Tis overlate to stitch even now," she insisted, pushing him toward the bench.

"God's bones, but I'd seek my bed."

"After." She began unlacing his overtunic, loosening it at the neck. "Ena, the cold first, else we'll not get this off him."

The woman finished pouring water into a pot, then brought a small basin and ewer to Arabella. Peering over her mistress's shoulder, she offered, "And ye want, I'd get Ewan to aid in undressing him."

"Ewan is as tired as I am," he muttered.

Arabella rolled a cloth and soaked it in the water, then pressed it against his arm, squeezing the liquid into the stiffened sleeve. Rubbing gently, she tried to loosen the blood-soaked wool from the wound, all the while taking care not to cut him with the jagged edges of his torn hauberk. He leaned forward until his head pressed against her breasts.

"How had you this?" she wondered aloud.

"I dinna remember taking the blow," he murmured, circling her waist with his other arm. " 'Twas a sword cut, I think."

"Thanks be to God that it wasn't an axe."

"Aye."

"I cannot get it loose without making it bleed."

"Leave it then."

"Nay. I need to see it."

He was tired unto death, and so cold that he did not think he ever could be warmed. "Then whilst she heats the water, I'd have her mull wine also." His arm tightened, bracing his body against hers as she pulled the woolen tunic sleeve out of the gash. "Jesu," he muttered.

"Would you that it healed with lint in it?" she countered.

"Nay." He closed his eyes, savoring the warmth of

her body, the smell of her rosewater. " 'Twas worth the blow," he mumbled against her chest. "They'll nae raid again this way."

"You caught them?"

"Aye, and punished them also." Despite the pain in his arm, he felt comforted by the softness of her breasts and the gentleness of her touch. "And Kenneth dies, I will hang one more for it."

"And he does not take a fever, he will live." Turning to where Ena poured honey into a cup for him, she said, "I'd have you aid me in getting him undressed."

"The wine . . ." he protested thickly. "I'd hae the wine before."

The poker hissed, and, immediately the air smelled of hot metal and spices. When Ena carried the cup to him he took it and drank deeply, letting the liquid warm his stomach. Twisting his head, he wiped his mouth on his torn sleeve, then drew a deep breath. Letting it out, he settled his shoulders in resignation.

"I am ready."

Between them Arabella and her tiring woman managed to strip the tunic, coif, hauberk, cuir bouilli, and gambeson from him, baring him to the waist. As Arabella pulled off the padded garment he weaved slightly, then caught the bench, hanging on. The ugly gash on his upper left arm exposed the raw muscle beneath. For a moment she fought the gorge that rose in her throat, then she swallowed it.

" 'Twill have to be stitched, my lord—'tis too deep." She looked again. "Holy Mary, but I know not how you can use the arm."

"It pains me now," he admitted.

She washed the wound again, this time with the heated water, then sprinkled basilicum to dry it where it still oozed. Taking her needle, she threaded it with silk and looked to Ena.

"I'd have you hold it together for me."

"Aye."

He winced visibly as she stuck his flesh with the

needle, drew the thread through his skin, and tightened it across the gap, drawing the edges close. She hesitated briefly.

"Nay, finish the task," he muttered through clenched teeth.

"I'd not hurt you."

"There is nae help for it—go on."

She worked quickly, taking stitches, closing the wound as his hands gripped the bench at either side. Every now and then she glanced at his profile, seeing the tightness of his jaw. His eyes were closed, the lids purple above deeply shadowed circles, and his hair, where it fell forward over his brow, was dark against his skin. When she'd knotted the thread at the end he exhaled, visibly relieved.

"Would you that I got you something to eat?"

"Nay." He leaned forward again, this time sliding both arms about her waist, resting his head against her chest. "So tired, Bella."

She held him tightly, then rubbed the thick, disordered hair, running her fingers through it. "I was afraid," she admitted, her voice low.

"I told ye: I dinna die easily," he murmured against her breast. "If anything, I feel the fool for taking the cut." Abruptly he released her and lurched to his feet. "Got to get into the bed now, else I'll nae get there."

He nearly stumbled over the pallet by the fire, waking Jamie. As the boy sat up Arabella caught her breath, for while he'd said her son could sleep with Ena he'd not meant here. For a moment the child stared upward, his eyes wide, then he wanted to know, "Did ye get them? Did ye kill them all?"

"Aye and nay." As tired as he was, Will managed a smile. "Ask me of it on the morrow, and I'll gie ye the dagger I brought ye."

"Ye brought me a dagger?" He rubbed the sleep from his eyes, as though he feared he dreamed. "An *English* dagger?"

"Aye."

"I'd see it! I'd see it now! And—"

"On the morrow, Jamie," Arabella cut in sternly. Turning to Ena, she told her, "I'd have you take him down to pallet below."

"Mama!"

"And he is quiet, he can stay," William murmured, moving toward the bed. "Peace—'tis all I'd ask this night."

He lay down, heedless of his chausses or his boots, and rolled over to face the back bed hangings. She struggled to pull off the boots, then eased the covers from beneath his heavy body. As Ena blew out the lamp Arabella crawled into bed behind him, drew the top mattress over them, and held him. When he said nothing, she feared he was angered over Jamie.

"My lord, I brought Ena here because I was afraid for you," she whispered against his back.

There was no answer. He slept.

For a long time she lay there, warming his cold body gratefully, listening to the even rhythm of his breathing. Finally, when her arm had grown numb from lying on it, she turned over, backing her body against his. Across the room she heard her son murmur sleepily, "At first light, I want to see my dagger. I canna wait, Ena."

For the first time in his young life, he fought sleep not because of the terror of his dreams but rather because he was too excited. And if she lived to be an old woman, she'd never forget the overwhelming love she felt for her husband just now.

Chapter Twenty-Five

His arm ached insistently, his head swam with the numbers before him, and Kenneth of Burwell had taken a fever during the night, making it possible that he'd have to hang another English prisoner. He could ill afford the loss of the ransom that would cost him. Not to mention that in the two days since he'd given James the dagger, Arabella had hinted yet again that the boy wished to go to Dunashie with them. It had taken a scowl from him to deter her, and God knew he did not want to rule her like that. He wanted her to do what he wanted her to do without questioning him, for far too often his answers shamed him. But he could not take the boy to Dunashie.

"My lord, I would speak with you."

William looked up from his accounts to see Ewan standing diffidently before him, and he felt a sense of foreboding. Whenever the older man approached him thus, it usually concerned the boy. For a moment his resentment rose: He'd given James a horse and a dagger, and now there seemed no end to what was expected of him. "Aye?" he answered warily.

That William was not in the best of humors did not

escape Ewan, but he mistook the reason for it. "How fares the arm?" he asked.

"But sore." Sighing, Will pushed his tally sticks aside and gestured to the bench opposite. "Sit you down and speak your mind."

Ewan dropped down to face him. " 'Tis about the boy," he admitted, confirming Will's suspicion. "I'd hae ye speak with him." When the lord was silent, he blurted out, " 'Tis the lessons—he'd nae learn them."

"He hasna the choice!" Will retorted. "God's bones, but you would bring this to me? Speak to his mother—aye, or to the priest."

"Father Edmund has little liking for him."

"What matters that? There wasna any love between Henry's clerks and me, but I learned what they taught me."

Ewan nodded. "Aye, but he fears to learn."

"Fears?" Will scoffed. "Jesu! 'Tis laziness, more like! Art grown saft like the rest, Ewan? I dinna give him over to ye that ye would coddle him, ye know. God's bones, but 'tis enough of that he's had already!"

"And ye asked it, he'd do it," the older man persisted. "And yer lady asks, he can see no reason." He lifted troubled eyes to William. "For all that he loves her, he'd nae be as helpless as she would hae him."

"I'd nae believe it," Will countered. "Whene'er mine back is turned, he is with her. He is like the vine against her wall. Jesu, but art as blind as she, Ewan."

"My lord . . ."

"Nay," William dismissed him. " 'Tis enough that I have said he will learn. Tell him I give Father Edmund the right to chastise him and he doesna do it."

The grizzled man rose to leave, then hesitated as though he sought the means to appeal. Finally, he shook his greying head tiredly. "Ye canna visit the sins of the mother on the boy, my lord. 'Tisna right."

William reddened, then lost his temper. "Afore God, but you take overmuch on yourself, Sir Ewan! 'Tisna your place to dispute with me!"

"Afore God, ye forget whence ye are come also," Ewan retorted, stung.

" 'Tisna your place to remind me of it!" Will shouted. "And ye would serve me, ye'll hold your tongue!" He lurched to his feet angrily. "Aye, and I'd nae hear ye speak of my lady either!"

" 'Twas of the boy I'd speak."

"And I told ye I'd nae hear it! Between ye and her, 'tis nigh to all I have heard since I wed!"

The man flinched before William's anger, but he held his ground. Looking up, he tried to speak more calmly, declaring, "I dinna think ye'd be one as could fault a boy fer his birth, my lord."

For a long moment Will stared hard at his liege man, and his jaw worked as he sought control of his temper. "I'd hae ye leave me ere I say what I would not," he said finally, keeping his voice even. "Too long we hae served together, else I'd not brook this."

"Art grown so high, Will o' Dunashie, that ye fer-get what we all were to each other?" As William's face darkened again, Ewan turned to leave. "High or low, ye answer to the same Father in Heaven, ye know. Aye, and if ye'd hae me leave yer service, I'd go back to Lord Giles at Dunashie."

Will had no answer for that. As the door closed after the man who'd served Giles loyally for eleven years and more, he turned again to the tally sticks on the table. Ewan had not the right to chide him, he decided resentfully. And he had not the right to remind him of Arabella's sin. God's bones, but did they *all* speak of it behind his back? Was he pitied for taking her? Did they count him a fool for it?

Resolutely, he sat down and began again the task of reconciling the rents with the expenses. 2d—pure wax candles for the chapel. 5s. 6d—a dozen tuns of clear wine. 3d—two barrels of pickled lampreys. His eyes scanned the page carefully until he came to an entry that made his blood rise. 3d—fine blue camlet for James of Woolford's shert. Jesu, but did she never tire of buying things for the boy? What was wrong with plain Scottish wool—or unbleached muslin, for that matter?

His arm pained him, making him unreasonably cross, and he knew it. And Ewan's words still stung. *Ye canna visit the sins of the mother on the boy. . . . Afore God, but ye forget whence ye are come also. . . . Ye canna visit the sins of the mother on the boy. . . . High or low, ye answer to the same Father in Heaven. . . .* It was as though Ewan's words beat like a musician's castanets in his ears.

'Twas unworthy of his liege man to say it, for had he not taken the boy when he did not have to? Had he not provided for James of Woolford far better than King Henry had provided for himself and Giles? Had he begrudged what Arabella had spent on her bastard? He'd given the boy the pony, hadn't he? Aye, and he'd brought him an enamel-handled dagger that Nib had admired, hadn't he?

For a brief, fleeting moment, he recalled the small boy's pleasure as his thin, pale hands had lovingly traced the design on the hilt. He would, he'd told William proudly, use it to kill an Englishman someday. As though he would ever fight anyone . . . And yet as Will remembered the shining in the boy's pale eyes, he felt anew the satisfaction of giving it.

It had reminded him at the time of a distant year, a year when he and Giles had been at King Henry's court. It had been the last day of Christmas then, and he'd sneaked from beneath the watchful eye of Henry's clerks to toss dice with the sons of wealthy lords. He'd won a jeweled belt then, and as it was too small for himself he'd given it to Giles. The look on his brother's face had been much the same as that on Jamie's. Giles had worn that belt, paying to have it lengthened each year until it had literally disintegrated, and once he was lord to Dunashie he'd had the jewels pried from it and set in another.

High or low, ye answer to the same Father in Heaven. Ye canna visit the sins of the mother on the boy. Jesu, but how was he supposed to help it? He was not a saint. Yet even as he asked, he remembered his earlier Christmas prayer. St. Joseph had been asked to do far more.

Abruptly he rose, scattering the tally sticks and the account sheets. If he would not speak to James of it, he'd speak to the priest. For all that he was overyoung, mayhap Father Edmund would provide guidance in the matter. Clasping his throbbing arm to ease it, William started for the chapel.

"My lord."

He spun around to face a grave Ewan, and he felt the sting of the man's words anew. Yet there was no rancor in the blue eyes now. Briefly Will wondered if he'd come to say he was leaving to Dunashie, but Ewan cleared his throat and spat ere he spoke.

" 'Tis yer pardon I'd ask, my lord. I know it isna in ye to be unkind, and I shouldna hae spoken so."

He could have accepted the older man's harsh words more easily than this, for they'd been justified. Yet, oddly, it was the apology that shamed him more. " 'Tis forgotten," he answered brusquely.

"I did but think that ye'd be able to make him do it, ye know. For all that ye scarce note him, he holds ye in regard."

Scarce noted him? God's bones, but it seemed 'twas all he noted. For a moment William's resentment seethed anew, then he forced it from his mind. "I'll speak to Father Edmund on the matter," he promised.

"He doesna like the boy," Ewan insisted. "He'll say he canna learn, when 'tis that he doesna want to. But if ye were to—"

"I'd speak to the priest first."

"Aye." The older man shifted his weight on his feet, then added, "Nib can tell ye the boy can ride unaided."

"What good does that do? He canna mount unaided."

"Nay." Ewan spat again on the stones below, then looked at the cloudy sky above. "My sire learned to walk without his leg, ye know."

"Your sire walked ere he lost it," Will reminded him. "And you speak of the boy, his leg is too short and the foot willna hold him. You see how 'tis for him."

"Aye." Despite the clouds, Ewan squinted at the sky where the sun was trying to break through. "But if the leg wasna overshort, and if the foot dinna turn o'er, mayhap . . ." His voice trailed off, as though he realized the impossibility of the thought.

"You would ask God's miracle, Ewan, for all that I have prayed in my life, never have I witnessed one."

"Aye," the older man sighed. "Still, it doesna seem right that he'll nae walk in this life, does it?"

" 'Tis God's will."

"And we believed that we'd nae ask fer anything, would we?" Ewan exhaled heavily again, then started away. " 'Tis a pity, it is. My sire learned to walk with two stout poles to hold him."

For a long moment William stared after him. Nay, but Arabella's son could not do it, he decided. Unlike Ewan's father the boy had not walked before, and he lacked the proper strength in his good leg. And he was too frail to support his body on two poles.

He found both the chapel and the priest's room behind it deserted. It was, he supposed, the difference between the young and the old, but he still considered it odd that Edmund of Alton spent so little time on his knees. For all that William had seen of the man, 'twould appear that he himself prayed more often than his priest. Not that Edmund had not gained a measure of popularity in the short time he'd been there. God only knew of any other who could sing his way through the liturgy any more quickly than he, nor was there any more eloquent at Blackleith when it came to his short homilies. The sand was scarce gone from the hourglass ere he was done: prayers, homily, Eucharist, and all.

'Twas what ailed the Church: There was naught else for bastards and younger sons. They learned either to read their prayers or to fight other men's wars, and for

many the choice was no choice at all. In the matter of
Edmund, Will had not a doubt that he lacked the stomach of a mercenary. And thus Holy Church was served
by yet another cleric of doubtful piety. But at least the
man was literate, and that was something, Will supposed.

As he surveyed Edmund's small room it struck him
that it bore none of the symbols of God's calling. There
was not even a crucifix above the narrow cot. The
small table held naught but a spiked tallow candle and
the floor was swept bare, giving an impression that
none lived there at all.

"You seek me, my lord?"

William spun around at the sound of the priest's
voice, to find him standing in the doorway. "Aye."
He gestured to the sparsely furnished room. Perceiving a certain contempt in the man's gaze, he forced
himself to speak properly. "You do not seem to require overmuch. 'Tis clean for a man."

Walter smiled briefly, but his eyes were cold. "The
monks taught me cleanliness at Kelso."

"And yet you did not stay there. You chose the life
of priest over that of a monk." Will's gaze moved
over the bare walls. "You have not even a Cross here."

"I moved it outside, hanging it above the chapel
door, my lord." Again there was that faint smile that
did not warm his eyes. "I do not need it to remind
me of my purpose here." He moved closer to face
Will. "But you did not come to inspect my humble
room, surely?"

"I am come to discuss James of Woolford, Father.
I'd know how he does."

"Poorly. He has not the mind for it." Walter's lip
curled disdainfully. " 'Tis a waste that I make him
try."

There was that in the priest's tone that William did
not like, and for all that he himself did not love the
boy he felt the need to defend Arabella's son. "Is it
that he cannot—or that he will not?" he asked bluntly.

"I think his brain as weak as his legs, if you would have the truth of it."

"It has not been long—mayhap 'twill take him time to learn. As I recall from mine own lessons, there were those who read as though they were born to it, while others mastered the task slowly."

"And which were you?" Walter asked.

"At first it came slowly, but then I did not want to learn at all, Father. In the end I mastered the work, for I'd not have it said that one who was five years younger could do it better than I."

"The Butcher?"

"I'd not have him called thus," William said coldly. "Giles of Moray does not deserve the name men give him."

"He burned Hamon of Blackleith's keep—e'en at Kelso we heard the tale. 'Tis said he is damned for it."

"Dunashie was not Hamon's—'twas Giles' patrimony that Hamon stole!" Will retorted angrily. "And you would have the truth of the tale ask me, ere you judge what you do not know."

Knowing that they would not serve his purpose, Walter bit back bitter words. His eyes flashed momentarily, then the veil lowered over them once more. He shrugged expressively. "Your loyalty to your brother is commendable, my lord, and I'd not dispute what you say, for I know not of him but by repute."

"Aye." William drew in a deep breath, then exhaled slowly. "But we spoke of the boy," he reminded Walter. " 'Tis early to determine that he cannot learn, and I'd have you attempt the matter still. Mayhap it is that he does not practice what you give him. Learning to read is like fighting the quintains, Father: And you do not do it enough, you cannot do it well."

"I have no great hope for him," Walter muttered. "I see no use to the boy at all."

"Whether we know of it or no, God made him for

a purpose," Will growled. "He doesna make mistakes."

"Then how is it He makes a lame boy who will never walk? How is it He makes one who can scarce drag his body through the filthy rushes on the floor? Nay, but there is no purpose to James of Woolford, my lord."

"Ye canna know that, Father—'tis not up to man to question God's will."

"And there is a purpose to James of Woolford, I have not seen it," Walter declared flatly. " 'Tis a waste to teach him what he would not know."

Will regarded his priest intently, and saw the arrogance in the handsome face. It offended him deeply. "You have not the love nor the humility required for your calling, Father," he said finally. "I see naught of the Savior in you."

Walter's expression never changed. "And I see no love for the boy in you, my lord," he countered. "Ere you would accuse me, you would do better to look within yourself."

"Were it not for your calling, Edmund of Alton, I'd dispute with you most heartily, but for all that I fault you I'd still respect the cassock you wear."

Will left his priest, feeling more out of sorts than when he'd found him, for in his eyes Father Edmund's was the greater sin. After all, a priest promised to love all, serve God, and practice humility in His name, did he not? He had half a mind to write the abbot at Kelso, asking what they taught novices these days. When he looked back, Father Edmund was already returning to the warmth of the hall.

William started back to his accounts, but halfway across the yard he stopped. If Jamie was not with Ewan and not at his lesson, then he must be with Arabella, or with Ena. And as he had no hope of Father Edmund's assistance in the matter, he supposed it fell to him to tax the boy about his unwillingness to learn. It was not something he relished, for he could expect that Arabella would come to her son's defense like a wolf over its cub. But he'd told Ewan he'd do it. May-hap 'twas that he was too new to this also, but there were times when he wondered if 'twas he who ruled his men or they who ruled him.

He climbed the steps to the solar slowly, considering what he ought to say to the boy, but each thing that came to mind he discarded as useless for one who could not even walk. What good did it do to tell young James that a man needed to know his letters and his sums, that he would not be cheated in his house? There was no hope that the boy would rule anything. And what good did it do to say that he ought to learn them that he could serve God? 'Twas equally as ludicrous to think James of Woolford would be ordained. But if the child had no hope, there was no reason for anything.

When he opened the door, Arabella jumped up from the pallet where she played at draughts with Jamie, and for a moment it looked to him as though she sought to shield the boy, moving between them. "Father Edmund finished early," she offered lamely.

"I said James could come here after his lessons," Will muttered, angered that she still could fear him.

Arabella turned quickly and motioned to the woman who sewed by the fire. "Ena . . ."

"Nay. I came to see the boy."

Her eyes widened. "Is aught wrong, my lord?"

"I dinna come to beat him, if 'tis what ye ask."

"Nay, I—"

"And I'd have ye leave us that I may speak to him."

"But . . . my lord, he has done nothing, I swear."

"Did I accuse the boy of anything? God's bones, Bella, but 'tis between him and me!" When she made no move to leave, he walked past her to where the child sat on the pallet. "Well, James, as she willna leave us alone, we'll go elsewhere ourselves."

"But what has he done?" Her voice rose as he leaned to pick up Jamie. "My lord, he is blameless!"

"If being coddled were a sin, he'd rot in hell, Bella!" William snapped.

Jamie twisted in his arms almost frantically, leaning as far as he dared. "Mine dagger! I dropped mine dagger ye brought me!"

Ena looked up, her expression bland despite her mistress's distress. "He willna sleep without it, my lord."

" 'Tis not to bed that I take him," Will growled. Nonetheless he stooped low enough for the boy to retrieve the precious knife. As he straightened, his eyes met Arabella's. "I will bring him back when I am done."

"Can you not speak before me?"

"I told ye: 'Tis between him and me."

She had no choice but to stand aside. Telling herself that he'd not harmed her son in six weeks and more, she forced a smile. "And 'tis outside you take him, I'd have you wrap his cloak about him, my lord."

"And ye'd leave us in peace, I'd not take him outside," he retorted. "Nay, he doesna need it."

But as they emerged into the yard and the chill air hit them, the boy turned into Will's shoulder, hugging him for warmth. "I showed it to Black Jock in the scullery, ye know, and he offered me a fat capon for it!"

For a moment William did not follow him, then he realized the boy still spoke of the knife. "Och, he did, did he? And what did ye tell him?"

"I told him the capon wasna his to give—'twas yers. They all want it, ye know." His arm tightened about the big man's neck. "Did ye kill the one as had it?"

"Aye."

"I would that I could hae seen it. I would that I'd been there."

" 'Tisna a sport like Hoodman Blind, ye know."

"But I'd hae seen ye punish 'em fer what they did to Burwell—I would!"

"Nay, ye wouldna like it—'tis a bloody business." He felt the child shiver against him, and instinctively he closed his great arms about the small body, sheltering it against the wind. "Ye kill to protect yerself,

then ye pray for them ye killed—there isna any sense
to it, Jamie.''

"But they raided into Scotland!''

"Aye, and 'tis why ye go after them, else they'd
come again and again,'' Will conceded. "But it doesna
mean ye like it.''

"I'd like it,'' Jamie declared positively. "I know
it.''

On impulse Will carried the boy to the chapel,
thinking to set him upon the altar rail where he could
look at him as he spoke. It was, he reflected dryly as
he pushed the door open, a place where they were
nearly certain to be alone. But when he got inside and
had Jamie perched before him he hesitated, seeking
the words. To the side of them candles glowed, lighting the feet of the Virgin. He cleared his throat to
speak as he knew he ought.

"Ewan says you do not attend your lessons,'' he
said finally. " 'Tis not what I'd hear, James. Two silver shillings I have paid Father Edmund that you may
learn, and I do not mean for you to waste them.''

As Will held him on the altar rail, Jamie looked
downward to avoid his eyes. "I dinna want to learn
it,'' he mumbled low.

"I'd not hear this either. And you *could* not learn
I'd accept it, but if you *will* not, 'tis another matter.
Look at me. And I think 'tis that you do not try, I will
ask Father Edmund to apply the rod to your backside,
James.''

"I have no wish to be a priest! I dinna want to learn
it!''

" 'Tis a godly calling, and I'd not disparage it. Besides, 'tis not a priest I'd ask of you: There are clerks,
and—''

"I'd nae be a clerk neither!'' The boy's eyes swam,
and his chin trembled as he lifted his head to face
Will. "I'd not!''

"Jesu, James! Ye've got to be what ye can be! God's
bones, but ye—'' He caught himself and flushed guilt-

ily. "Nay, James," he said more kindly, "but ye've got to consider that—"

"Nay! And I must sit and cipher forever, I'd as lief die!" Jamie cried vehemently. "I canna stand it! I canna!"

This was not what Will had intended, and now there was no easy way to achieve what he'd attempted. As the boy sobbed before him, he groped for words of comfort. "Och, James, but ye mustn't cry over that which ye canna help," he said gently. "God made the lion and he made the sparrow, each for a purpose."

"I don't want to be a broken sparrow! I tire of what I am!" His small bosom heaved as he choked back his tears. "Ye canna know how 'tis—I'd not hear what is said of me! I'd not hear the devil made me—I'd not! And I'd not hear Wee Tom nor the others laugh because I canna walk! I would I had died ere I was borned!" Before Will could stop it he had slipped from the altar rail and lay in a sobbing heap at Will's feet. "I know not why God cursed me!"

The big man reached down, pulling him up to half-stand before him. " 'Tis enough, James! Pity yourself and ye are pitied—d'ye hear me?" But even as he said the words, they rang hollow in his own ears. Still he forced himself to go on, speaking harshly: "Think ye are the only one who counts himself a freak, James of Woolford? Look up at me, and see one as has been laughed at since he was twelve! D'ye know what they called me at King Henry's court? A great fool! The 'Scots ox'! Ye behold one who was as big then as I am now, James! There wasna a maid as looked and did not laugh at the sight of me!"

" 'Tisna the same! Ye could walk!"

"A freak is a freak!" He lifted the boy higher, holding him until their eyes were level. "Look down, James of Woolford: 'Tis a long way to the ground!"

For an awful moment the little boy thought he meant to push him, but then William pulled him close and spoke again more gently. "A freak is one who thinks he is. A man is one who learns to use what God gave

him, that he prospers.'' His hand smoothed the pale
hair against the small head. ''Be what ye can be,
James—'tis all any has the right to ask of ye. 'Tis all
your mother or I would ask of ye.'' Will half turned
his body so that they faced the statue of Mary. ''When
ye think ye canna stand it, pray for acceptance, and
God willing, 'twill come to ye.''

''I'd pray for two stout legs.''

''Nay—'tisna how 'tis done. For years I prayed that
I would grow no more, but I dinna stop until 'twas too
late. 'Twas then that I realized these overlarge arms
could swing an axe.'' When he perceived that the boy
was about to cry again, William ruffled his hair. ''Och,
nae more of that—if God dinna give ye legs, he gave
ye a mind to make up for it.''

The child stared at the Virgin Mary, then shook his
head. ''Ye canna ken, can ye?'' he asked, his voice
breaking. ''Ye canna ken.''

''All right, then—aside from the legs, what would
you have? A good mind is a treasure also, Jamie.''

''I dinna want a good mind, neither!'' The child
swallowed, then raised his eyes to William. ''And God
answered my prayers I'd be as ye, my lord: I'd be a
knight like ye,'' he choked out. ''I'd be as ye are!''

The boy's words hung in the air between them,
shaming Will with the implied admiration. He fell silent, for anything more he might say would not serve.
His own eyes burned, and he ached from his throat to
his breastbone for the child's pain. He had no answer,
nothing to offer that could ease James of Woolford this
day. Instead he held the little boy so close that he could
feel his heartbeat, and he was reminded of the fact that
James was a living, breathing creature with the same
hopes and aspirations as any other. The only difference was that he had not the body to live his dreams.

Whether it was the wind against the metal roof, or
whether 'twas his own conscience speaking, Will heard
it clearly, a voice to his soul: *'Tis to you he looks,
William of Dunashie. 'Tis from you he'd learn.* And

he heard himself ask of it: *What would you that I did for him?*

Above him the wind grew stronger, the cross-rafters groaned, and the shutters banged against the wooden sills. Before him the ever-present candles flickered, then went out—except for one. Its flame bent in the draft until it lay nearly over, then as the wind eased it stood alone again. 'Twas the tallest of the candles.

And again he heard the voice speak to him alone: *'Tis to you he looks, William of Dunashie. 'Tis from you he'd learn.* He knew not whence it came, but he knew 'twas not his own. And he knew not what it would have him answer.

It was then that he realized the boy also spoke to him, his small voice contrite. "I dinna mean to anger ye, my lord—I dinna. And ye will it, I will try to learn. And ye'd let me, I'd please ye."

William set him again upon the altar rail and looked into his pale, pinched face, meeting the solemn gaze of his eyes that seemed too large for their setting. " 'Tis a bargain I'd make wi' ye, Jamie of Woolford," he heard himself say.

"Aye."

"Nay, hear me before ye answer, for 'tis not an easy thing I'd ask of ye." Will hesitated, looking upward to the statue of the Blessed Virgin, then back to the boy. "And ye learn your letters of the priest, I'd see ye taught the other also."

Hope flared briefly in the boy's eyes, then reality reasserted itself. "Nay, I canna," he whispered, looking down. "I canna even walk."

"And I canna know if ye can until ye try, but I am willing to aid ye in the trying, Jamie. When I am back from Dunashie, I am willing to take ye to Edinburgh to see the king's physicians."

"They canna heal me!"

" 'Tis for them to tell us. And they canna, then we'll have to try for ourselves, ye know." Seeing that the child regarded him gravely now, he went on,

"Ewan's father walked on one leg, James. But it willna be an easy thing to do."

"I'd gie mine arm for a leg, my lord."

"And how would ye wield a sword then?" William countered. "Nay, but ye'll use what ye are given. Where's the dagger?"

"Here."

"I'd hae it—just for now." Reluctantly, the boy pulled it from his belt and handed it to Will. For a moment William weighed it in his hand, then he held it up before the boy by the tip of the pointed blade so that it formed a cross. "James of Woolford, and ye are willing to suffer for it, I swear ye'll walk unaided. 'Tis a promise I make ye at peril to mine soul, and I do not keep it. D'ye ken me?"

"Aye."

"And I'd nae have your mother know of it, for she'll but say ye canna do it—d'ye ken that also?"

"Aye."

"Now—there's two things as I'd have ye swear to me, James."

"I will."

"Ye'd best discover what they are first, ye know," Will observed dryly. "Never promise that which ye willna keep. God forgives what ye canna, but not what ye willna, I think."

"Aye."

"First, I'd have ye learn your lessons that your mother may be proud of ye." He paused, waiting for the import of what he'd asked to sink in, then he added, "And in the second case, I'd have ye promise to do all the physicians or Ewan or I ask of ye, e'en when it pains ye."

"Aye."

William held up the knife again. "Then swear it."

The boy swallowed, then took a deep breath. As William held the tip, Jamie placed his fingers on the hilt and said haltingly, "I, James, borned at Woolford, swear I will learn mine letters . . . and that I will learn to walk."

"Nay—that ye will *try* to learn to walk."

But the boy shook his head. "I swear it." His pale eyes met Will's steadily. "And I'll nae tell Mama until I can do it."

Later, after William had returned the boy to Arabella, he went again to study his tally sticks. But as the parchment lay before him, 'twas not numbers nor letters that he saw. He'd promised Arabella's son he'd make him walk—and he knew not how to do it.

For a long time he puzzled, staring at the half-empty parchment. If the twisted leg were longer . . . if it were straight . . . if the foot did not turn over . . . But none of that could be helped. The physicians could not lengthen a leg, nor was it likely they could straighten it. And even now the foot would not support the weight of a small boy.

He was almost angry with himself for having promised that which he doubted he could do, but then he remembered the voice. And very carefully he began to consider each aspect of the problem separately. Hours later, when the winter sun had lowered and William was leaving his tiny workroom in the near darkness, Arabella found him there.

"What is it that you do, that you would forget to sup, my lord?" she asked, coming up behind him. Curious, she peered over his shoulder at the parchment that lay open on the table before him. On the first half of it were columns of words with numbers after. And on the bottom he'd drawn pictures.

"Boots?" she asked, mystified. "I'd not think you'd want one like that, for you'd not be able to bend your knee in it."

"Aye." He rolled the sheepskin up and laid it aside, then put the stopper in his ink. Rising, he shrugged his shoulders to ease them. "God's bones, but the arm pains me. Is it time to sup already?"

"Nearly." She could scarce contain her excitement at the news she brought him. Finally, unable to hold her tongue any longer, she blurted out, "A messenger has come from Dunashie, William: Elizabeth of Ri-

vaux is delivered of *two* sons! And Count Guy comes
to the christening!''

"*Two* sons?'' For a moment William's expression
was blank, then his face broke into a broad grin. ''Two
sons! Aye, she's pleased o'er that, I'll warrant. Two
sons! Jesu! Did he say when?''

"But three days ago, as I count it.''

"Did he say they are named?''

"Aye." It was her turn to smile broadly. ''The elder
is Guy, and the younger she has called David, for the
king. You are to hold the king's namesake over the
font, William.''

" 'Tis not meet . . .''

"The man of Dunashie said Elizabeth of Rivaux told
him to say she'd have none other.''

"Two sons!'' He shook his head. ''And 'twas
thought she was barren! 'Tis a pity Reyner of Eury did
not live to see this. 'Twould have served him, and he
did. God's bones, but I'd write Giles, for I doubt not
he is swelled with conceit o'er this. Two sons. Sweet
Jesu.''

She came up behind him and laid a hand on his
shoulder. ''Jamie has worked his letters ever since you
brought him up to me.''

He tensed, wondering if the boy had already betrayed him. ''Och, and what makes ye think I had
anything to do with that?'' he asked her. ''Did he tell
ye?''

"Nay, but he would scarce look at them before.''
She moved behind him and rubbed between his shoul-
der blades, savoring the feel of his taut muscles.
"Mayhap 'tis that the dagger pleases him,'' she mused.

"Mayhap.''

"You make him very happy with it. I've not thanked
you for that,'' she added softly.

When he turned around to face her, there was no
mistaking the mischief in his hazel eyes. ''And ye'd
retire early, mistress, I'd let ye do it.'' His eyes swept
the tiny room, and his mouth quirked into a crooked,
almost boyish smile. ''When is it that we sup?''

She felt the now familiar excitement course through her, as her whole body went hot with anticipation. "As they set the trestles now, 'tis soon," she answered lightly.

"Och, and I'd thought to kiss ye, but . . ." His voice trailed off regretfully, but his eyes gleamed still. There was no mistaking his meaning.

"Here?" she said weakly.

He'd moved closer, and she could feel his heat also. She had to close her eyes to hide her desire. His big hand brushed at the tendrils of hair at her temple, smoothing them back, and his breath caressed her face softly as he bent his head to hers. She clasped his arms to steady herself as he kissed her deeply. His lips teased and his tongue probed, tasting of her, as his body pressed against hers. When at last he drew away, she felt disappointment until he answered.

"Aye."

"There is no bed," she said, her pulses racing.

"There is the bench," he reminded her. "Or the table. And ye choose the latter, ye can ride." His hands tugged at the laces beneath her arms, loosening them. "Or we can wait until we sup," he murmured, sliding his hands up her wide sleeves.

"The table," she decided.

His hands found her breasts as he nuzzled her ear. "And I'd only ask one son of ye, Arabella of Byrum," he whispered.

Chapter Twenty-Six

Despite her years at the English castle of Woolford, Arabella was unprepared for Dunashie. She'd expected it to be a crude shell keep, like most of the others on the border. But it was as fine a place as she'd ever seen, and she found it difficult to believe that Guy of Rivaux once had not thought it worthy of his daughter. To Arabella, it was as though she came to a palace.

The whole of Dunashie was stone, and instead of one tower Giles of Moray now had three to guard the approaches. And inside, the hall, its walls hung with red-and-black bunting, was spacious enough to hold a royal court. Every table therein was covered with red cloth in honor of Guy of Rivaux, who came to his grandsons' christening. Even the raised dais was impressive, for in the center was a single, richly carved high-backed chair wide enough for two. It was there that Giles of Moray sat beside his highborn wife to preside at table.

But of all whom Arabella saw at Dunashie, perhaps the most overwhelming was Count Guy's daughter herself. Elizabeth of Rivaux was taller than most men—some said she stood six English feet from the ground—and she was possessed of the blackest hair and the greenest eyes Arabella had ever seen. Aye, and she was so beautiful that it was difficult to believe she breathed like a mortal woman. 'Twas not a wonder that William's brother had carried her off: What man could look on Elizabeth of Rivaux and not want her?

Yet when she'd observed as much to William he'd merely grinned, saying most would not stomach Elizabeth's high temper. But she could tell that even he was not proof against Rivaux's daughter, for he greeted her warmly, enveloping her in an affectionate embrace. And she'd kissed him full on the mouth, as though she counted him as much a kinsman as those in her own family.

"I make you known to my wife, daughter to Nigel of Byrum," he'd said, beckoning Arabella forward. "Arabella, 'tis Elizabeth, born of Rivaux."

Arabella dropped to kneel before the tall woman, both because she was wife to William's overlord and because she was a count's daughter, but Elizabeth caught her under the arm and pulled her up. Kissing her lightly on each cheek, she stood back to admire her sister-in-law.

"Arabella, is it? Well, I had hopes he'd find a wife I would not tower over, but at least you are not small." Incredibly, she smiled. "Aye, and you are lovely: 'Tis no wonder he told me you were as a gilded rose."

"There are those who count me tall also, Lady Elizabeth." As soon as the words had escaped her, Arabella felt foolish for having said them.

"Then they have not seen me." Linking arms with her, Elizabeth turned again to William. "Well, do you stand here gaping—or would you see my strong sons? Come, the both of you—I'd have you see what the barren horse of Rivaux has given her lord."

"Aye. And your sire—is Count Guy yet arrived?" William wanted to know.

"He rode out forthwith at the news," Giles answered for her. "And you seek the cradle, you'll find

him there. There is something about a babe named
Guy that pleases him.''

"I'll warrant there is.''

Elizabeth stopped on the steps. ''I'd have named the
second son William, I'd have you know, but the day
they were born word came that King David had bestowed another manor on Giles. 'Twas decided more
politic to recognize him this time, but I give you my
word on your knife that the next boy will be our Will
o' Dunashie." She flashed him another grin. ''You
still have the knife, do you not?''

"Aye.''

"He made me swear on my soul, my babe's soul,
his knife, and all else he could think of that I'd return
to Giles from Harlowe," she explained to Arabella.
'' 'Tis a wonder the babes were not marked for all the
oaths I swore over them.''

"I dinna know ye well then," William protested.

"And you are not watchful, he'll have you swearing
to everything, Arabella. 'Tis his way of leading you.
William is more pious than the rest of us, I fear.''

'' 'Tisna a verra hard thing to be," he shot back.

"He still prays ere he retires," Arabella volunteered.

"Before or after, I wonder?" Elizabeth teased him.

Despite her earlier awe of her, Arabella was drawn
to the younger Elizabeth. Her own eyes sparkled mis-
chievously as she answered, "The first two days he
prayed not at all.''

"Aye—Berta wagered that you would not sit after.''

"Liza . . .'' William growled.

"Berta?" Arabella asked innocently.

"Elizabeth, I'd nae—''

"Dunashie's whore. She overcharged him, I am
told," Elizabeth answered blithely. She leaned closer,
her sparkling eyes on William, and whispered loudly,
"When we are alone, Arabella of Byrum, there is no
end to the tales I can tell you of him.''

"I am naught but ears.''

"I like her, Will—mayhap when summer comes,

you'll bring her to stay with me. But for now we tarry, when you could be looking on the two bonniest babes on the border.''

If the hall was richly decorated, it was as nothing before Elizabeth of Rivaux's solar. Every wall was hung with great alternating sheets of red and black silk, and the floors were swept bare beneath mats woven of reeds painted red. And over the red had been drawn the bear of Dunashie. The bed was many-curtained, the inner layer being gold-shot baudekin, then black silk, and finally on the outside was crimson velvet embroidered in gold. Even the boxes and cupboards that lined the walls were painted in black and decorated with gold.

'' 'Tis beautiful,'' Arabella breathed. ''I've not seen the like before.'' Then, realizing she'd not even mentioned the flames-of-fire fabric that Elizabeth had sent her, she tried to stammer out her thanks. ''Your pardon, gracious lady, but I'd forgotten: my thanks for the cloth—'twas my wedding gown.''

''You are most welcome. And ere you leave, I've far more than that to give you.'' She caught Arabella's hand, dragging her to where several men sat beside a double cradle. ''But for now—behold Guy and David of Dunashie!''

The men rose, and as Arabella looked from Elizabeth to the tallest of them she knew him for Guy, Count of Rivaux, Earl to Harlowe. It was as though her skin turned to gooseflesh as she stared. This then was the man she'd heard of for as long as she could remember. This was the man they sang of at hearths from Paris to Rouen to London to Edinburgh, and all places between. This was the man who'd brought down the evil Count of Belesme. It was like seeing a saint in the flesh.

Smiling, Count Guy addressed William almost familiarly. ''So Giles has seen fit to raise you, has he? When I heard it of him, I told him 'twas due you overlong. Nay—no ceremony is due me, for you hold no

lands of Rivaux," he hastened to add, when Will
would have gone down on his knee.

"I'd honor ye for Belesme, my lord."

" 'Twas long ago."

As Will took Arabella's arm, Elizabeth stepped
back. "My lord, I'd present Arabella, lady to Blackleith—my lady," he announced proudly.

Despite what Count Guy had said to her husband,
Arabella swept the flowing skirt of her gown behind
her and made a low obeisance before him. Looking
up though the veil of her lashes, she thought she detected a glimmer of amusement in his strange, flecked
eyes. Reddening, she managed to say, "My lord of
Rivaux."

"Sweet Mary, but you've got yourself a beauty, William of Dunashie," Guy murmured as he reached to
take her hand. "Lady."

When she dared to look at him directly, she could
see he was older than she'd thought, and it surprised
her. Men like Guy of Rivaux were not supposed to be
mortal. Yet his black hair was flecked with grey, and
small lines of age marked his eyes. But his grip was
strong, and his smile for her obviously genuine.

" 'Tis honored I am to meet you, my lord."

"Nay, the honor is mine." He smiled yet again,
which set into motion the fine scar that divided his
cheek. Releasing her hand, he directed her attention
to the double cradle. "My daughter would not forgive
me were I to fail to show you the fine grandsons she
gives me." Looking up at William he asked, "What
say you? Will either of them wield the Doomslayer, do
you think?"

"I think it likely they will fight over it, my lord."

"Nay, it goes to the firstborn."

"Papa, it ought to go to Richard," Elizabeth reminded him.

"He has Belesme's Hellbringer to give to his son.
'Tis more meet that one called Guy should have my
sword, I think."

"Lord Richard's wife is delivered also?" Will asked, peering over the cradle at the two babes.

Guy smiled. "Aye. Gilliane de Lacey gave him Roger of Harlowe ere Christmas, but the birth was a hard one, so he does not come. He sends one hundred silver pennies to each babe instead. You'd admire the babe, William, for his hair is as red as yours."

"Nay, then I'd pity him for it."

One hundred silver pennies each. Two hundred silver pennies. 'Twas as much as Arabella's entire dowry that Elizabeth's brother gave as birth presents for two babes. And Guy of Rivaux spoke of it as though 'twas to be expected. Arabella looked down on her woolen traveling gown and felt as though she were little more than a serving maid to them.

One of the men who'd been seated with Count Guy rose to speak to her. "Art Byrum's daughter, as was wed to Elias of Woolford ere he died?" he asked.

"Aye."

"My son served there then." He moved closer. "Aye, he said you were a pretty girl—too pretty for the likes of Woolford. He spoke of you often."

"Your son?"

William, who had been standing behind her, laid his hands on her shoulders. " 'Tis Duncan of Ayrie," he whispered tersely. Speaking more loudly to the other man, he said almost defensively, "She is lady to Blackleith now."

" 'Tis as well. Aidan would have it that Elias was a hard man, and 'tis said Donald is much like him." Duncan favored her with a smile. "He will be pleased to renew your acquaintaince."

"Aidan?" she asked cautiously, hoping he did not mean Donald. She'd not have Elias' son accuse her again before her husband. " 'Tis Aidan as comes here?"

"Aye."

William's grip on her shoulders tightened almost painfully. "I hope he is well, my lord," was all she could think of to say. "It has been many years since last we were met."

"He is."

"For shame—all of you!" Elizabeth chided. "You stand over my babes, and speak of all else. Will, I'd have you tell me they have as much promise as Giles."

He released Arabella and peered into the cradles, looking from one to the other. "I dinna remember him being so little," he teased.

"Fie on you, Will of Dunashie! Arabella, tell him that all babes save he come into this world like this." Elizabeth bent over them and lifted the one closest to her. As she nuzzled the small, red face, there was no mistaking her pride. "Your godson," she murmured, handing the babe to him.

He held it up gingerly, peering into the slate-grey eyes. "David of Dunashie," he said softly. "May ye grow half so great as your sire—aye, and may you be possessed of a tenth of your grandsire of Rivaux's honor. 'Tis all I'd ask for ye."

"Give him over—'tis no way to hold a babe." Arabella reached to lift Elizabeth's second son from him. "Ah, he is a big one." She looked at him, then at the one still in the cradle. "In truth, I think this one bigger than the other."

"He is."

"Art a fine, bonny fellow, Davy o' Dunashie," she crooned. "For shame, Will—naught's amiss with this babe." She hugged him closer for a moment, then laid him again in his cradle. "And you—you are a fine fellow also, aren't you?" she murmured, picking up the other. "Aye—Guy, is it? My, what a name you are given—God grant you are like the other who bears it."

"They are so alike that we have put beads on their ankles to tell them apart—red on Guy and black on David," Guy pointed out. Briefly, his expression clouded. "I would that Cat were here to see them—aye, and Red Roger also. Three grandsons born within a month."

"My mother," Elizabeth explained. "She remains

at Rivaux, that those who choose Stephen do not take it." She leaned over to pick up the infant David. "And you do not mind it I'd sit apart with you, Bella. Nay— bring him. Men," she said pointedly, "are easily made tired of babes." As she crossed the room to where silk-covered cushions lined the wall, she half turned back to Arabella. "You have a son also, do you not?"

"Aye."

"I'd hear of him."

Arabella looked down on the small, perfect head and the round, plump body she held against her shoulder, and she felt as though she herself had been cheated in her firstborn son. "He is lame, my lady," she said simply.

"Then God aid him." Elizabeth's green eyes softened perceptibly. "Bella, I would that you called me Liza—mine own sisters do."

In another corner of the room, William growled low to Giles, "You dinna tell me Ayrie's son came."

"I could scarce forbid him, when full half the border is invited." Giles' gaze traveled to where Arabella held his son close. "Unless I mistake the matter, Will, she is content enough with you."

Although Will nodded, he could not help hoping that Duncan of Ayrie's son was ill-favored.

Chapter Twenty-Seven

Although it was cold, January 20th was a good day for a christening, in that it neither rained nor snowed. The sun shone brightly in the winter sky, an auspicious occurrence by everyone's reckoning. As Elizabeth waited outside the church door her father carried Guy of Dunashie inside, and William followed him with the infant David. Since the mother had not been purified yet Arabella offered to stay with her, but Elizabeth would not hear of it.

"Go on," she urged. "I'd have you see them blessed."

Once inside, she was seated at the front, in honor of the role her husband would take. Like everything else she'd seen at Dunashie, the chapel was far better than that of Woolford—or even that of Byrum. There were above her blue glass windows that admitted light. It was fitting, for William stood under them in his new blue Christmas tunic.

The service itself was short, with Guy of Dunashie being baptized first, and the chapel seemed to reverberate with the pride of Guy of Rivaux when he named him. The priest, in honor of his illustrious godfather, blessed the babe thoroughly. But as Will lifted David over the font there was the sound of water hitting water, and heads craned to see what had happened. The priest never paused, asking only what the babe would be called, then he baptized him quickly, and gave him a shorter blessing than the other. William murmured something but she could not hear it, and the priest shook his head. It was over.

She hurried up to her husband, then walked out with him. Outside, William was asked about it, and he answered that the sound they'd heard was when the babe had passed water into the baptismal font. It was, he hoped, not an ill omen.

"Lady Arabella . . ."

She turned around to face an older Aidan of Ayrie, and her breath caught in her chest. For all that he'd changed in the intervening years, she still would have recognized him anywhere. And like herself, she counted him a survivor of Elias of Woolford's cruelty. She managed a smile.

"Aidan."

"You look well—far better than when last I saw you."

"I could scarce look worse than then, but I shall consider that you praise me."

"As I did ever—and with good reason," he insisted gallantly. He hesitated briefly, then blurted out, "Your babe—he survived? He is well?"

She saw William scowl, and mistook the reason. "He cannot walk, sir, but his mind is as good as any." Turning to her husband, she asked with forced brightness, "Do you not think he does well at his books, my lord?"

"Well enough," Will muttered.

"It gladdens me to hear it, lady, for when I left I was sorely worried for the both of you."

Thinking William resented speech of the boy he wished to hide from others, she changed the subject abruptly. "Elias died that night, you know."

"Aye. I had heard, but I could not regret the news.

Indeed, but I counted it God's blessing that he did. He
was not a kind husband to you, nor was he a good
master to any.'' He shifted his weight slightly, then
added, ''I would have come to Byrum, but after—Well,
I did not think it meet.''

''Nay. Nay, he was not,'' she agreed. It seemed to
her that with each word she spoke William's frown
deepened, warning her that he was displeased. Still,
after all the years that had passed, she would know
how Aidan fared also.

''And you?'' she asked hastily. ''Did you wed? Little news reached us at Byrum.''

''Aye, but she is dead these two years last. 'Twas
childbed, and I have a daughter from it.'' He favored
her with a twisted smile. ''There was much to admire
in her, sweet lady, for she oft reminded me of you, so
much so that I have called the child Arabella for your
kindness to me.''

She felt William's body tense beside her, and she
knew she ought to go. ''I am sorry she perished, my
lord. I will remember her in my prayers.''

''Her name was Margaret of Kenreith.''

''Aye—I will remember it.'' Grasping her husband's
arm, she tried to direct Aidan's attention there. '' 'Tis
two months and more since I wed William of Dunashie.''

''Art a fortunate man,'' Aidan murmured, his eyes
still on her.

''You chill,'' Will told her bluntly, ignoring the other
man. '' 'Tis time we were inside, Bella, lest you sicken
ere we are able to return home.''

''Mayhap I will see you and the boy at Dunashie
one day, Lady Arabella.''

William had had enough. ''And mayhap ye willna,''
he snapped. ''I've nae invited ye.''

Arabella's face reddened at his rudeness. ''My lord . . .
There is no need. . . .''

Lang Gib, who'd been behind them listening to the
whole, stepped forward quickly to address the younger
man. ''Art Ayrie's son?''

"Aye. And you?"

"Gilbert of Kilburnie. I have heard you are possessed of a gyrfalcon of repute."

"Aye."

"Mayhap I'd be interested in a hatchling of it. I'd pay good gold for a prime bird."

"Then you speak to the right man, for I have the best," Aidan declared proudly, momentarily diverted from William's lack of courtesy. "And you would see for yourself, I have brought it to compete with Moray's best."

William's hand slid down Arabella's arm to possess her hand. "Come," he growled. "I'd go inside." But as he pulled her after him on the cobbled stones, he felt great unease now that he'd seen Duncan's son. For all that he had hoped otherwise, Aidan of Ayrie was far comelier and better favored than he—aye, and better born also. Compared to him, Will could look naught but big and clumsy to her. And it did not help that Aidan had asked of the boy. God's bones, but did he think that none knew? Or was he so careless of Arabella's honor that he dared speak of what had happened at Woolford? And she'd been brazen enough to answer, brazen enough even to ask if he'd wed. No doubt those who'd already heard the tale felt pity for William of Dunashie. His stride lengthened as his fury grew.

She nearly tripped trying to keep up with him. Finally she pulled free, and bent to draw her soft kid shoe back up on her heel. When she looked up, he had already reached the hall. When he turned around, he was clearly angered. Gathering the full skirt of her gown above her ankles, she hurried after him. Catching up, she touched his arm tentatively.

"William . . . My lord . . . What. . . ?"

He jerked away. " 'Tis nothing. Get ye inside, ere we are remarked more."

"Is it nothing that you will but snarl and snap?"

"I dinna say anything to ye!" he retorted angrily.

"You dinna have to: 'Tis as clear as the sky above

that I have vexed you, William of Dunashie, and I know not why or how!''

"And I'd nae hae ye mock me, Bella! I can speak as well as you, and you want it!''

"Then tell me what I have done!''

He raised his hand, and for a moment she feared he meant to strike her before those who were yet in the courtyard. In defense she lifted her arm, infuriating him more.

"Nay, Bella, I'd nae hit ye, for all that I ought to do it,'' he muttered, turning away. "Get ye inside, I said.''

"For what? What is it that I have done?'' she demanded again.

"Come, ere ye make greater fools of the both of us.''

The old fear washed over her, fear that she was returning to the hell Elias and Nigel had given her, fear that once again she was unable to please no matter what she did. Fear that she'd carry this babe like the last. And she'd almost rather die than live like that.

She caught his sleeve again, this time pulling it. "Is it that I spoke with Ayrie's son?'' she demanded. "I could scarce do aught else, for he was kind to me at Woolford, and I—''

"I'd nae speak of it, Bella! Now, do ye come with me or not?''

She could see that several of Dunashie's villeins watched curiously, and she did not think she could stand their pity. Her pride rose like a gorge in her throat, and beneath her breastbone she ached. She swallowed, then breathed deeply of the cold air, striving to calm herself. And she quarreled with him before them she risked a beating, she told herself, and that she could not bear. Not in Elizabeth of Rivaux's keep.

"Aye.''

" 'Tis better,'' he muttered. "So long as we are here ye'll be the obedient wife, d'ye ken me? Ye'll nae go about so free with your speech, Arabella, for I'd nae remind any what ye are.''

It was as though a cold chill gripped her heart as he spoke. Tears welled in her eyes, nearly blinding her. Blinking them back, she managed to whisper, "What I am? Sweet Mary, but what am I, William? What is it that you think me?" But even as she asked, she *knew*. He'd heard the tale, and he'd believed it.

"I said I'd nae speak of it."

"But I am blameless, my lord."

"And ye'd nae anger me further, Bella, ye'll do as I ask. Speak to him again, and I *will* beat ye for it."

"My lord . . ."

"Nay. I'd nae hear his name again—d'ye ken that also?"

She felt as though she suffocated, as though her life ebbed before her eyes. Swallowing hard, she managed to look up and ask, "Then how could you wed with me?"

For a long moment he met her gaze, then he looked away and answered low, "I was contracted to ye. I told myself my desire for ye was greater than a bastard's honor." Settling his shoulders, he sighed heavily. "But I have found that even a bastard values his honor, Bella."

"William, I swear to you that I—"

"Nay. We will return to Blackleith, and we will never speak of this again—not now, not ever," he declared grimly. "I forbid his name to your lips, Arabella of Byrum." When he swung back around he could see she still would speak, and he shook his head. "I've nae hit ye before, but afore God, if I ever hear ye say aught of this again, I will."

"Will!"

There was no mistaking the imperious quality of Elizabeth of Rivaux's voice as she came up to them. Oblivious to what had just passed, she laid a hand on Arabella's arm and smiled.

" 'Tis too cold to stand without, when there is a goodly fire inside," she chided. "What say you, Bella: Shall we leave your bear to the other men and withdraw where we may be more comfortable?"

"Ah . . ."

For all that his face was still grim, William nodded. "Go on. I'd find Giles, to tell him we leave on the morrow."

Elizabeth's smile faded. "So soon? But I'd thought you would stay after the company left, Will."

"Nay."

Instead of going inside, he left them. Elizabeth's gaze followed him for a moment, then she shrugged expressively. " 'Tis best to leave a man to stew in his own bad temper, Bella." But as she said it, her green eyes met Arabella's and she smiled ruefully. "Alas, but I was never one to try it, though. My wicked tongue leads me far too often."

Despite the other woman's kindness, Arabella scarce heard half of what she said during the hours they were together. Even though she smiled politely and said all the right things, as the many guests climbed up to the solar to admire the babes, her mind was on what William had said to her. And with each reliving of his words, her heart grew heavier within her breast. Just before it was time to go down to sup Elizabeth dismissed everyone else, saying the excitement was too much for two infants, then sat beside her.

"Art troubled?" she asked gently.

For a moment Arabella longed to unburden herself, to tell the other woman of Elias, of Aidan of Ayrie, and of the beatings and lies she'd endured, but she knew she could not. If Elizabeth of Rivaux did not know the tale, William would not wish her to learn of it. Besides, there was no certainty she'd believe the truth, anyway, and Arabella could not stand it if the woman's kindness turned to condemnation.

"Nay," Arabella lied. "I am but tired."

"You do not look well."

"I am all right." She twisted her hands in the folds of her skirt, then looked to the neat, woven mat at her feet. " 'Tis most likely the babe I bear."

"Will did not tell me."

"He does not yet know." Arabella lifted her eyes.
"I am waiting until I am sure of it."

"I've half a mind to tell him myself, saying that you
ought not to travel. But he would know better, I suppose, for he rode all the way to Harlowe with me when
I was in like case." Briefly Elizabeth squeezed Arabella's hands, then she rose. "And you wished you
could lie abed, and I would send Helewise up with
food for you."

"Nay."

"I could scarce abide food in the early days. But I
forget: You have borne a babe also, so you know what
you are about." The rich, heavy samite of her gown
swished over the mats as she moved. "Well, if you
come, we'd best go down now, else some of these border louts will bang upon my tables for their food. And
Papa will be aghast at the roughness of the company
we keep."

William was waiting impatiently when they came
down, and by the looks of it he'd consumed more wine
than was his custom, for his color was heightened beneath his dark red hair. Saying little, he offered his
arm, then led Arabella inside.

The great hall was filled to overflowing, and the tables seemed to groan with the feast that celebrated the
heir's christening. On another day she would have been
wide-eyed with excitement to see such a place, but
now Arabella was too miserable to note it. William sat
beside her, first cutting their meat without comment,
then toying with the food on his end of the trencher,
scarce tasting anything. Instead, each time the serving
man refilled his cup he drained it, as though he could
drown his ill temper.

She felt too sick to eat. Each bite lay upon her stomach like a heavy, sodden mass. Thinking it would ease
her, she grasped his newly filled cup ere he could finish it again and drank deeply. It was as though the
wine met her food coming up on its way down. Heedless of those around her, she clamped her hand over
her mouth and fled from the dais, passing Lang Gib

and Wat on her way out. Gib hesitated, then lurched
to his feet to follow, with Wat close behind.

She had not reached the garderobe before she began
to wretch violently. Gib caught her from behind and
pushed her forward, shouting to Wat, "Get Will—get
Lord William—now! Jesu, lady, but you are sick," he
muttered, trying to hold her gown out of the mess. He
half lifted her, half dragged her into the garderobe,
then held her over the hole as wave after wave of nausea hit her. Finally it passed, and she straightened
shakily.

"My thanks, sir."

" 'Tis fortunate I saw ye in the crowd."

"And I'd thank you for what you attempted earlier
with Aidan of Ayrie."

"Och, but there's none as doesna have a prized fal-
con—'twas a safe enough guess," he answered, smiling. He saw her pass the back of her hand across her
brow, and he thought she meant to be sick again. He
reached out to hold her, steadying her with his arm
again. "Art all right, lady?"

"Unhand her."

Gib twisted to see William standing in the doorway,
and he reddened. It was obvious that his lord was more
than a little drunk from the wine—and completely out
of temper. "And I do, she'll fall," Gib retorted.

Again Arabella straightened, and pushed damp hair
back from her face. Everything—her veil, her gown,
her shoes—was ruined. As Gib released her she leaned
against the coolness of the stone wall, clinging to it.

"I told ye she was sick," Wat insisted.

But William was watching Lang Gib. "I'd nae wear
the horns for any—ye hear me? Not for ye, nor for
any! Not for ye or Ayrie, I tell you!"

"She was sick, Will!" Gib snapped, forgetting the
difference in their station now. "God's blood, but
would ye that I left her to fall in her own puke?" When
William did not answer, the younger man pushed past
him angrily. "Art a fool, Will o' Dunashie!"

"He dinna mean it, my lord—he dinna! Gib! Jesu, Gib!" Wat ran after him. "Where do ye go, Gib?"

"Dunashie!"

"But ye are at Dunashie!"

"Aye, and I am like to stay here!"

"My lord, I would lie down," Arabella said tiredly. "I am all right now—go on back and eat."

"Nay. I'd take ye."

He reached for her arm, but she jerked away. "I am scarce fit to tryst with any," she reminded him bitterly. "not even a swine would wish to lie with me like this."

"I said I'd take ye," he muttered. "And I am more like to beat than lie with ye."

Although he did not touch her, he walked beside her along the deserted kitchen passage and up the tower stairs. And with each step, her fear grew. But while Holy Church taught that a husband had the right to beat a wife, she knew in her heart she'd done nothing wrong. If he lifted his hand to her, she'd not cower tamely. If he lifted his hand to her, there'd be none in the castle as did not know of it, she told herself. And he'd not want that—he'd not want all to hear, for then there would be no hiding what he thought her. If he beat her, his pride would suffer as much as her body.

The steps were steep and she stumbled once, falling into him, but as soon as he'd righted her she went on. When they reached the tiny cutout chamber they'd been given, Ena was waiting. For a moment, despite all her brave musings, Arabella felt intense fear. If he hit her hard enough, he could kill her—if he hit her hard enough, she would not be able to cry out. He caught her shoulder roughly, thrusting her inside, and this time the sickness came from terror.

"I'd hae ye get her to bed," he told Ena curtly. "And ye'd best keep the basin near, for her food does not sit well upon her stomach." As he spoke, he pushed her into the woman's arms. "If she worsens, send to me below."

"Aye, my lord."

It was not until she heard his footsteps again in the stairwell that Arabella realized he did not mean to beat her at all. And as her fear receded it was replaced first by relief, then by anger. He had no right to frighten her like that, not when she'd done nothing to deserve it. He had no right to believe wrongly of her, then to refuse to hear the truth.

"Sweet Jesu, lady, but naught's left in your stomach, I'd say," Ena murmured, pulling the soiled gown over Arabella's head. Working quickly, she stripped the undergown also, then bent to untie the stockings. "Mayhap if ye told him of the babe, he'd nae be angered with ye."

"It did not matter to Elias."

"He is not Woolford."

She rolled gratefully into the bed and drew up her knees, as Ena settled the thick covers over her. Shivering as much from emotion as from cold, she considered a dozen harsh words she ought to have flung at him. But she was a coward, and she knew it, else she'd have faced him down in the courtyard earlier, else she'd have shouted that any who accused her and Ayrie to him had lied. But he'd not wanted to hear the truth. He'd not even acknowledged that he knew the tale, but there was no mistaking that he did. Her anger faded to despair. If he would not hear her, he could not believe in her.

What had he answered when she'd asked how he could have wed her? *I was contracted to ye. I told myself my desire for you was greater than a bastard's honor.* He'd believed the worst of her, and yet he had wed her. *I was contracted to ye.* He must have heard the tale after his first visit to Byrum, after he'd given her the golden chain. 'Twas why he'd never given her the stone to wear on it.

But he had wed her. And unlike Elias, he'd not beaten her for every word. Unlike Elias, he'd not beaten her for every look. Unlike Elias, he'd not beaten her for having been born on the Scots side of the border. Even now, after all these years, she still spoke as the English, for Elias had beaten her for the "dinnas," the "cannas," and all else that reminded him of her birth. And yet William, as much as she had angered him over Jamie, had never hit her once.

Hope soared briefly, then it too faded. It was no longer enough that he did not beat her. When she lay beneath him, she wanted more than that. She wanted to be more than the means to ease his body. She wanted him to love her. And what man could love a woman he believed unworthy of him? For all that she had tried, to him she was not even worth the stone he'd once promised her.

There had to be some way—there had to. And yet if he would not speak of it, if he would not allow her to tell him, she could think of none, for she dared not rouse his temper, not now. Her only hope lay in the child she carried, and what if he, like Elias, found reason not to claim it? What if this second babe was as ill-formed as the first? Nay, but for all that she wanted to shout her innocence to him, she feared what a beating would do to her babe.

For hours she lay awake, and still he did not come to bed. Gradually, she slipped first into that fanciful world where every fear took form, torturing her, then finally into the oblivious ease of sleep. Sometime far into the night the bed creaked with his weight as he lay down beside her, but she did not feel it when his hand awkwardly smoothed her hair against her shoulder, nor did she hear him mutter thickly, "God aid me, Arabella of Byrum—for all that I know of Ayrie's son, I'd still have ye."

Chapter Twenty-Eight

Walter paced his small room as though it were a cage. Behind him James of Woolford copied his letters carefully, repeating the words as he wrote. And for all that he did not like the boy, Walter had to admit young James had a good mind when he wished to use it.

He walked to the window and opened the shutters, peering down on the snow-dusted hills that seemed to roll endlessly southward. His land, and he could not claim it. Instead, he lived this lie he could not stand. He was no closer to killing Giles of Moray than ever, and still he waited, hovering, biding his time, hoping for the chance that seemed to elude him. He'd wanted to go to Dunashie, but he'd been left behind with the boy. His resentment seethed, for he could not stand it.

Though they had been gone less than a fortnight, Walter so longed for Arabella of Byrum that she haunted both his dreams and his thoughts. And all the while he knew that William of Dunashie had her, had the right to lie with her at his will, while he, Walter FitzHamon, could but watch and wait.

'Twas impossible what he wanted, and he knew it.

He'd have Blackleith—and Arabella of Byrum with it. And yet even if the Butcher and his brother were dead, there would still be the matter of getting King David favorably disposed to him. And the matter of explaining how he'd come to Blackleith a priest called "Edmund of Alton." What could he say: that he'd come in disguise to look at the place? And Arabella: Would she be inclined to his suit, once he'd let his hair grow? Nay, she would only know that he'd deceived her.

To gain Blackleith, he'd have to kill every heir and force her into a marriage with him. And then he'd turn to King David, asking as the last of Hamon's blood that the keep be bestowed on him. Why had he chosen a disguise? 'Twas to gain entry inside. The problem was Arabella. If she knew, if she suspected even, that he'd killed to gain her, she'd not want him.

Now he was her confessor. Now he taught her to read. Now he listened and advised. And for all that she disputed with him over the boy, she trusted him. But he wanted more than her trust. God's bones, but after years of living in a monastery with naught but the company of men, he was ready for more than that. He wanted to know the feel of a woman's body beneath his. He wanted to know the ease of lying with Arabella of Byrum. He wanted to see her naked.

"Father . . ." A young girl, one of the maids that served Arabella, peered around the corner of his door. "Would ye that I brought ye and the boy fresh oatcakes from the ovens?" she asked shyly.

His gaze rested on her curiously. Though she was small, her breasts thrust against the coarse wool of her gown. And her hair was blond, though not the pale, shimmering gold of Arabella's. His mouth went dry with the thought that crossed his mind.

"How are you called, child?" he found himself asking.

"Ye know me, Father—ye give me the host every Mass."

"Aye, but I know not the name you are given."

" 'Tis Avisa, Father."

" 'Tis a Norman name."

"Aye." The girl's chin came up, as though she dared him to dispute it, then she added proudly, "My sire was a Norman knight. He bedded my dam when he came to visit the lord Hamon."

"I see," Walter responded gravely. "Then you are half gentle-born yourself, aren't you?"

She nodded, pleased that he saw it that way. " 'Tis why my dam called me Avisa."

"Well then, Avisa—how many years have you?"

"Nearly seventeen."

"Art a pretty little maid."

She giggled, then volunteered, "My dam doesna let me lie with the boys, for she'd hae good silver and I am a virgin. I was promised to the miller, but he died ere I was wed. His sons disputed it, but we kept the money," she explained artlessly.

"Aye, come back, little Avisa, and share the cakes you bring with us. We have spiced wine to wash them down."

"I am more used to ale, Father."

"Then wine will be my gift to you."

He watched her leave, thinking it unlikely that she was in truth a virgin still, but it did not matter. Despite his limited experience of women, she looked ripe for the plucking. And his body was ready to taste that which had been forbidden him at Kelso.

Briefly he considered whether to call for someone to come for James of Woolford, then he decided against it. Should the maid prove skittish, the boy's presence would assuage her fear until Walter could gain her trust. Avisa. 'Twas a foolish name for a villein's daughter, but if it fed her pride 'twas useful, he supposed.

For want of anything else to do he walked to where the boy still copied his lesson. Looking over the thin shoulder, he was surprised by the neatness of the characters. " 'Tis good. Your mother will be pleased when she comes." But when he looked more closely he

could see that the boy had copied a short prayer, and
had inscribed it to William of Dunashie.

"You'd best pray for yourself, James," Walter told
him coldly.

But the boy shook his head. "Nay. Me and Lord
William shares an oath betwixt us. 'Tis for him that I
make this."

Walter snorted. "He scarce notes you."

"He brought me an English dagger—aye, with a
painted hilt—and he gave me Minette that I may ride."
He laid aside his pen and dug into the small leather
pouch at his belt, drawing out a silver coin. "And this
I had of him ere he left for Dunashie."

"It does not cost him much to give what he has
stolen," Walter muttered under his breath.

" 'Tis for him that I study my letters, Father—and
I do them right, he will see that I walk."

"A fool's promise—worth scarce more than prayers."

To Walter's chagrin, the child merely shrugged and
retrieved his pen. "He wouldna told me, else he meant
it." He labored, making the final strokes on the last
word, then held it up. "I could hae done better, but
I'd make my lady mother one also ere she returns."

The girl came back, carrying a small wooden plate
of steaming oatcakes drizzled with honey. Walter in-
dicated the table where Jamie worked, then he turned
to find his wineskin. He'd sweeten it more than usual
for her first taste, for he'd have her like it. Aye, he'd
have her drink plenty of it.

The courtyard below looked as though it were covered with crystals beneath the moon, and all was silent
within the keep save for the lone sentry that walked
above each hour. The rest of the time he kept to his
guardroom, close to the fire. Walter closed the shutters
to his small room, and waited for the girl. On the table
sat the pitcher where he'd mixed the wine, this time
adding poppy juice with the honey and the precious
spices. He hated to waste the cinnamon and the gin-

ger, but if it gained him what he'd have of her, he'd
have to count her worth the cost. If only she did not
scream or cry out . . .

He left but one candle burning, for the near darkness
suited him also. Where was the silly, foolish creature?
Had she taken his earlier wine and decided not to
come? Surely he'd not given her so much that she'd
sickened from it. Cursing the wait, he sat down and
poured himself a cup from his wineskin, saving the
other for her. He'd not be senseless the first time he
took a woman.

He thought he heard the soft scrape of slippers on
the steps, and it was as though every inch of his skin
came alive. His door creaked inward, and she peeked
cautiously inside.

"Father . . ?"

"Come in, daughter."

"Should we not pray in the chapel?" she asked nervously.

"Would you not share a cup of God's fruit with me
first? Sit you down, little Avisa, that we may speak
with each other. Your mama. . . ?"

"She sleeps."

"Aye. The spices are too precious—I'd not share
them with any but you."

The light of the single candle reflected eerily in his
eyes, and for a moment she was afraid. And yet there
was something exciting, something forbidden about
drinking alone in the dark with the priest. And a priest
would not harm anyone, for he was of God. She sat
down, spreading her skirt demurely as she thought a
lady would. He poured her a cup of the liquid and
swirled it with his finger ere he handed it across the
table.

"There may be too much honey for you, child."

She knew she ought not to be there, but did he not
call her "daughter" and "child"? She sipped the
sweetened wine, feeling quite the grand lady. "I like
it," she murmured, watching him over the cup. " 'Tis
like a sweetmeat."

"The best fruit of God's vineyard, my daughter." He leaned his elbows on the table and clasped his hands beneath his chin. "I'd have you tell me what troubles you, little Avisa," he said softly.

The thought crossed her mind that despite his tonsure, he appeared not much older than the boys who teased her in the stableyard. 'Twas strange how some men aged not at all, and others were toothless ere they were wed. But this one was far handsomer than any she'd found below. She sipped deeply, letting the sweetness linger in her mouth ere she swallowed, wondering what she ought to say to him.

"Who gives you pretty things?" he asked, when she did not answer the other.

"There is none, Father."

"A pretty child is deserving of a jewel, I'd think." As he said it, he pushed a small pin across the table. Four smooth black stones gleamed around a silver center, in a shape much like St. Patrick's shamrock. " 'Twas my mother's," he lied. "And until I saw you, I thought none pretty enough to wear it."

"Nay, I—"

" 'Tis of little worth to any but myself, child. Go on—take it."

"My mother would ask where I'd gotten it."

"I will look away, and you may say 'twas found." He reached for the pitcher and refilled her cup. "But if you fear . . ."

Afraid that he meant to take it back, she snatched it up and stuck the pin into the shoulder of her plain gown. Then, unsure of how to thank him, she drank instead, and he did not appear to note the lapse.

He talked low of many things: of English gardens and castles too big to be believed, of river barges and pretty lakes she'd never seen. And all the while he watched her, again refilling her cup. The room grew warmer despite the smallness of his fire, and it seemed that her mind floated above her body. She blinked as his face swayed before hers. She pushed her cup away and tried to rise, but her legs were too weak to hold her.

"I think I've had too much," she said as he caught her, steadying her in strong arms. But instead of helping her to the door, he pushed her to his cot. "Nay, I canna sleep here," she whispered. "My dam—" But already his hand was beneath her skirt, lifting it to expose her legs. And as she tried to wrench away, he reached for a cloth. "Nay, I—" She said no more as he stuffed it in her mouth, stifling her words. Her head turned from side to side, and she kicked and flailed to escape him.

"I'd not want to hurt you," he whispered by her ear, as he pulled up his cassock and lay over her. "Cry out, and you'll wish you hadn't."

"Mumph!"

He removed the cloth only to cover her mouth with his. His knee forced her legs apart, then he pinned her down and thrust hard. She stiffened, then tore open beneath him, and he was inside. As her legs fell slack he rode her hard, discovering for the first time Eden's sin. He lost himself in what he did to her until he had no mind, no reason, and then it seemed there was naught but the pulsing explosion that finally fed his need.

When he eased himself off her he could see her eyes were huge, and at first he thought 'twas fear. Then he realized 'twas from the drugged wine. She lay docilely now, and did not even try to rise when he stood above her.

For a long moment he looked at her white legs, exploring them with his eyes. Raising her gown higher, he gazed on the wet thatch where he'd been. He bent over her, lifting her hips, and eased the gown upward over her body. As he bared it he saw for the first time her white belly, her small breasts, and the smoothness of a female's skin. The temple of Venus before him.

But her eyes were glazed, and he'd not have her lie as though she were dead for him. He wanted what he'd heard in the furtive gropings behind the stable. He wanted to feel the life beneath him. Leaning over, he bit her breast, and felt her body tense, and he knew what to do. Aye, until he could have Arabella of Byrum, little Avisa would have to serve him.

Chapter Twenty-Nine

When Arabella returned to Blackleith with William, there was no hiding the strain between them. And for all that he had grudgingly apologized to Lang Gib and Wat, there was a lingering breach there also. Indeed, every man in the small mesnie seemed unusually quiet, despite the shouts of welcome that greeted them.

As soon as her husband had lifted her from her saddle Arabella knelt to hug her son eagerly, but 'twas to William that he reached, leaving her feeling even more empty and disappointed. Again it was as though some cruel jest stole him from her, and she could not forbear chiding him, saying that had she not known better she'd have thought 'twas only Father Edmund as had missed her.

In that at least she was right, Walter hastily assured her, for there was none other to play at chess and draughts and tables with him. William frowned at his familiar manner, but said nothing. He reminded himself that Edmund of Alton was, after all, a priest. And yet he could not like him.

After two days of riding in the silence of his wife and his men William warmed to the boy's eagerness, returning his embrace, feeling a new kinship with Arabella's crippled son. For all that could be said of James of Woolford there was no denying that he admired his stepfather, and William could not help responding to that now.

"I did as ye asked me!" Jamie chortled proudly. "Tell him, Father—I have written and read all I am given."

"Aye," Walter answered shortly.

"And ye'd carry me there, I'd gie ye what I made ye," the child offered. Twisting in William's arms, he looked to his mother. "And I made ye one also, Mama."

"And what of me?" Ena asked him.

The boy's face fell. Then he brightened. "Ye canna read, Ena!"

"Well, ye could have carved me something with your fine dagger," the woman protested.

"Nay, but I'll nae let ye shame him, Ena!" Even as he spoke Ewan held out his hand, revealing a decorated cross. "Fer ye, woman." Looking to William, he sighed. "Ye left me here to nurse one as kept his head in his letters, my lord—there was naught else to do." In an offhanded manner, he nodded again toward Arabella's maid. "Thought she might value it summat, ye know."

"Put a hole in it, and I'll wear it," Ena declared. "I've a need for something to ward off the evil spirits."

"There hasna been much to do," Ewan repeated. "And your lordship was wishful of it, I'd say 'twas time we hunted at Blackleith."

"Nay." Hoisting Jamie higher on his shoulder, William took a deep breath, then turned to Arabella. "I promised him, and he did not go to Dunashie, I'd take him to Edinburgh."

She stared blankly, then her voice betrayed her consternation. "Edinburgh! But *why?*"

"He canna tell ye, Mama! We are sworn over it."

"But naught's at Edinburgh save the king, and I can-

not think—'' Her eyes darted fearfully to her husband's. "Do I go also, my lord?''

"Nay. 'Tis but Ewan and me and the boy. And it
willna serve ye to ask, for I'd tell ye nae more." As
he spoke, Lang Gib and Wat exchanged glances that
did not miss Will. "I dinna favor traveling with two
sour faces," he added, reminding them of the breach.

"Nor do I!" Jamie chimed in, adopting the big
man's view immediately.

Ewan looked uneasily at Ena. "When do we go, my
lord?''

"The day after the morrow. 'Tis time, dinna ye
think, James?''

"And ye wish it.''

" 'Tis settled then. Now—what is it that ye made
me? I'd hae proof of these studies, ye know.''

Arabella watched them cross the yard, leaving her.
Once she would have given anything for someone to
show kindness to her son, but now she felt only un-
easiness. Although 'twas what she herself had asked
of William, this attention he gave Jamie, she mis-
trusted it now. Edinburgh? For an awful moment, she
considered that William took him away to a monastery
someplace, that 'twas a ruse to remove her child from
her. That she would never see her son again.

"Lady, you *have* been sorely missed. 'Twas as
though the light was gone from my days.''

She turned to face Father Edmund, and sighed.
"Only by you, 'twould seem." Nonetheless, she
forced a smile. " 'Tis glad I am to be again at Blackleith, Father. For all that Dunashie is grand, I'd rather
be here.''

"Did you see Rivaux's daughter?'' he asked, returning her smile. "I have heard she is overproud.''

"She comes from great wealth, and therefore is
given to speaking her mind with authority," Arabella
admitted. "But she is surely the Helen of all Christendom for her face. Father Edmund, I swear I have never
seen another like her in all my life.''

"And I'll warrant there were those who admired

Arabella of Byrum also, those who thought her as lovely as Rivaux's daughter.''

Her expression sobered, and her eyes betrayed her unhappiness momentarily. ''Aye. But 'tis like much else that befalls me, and I count my face a curse more than a blessing.''

''Nay. Only God makes beauty such as yours, lady.'' Seeing that Lang Gib had turned around to frown at him, Walter changed the subject quickly. ''And Moray—how fares the Butcher?''

''He prospers. Scarce a month passes that King David does not reward him in some measure for his service at the Standards. Sweet Jesu, Father, but you've not seen the like of Dunashie.''

''I have been there.'' Then, realizing he risked betraying himself, he added more smoothly, ''And you've not seen Harlowe or Rivaux, or even the Condes,'' he reminded her. '' 'Tis said Dunashie is a mean place in comparison to those Count Guy possesses. Nay, but the Butcher wed well—too well, some would have it— when he took Rivaux's daughter.''

''I could scarce believe that I saw Guy of Rivaux with mine own eyes, but I am glad he comes not here, for he travels with no less than fifty in his mesnie.'' She looked around her, then sighed again. ''For all that I have come to love it, Blackleith would be a poor place to him.''

'' 'Tis a prettier place here, now that you are come home.''

After William's sullenness, she could not help but respond to Edmund of Alton's kind words. ''Father, you are ill suited to your calling. You should have been a gallant knight rather than a tonsured priest, for you lighten my heart this day.''

Seeing that Lang Gib had moved out of hearing, Walter reached out and laid a hand on her arm. ''And you lighten mine also, repaying me for my poor words, gentle lady.''

The smell of bread baking in the ovens wafted past her on a chill breeze, and she felt a wave of nausea wash over her. And then it passed. Impulsively, she looked up at the priest.

"Father, I would that you heard me confess this day, for I am heartsore, and I'd speak to someone."

There was no mistaking the sudden sadness that came again to her eyes. Walter felt a surge of hope. His eyes took in the shimmering veil that seemed to float over her pale gold hair. With an effort, he looked away to hide the intense desire he felt for her.

"What sins could burden a lady as kind as you? Nay, but I'd not believe ill of you. I could absolve you without the hearing, I'd warrant."

She looked around her, then shook her head. " 'Tis not sins, so much as what mine husband believes of me, Father. I am afraid, and would ask God's guidance."

"You behold one who would heal you and he could. Lady, there is naught I would not do for you."

"Bella!"

She looked up to see William striding toward them, and she leaned closer to the priest to whisper, "Later— I'd speak of this later, and you do not mind it. I'd not speak before him of this."

"Lady, ever am I ready to serve you," Walter murmured low. "You have but to tell me what you would have."

" 'Tis too cold for you to stand about outside like a washwoman!" Will called out to her. "Get you inside."

"I'd have my husband's belief in me," she said low, for the priest's ears only. "I'd have you pray for that, Father."

William watched as the priest bent his head close to Arabella's, sharing confidences with her, and he felt an unreasoning surge of jealousy. Again it seemed to him that Edmund of Alton was too young and too well-favored for his calling. And for all that the young man was tonsured, there was no mistaking his admiration for her. Too often Will had seen that moonling look on men whose minds were between their legs. He

walked up to Arabella and pulled her traveling cloak
about her shoulders in a proprietary manner.

"The boy would show you his work," he told her
tersely.

"Aye. Father, I will come to chapel later that I may
confess. Until then, I'd bid you a good day."

"And I will await you," Walter promised.

Walter watched them walk, she trying to match her
husband's long stride, and he felt a surge of elation.
So all was not well between the Bastard and Arabella
of Byrum? And she would turn to him to mend matters, would she? Aye, but Lucifer would deliver her
into Walter's keeping yet, and he would have her when
William of Dunashie was no more. Well, he was ready,
more than ready, for that to happen. All he needed
was the opportunity, for he'd not be suspected, not
when he would appeal later to King David for Blackleith and for her. Stuffing his cold hands into his wide
sleeves, he hurried toward the hall.

"Jesu, but what ails you now, my lord?" Arabella
asked. "Can I now not even speak to a priest?"

"Nothing," William muttered. " 'Tis too cold outside."

As they went inside the outer door to the tower, they
passed one of the young maids hurrying downward.
Arabella could scarce fail to note her sullen expression, or the deep circles beneath her eyes. "Sweet
Mary, Avisa, but art all right? Is aught amiss, child?"

"Nothing," the girl mumbled.

" 'Tis a pretty pin you wear."

"Aye."

Scarcely civil, Avisa brushed past them and ran to
catch up to Edmund of Alton. When he would have
pulled free, the girl hung onto his sleeve. As Arabella
turned back briefly to watch, she thought the girl's
manner odd. 'Twas Avisa's age, she supposed, for at
sixteen and more she ought to be wed. Gathering her
skirts she turned away, thinking she had other thoughts
to trouble her just now. Her husband was taking Jamie
away from her. And she knew not how to make him

believe in her. She knew not how to make him love
her for more than what she did for him. She knew not
how to make him want more than that from her.

In the yard, Walter disengaged his sleeve from the
girl's clutch irritably. "Not here," he muttered.

"I'd come up to ye, and ye'd gie me the wine
again."

"Mayhap," he answered, shrugging.

"D'ye think her prettier than I am?" she asked,
pouting. "Ye canna have her."

"I know not who you mean."

"Lady Arabella. I saw the way ye looked on her,
ye know."

" 'Tis your fancy."

He started away, but she caught up to him again.
"Nay, 'tis not." Moving in front of him to block his
way, she raised reproachful eyes to him. " 'Tis the
way ye look on me when ye hae me in yer bed." As
his scowl deepened, she dropped her gaze. "I've told
no one, ye know."

"There's naught to tell."

"Think ye I canna remember?" She leaned forward, this time suggestively. "Think ye I come up
only for the wine ye gie me? Think ye I canna feel
what ye do to me?"

Walter's mouth went dry with the fear that she'd be
heard, that Arabella would discover what he'd done to
the girl. "I'd not talk of this here," he muttered, starting around her. "Come up tonight, and I'll give you
enough wine to take to your own bed with you."

"After ye are done? I like the feel of ye in me, ye
know," she said eagerly. "I dinna even mind the biting."

"After," he promised. With unusual gentleness, he
brushed back her tangled hair from her face. "I'd not
forgo that, little Avisa."

"Some priests wed, e'en though the Pope doesna
like it," she reminded him hopefully.

"Not in England, I'm afraid."

" 'Tisna England—'tis Scotland."

She let him go finally, and as he walked on he decided regretfully that it was time to end his liaison with her. Otherwise she was like to tell Arabella of Byrum, and he could not allow that.

There was the sound of shouts and running feet in the courtyard below. Roused, William groped in the darkness for his chausses and his sword. "God's bones, if 'tis the thieving English . . ." he muttered. "Arabella, there isna time to send for another—I'd hae ye arm me."

"What?" She sat up. "Sweet Mary, but what . . ? Oh—aye." Throwing back the covers, she rose and pulled on her discarded gown, while he tried to spark the wicks on the cresset lamps.

Already someone pounded on the door. "Two are dead, my lord!" And behind him a woman wailed, " 'Tis a plague, and we are all dead!" Then someone else shouted, "Art daft, woman! There wasna any sickness!"

"Is it that we are attacked?" William shouted.

"Nay! Two of the women are found dead!"

" 'Tis a plague, I tell ye! They died in their beds!"

"And I say ye are daft!"

Giving up on the flint stone, William threw open the shutters and looked outside. Already the faint rosy light of dawn could be seen like a thin line along the horizon, and above it the sky was more grey than black. "Jesu, but 'tis cold," he muttered, closing the window and plunging the room into darkness again.

He managed to stumble over a couple of benches and unbar the door. Someone thrust a pitch torch up at him. He half turned to order Arabella, "If I am not to be armed, I'd have ye back to bed. Ye've nae been well since Dunashie, and if 'tis a plague I'd nae have ye take it. Besides, if they are dead, there's naught ye can do."

She would have argued, but then she thought of her babe. And for all that she believed it was Elias' beatings that had marked Jamie, she'd not risk harming the child within her. And 'twould be better if she did not see, she supposed, yet she felt guilty for staying. Reluctantly she returned to bed and waited, listening to the near hysteria below and wondering what had happened.

Two women had died, they'd said—but how? Now that Kenneth of Burwell had finally healed enough to go home, there were none as ailed at all. In her head she ran through all those who lived within the walls, wondering who'd perished. There was Old Gerda, to be sure, but for all that she was old, she was well. And despite failing sight, the woman still baked bread better than any.

Even the thought of the bread made her queasy. Resolutely, she considered the others. Had it been Ena they'd have said so when they came up, for 'twas known how valued she was. Mayhap 'twas Sibyl, for she was near her time, but a woman seldom died until she labored overlong. Sweet Mary, but who?

The shouting had stopped, and a hush descended over the place. Unable to stand it, Arabella rose and pulled William's heavy cloak over her gown ere she unhooked the shutter. She'd do that much at least: She'd not sicken while she carried this babe.

It was lighter now, affording a clear view of the scene below. She could see Father Edmund leaning to comfort a woman who wept, bending so low that his crucifix nearly touched the ground. And then she saw the men carrying two wrapped bodies into the chapel.

It didn't make sense. To be sure, people died every day, carried off by ailments oft unknown, but two of them at once. . . ? Had she not feared marking her babe, she'd have gone down to see for herself. Instead she withdrew from the window and shuttered it again.

"Would ye that I made ye a fire, my lady?" a boy from the scullery asked her.

"Aye." She turned around and removed William's cloak. "Who was it that died?"

"The girl Avisa and her mother, lady. When Old Gerda sent one to waken them, both lay upon their pallets cold."

"Sweet Jesu! Does any know why?"

The boy shook his head. "Nay. There wasna a mark on them. The girl was all huddled up, but the woman looked as though she slept. There wasna but one empty cup on the floor," he went on, "and they ate and drank at table with us all. Father Edmund thinks 'tis something in the air, and Lord William has ordered that the pallets there be burned—aye, and the floor washed with lime lest others sicken."

Arabella made the sign of the Cross over her breast, murmuring, "God rest their souls. But others slept about them, did they not? Did none know they ailed?"

"Aye, and nay. Whatever took them from this world into the next, 'twas quick, for there's none as heard 'em."

"But my lord thinks Father Edmund has the right of it?"

"I think ye ought to be abed, Bella." He walked into the room almost silently. "God's bones, but 'tis strange," he observed, kicking the door shut after the boy. "They died without violence, yet the girl lay as though she were pained," he mused, as much for himself as for her. "And as the boy said, the woman's face was peaceful. Had there been but the one I'd hae thought mayhap poison, but the other . . . nay, even poison would have wakened those around them. 'Tis a bad thing, Bella—a bad thing—and there is no answer." He came up behind her and caught her to him. "Father Edmund fears there will be more, but I hope he's wrong. Until 'tis known, I'd send ye again to Dunashie."

"Nay. I'd rather sit alone in here, served by none but Ena, than ride again in the cold." She twisted her body to look up at him. "Do you go to Edinburgh still?"

"Aye, as soon as the women are interred and the

words are said over them." He frowned. "Mayhap ye ought to go to Elizabeth at Dunashie, Bella."

"Nay. I am too tired for the ride," she lied.

He released her, stepping back. " 'Twas a mistake to take ye to the christening, for ye've ailed ever since. Still . . ."

His voice trailed off as the bitterness nearly overwhelmed him. Aye, it had been a mistake, one of the worst in his life, for it had changed everything between them. Now, after having seen Aidan of Ayrie, after having seen her with him, he could not lie with her without wondering whether she thought of the other man then. It had been wrong to wed when he could not forget, Giles had told him at Dunashie, and mayhap he had the right of it. But for all his disappointment, for all his anger with her, he'd never stopped wanting her.

She turned around at his silence, and once again she saw the hardness in his expression. Her heart ached for what she knew he believed her.

"William . . ." She hesitated, searching his face for some sign that he would listen, then blurted out, "I'd speak of Dunashie, William—aye, and of Woolford also. I'd have you know—"

"I have no wish to know!" he cut in harshly, interrupting her. "Can you not understand that? I don't want to know! I'd hear of nothing ere we were wed, Bella—nothing." He lifted his hand, then dropped it as she cringed. "Get you back to bed. I did but come to tell you 'twas the girl and her mother that died."

"You cannot ask me to hold my tongue when—" But he would not listen. Already he was more than halfway to the door, leaving her to speak to naught but the air.

She sank onto the nearest bench, sick both in heart and body, and once again the awful nausea washed over her. Nay, but she would not weep again, for 'twas not good for her babe, she told herself. Instead she crossed her arms, holding herself tightly as she fought

Chapter Thirty

A cold mist hung over Blackleith, dampening her cloak and wetting the grass beneath her feet, as Arabella watched the crude wooden boxes being lowered into the muddy graves. Father Edmund sprinkled blessed water upon them, commending first the girl's spirit, then the mother's, to God. In the absence of a male kinsman, William reached down to toss a clod of earth over each casket as the priest spoke the familiar words of "dust to dust." The odd thought crossed Arabella's mind that 'twas mud, not dust, that received them.

William straightened to wipe his hands on a cloth offered by one of the kitchen boys, then he prayed silently ere he made the sign of the Cross over his breast. As two men began shoveling the wet earth into the mother's grave, Arabella could only think that Avisa, the girl who'd taken such pride in being the bastard of a Norman knight, was no more. Her gaze traveled to Father Edmund, and with a start she realized that Avisa's pretty pin was fastened to his sleeve. She'd meant for it to be buried with the girl.

As he walked quickly back toward the chapel she

hesitated, then hurried after him, thinking that there was yet time to put the pin in Avisa's shroud—a pagan practice, she supposed, but one that somehow seemed fitting. For all her airs, it was the only thing of value the girl had possessed.

But Walter went instead into his small room, where he poured himself a cup of wine before moving to stand over the fire in his brazier. Arabella rapped on the door jamb to gain his attention.

"Father Edmund . . ."

He looked up, then beckoned her inside. When she hesitated, he waved his hand toward the table where the precious parchments were rolled. "Ere you say 'tis not meet, I'd say 'tis the same place where you and the boy have studied, Lady Arabella."

"I did but come to ask for Avisa's pin, Father. I'd bury it with her," she said, moving to face him.

"We are Christians rather than Vikings, daughter," he chided. "Leave the things of the living to the living."

"They had no heirs."

"Nay, but 'twill buy good candles for God's altar."

"I'd still send it with her."

For a moment his face darkened as though she'd angered him, then he shrugged and unpinned it, holding it out to her. " 'Tis a waste, gentle lady, but I'd not deny you."

"Bella, what are you doing here?" William demanded from the doorway.

Her hand closed over the enameled pin as she spun around. "I am come to see Father Edmund."

"What is it that you hold?" he asked, his eyes narrowing. "What did he give you?"

" 'Twas Avisa's," she answered, opening her palm for him to see. "I came for it."

"Why?"

"I'd put it in the box with her, my lord—I'd let her wear it in eternity." But he was watching the priest rather than her, and there was no mistaking that he struggled with his temper, for his jaw was tight.

"Sweet Mary. William, you surely do not think that I
. . . that Father Edmund . . ."

"I am come to tell him that he goes to Edinburgh
with me, Bella. We will leave at first light on the morrow."

She stared, incredulous at first, then her own anger
rose, making her reckless. "Why? Is it that he smiles
on me? Is it that he is kind to me? For if it is that,
then you'd best take Lang Gib with you—aye, and Wat
also, and Ewan, and all the rest! Oh, and you'd best
not leave any of the scullery boys, or the ostlers either!
Take all of them and leave me with naught but the
women! Is that what you would have, William?"

"Lang Gib stays to protect you, as do the others."

"Are you not afraid he is too comely? Are you not
afraid he will succumb to my wiles also? Jesu, a *priest!*
What you must think me, my lord!"

"Have done, Bella!"

"Nay!" She pressed the pin into his hand. "Look
at this, William! For all that you never gave me the
jewel you promised, do you think I would lie with a
priest for this? 'Twas Avisa's, I tell you!"

He did not want to quarrel with her before Edmund
of Alton. He did not want to quarrel with her at all.
"I did not think it."

"Aye, you did! You think me no more than a whore,
but you will not say it! Say it, William—say it!"

"Jesu! Art daft, woman!" He caught her roughly by
the shoulder and pushed her from the room. "I'd nae
hear ye say such things before him!"

"Ye'd nae hear me say anything!"

"I'd nae hear ye mock me!" He looked toward the
spot where they still filled the graves, and saw that
there were none there who had not turned to stare.
" 'Tis not the place for this, Bella," he muttered,
lowering his voice.

"Where? Where is the place, my lord? And you had
your way, I'd say naught but 'aye' to you!"

He raised his fist, then opened it as though he meant
to slap her there in the courtyard. The old fear washed

over her, fear that she was returning to the hell Elias and Nigel had given her, fear that once again she would know naught but a heavy hand. Fear that she'd carry this babe like the last. And she'd almost rather die than live like that. Still, she managed to meet his eyes without wavering. Finally he dropped his arm and started to walk away from her.

She caught his sleeve and held on. "You've scarce been civil since I spoke with Ayrie's son, William, and I'd speak of that. I'd have you tell me to my face what you think me!"

"I'd nae speak of it, Bella! Get you upstairs until you are calm."

She could see that everyone watched curiously, and she did not think she could stand their pity. Her pride rose like a gorge in her throat, and beneath her breastbone she ached. She swallowed, then breathed deeply of the cold air, striving to master her own fury.

"Aye, but you will come with me, William. And you do not, I'd go back to Byrum," she stated evenly.

Her words hung between them as he stared hard. "Ye belong at Blackleith. Ye canna leave without cause, and I'd nae let ye."

"You are going to Edinburgh." Tears of anger rather than hurt scalded her eyes. Blinking them back, she told him bitterly, "You make Blackleith the greater Hell for me."

"I'd nae stand here disputing for all to see," he retorted, reaching for her arm. "Ye'll go up, I said."

"Are you not afraid I will tryst with another whilst you are gone?" she gibed, jerking away.

He followed, not answering her, but she knew he was as angered as she was, and she no longer cared. Whether he beat her or not he would hear her, if she had to shout everything for all to hear. No matter what it cost her, she'd tell him how much he wronged her.

The steps were steep and she stumbled blindly, falling back into him, but as soon as he righted her she went on. A silent, disapproving Ena awaited her.

"I'd hae ye get her to bed. The woman's taken leave of her senses," he told the tiring maid.

"Nay—I'd have you leave us," Arabella ordered her. As Ena slipped past them, she whirled to face her husband. "Behold the whore you have wed, my lord! I'd hear you call me thus to my face!"

"Keep your voice down, Bella!"

" 'Tis what you think of me, is it not? I'd expected more of you, William of Dunashie!"

"I dinna say it!"

"You all but accused me after I spoke to Aidan of Ayrie, William! And if you did not say it, you made it plain that you believed the tale!" Too furious to care, she let the tears spill from her eyes and run unchecked down her cheeks.

"I've nae accused ye," he muttered.

"Think you I do not know what is in your mind? Think you I cannot remember how it was with Elias, William? He beat me so many times without reason that he marked Jamie! And 'twas for foundless jealousy, nothing more!"

"I never beat ye. . . . Ye canna say it."

She tugged at the lacings, loosing them, then pulled her gown over her head. Tossing it across the room, she faced him in her thin linen undergown. "Then beat me now!" she shouted at him. "Or do I have too much on to mark me yet? Have I not made it easy enough for you to do it?"

"In the name of God, Bella, have done! I . . ."

She lifted the undergown up and wrenched it off also. As it fell at her feet she stared at him, her bared breasts heaving. "Now? Would you hit me now for what you think I have done? Papa hit me also—too many times to count, William—but I dared to think you were better than they were! I dared to think you could love me! Can you not understand: They hurt me for naught!"

"I have never hurt ye, Bella! Ye canna say I have!"

"Nay, there is greater hurt than beating when you mistrust me, when you would have it that I am without

honor.'' She moved closer, standing before him.
''Punish me for what you believe I've done, William
of Dunashie! And you believe I have lain with Aidan
or any other save Elias, beat me for it! 'Tis your right,
isn't it?''

''I'd not speak of it. . . . God's bones . . .''

''Aye, you will! This night you will!''

''Bella, I cannot stand it—I cannot stand to think of
Ayrie!''

''*You* cannot stand it! *You* cannot stand it!'' she
fumed. ''There is nothing for you to stand, my lord!''

''I have tried to forgive ye, I swear. Give me time,
and I'll forget about him. 'Twas that I dinna know
until after—''

''Forgive me? For what? For the face God gave me?
Afore God, William, but I've done naught to dishonor
you or me! Can you not hear me? You have naught to
forgive!''

''They can hear ye below. Jesu . . .'' His eyes
moved over her bared body, and he knew he did not
want to quarrel anymore with her. His mouth went
dry, and the heat rose within him. ''I'd lie with you
and forget this, Bella.''

''I'd be more to you than that, William of Dunashie!
You can get a whore for that!'' Casting about for the
basin and pitcher, she lifted the latter. ''D'you burn?''
she demanded sarcastically. Before he realized what
she meant to do, she flung the water on him. As it
dripped from his tunic and ran down his legs, she surveyed him with disgust. '' 'Tis all the ease you will
get of me this day. I'd not lay with any who believes
me false.''

''The boy. . . . D'ye deny . . . ?'' He could not
bring himself to say the words to her. He combed his
wet hair with his fingers and tried to reason with her.
''For all that we have shouted at each other I'd have
no other, I swear it.''

''I'd hear you tell me what sin you think I have committed, William. I'd hear it of you.''

He sucked in his breath, then exhaled fully. ''Nay.

It matters no more that Aidan got the boy of ye. And ye swear he isna in your thoughts, I'd forget this.''

"I'd not ask you to forgive or forget, Will. I'd have you believe me blameless.''

For a long moment he watched the tears spill from her eyes, then he could stand her pain no longer. He tried to force a smile and could not. "Nay, Bella—I'd nae have ye weep. And ye tell me ye never lay with him, I'd believe it.'' And for the first time since he'd had the tale of Milo of Woolford, he knew he meant it. "I never thought ye lay with Edmund of Alton nor any other. 'Twas only Ayrie, and if ye say 'twas not so, I'll accept it.''

There was no mistaking the appeal in the hazel eyes, and yet she was not certain he meant his words. Oddly, she remembered what Elizabeth had said, that he put such faith in oaths. "Do you swear it?'' she asked suddenly. "Would you swear it now?''

"I swore to ye when I wed ye.''

"Not of this, my lord—not of this.''

"Aye.'' He drew the dagger from his belt and held it up so that she could see the cross formed by the hilt above the blade. "What would ye that I said, Bella? What would ye that I swore? I'd say anything, and 'twould ease ye.''

"I'd have you swear that you believe me, William. I'd have you acknowledge that you believe I never lay with Ayrie's son. Aye—and I'd have you say that you would love me.'' She watched him hesitate, and she felt defeated. Still, she would gamble one last time. "Else you swear it, I'd go back to Byrum, my lord, for the only marks Papa put on me were on my body.''

He held the knife higher, his eyes on the stones on the hilt, then he drew a deep breath. "Aye. And ye tell me ye never lay with Ayrie, I'd believe it. And despite the boy, despite all else, I have loved ye since we were met, Arabella of Byrum, I swear it.'' He looked from the dagger to her. "Is there aught else ye'd have me swear?''

She bit her lip to still its trembling, then nodded.

"Aye," she whispered. "I'd have you say you will try to put my son in your heart."

"I canna swear it, Bella, but I believe a wee bit of him is there already." A crooked smile twisted his mouth down at one side. "And ye'd leave us be, I think we'd learn to love each other without ye." With his free hand he reached to hold her chin up, that she could not look away. "He is in a fair way to winning me for himself, ye know. Now—would ye hear what I'd have ye swear to me?"

"I have naught—"

"Ye do. I'd have ye say ye'd put me before him in your heart and mind, for 'tis where I'd be. And I'd have ye say ye'd love me also. E'en if there are a dozen to join him, in the end there will be naught but ye and me, Arabella."

"I have always wanted to love you, Will. From the first, from when you gave me this chain, I have wanted to love you," she answered, her voice husky. "And I do."

He tossed the dagger onto a low table, then faced her again, grinning crookedly. "And I do not touch ye wrongly, would ye kiss me?"

"And you do not touch me wrongly, I'll be sorely disappointed," she murmured, standing on her toes to twine her arms about his neck. "As I remember it, you told me there were a dozen ways. . . ." Her voice trailed off as he parted her lips beneath his.

He would have nibbled, he would have wooed to win her after the quarrel, but she pressed against him with an ardor that matched his own. Her mouth, her breasts, her hips—all of her—invited him eagerly. His hands twined in her braids as his mouth explored hers, until the heat between them was nearly unbearable. When he raised his head his hands were on the ties to his chausses, tugging them loose. They fell away, bagging above his leather garters. Without waiting to undress further, he lifted her and carried her to the bed. As he laid her within the deep feather mattresses, she pulled him down over her. When he would have nuzzled her neck and teased her breasts, she grasped his hair, pulling his head back to her. It was *her* body that tantalized, *her* tongue that played against his, and it was *her* hands that urged him, moving over his bared hips as she twisted eagerly beneath him. The next time he would love her slowly, savoring each small taste of her. But for now, he would lose himself in her mindlessly.

Her legs parted, welcoming him into the heat of her, taking as much as she gave. It was as though she could not have enough of him as she rocked and bucked beneath him. He plunged again and again, striving to reach the precipice that would send him over the edge. Her hands were everywhere, and beneath him she panted and moaned as she strained to meet him ere he fell. There was nothing beyond the feel of her body around his. Only dimly was he aware when she cried out loudly, then there was the ecstasy of union, that final peak ere he floated slowly back to earth.

When he looked down, her eyes were closed and her hair clung damply to her forehead. She swallowed visibly as she tried to gain her breath. Jesu, but she was beautiful, and for the first time he felt that she was truly his. He lay over her, resting his weight on his legs and elbows, waiting for her to look at him.

"Twas good," she murmured finally.

"Aye, and there are eleven more to go."

Her eyes flew open, and the rings around the grey seemed even darker than usual. "Are there really that many ways?"

"Probably more," he assured her.

"I think I'd hear about them first," she decided, blushing beneath his gaze.

Reluctantly he rolled away, then pulled the covers up over them. "Well, the next time I take off my boots, and after that 'twill be without my clothes. And there is when we unbraid your hair. And I'd let you ride at least once before I leave for Edinburgh, I think."

" 'Tis only four more," she reminded him.

"There are two sides—and the back."

"Sweet Mary. Berta must have taught you well. Elias counted all but this a sin."

"Then he was a fool in that also." He pulled her closer, easing her head onto his shoulder. "And he was wrong to say you were naught but skin and bones."

She sighed. "I expect I will be much fatter ere long, my lord. 'Tis neither the weather nor the food that sickens me." She rose up slightly and traced along his ear lightly with a fingertip. " 'Tis the babe."

He was very still for a moment, then he grinned broadly. "When?"

"Well, I have missed my second course but lately, so Ena thinks 'twill be late August. I will be fat and ugly in the heat."

"Nay. Elizabeth was never ugly," he reassured her. "Fat mayhap, but not ugly." He pulled her down again, wrapping strong arms about her, holding her so close she could feel as well as hear the beat of his heart. "Jesu, Bella," he complained, "and you would have had me beat you?"

"I had hopes you could not."

"But what if I had?"

"I'd have told you then—and hoped you would not accuse Lang Gib or another for it," she answered simply. Before he could protest she went on, " 'Twas only Elias' vanity that denied Jamie, Will. 'Tis odd, is it not, for I believe 'twas his beatings that marked his son."

"Aye." His hand combed at the ends of her braids, loosening them. "Well, I'd like a daughter. I'd name her Rose for ye, but I will take whatever God gives us, praying only that he or she is whole. I'd have no other child suffer like Jamie."

"I have hopes of a Giles."

"Mayhap."

She fell silent for a time, then could not help asking, "Why is it that you go to Edinburgh, my lord?"

"Nay, but I am sworn to secrecy in that, Bella. You will have to wait to discover the reason." But he knew she still feared for the boy. "Would it ease your mind if I swore I mean to bring him back?"

She appeared to consider the offer, then shook her head. "As you have sworn you love me, I know you will bring him home to me."

Chapter Thirty-One

The journey to Edinburgh had been a hard one, and the boy was stiff and sore, but he made less complaint than Edmund of Alton, who'd been loath to go. Then for three days they'd waited to see King David. In the end it was a letter William brought from Giles that gained them an audience with the sovereign. And when the appointed time came, they all went, and as the royal page announced, "William of Dunashie, sire!" Will carried James of Woolford into the room. There were audible murmurs, but Will went down on bended knee, the child still in his arms.

"Rise you, William of Dunashie." David referred to the letter handed him by a clerk, then looked up from his carved chair. "So Giles of Moray asks our indulgence, does he?"

"For the boy, Sire." Knowing that David was by custom more Norman than Scot, William forced himself to speak properly before him. "He cannot walk, and I have brought him to seek the opinion of your physicians. Although I have money to pay they would not see him, saying there was naught to be done, but I'd have them look on him ere they decide."

"Your son?"

"He is James of Woolford, Sire—son to my wife by her first husband."

"Woolford?"

" 'Tis English, but there were too many sons already in the house. With their consent, I have the boy." He lifted his cloak from around Jamie, revealing the twisted leg. "We do not ask that he be cured, for that is in the hands of God, Sire, but we'd know if aught can be done that he may walk."

He'd chosen the right words for David, who prided himself on his piety. He leaned forward in his chair to look more closely at the leg. " 'Tis shorter than the other," he observed.

"Aye—and the foot turns half over so he cannot stand." He set the child down before the king, holding him up by his shoulder, showing that the foot alone would not hold him.

"I cannot order miracles, William of Dunashie."

"And I'd not ask that." Will reached into his cloak and drew out a rolled parchment from the pouch within. "I'd have the physicians' opinion ere I attempt to remedy each thing. I have brought drawings of what I'd do, but afore I attempt it I'd know I do not harm him further."

Walter watched, his lip curled derisively, as the big man held out his parchment. But David unrolled it curiously, looking at the pictures William had made, then handed it to a clerk. "Tell the doctors that this man comes to them with our consent—aye, and with our hopes also. They are to look on the boy and determine a course of treatment." He looked again to where Jamie balanced himself against Will's big leg. "God grant that they can aid you, young Woolford, for I'd see none of His creatures like that."

When the child nodded mutely, William spoke for him, "And God grant his blessings to you, Sire, for the kindness you do this day." Picking Jamie up again, he started to leave. But King David's voice stopped him. "You have been to Dunashie—how fares our namesake there?"

"I stood at the font for him," William answered proudly. "He is as strong as his king."

David nodded, pleased. "Tell the physicians also that they are not to take this man's silver. Make it known to them that we consider such service a gift to God."

"Nay, I can pay them."

"There is no need. Buy the child what he requires instead."

The brief audience was over, and it was not until they were outside the room that William realized his own knees were weak. Walter fell in beside them, and Ewan followed.

"They are physicians, my lord, not workers of miracles," Walter muttered. "I know not what you think they can do."

"I mean to see. Had I the money I'd take him to the hospital at St. Gall, but I cannot."

For the better part of the next day, those who counted themselves skilled in everything from the humours to surgery examined James of Woolford, pulling, twisting, and stretching on his bad leg. Finally, Androchus of Ravenna came forward to meet with William, who sat across a littered table from him. Clearing his throat, he examined Will's drawings carefully, then looked up.

"These are yours, my lord?" he asked in Latin.

"Aye," Will answered in kind, surprising the physician.

"He will not walk as you or I."

"I do not ask that. I would that he walked at all."

"The boy is your son?"

"He is my wife's."

"He is fortunate then to have one with such a care for him."

"He is dear to us."

Androchus cleared his throat again, then traced with his finger along Will's first drawing. "There is more than one problem, as you know, my lord. But the worst are that the leg is weak and the foot will not support him,'' he murmured, stating the obvious.

"Aye."

"And when you put the steel rod in the boot, two things will happen. First, he cannot bend his knee, and second, the steel foot is heavy.

"Aye."

"He is not a strong boy, my lord."

"But he is willing."

"He is that," the physician conceded. "He bore much today." For a moment William thought he would say that it had all been for naught, that the device was useless—or worse, that it would harm the child. Instead, the man nodded. "The boot is fine, my lord. 'Twill keep the leg and foot straight. But the third problem is the length of the leg."

"I'd thought mayhap a block of wood on the bottom."

"Aye—or a metal stirrup that extends down beyond the sole. Again, 'twill be heavy."

"Aye."

"I'd measure poles to support his arms until he is used to the weight of this. 'Tis all I'd suggest that you have not proposed. As for whether he can learn to walk thus, only time and his effort will show." He looked directly at William for a moment. "Your Latin is good, my lord."

"I studied with King Henry's clerks."

"They taught you well." Faint amusement lurked in the dark eyes. "Why did you bring him here, when you had already reasoned this out?"

"When his mother says he cannot, I'd tell her you said he could," William answered honestly. "And I'd know I do not harm the child. It pains him to be as he is, for he'd dream of being whole."

"I wish I could say there was the means to straighten the leg—or to make it grow—but there is not." Androchus rose to leave, indicating that the interview was over, then turned back. Drawing a small vial from within the folds of his gown, he held it out. " 'Tis oil from the Holy Sepulchre, my lord, and I'd not thought to give it. But ere you put the boot on the boy, I'd have you rub three drops on the leg, and invoke the Savior's healing grace each day for a week.''

"You honor me with it," William managed, taking the precious oil. "I'll not waste it."

The physician smiled. "As you can write, William of Dunashie, I'd have you inform me of the boy's progress. Someday I may discover another so afflicted, and I'd use what you have shown me."

When William finally came out, Ewan was waiting with a very tired Jamie. "They said I canna walk," the child decided.

"Nay, they dinna," Ewan insisted. "They said ye can, and ye are willing to suffer for it, I'd expect.''

"How?"

"Well," Will joined in, "first we find a bootmaker as can make one that comes high above your knee." He held up the vial. "And to ease the pain for ye, we are given oil from Christ's tomb."

"A boot!" Jamie snorted in disgust.

" 'Twill not bend, ye know, for there is to be a metal rod the length of the shaft on either side to hold the leg stiff. And the foot will be encased in armorer's steel inside the leather, that the foot does not turn," Will explained patiently. "And beneath the sole there is to be something to make the leg as long as the other." He reached to ruffle the pale hair. " 'Twill be no thing of beauty, I grant ye, but God willing, ye can learn to walk a wee bit with it."

" 'Twill be heavy, Jamie, but ye can do it."

"Aye, but we put poles beneath his arms until his legs are strengthened enough to walk without them." William reached for the boy, taking him from Ewan. "All I'd ask of ye, James, is that ye try. We canna do it for ye, ye know, but we can pray." Shouldering Arabella's son, he noted the priest's absence. "And where is Edmund of Alton?''

"When he left he dinna say, but he is to meet us at our lodging. Unless I mistake me, he is gone to pur-

chase herbs.'' As they emerged outside, Ewan spat on
the ground. ''Coming from Kelso, he is skilled with
them, he tells me.''

The child's arm tightened around William's neck.
''When do I get my boot, my lord?''

''As soon as it can be made as I'd have it. And then
I'd nae go home until ye can make a step for your
mother.'' He hoisted the boy higher. ''And tonight,
wee son, we rub ye wi' the sacred oil.''

The bootmaker puzzled and argued over William's
design, and in the end agreed to consult with a smith.
'Twould take at least three days, he said, ignoring the
boy's eagerness.

''Nay, but for six years ye have not walked,'' Will
told the disappointed Jamie. ''Three days is as nothing. We'll wait for it.''

Walter waited for them to return and seek their beds.
It had been a near thing earlier at King David's court,
for he'd recognized one from Kelso amongst the royal
clerks. Nay, he dared not tarry where any might know
him. And so he had spent the day separate from the
others, replenishing his bags of poppies and of belladonna berries, the two most useful tools he'd discovered, for the one lulled while the other did its deadly
deed.

He'd considered giving all three of them his mixture
here, to say later that they'd succumbed to the strange
sickness from Blackleith, but the time was not yet
right. When he did it he'd be where he could comfort
Arabella of Byrum—he'd be there to hold her, to
soothe her while she wept. Nay, 'twould be better even
if he were not where they died, for then when he revealed himself there'd be none to suspect him. Mayhap
he ought to excuse himself, leaving them with his
deadly potion, that he would be at Blackleith when the
word came.

He was restless, for thus far his plans had come to
naught: He was no closer now than ever to killing Giles
of Moray. And lately Arabella of Byrum seemed to be
truly enamored of the great lout she called husband.

But would Moray not come to Blackleith to bury his brother? That still left the matter of Elizabeth of Rivaux and her infant sons. The list of those he'd have to kill seemed to grow ever longer. The way he saw it now, nothing less than a selective epidemic would serve. And it would not be enough for only those of Moray's blood to die. Nay, there would have to be others as perished from his plague. Mayhap the woman Ena, for he knew she did not like him, and a kitchen boy or two . . . and possibly an ostler. It didn't matter who, beyond those sharing the blood of Giles of Moray. Mayhap he would but make up enough of his poison, and leave it to the Devil to determine who shared it.

He had only just finished his work when he heard them, and he slipped his newly made powders into his bag. William of Dunashie wanted piety, did he? Carefully Walter readjusted his crucifix over his breast, then took out his small sheaf of prayers and bent his head over them as though he would commune with God. As the door opened before him, his lips moved silently.

"Father Edmund! Father Edmund! God grants that I may walk!"

William silenced the child with a finger to his lips and murmured, "Nay. 'Tisna right to disturb a man at his prayers. And He doesna grant it yet—He but gives ye the chance to try."

Walter crossed himself and looked up. "It went well then?"

"Well enough, I think."

"I dinna like it when they would pull my leg," Jamie protested. "One called Ambrose would have put a rope and rock on it, but another said 'twould but separate my joint."

William set the boy down on a bench opposite to Walter and reached into his pocket for the vial. Taking it out, he showed it. " 'Tis holy oil. And ye do not mind it, I'd have ye put it on his leg ere we retire."

"Me? Surely—"

"There canna be enough prayers, Father."

Later, when all was done and Ewan and the boy had taken to their pallet, Walter broached his departure with William. "And it takes days or weeks here, my lord, I'd return to Dunashie. Ere we left there was sickness there, and I'd be where I am needed." When William said nothing he went on, "The physicians have seen the boy, after all, and 'twould appear your prayers are answered. Nay, but I'd minister to mine flock ere I am counted remiss."

William knew he had no real reason to keep him, yet he hesitated. For all that he now truly trusted Arabella, he did not trust Edmund of Alton. There was something wrong with the man, a coldness that belied his mission. For a man of God, he attended to his soul less than William himself did.

"While I am here, no masses are said for the dead or any other," Walter reminded him.

Aye, and William knew not how long it would take James to make that first step. He knew not even if the boy would make it at all. And it was no small thing to deprive his people of the sacraments. With Edmund of Alton in Edinburgh no babes were baptized, no marriages blessed, and no dead shriven. Nay, he had no good reason to demand the priest's continued presence. Finally, he nodded.

"When you are returned, I'd not have you tell my lady why 'tis we are come here," is all he said. "I'd not have her hope until we know. Promise me that, and you may go."

Chapter Thirty-Two

Arabella lay upon her bed fully clothed, unwilling to move, for fear the sickness would return. Sweet Mary, but Ena had said it did not last long, and yet for three weeks and more it seemed that naught but dried bread and stale cheese would stay in her stomach. And still William did not come.

"Gentle lady . . ."

Too miserable to rise, she opened her eyes and saw Edmund of Alton leaning over her, his face betraying his concern. "Forgive me, Father, but I'd not rise," she whispered.

"Aye. The woman says you cannot eat. Would you that I brought you something—a little fowl is easy on the stomach—or some sweetened wine, mayhap?" he asked.

"Nay."

He'd returned to Blackleith to find her sick, and while it served him by making an epidemic plausible, it also worried him. She was the one thing he'd not see perish there. He pulled a bench beside the bed and sat down, possessing one of her hands. It was damp, despite the chill in the room.

"Would you that I summoned Burwell's barber to bleed you? Or I'd even brew you a soothing potion, and you willed it. At Kelso, I studied the use of herbs for many maladies."

" 'Twill pass—'tis but the babe."

It was as though his blood chilled. He felt actual pain in the center of his chest and his stomach knotted, sickening him. And then he felt an impotent anger: at her, at the Bastard, at everything. In letting William of Dunashie's seed take hold within her body, she'd betrayed him. She gave the Bastard what Walter could not allow: She gave him an heir to Blackleith. He recoiled, drawing his hand away.

"I'd thought mayhap 'twas the sickness that plagues us here," he said, his voice strained.

"Nay. Sweet Jesu—there are others?"

"The old man as lowers the gate. 'Twas this morning," he added, recovering his composure.

"But it has been weeks. Surely—"

" 'Tis a strange malady, to be sure, but there is no mistaking 'tis the same, for he was discovered in his bed like the other two."

"But he was old. Mayhap 'twas his heart that ceased."

"I'd not think it. His face bore the same expression as that on the girl Avisa. E'en though he was not warm, I shrived him," he added. Thinking he had to leave ere he betrayed himself, he rose. "But I can hope you are right, of course."

She turned her head away and closed her eyes. "I would that William came home, Father."

And to him, it was as though her words sealed her fate. He wanted to wound, to tell her that the Bastard would never come again to Dunashie, that her precious brat died—aye, and Ewan with them. And he wanted to tell her that she would join them, she and the babe she carried. But he dared not. Instead, he forced himself to pat her arm and murmur soothingly.

"As 'tis but the babe, sweet lady, I'd send you a draught to ease the sickness."

" 'Twould not stay down, Father.''

"I will add enough poppy juice,'' he promised. "It seems to stop the retching.''

"Aye.''

"Rest you, daughter, and I will return forthwith, bringing it.''

He left her then, but instead of hastening he walked slowly back to his small room. And when he got there he sat for a time at his table, the two pouches open before him. It had been too easy before, and he realized it now. Like any who bargained with Lucifer, he now was discovering the price higher than he would pay. It was as though the Black Angel had lured him, dangled the woman before him, then pulled her away before Walter could have her. It was the cruelest jest of his life, for he'd had not much to love in his life, and he believed he loved her.

But what if the child she carried were a daughter? Walter argued within himself. And what if it were not? Whether William of Dunashie came home or not would not matter then, for the Bastard would have left yet another mountain in Walter's path. As he climbed one, it seemed another always rose before him. Once he would have needed only to kill the Butcher after Edmund, knowing it unlikely that William would inherit, but then he'd found the Bastard already there before him. Then he'd had two to kill. But that was before Elizabeth of Rivaux bore her sons, making it four. And now Arabella of Byrum stood ready to cheat him also. There appeared to be no end to it.

He'd wanted her, he wanted her still, and even when she was dead he'd think on what he'd been denied. For a moment he considered letting her live, in the hope she bore a girl. Torn, he did that which he'd not done since the Butcher had burned Dunashie: He laid his head upon the table and wept for himself and for her. Six people he'd murdered for Blackleith—and he expected to hear of the other three at any time—and he was not yet done.

He sat back and shrugged his shoulders to ease them.

Then he wiped his wet cheeks with the back of his hand, drying them. As great as the cost, he had to pay it. He had to keep to that which he'd promised his uncle at Dunashie.

For the time the sickness had passed, and Arabella rose to wash her face at the basin. She was tired, she was hungry, and yet she dared not eat. She looked down, seeing that her dress hung loosely about her. When William came back, he'd think she looked more like a stick than a woman.

William. What was it that kept him in David's city, when she had need of him? And what need had he of Jamie's company, when her own for her son was greater? Sweet Mary, but he'd left her to suffer alone, and she resented it. Nay, but he did not know she was sick, she reminded herself—there'd been none to write him until Father Edmund had come home.

"Och, but ye are up now, are ye?" Ena asked from behind her. "Ye've fair worried Father, ye know, for he sends ye something for yer stomach, my lady."

"I'd not put anything in it," Arabella responded tiredly.

"He fears ye have the malady, but I told him 'twas the babe. Being a priest, he canna know of that, I suppose." The woman carried a small pitcher to the table near the bed. "He said I was to tell ye to lie down after ye drink."

"All I would have is my husband, Ena."

"He'll come back ere the month changes, and ye can mark that I said it."

"And I long for my son, also."

" 'Tis two things ye ask," Ena chided her, "nae one." Sighing, she turned back to face Arabella, and her own eyes were reddened. "Och, but I ken ye, mistress, for I'd see that Ewan myself." Her fingers played with the carved wooden Cross she wore at her breast. "I been prayin' for him to come home. E'en with the boy between us, he keeps me warm." Moving back to the table, she poured a small amount of Edmund of

Alton's medicinal wine into a cup. "Ye might want to try it."

"Not now."

Carrying it closer to the fire, Ena sniffed it curiously. "He says 'tis herbs and honey blended for ye." Regretfully, she set it by the brazier. "I suppose 'tis the honey as hides the taste of the other, ye know. Sometimes I wish I was as skilled in the simples as ye are, but I—" She stopped, hearing running footsteps on the stairs outside.

Edmund of Alton burst in with unseemly haste, then, as his eyes took in the two women, he seemed to recover. "Ah, you are up, dear lady."

He'd not been too late. Relief washed over him when he saw that she lived. In the minutes since he'd given Ena the poisoned wine, he'd died a hundred deaths of his own. And during that time he'd realized that he could not kill one of the two things he wanted in this life. He'd rather wait and dispose of her babe than lose her with it.

"My thanks for the wine, Father, but I've not yet partaken of it. My stomach is better for now."

" 'Tis why I am come." He looked around him, then spied the pitcher. "When I mixed it I forgot about the babe, and I fear 'tis overstrong. And after the other boy, I'd see you take care lest this one be marked also." As he spoke, he crossed the room and picked it up. " 'Twould be better mayhap if I made you another without the poppy in it."

"I'd not take any of it. There cannot be much more of this before the babe sits better within me." She walked toward him, her hands clasped before her. "What you would do for me is appreciated, Father, but all I need is for my husband and my son to come home again to me."

"May God grant your wish, daughter," he murmured. "And you have the need, I pray you will send to me."

He left nearly as precipitously as he'd arrived, but neither woman thought much of it. Arabella halfheart-

edly tried to stitch an embroidered band about the
sleeves of a new tunic for her son, then abandoned
the effort, while Ena plied her own needle silently by
the fire. Finally, too restless to lie upon her bed and
too weak for much else, Arabella carried the small
writing box she'd assembled to the table closest to the
fire. Moving the wine cup out of the way, she unrolled
a piece of the precious parchment. Crude though it
would be, she intended to write her first letter to her
husband.

Very carefully, she dipped her pen into her ink bot-
tle and held it poised above the skin, not knowing how
or where to begin. Her skills were not many and her
spelling yet poor, but she'd have him know she missed
him. Finally she began tentatively with ''William,
husband to me.'' It ought to have read otherwise, but
she knew not how to make the word ''recommend.''
Indeed, as she considered the parchment, she realized
she knew not enough words to make sense, but still
she would try. ''On this twi—'' She stopped and
scratched that out, for she could spell neither ''twenty-
second'' nor ''February.''

There was a polite tapping at the door, and when
Ena went to answer it Lang Gib stepped inside.
Bounding from behind him was one of William's
wolfhounds. In William's absence the dog lunged for
Arabella, licking at her face, turning over the ink and
the cup. She pushed him off, and pulled the parchment
away before the ink spread to it.

''Fie on you, you silly creature!''

'' 'Tis sorry I am, lady,'' Gib apologized, pulling
at the beast's collar. ''Down, Brut!''

Ena dropped to her knees with a cloth and tried to
sop up the wine from the rushes to no avail, while her
mistress blotted at the ink. When it appeared that Brut
had no further interest in Arabella, Gib let him go to
lap at the wine. Reaching into the neck of his tunic he
drew out a parchment case, and for a moment Arabella's hopes soared.

"I ordered the messenger fed ere he leaves, my lady. And ye'd reply, ye hae but to call down to the yard."

She barely nodded as he left, dragging the dog after him. Instead she slit open the wax that sealed the case and unrolled the letter within. Her face fell as her eyes found the word "Woolford" in the greeting. It came not from William but from England, and she feared to try to read more of it. Any news from Woolford could not be good. Later, when she was calm, mayhap she'd ask Father Edmund to help her with it. Putting it aside she cleaned the table, then washed the spilled ink from the bench.

She'd not think on anything that came from Woolford—she'd not. She sat for a moment, wondering what Donald could want now. Nay, she'd not know, she decided, for she'd have nothing to do with Elias' sons, not after what they'd done to Jamie. When William came home, 'twould be soon enough to answer. Still, it was in truth strange to hear anything after so many years. Very gingerly she unrolled it again, and looked to the seal at the bottom. Tracing over the words beside the imprinted wax, she read carefully, "Hugh, his mark," thinking they made no sense. Why would Hugh write to her?

Uneasy, Arabella took up her pen to continue her letter. Call it fancy or call it a woman's silliness, she was afraid, and even she acknowledged 'twas probably without reason. But aside from whatever came from Woolford, there was the mysterious malady that had come upon them. In the four months she'd been at Blackleith four people had died suddenly—'twas many for a small keep. With great care she formed the letters, using an economy of words. Beneath "William, husband to me," she added, "I would you came home in all haste, for I am fearful." She read it, thinking he would surely think her foolish. Then, knowing he loved her enough to come, she signed it, "Arabella, not her mark," betraying her pride that she could write the words. And as she had no seal of her own, beneath her name she drew a rose like those in the hall.

Summoning Wat, she ordered him to Edinburgh, telling him to seek William at King David's court first, then to go house to house if need be. To speed him on his way, she parted with three of William's pennies.

Later, as she lay upon her bed in the winter greyness, she heard the door open. "The woman says you are too ill to come down to sup," Father Edmund said. "I have brought you another potion. Aye, and some bread and cheese also, daughter, for the sooner you keep your food, the sooner the sickness will pass."

"Where is Ena?"

"She sups below. Would you that I summoned her?"

"Nay."

He poured a small amount into the cup, then pulled a bench closer to sit beside her. " 'Twill ease you," he promised. " 'Tis not so strong as the other."

"I do not thirst, Father."

" 'Twill keep the food down."

" 'Tis not the sickness now. I am but tired."

"Then I would that you ate, gentle lady. Your woman says you are become but skin and bones beneath your gown." Setting the cup aside, he took out a small knife and pared a sliver of cheese for her. "And you chew it slowly, mayhap 'twill stay down." When she did not answer Walter hesitated, for her babe angered him yet. Finally he forced himself to say, "You must eat for your child."

"Aye."

He fed her doggedly, cutting small pieces of the cheese and bread and holding them to her mouth, waiting for her to swallow. When she would have stopped he urged her on, telling her that her lord would expect her to eat. As darkness descended the wolves howled in the distance, and still he sat with her, covering her hand with his own, speaking low until she slept.

Somewhere in the netherworld she heard Ena ask if she'd eaten, and the priest answered aye and that it had stayed down. She tossed restlessly, plagued by dreams—dreams that Elias came for her from his grave, dreams that William fought him for her. She roused from her nightmares, saying that she thirsted, and it was a man's arms that lifted her to drink wine so bitter she nearly gagged from it. But then peace descended, and she knew nothing more until Ena drew the hangings in the morning.

She felt better, and when one of the kitchen boys brought a wooden plate with bread and salted meat she was actually hungry. Ena helped her dress, then arranged the food on the table.

"The babe sits more kindly within ye," the woman observed, as Arabella reached for a piece of cheese.

" 'Twould seem so.''

" 'Twas the medicine Father Edmund brewed ye. Ye know he dinna leave ye until the cock crowed.''

"I know only that I ate and slept.''

"Well, he sat there with ye, a-holding yer hand until ye was calm. Did ye good, it did.'' She leaned over Arabella to pour a small amount of ale into her cup. "Do ye think he'd teach me to make his potions?''

" 'Twas foul-tasting,'' Arabella recalled.

" 'Twas because he left the sweetness out of it. He said ye dinna need it. I expect 'twas the poppy juice ye tasted, for ye slept.''

"No more have perished, have they? From the sickness, I mean?''

"Nay. And I still say that for all he is learned, Father Edmund is wrong in that. Auld Ben wasna sick—'twas God as took him at his time to go.'' Moving to straighten the covers on the bed, she added offhand-edly, "Lang Gib was asking about the master's dog this morning, for they canna find him. He dinna come to eat.''

"Which one?''

"The one Lord William calls Brut.''

Chapter Thirty-Three

William hurt for the boy, wincing with each painful step Jamie took. The boot was heavy and awkward, and it had chafed against the child's skin, leaving red, nearly raw skin before they'd thought to line it with lambskin. But still the boy would try, falling, stumbling, struggling for each small victory, until Will thought he could not stand to watch. Yet when Will had said 'twas enough, James of Woolford would not quit, and with his lip between his teeth, his forehead furrowed from the intensity of his effort, he'd dragged the boot some more.

They'd stayed longer than expected, making adjustments, changing the way the device was attached so many times that it no longer resembled William's design above the knee. Now it was attached by crossed belts at the waist, like half a pair of leather chausses, and the iron rods that held it straight went up past the knee, visible on the outside. Another iron foot piece went beneath the sole, holding it a full handbreadth above the ground. But the worst torture was on the inside, for the boot was lined with a metal slipper that kept the foot from turning on its side. When Ewan had seen it, he said it looked like a torture device. The result was almost more than the boy could bear, but somehow he began to master it.

On this cold, rainy day, Jamie hobbled in the muddy lane with the two poles beneath his arms, resting on them between every step, as William and Ewan watched him. There was no denying the boy walked—there was only the accounting of the cost, not in silver, but in suffering. As far as William was concerned, James of Woolford deserved to be sainted for what he bore.

" 'Twas four, my lord!" the boy called out to Will.

"Aye! 'Tis enough for now!"

"Nay, but I'd do ten ere I stop."

"Jesu! 'Tis enough, I said!"

The boy did not make it, collapsing against a building at seven steps. At first Will thought he cried, but as he bent to lift him he could tell Jamie breathed hard from near exhaustion. " 'Twill take time," he murmured soothingly, "for the limbs are but weak from disuse. Come—'tis time we warmed and dried ourselves. Later, when the rain ceases, we'll try for more."

"I'd nae wait," the boy insisted stubbornly. "I'd do it again now."

"Nay. 'Tis enough. Ewan, unstrap him."

" 'Tis well ye do," Ewan told Jamie, reaching to remove the boot. "Ere summer comes, ye'll walk across the yard at Blackleith. But," he added soberly, "ye've got to eat and grow." Turning away, he used his knife to scrape the mud from the metal bar. " 'Tis patience ye've got to have."

"But I'd try again, Ewan—just this time."

"Ye heard the lord, dinna ye? Besides, the rain worsens, and we'd nae take ye home too sick to show yer ma what ye can do. Mayhap when it clears, we'll come out again."

They went inside to the room they'd taken at the edge of David's royal city. It was a tiny, dark, nearly airless room, but at three shillings a week it came dear.

Tense from the intensity of watching him, William laid
the boy upon the bed they all shared at night. As the
disappointed child rolled over and closed his eyes, Will
reached for the wineskin Edmund of Alton had left
him, taking it to a bench by the small, smoldering fire.
He'd not wanted to drink it yet, thinking he'd save it
for the journey home. But this day he was cold and
wet, and the boy's steps seemed worth more than the
ale Ewan bought them.

"Would ye have a drap to mark the victory?" he
asked James. "And ye also, Ewan?"

Jamie did not even open his eyes. "Nay."

The older man shook his head. "Father said he'd
sweetened it for ye, and I'd nae favor it. Too much
honey and the teeth ache." Laying aside the boot, he
reached instead for the ale. "But I'd drink to the boy
wi' this. 'Tis courage ye've got, Jamie of Woolford,"
he pronounced definitely.

Unstopping the skin, Will poured himself a small
amount of the wine and took a seat, leaning back and
thinking of Arabella. In all of his nearly thirty-three
years, he'd never missed anyone so much. In the beginning he'd set a goal for them: They'd not go home
until Jamie could walk to his mother unaided by any.
Now he was ready to have Minette ride up close to her
and let the boy take but a few steps. Nay, he chided
himself, he was but overeager, and the boy was not
yet ready. Another week. 'Twould take another week.

Lifting the cup, he sipped almost absently of Father
Edmund's precious wine. "Aaargghhh!" His bench
came down with a jolt as he leaned to spit into the
rushes. "God's bones, but 'tis too sweet for any!"
Wiping his mouth with the back of his hand, he looked
to Ewan. " 'Tis as well ye dinna take it, I can tell ye.
'Tis fit for naught but the swine!" Rising, he carried
the skin across the room to unshutter the small window, then emptied it into the street, where it mingled
with a puddle. "Jesu, but he must think he makes a
confection rather than a drink!"

"If 'tis sweet, I'd hae some," Jamie decided.

"Nay—'tis gone. And ye'd drink ye'll take ale like a man, James. 'Twas overspiced, anyway," Will added, spitting again. "God's blood, but the mead is sour compared to that. Ewan, get him a cup of yours."

He looked around the room. It was a grim and lonely place within the city, made even gloomier by the rain and by his homesickness. A bed too short, shared by three, was not the same as his own, particularly since he lay awake nights for want of his wife. Each morning he'd rise, thinking 'twas not worth his loneliness, and then the boy would struggle to walk, shaming him, and he'd promise himself the patience to wait. 'Twould be enough to see Arabella's face when her son stood unaided before her.

But within a short time, his mouth felt odd and his hands tingled strangely. He became aware that the brazier weaved in front of his eyes, and that there was a weakness to his limbs. He passed a hand over his face, as though he could clear his head. His skin was damp from more than the rain. His flesh seemed to crawl. He felt sick, and it had come upon him far too suddenly. He was so preoccupied with the strangeness of it that he scarce heard the knocking at the door, and scarce noted when Ewan answered it.

"My apologies, my lord, but the weather made the journey overlong," Wat explained, shaking the water from his cloak. "And I couldna find ye. I've been to the court, to the physicians, and to the armorer, seeking yer direction, and each gave me to the other."

Will looked up, seeing the man, wondering if he dreamed. But the water from the cloak was real. "Aye," he managed.

"My lord, art all right?" Ewan asked, peering over Wat's shoulder at him.

" 'Tis dizziness—'twill pass."

"I bring you greetings from your lady," Wat said, drawing out a parchment case.

Arabella. Word came from Arabella. "Open it," William ordered. The two men looked at each other, then the messenger complied, removing the letter. As neither of them could read he unrolled it, stretching it out in front of his lord. The words blurred. Will blinked, trying to make sense of them. There were not many.

His speech was thick as he read aloud, "I would you came home in all haste, for I am fearful." He looked up at Wat. "What know ye of this?"

"She dinna tell me anything, my lord." Then, having heard her words, he added, "Mayhap 'tis that another died from the sickness."

"When?"

Uncertain as to the day, Wat answered, " 'Twas shortly after Father Edmund returned to us. He said 'twas the sickness, but the man was old—'twas Auld Ben at the gate." When Will said nothing Wat hesitated, then blurted out, "Ye dinna look too well yerself, my lord."

"Nay, I am all right. I'm overtired, 'tis all."

"Ye were all right when ye came in," Ewan reminded him.

Jamie rolled over on the bed and sat up. "Aye—ye carried me in."

The weakness seemed to overwhelm William, and it was an effort to think. He leaned forward, bracing his head with his hands. It was too heavy. He tried to speak, and his tongue seemed too thick for his mouth.

"I'd hae ye get me to the bed."

They did as he asked but he stumbled between them, his legs too weak to hold him unaided. Tumbling heavily onto the mattress, he pinned the boy beneath him. With an effort he raised himself enough for Jamie to roll aside, then he lay upon the spinning bed and willed himself to stay awake.

The two men looked at each other, then at William, "My lord, would ye that we fetched ye aid?" Wat asked him anxiously. "Ye dinna look good."

"Nay. I am cold."

A gust of wind banged the shutter, then it flew open, sending a spray of cold rain into the room. Ewan went to relatch it, peering outside first, and what he saw made his blood run cold. Turning back to Wat he said with a calmness he did not feel, "I'd get the physician—aye, and the priest also." Motioning the other man to look, he pointed. "There are two dead rats below."

Wat stared blankly into the muddy wine. "They drowned."

"They were not there when we came in, Wat—'tis the wine."

"They drowned in wine? Surely—"

"Nay. I'd say they were poisoned."

"Holy Jesu!"

William tried to shake his head, and could scarce move it. "Nay," he croaked, "I dinna drink . . . enough of it."

But Ewan moved to stand over him, addressing Jamie, "I'd nae leave ye, James, but there is nae help for it—d'ye ken? Ye must watch o'er him until we return." Speaking as calmly as he could, he added, "Wat goes for the priest and I to seek a physician for him. 'Tis up to ye to care for Lord William."

"Aye." The small hand crept to the English dagger he kept at his belt. "I'd guard him for ye."

"See as ye do." Ewan clasped the thin shoulder quickly, then backed away. "And he worsens, get ye to the window and call to any who would pass."

For once, the child did not protest that he could not walk. He merely nodded, his eyes large. But as soon as the door closed behind them he touched William's face gingerly, telling him, "Ye are all right—I know it—ye are all right."

" 'Twill pass."

But tears streamed down the boy's cheek as he laid his head against William. "I'd nae go back to Byrum—I'd nae," he whispered, reaching around the big man's neck. "I'd stay with ye."

Will lifted his arm weakly, then wrapped it about the small body. "Nay," he murmured. "We dinna come this far for naught, Jamie."

For a time they lay there, embracing each other, one

frightened, the other telling himself he could not die, that he was not done loving Arabella. He had too much left to do to perish. He'd see her again, he'd see the babe she gave him, he'd see James of Woolford walk. He was not done. He felt the small shoulders shake against his.

"Ye mustna weep—'twill pass."

The boy struggled to sit, wiping at his eyes. "I'd get ye ale. . . . I'd get ye a cloth. . . ."

"Nay. Lay down and be still. I'd hold ye."

"But—"

"Ye comfort me. I'd hear ye speak—I'd hear ye tell me of anything."

The child rested his head above the man's heart, hearing the beat of it, and tried to think of something to say. Until William, he'd thought of himself as worthless in all eyes but his mother's. Then the big man had given him the horse and dagger. Now the awful fear that, if aught happened to William, he'd never walk, nearly overwhelmed him. Burying his head in his stepfather's damp tunic, Jamie mumbled, "I'd nae have ye leave me."

"And God wills it, I'll not."

Wat was the first to return, bringing with him a priest he'd found at the nearest church. As he bent over William, smelling of his breath, then feeling of his pulse, the cleric decided it was premature to shrive one whose heart was still strong if not steady. Turning to Wat he said, "Although I am not a physician I have some knowledge of herbs, and I'd think poison also. I'd know how much he drank of it."

"I wasna here."

"He dinna drink—he spat it out," Jamie told him. "He said 'twas too sweet."

"I swallowed a little," William admitted.

"Hmmm." The priest lifted Will's eyelids, peering intently into the eyes, then felt of his skin. "What feel you in the limbs, my lord?"

"They sleep. 'Tis as though I have sat overlong on them."

"Art confused?"

"Aye."

"The heart is fast? It feels as though it would leap from your chest?"

"Aye."

"The limbs are weak?"

"Aye."

The priest looked at Wat. "Mix ale with water, one part to three, and have him drink as much as he will until there are no fewer than six filled cups down him. And after each say one Pater Noster and three Aves, that he will again be healed."

"You do not shrive him?"

"Nay. 'Tis God's will he recovers."

Turning his attention again to William, he explained, "As you did not succumb quickly, and you do not vomit as with some poisons, 'tis probable you swallowed but a small amount."

"What was it?" Wat wanted to know.

The priest shrugged. "There are those that affect the stomach, causing great griping, vomit, and bloody flux, and there are those that cause the body to convulse and the heart to beat rapidly ere it stops. If 'twas poison, and 'tis probable, 'twas likely nightshade or belladonna."

"'Twas wine," Jamie volunteered. "'Twas Father Edmund's wine."

"A man of God does not administer poison," the priest declared coldly.

"He only liked my mother—he doesna like any other. He says I am a misbegotten brat."

By the fourth cup of watered ale, with its accompanying prayers, Will's numbness had seemed to ease and his mind to have reunited with his body. In gratitude to the priest, William parted with another of his silver pennies, saying he'd have a candle burned at the altar in thanksgiving. He was sitting up drinking the fifth cup, when Ewan finally arrived to explain tiredly that he'd not been able to rouse any but a barber to bleed his lord. After much haggling, and with obvious disappointment, the fellow went on his way, but only after he'd declared that William would not recover until a balance between the four humours had again been achieved.

"Ye look better," Ewan observed.

"I know not of humours," Will admitted, "but whatever ailed me passes."

"I took care of him, Ewan—I did as ye asked me."

"And I dinna leave ye, did I?" Will countered.

"Nay."

Ewan glanced at the empty wineskin, then asked, "What would ye that I did with that?"

William followed his gaze, and his expression grew grim. "I'd hae ye fill it with water ere we go, and when we are arrived at Blackleith I mean to ask Edmund of Alton to share it with me. I'd hear what he says." Reaching his hand to ruffle Jamie's hair, his face lightened. "What say ye, James of Woolford—would ye that we went home again? Would ye walk to your mother? Nay, I know the answers, don't I? 'Tis both of us as are homesick to see her."

"We go back, then?"

"Aye—by way of Kelso," William decided. "I'd ask of Edmund of Alton there."

Chapter Thirty-Four

For nearly a fortnight it had rained, but now the sun emerged from the clouds, lifting her spirits a little. And although the air was still crisp there was a faint mingling of green amid the brown on the hills, promising spring within the month. With her cloak held tightly about her, Arabella walked the wall between the tower and the gate and tried not to think of the burns and rivers flooded between Blackleith and Edinburgh. If the rains did not come again the waters would recede, she told herself, and William and Jamie would come home to her again.

The sickness had passed—a good thing given 'twas Lent, for fish had not set well upon her stomach earlier. Now it did not matter, for she could even savor the smell of baking bread. Now she could turn her attention to the babe, thinking on it when her spirits flagged, planning for it, praying for it, and though 'twas early, sewing fine gowns for it also. This babe, God willing, would be whole. When Father Edmund had asked if she would have him light a candle for it, she'd answered that her only prayer was that it be born well formed and healthy. She'd not want another to suffer as Jamie. If anything, she would pray that Jamie would not feel abandoned when the babe came.

She looked out over the burn, seeing the water that lapped at Blackleith's wall itself. Five feet above the bank, Lang Gib had said. And for all that Wat had ridden out with her letter two weeks before, neither he nor an answer had returned. 'Twas the weather, and she knew it, yet she could not help hoping. Before she was fat and ungainly she'd lie in her husband's arms, and hear him say he loved her once more. She'd hold Jamie close, smoothing his hair, and she'd tell him that as much as she would love the babe she carried, he was still the firstborn of her heart.

But there was still the matter of the letter from Woolford to plague her. Two weeks and more she'd had it, and still she feared to know what Hugh of Woolford wrote William. There was naught she wanted of the Woolfords now, save to be forgotten. For nearly seven years Elias' and Donald's words had wounded, but now that William understood she no longer cared. Woolford was her past, Blackleith her present and future. But why had Hugh written, after all those years?

"Art overquiet, gentle lady."

"My thoughts plague me."

"I would that I could aid you."

"Nay, Father. Nothing ails me that my husband and son cannot cure. I'd see them, 'tis all."

"Would you that I heard your confession this morning?"

"As mine husband is gone from me, there is naught to confess—unless you would have me say that I curse the rain that keeps him away."

"What? You have no vanity, no sloth to admit?" he teased lightly.

" 'Tis difficult to be vain when there is none to praise me, Father."

"Your mirror praises you, Arabella of Byrum," Walter said softly. "Art possessed of as much beauty as any I have ever seen."

His manner and his tone had changed, and there was

a warmth in his eyes that discomfitted her. It was the gaze of a lover rather than that of one who would guide her rightly. Too often lately it had been thus when he was with her. She moved away to lean on the stone ledge.

"Ah, but you have been with monks at Kelso, have you not? There are no ladies there."

"But I have the eyes of any man." He followed her, his smile broadening. " 'Tis a pity you have not heard the pagan tales of Greece and Rome, gentle lady, for I'd liken you to Helen—or Venus even."

"Nay, I am but flesh-and-blood woman."

Always it was thus, and Walter would have to tell himself to wait, to bide his time. When word came that the Bastard did not return, that he'd sickened and died, then would Walter console the widow, then would he help her write to Giles of Moray. And when Moray was dead also, he'd travel to see King David, asking for justice, saying that he did not dispute Elizabeth of Rivaux's sons right to Dunashie, but that as the last of Hamon's blood he had the greater right to Blackleith. Then he'd return, not as Edmund of Alton but as Walter FitzHamon, to tell Arabella she need not return to Byrum, that he welcomed her presence here. She'd be stunned at first to learn of his deception, but he would explain it away, saying he had but wanted to return to Blackleith.

'Twould be no easy thing, and he knew it. He would have to account for Edmund, but he would say the poor old fool had drowned, and that rather than turn back he'd come in his stead. To those who would call it blasphemy that he'd claimed to be a priest, he'd say that he'd all but taken his last vows. But now 'twas Blackleith that had the greater claim on him. But that would come after the Bastard and the Butcher had died.

He cleared his throat and said aloud, "Mayhap if you returned to your studies, 'twould ease your mind. You are an able pupil, daughter. We could read and pray together."

"You flatter me," she murmured, forcing a smile.

" 'Tis Jamie who has the skill. 'Tis Jamie who learns easily. Alas, but I toil over the words.''

"Come up, and I will aid you. We will share a cup of wine and my small fire, while I show you the stories I have copied. Together we will read them, and 'twill improve your Latin,'' he coaxed. "I'd teach you of Venus—and of the others.''

"Pagan gods?''

"There is no sin in the reading, lady, for 'twas at Kelso I learned them. They are but tales for your fancy.''

"I ought to be at my needle.''

"Would you improve your sewing or your wits?'' he countered. "And it eases your mind, we will pray after.''

She looked down into the swirling water below, seeing that which kept William and Jamie from her. And once again she felt the intense longing. Nay, and she sat over her mending once again, she'd go mad from the wait.

"I would that I knew how he fares—that he and my son are well. Indeed, Father, but I'd have them home now. I know not why they tarry, or even why they have gone.''

"Life is uncertain, sweet lady, and 'tis not our lot to know the why of everything. 'Tis God's will that we wait.''

"Is it God's will that I worry?'' she demanded almost angrily.

"Aye.''

She moved away again. "If aught harm has befallen them, I could not stand it.''

"You would do as you did when Elias of Woolford died, lady: You would mourn and then you would live again. Nay, but William of Dunashie is unworthy of your tears. When all is said and all the pain is past, there will be another to love you.''

"You speak as though he does not come back, Father—and I'd not hear it.''

"Nay—I speak as though I do not know.'' This time

when he came up behind her, he laid a hand on her shoulder. "Come—let us study together. 'Twill divert your mind," he promised. "We will speak of other things until we know."

"I ought to bring Ena."

"Leave her to ply her needle." He favored her with a strange smile. "Surely after all these months we have been at Blackleith together, you've learned you have naught to fear of me, daughter."

"There are those who would say you are overyoung, Father, and that I am too much in your company."

"And 'tis so, 'tis the evil in their minds that says it. But if it disturbs you, I'd leave the door open that all can see we do naught but read together." Again he moved closer. "Think you I do not miss the boy also? I came to treasure the time you and James of Woolford spent with me," he lied.

"Aye," she sighed. "I have missed the lessons, Father."

"Then we will share a cup of wine and begin them anew. By the time your lord returns, you will be able to show him what you have learned."

"I have hopes he will not be gone that long," she retorted, starting down the outside steps.

Walter felt a grim satisfaction as he followed her. Long? Though yet there had been no word, Walter expected William of Dunashie already waited across eternity. And the very lack of that word probably meant he'd taken Ewan and the boy with him also. He felt a small pang of regret, knowing she would mourn her brat, then he shrugged it off. He would be there to comfort her.

Walter studied the way the firelight played upon her pale golden hair, thinking yet again how beautiful was Arabella of Byrum. How could he even have looked at the girl Avisa when this woman lived and breathed before him? As Arabella bent her head low over the unrolled parchment, studying the words he'd written, he imagined what it would be like to have her, to feel

the softness of her body beneath his. Patience, he
counseled himself, 'twas only patience he would need,
if he would see her come to him.

She stopped, spelling out a word with her lips, then
raised her lovely grey eyes to his. "I do not know this
one, Father."

He rose, moving behind her to look over her shoulder and see where she pointed. "It says that Arabella
of Byrum is the equal of a goddess," he murmured,
reaching to touch where one of her braids lay against
the soft blue wool of her gown.

She ducked from beneath his hand. " 'Tis a flatter-
ing jest at best, and I'd not hear it. I'd know the word,
Father."

" 'Tis *pense*—'think.' *Mal pense*," he repeated,
pronouncing the words.

"Evil thoughts?"

"Nay. Thinks evil. 'Tis the lot of man to think
evil."

She rose to stretch shoulders made tired by hunching over the parchment and walked to the tiny window,
where she peered through the crack between the shutters. 'Tis full light, and I've much to do, Father, yet
I'd work at none of it."

"Would you share a cup of wine ere you go?"

"Aye." When he would rise, she shook her head.
"Nay, I'd get it," she said, walking to another table
to pick up a wineskin. "Where keep you the cups?"

"Nay, not that one." He moved with such haste that
he knocked over the bench behind him. Reaching for
the skin, he explained, " 'Tis rancid, for I have kept
it overlong."

But she'd already removed the stopper. Smelling of
it, she shook her head. "Nay. 'Tis as sweet as any."
Dipping her finger into the neck, she would have tasted
the wine, but he snatched the skin away so quickly
that she dropped it, spilling it over her and onto the
floor. The stain spread down the front of her dress.

" 'Twas clumsy of me," he muttered, turning to
find a cloth for her. There was no water in the ewer

or the basin. "Sit you down and I will get it wet," he promised. "And I will bring more wine to you."

As he went out, she dropped to her knees and used the skirt of her already ruined gown to sop at the puddle ere it seeped through the wooden floor. Moving on all fours she dabbed at that which ran beneath the table, and it was there that she saw the black berries. Two of them. She touched them gingerly, recognizing that they were of the deadly nightshade, then her fingers closed over them. Rising, she tucked them into the pouch that hung from her girdle. And as she looked down, she could see the tiny specks of black that clung to the stain on her gown. The wine she'd spilled had been poisoned.

Deadly nightshade. The belladonna. That which convulsed, then paralyzed, ere it killed. It was as though the hairs at her neck stood on end and her blood ran cold in her veins as horror and fear mingled within her. Was this the strange malady that had claimed four people and the dog? And yet even as she asked, she denied the answer. The priest had no reason.

He came back, a wet cloth in one hand, a new skin in the other. " 'Tis sorry I am for the gown," he murmured, bending to rub at the hopeless stain. "Mayhap the woman . . ."

"Aye. I will have her wash it." Even her words, when she said them, seemed strained. She pulled her skirt away and tried to speak more lightly. "Mayhap if I give it over now, the spots are not yet set and will come out."

"Do you come back that we may share the cup? I have found a better, sweeter vintage I brought from Edinburgh."

Edinburgh. He'd been to Edinburgh with William and Jamie, and he'd returned alone. *When all is said and all pain is past, there will be another to love you.* The words so lately said echoed within her ears. Had they perished already, and she did not know of it? Nay, for that would not explain why Wat had not come back.

He'd not gone to Edinburgh until after Edmund of Alton came back.

"Art all right, lady?"

"Ah . . . aye. 'Tis that I am overtired, I fear."

"Would you that I helped you to your woman?"

"Forgive me, Father, but I'd be alone with the thoughts that plague me. When William comes home, I will be better."

He watched her go uneasily, wondering at her change of mood, then sat to drink alone. 'Twas the babe that overset her, he decided finally. Leaning back, he drank deeply of the good wine, wondering if William of Dunashie had suffered as he'd died.

Arabella walked quickly to the tiny solar, then dismissed all of the girls who worked there ere she showed her discovery to Ena. Barring the door, she dug into the pouch and drew out the berries, holding them in her open palm. "What see you here?" she asked the woman.

Ena stared for a moment, then without hesitation answered, "I see poison, my lady."

"As do I."

"But. . . . where. . . ?"

"I found them upon Father Edmund's floor."

"Sweet Jesu! You do not think . . ?"

"If William comes not home, if word arrives he is dead, I will have Lang Gib arrest Edmund of Alton," Arabella declared.

"Ye canna accuse a priest!"

"Ena, do you remember Brut? Do you remember my lord's dog? Think on it: He drank the wine Father Edmund brought me, and he died."

"Father dinna let ye drink it," Ena reminded her.

"Why? Was it that he decided not to poison me also?"

" 'Tis yer babe as oversets ye."

"Now he as much as says mine husband does not come home, Ena. 'When all is said and when all the pain is past, there will be another to love you,' he told me. Ena, he was in Edinburgh with William and Jamie and Ewan, and he came back alone.''

The woman paled visibly and turned away. ''Nay, I'd nae believe it, lady.'' Her voice dropped to little more than a whisper. ''I'd nae lose another—I canna bear it.''

''That first night we were here—the night the gatehouse guard died—do you remember that?'' Before Ena could answer, Arabella continued, ''I could not sleep for worry over Jamie, and I went outside. There was none but me and Father Edmund there when word came that the man had suffered a seizure and died.''

''It doesna mean—''

''And the girl Avisa? Do you remember her?''

''Aye.''

''I know not what passed between them, but I saw her hold his sleeve, and I saw him shake free of her. Whatever 'twas, the girl was overset that day.'' She paused, waiting for the import of her words to sink in. ''Ena, that night she and her mother died.''

''But none heard anything,'' Ena protested.

''There was an empty cup. D'you recall saying you would that you knew of simples?''

''Aye, but—''

''What did Father Edmund speak of when he offered to make me a potion for the sickness?''

''Poppies.''

''Ena, the nightshade kills, and the poppy dulls the senses!''

''E'en so—''

''They slept ere the poison stopped their hearts, I'd think.'' As the woman stared with dawning horror, Arabella nodded. ''Who would have it that we are beset by a malady that strikes without warning?''

''The priest. Oh, lady—I'd nae live without Ewan!''

''The only thing that would make me doubt it is that he has no reason.''

Tears welled in Ena's eyes. ''But what if 'tis that he is mad? Madness needs no reason.''

''And Lang Gib will think 'tis I who is mad if I

accuse Edmund, I suppose," Arabella mused. "Ena, on the pretext of cleaning for him, I'd have a girl bring me the empty wineskin. And if there is even a drop in it, I'd have Gib watch me feed it to the fowl. When the bird dies, I will ask that he arrest Father Edmund."

"Ye canna charge him—the Church willna stand for it. 'Tis only they as can judge their own, ye know."

"If word comes that William or my son is dead, Ena, Gib and I will hang him from Blackleith's gate. If the fine beggars me, I will pay it."

"But ye canna know—the burns and rivers is flooded. Mayhap Wat couldna find him. Mayhap they canna cross the waters. I'd nae do it. I'd—" Her gaze dropped to where Arabella still held the poison in her hand. "Oh, lady—I'd pray with ye for Lord William, for Jamie—and for Ewan!"

An oliphant sounded in the distance, but neither noted it. Very carefully, Arabella wrapped the deadly berries before she put them again into her purse. "Ena, I'd have you strain all that we drink through a white cloth. We do not partake of anything that has any black in it."

"But the pitch as seals—"

"Nay. The pitch can be recognized. 'Tis the berries I mean."

"Lady, he was going to ask ye to wed me," Ena whispered pitifully. "He said he was as tired of a cold pallet as I, ye know." Tears flowed freely down the woman's cheek. "There's been nae a one since Thomas until now. Ewan was going to ask Lord William to let Jamie lie separate from us on a pallet of his own."

"Lady—"

They looked up and both recoiled, for Edmund of Alton stood in the doorway. If he had heard he gave no sign, but still Arabella was afraid. Smoothing her hands on her soiled gown, she managed a wry smile. "As you can see, I have not yet removed my gown. Ena, goose that she is, has finally confided to me her intent to wed Ewan. She'd thought I would be displeased.''

The woman flushed guiltily, then knew she ought to say something to corroborate it. "Aye—when Ewan comes back, we'd hae ye cry the banns for us, Father.''

"Ewan does not—''

He stopped, aware of the shouting below. Ena ran to the window and threw open the shutters, leaning into the slit. "Lady, I would that ye came—'tis Lord William! Aye, and he brings Ewan! And Jamie and Wat also!'' When she withdrew and turned back to them her eyes still streamed, but she was laughing. "We was wrong—we was wrong! Lady, we was wrong!''

Walter's face froze as the sickness he felt nearly overwhelmed him. By rights William of Dunashie ought to be dead, and yet he came to Blackleith. He came home to Arabella. With an effort Walter regained his composure, only to find that both women had run down the stairs to greet the Bastard. Unable to face Arabella's husband yet, he watched from the unshuttered window instead.

William reined in at the end of the courtyard and called out to Arabella, "Stay where ye are, Bella!''

She stopped uncertainly and her face fell. Her husband dismounted there and lifted Jamie down. Sweet Mary, but what was that on her son's leg? The boy teetered precariously, his hand clutching William's. Despite his words she started forward, but her husband roared, "For once, I'd hae ye do as I tell ye!''

The boy looked like an elf beside a giant, as he gazed upward for reassurance. Then, when his stepfather nodded, he lifted his leg stiffly and moved forward, not once or twice, but a dozen times, each step halting but determined. The limp was painful and pronounced, but he walked. When they were about twenty feet from her William released the child's hand, and Jamie took another two steps alone.

"He needs much practice, but with God's aid and

ours, he'll do it." Though his own eyes were bright
with tears, Will smiled broadly and beckoned her.
"Well, ye can come get him now, ye know. 'Tis flood-
water we've crossed, and the longer road we've traveled to see ye."

Her chin quivered dangerously, and her chest ached
with what she felt. She stumbled blindly for her son.
Kneeling, she enveloped him in her arms. "God gave
us a miracle, Jamie—God gave us a miracle," she said
over and over again as she kissed his hair.

Finally, he struggled free. " 'Twasn't God, Mama—
'twas Lord William.''

"Ena, I'd hae ye take the boy up, for he is tired
unto death from the ride," Will ordered. "Aye, and
ye can take Ewan with ye."

Arabella stood, wiping her wet face with both hands,
then looked up at her husband. Her mouth twisted as
she tried to smile, then she flung herself into his arms.
" 'Twas God, my lord," she sobbed, "for he gave you
to me." She leaned into him, smelling the smoke, the
oiled mail, and the leather as she rubbed her cheek
against his shoulder. "Sweet Mary, but I'd feared for
you, my lord—I'd feared for you. I prayed to God for
another time to tell you how much I love you."

His arms tightened around her and he stood there,
oblivious to all else save her. Rubbing his two days'
growth of beard against her hair, he breathed deeply.
"Ye canna know how many nights I've wanted to smell
the roses in your hair, Arabella of Byrum. There's nae
been anything in mine life I've missed half so much
as ye."

He was there in the flesh. He lived and breathed
before her. Slowly the sobs subsided, and she was able
to step back shakily. "After I found the berries, I was
afraid something had happened to you."

Setting her from him, he looked around the yard.
"Where is Father Edmund?" he called out. "I have
brought his wine back to share it with him!"

"William, I fear 'tis poisoned!" she hissed loudly.
"I found the black berries in his chamber, and—"

"Aye," he agreed grimly. "And I'd see him drink from the skin ere I charge him."

Above them they heard Ena scream, and all else was forgotten. William and Lang Gib pushed past the crowd to run for the inner stairs. But the outside door opened ere they'd reached it, and Walter FitzHamon emerged, dragging Jamie. The knife in his hand gleamed in the rare sun. One hand smothered the boy's mouth, the other arm circled beneath his chin. "Stand away, and you would the boy lived!"

"Sweet Mary—nay!" Arabella cried. "He is but a child!"

Walter's arm tightened further, holding the blade at Jamie's throat. "The first man as moves sees the boy die." His eyes met William's, and there was no mistaking the hatred in them. "My life for the boy's, Bastard."

"I spared ye once."

"Ye took me to Kelso!"

"And I could have hanged ye."

" 'Twas a weakness that you did not." Walter edged away from him, shouting again to the others, "Stand away from the horses!"

Ena ran out, crying, "He's stabbed Ewan—afore God, he's stabbed Ewan!"

Lang Gib started forward, but William shook his head. "And ye kill my boy, Walter, ye'll die slowly."

"You cannot touch me!"

"I have been to Kelso—ye took no vows." Staying well back, he moved sideways, hoping to stall until he could flank him. "What did ye to Edmund of Alton?" he asked.

"The fool could not swim! Nay—stay back, I said!"

"Did ye poison the rest—or was it just me ye wanted?"

" 'Twas any of Moray's blood!" Walter pressed the knife harder, and as the boy cried out he thrust him forward again. "I'd delay no longer, Bastard! And you'd have the boy, you'll let me go!" When none moved, he reminded them, "Aye—four I poisoned with nightshade and poppy, and one I pushed from the wall—now would you see another before your eyes?''

"Nay! Leave the boy, and ye can go!"

"Hamon did not sire a fool! The boy goes with me!"

"Ye've no need for a crippled boy, Walter! Leave him, and I'll swear to your safety! Ye can ride for England!"

Walter had reached the horses. With his arm still around Jamie, he managed to swing up and right himself ere any could charge him. "I'll take him with me—to safety or to Hell! And ye want him, I'll leave him where I cross the Tyne!"

Arabella ran forward before Will could stop her, and she caught at Walter's foot. "I pray you will leave him now."

"Do you come with me, and I do?"

She looked back at her husband, then again to her son. "Aye. For my son's life."

He wavered momentarily, for 'twas what he'd always wanted, then he shook his head. "Nay. I'd not be able to keep you," he decided. "The Bastard would not rest until he killed me for it." He pulled hard at the reins, making the horse rear above her. "And you'd lie beneath me, wanting him."

"Leave me my son, and he will let you go!" she pleaded. "He said he would!"

For answer he spurred hard, and the beast shot past her for the lowered bridge. Behind her, the men of Blackleith scrambled for their horses. She turned and stumbled for William. "I pray you—"

But he caught her by both arms and thrust her aside. "There isna any time, Bella! The water's high, and the roads treacherous!" Swinging up into the saddle of his already wearied horse, he leaned down but briefly. "I dinna bring him home on his feet to lose him for ye."

"Have a care for yourself also, for I love you both!"

"Aye!"

The big horse thundered across the bridge, and the

others fell in line behind him, leaving her to wait and watch again. It was as though God could not leave her happy, she thought. She crossed back over the nearly empty yard, passing the silent kitchen boys and the women who, scarce a dozen minutes before, had been cheering her lord and her son.

The terror she felt was nearly numbing, and yet she could not give into it. William would come home again. He would deliver Jamie safely into her arms once more. She climbed slowly, feeling the weight of a lifetime with every step. Until she saw that Ewan still lay within the solar door. Ena knelt beside him now, cradling his head in her lap, crooning to him as though he were a babe.

There was a rent in his mail, and it took no skill to know the wound was a grievous one. Turning back briefly, Arabella called out loudly, "To me! To me! To Blackleith!" And when the first stable boys and scullery lads reached her, she ordered, "Put him into the bed."

" 'Tisna meet," he gasped.

"I'd not get down to the floor to tend you," she told him. "Put heavy cloths beneath him, that his boots and the blood do not soil the covers. Ena, get both hot and cold water—aye, and heat the poker in the fire."

When they had him laid upon the bed she began unhooking his hauberk at the neck, pulling it down, but she could see nothing for the blood that soaked his shert. " 'Twill take two different layers of stitches," she murmured. "One for the muscle and one for the skin."

"Aye," he croaked. "Lady, 'tis sorry I am. I tried to stop him."

Ena carried up two pans of water and set them on a table near the bed. "He surprised us, lady: Ewan was carrying Jamie on his other shoulder, and there wasna any time."

" 'Tis all right."

The older woman looked ready to cry again. "Can ye aid him?"

"If we can stop the blood, I can sew him." Arabella looked to one of the boys who hovered nearby. "I'd have as many cobwebs as you can gather." Rolling her sleeves, she proceeded to wash around the wound, revealing it more clearly. "His blood clots well, and 'tis a good sign, Ena. God willing, there'll be enough life left after this that he'll sire a babe or two of you."

"She told ye?" he gasped.

"Aye. And I give my blessing. But first you must live."

Chapter Thirty-Five

The way was hilly, the road but mire, and at every small burn Walter had had to turn aside for the high water. Beneath him, his tired mount was made even more so by the mud. Every few minutes Walter looked over his shoulder, seeing those who followed, keeping nearly the same pace as he, always staying just behind him. He doubled back again, unable to cross the swollen river, and took the road westward.

He had to reach the safety of England—he had to—for there he could throw himself upon the mercy of an English lord, saying he fled the maurauding Scots. And mayhap 'twould be William of Blackleith they turned on. 'Twould be almost a cruel jest, Walter supposed, if after all he'd done 'twas the English as felled the Bastard.

The boy rode before him, saying nothing, which suited him, for he still had no liking for Arabella's brat. And now that he had no hope of her, Walter had not even a single reason for kindness. He could almost curse himself for having let her live to love the Bastard.

The sun lowered in the sky, promising no more than

two hours or so of light, and he knew that once it fell below the horizon he'd be at greater disadvantage. Then 'twould be William of Dunashie, not he, who knew every road and burn that Walter had forgotten. Nay, he would have to go southward now, or not at all. Resolutely he spurred his tired beast, taking it off the path and over the darkening hills.

"Ye canna escape him, ye know," Jamie said finally.

"Close your mouth," Walter growled. "He comes not for you, you misbegotten brat."

"The wine ye gave him made him sick."

" 'Twas supposed to kill him."

"Aye, but it dinna."

Both fell silent again as the poor horse plodded on. Walter's only consolation, and it was a small one, was that William of Dunashie rode a beast as tired as his. He was lost now, and he knew it. As far as his eyes could see there stretched naught but more of the same topless hills. When the sun went down, he would not know which way lay England.

"Did he in truth go to Kelso?" he asked after a time.

"Aye."

"What said they there?"

"That Edmund of Alton was nae young as ye."

"And?"

"That you were Walter, the same as Lord William brought to them when you were a boy."

"But did they say I was not tonsured?" Walter wondered, clinging to that last hope despite what the Bastard had said. "Did they say I was not ordained?"

"I dinna listen."

The boy was good for naught, for naught at all, Walter decided sourly. Of all he'd have him remember, 'twas the most important. He'd know ere he was cornered if he could claim clerical privilege or not, and to that the boy had not listened. When darkness came and they could not see him, he'd not rely on the worthless child. Though James of Woolford did not weigh much, the horse would travel better without him.

"I hunger."

"As do I," Walter responded dryly. "There is naught to eat."

"Ye do not mean to set me down at the Tyne, do ye?"

"Nay."

"Ye promised my mother."

"I'd have William of Dunashie go back to Blackleith without you, that she will see he fails."

"I'd nae go to England."

"And I'd not take you."

For a moment Jamie considered asking what Walter did with him, but then he did not have to—he knew. "Ye could take me to Woolford, ye know."

"And you think they would thank me for it? You think they would want one as cannot walk?" Walter gibed cruelly. "Were it not that he has a care for your mother, William of Dunashie would wish you dead. And when the babe comes, do you think any will care for you? When there is one who is whole, what use will they have for Jamie?"

" 'Tisna true! 'Tisna true!" The boy craned his neck to look up at Walter. "Do ye mean to poison me also?"

"Nay."

Walter looked over his shoulder, seeing that William and the others were but a hill behind him. And then he heard the water. Unless he could cross it, he was caught like a hare in a trap.

"And he said he wouldna follow ye, he wouldna," Jamie said hopefully.

"He said it for her. Do you think he'd do it now?"

"Aye."

"Art a fool as much as a cripple then," Walter snorted.

"And ye kill me, he'll kill ye for it."

"He'll not cross into England with no more men than that."

"He and the Butcher have been all the way to London," Jamie recalled proudly.

" 'Tis the Butcher, not the Bastard."

Walter allowed himself the luxury of reining in for a moment to get his bearings. Unless he was mistaken he'd turned wrong somewhere, and made naught but half a circle. He eyed the sun, knowing he had not the time to find another road. As his gaze traveled over the hills, he thought he recognized the place. Jesu, but how could he have been so stupid? Ahead lay the ford where he was to have led Edmund of Alton, in what seemed another life. Only now 'twas flooded, and the water rose to where there was no sign of it.

Behind him the men of Blackleith, a few though they were, spread out, forming a curtain of mounted men to cut off his escape. Well, they'd not take him, not if Walter had to swim. He'd not swing from a scaffold at Blackleith. He'd not let the crows pick the flesh from his face in front of Arabella. He'd live to take his revenge another day.

He spurred his horse ahead, kicking it furiously when it balked. "On, you whoreson beast! And you stop now, I'll slit your throat!"

"But ye canna cross the water! Ye canna!" Then, when he perceived that Walter meant to go ahead, he turned to clutch at the man's cloak. "I canna swim!" And as long as he would live, he would never forget the expression in those cold eyes as Walter said, "Aye, I know."

William, who'd been pursuing doggedly, saw where his quarry rode, and knew the time to close with him was now or not at all. His heart in his throat, he waved to Lang Gib.

"Holy Jesu!" he shouted. "The fool thinks to swim it!"

"His horse is overtired!" Gib shouted back. "He canna!"

William rose in his saddle to lift his cloak and throw it, then he pulled off his gloves and tried to unhook the neck of his mail hauberk, lest it weight him down.

Ten minutes it took for a squire to put him into it—less than one tenth the time he had to get out of it. It was no use: He could not divest himself on the back of a horse. Instead he dislodged his heavy helmet and dropped it to the ground, then prayed that the greater size of his mount would carry him through the swirling water.

"Move downstream, that you may get the boy and he falls!" he yelled.

The water was deep, Walter's horse afraid. When the younger man saw William come into the river behind him, he loosened the boy's almost convulsive grip and pushed him. The child screamed as he fell, then went beneath the surface, his hands reaching upward still. Let the fools look for the boy—Walter Fitz-Hamon would escape.

Down current, William leaned from his horse, scooping frantically at the water where he'd seen the boy go under. For a moment he hesitated, thinking Arabella would mourn the both of them, then he dropped from his saddle into the cold water. He went under, groping until he thought his lungs would burst, then he tried to rise, carrying thirty pounds of mail and a soaked gambeson on his back. Ahead of him the child surfaced, bobbed, and flailed desperately. But before Will could reach him, he disappeared again. This time William went down, grasping with his fingers in the mud, and as he came up the metal links of his mail caught in James of Woolford's shirt, dragging him up also. Gasping for air, William managed to get his own head above the water, then he lifted the boy. Small hands grasped his neck, and the child's body struggled.

"Nay—ye dinna hold me—I hold ye!" Will gasped. "Be still, and I'd nae drap ye!" Somehow he managed to disengage the boy's hands and tuck his head under his own arm. Turning on his side he pulled Jamie after him, getting his wind as he rode the current, then striking out for the bank.

Gib rode along, then eased his horse into the water

to lean for the boy, grasping his shirt to pull him up.
Will grabbed his stirrup and held on, letting the animal drag him to safety. For a time he lay in the mud,
too exhausted to speak. But as the shivering child crept
to lie upon him, his arm closed over James of Woolford. Someone carried a blanket to lay over them.

"He said ye wished me dead," Jamie said finally.
"He said ye were only kind to me for Mama."

William opened his eyes and met the pale ones above
him. "Och, but ye know better than that, don't ye? If
I dinna let ye drown, 'twas that I loved ye."

"Aye. And he said when a whole babe comes, ye'd
nae want me."

"And ye believed him?"

"Nay." The boy raised up and wiped at the mud on
William's face. "I knew ye wouldna have taken me to
Edinburgh else ye loved me. Besides, and ye didna,
ye'd have punished Walter first, but ye let him go."

"I have hopes God punished him for me."

It was not until he was back astride his big horse,
with the blanket wrapped about him and Jamie, that
William felt the need to speak to the boy's fears about
the babe. Drawing the blanket closer, he leaned forward to shelter the Jamie's wet body from the wind.
"Ye know your mother and I are like to have more
sons and daughters, don't ye?"

"Aye."

"But for all that, ye'll always be first in her heart,
for ye were the firstborn of her body."

The boy nodded, then waited warily, for the big man
had said nothing of himself.

"And while I canna deny the bond I will feel for
the flesh of my flesh, Jamie, ye'll always be the first
son your mother brought to me."

"I would I had been born to ye."

"Ye know when you are baptized? Ye know ye are
born again in the spirit then? Well, as we have been
in the river together, James of Woolford, I guess we
could say ye were born again to me." When the child
made no answer, William added, " 'Tis proud ye make

me to claim ye. I know none other as would have tried
so hard to walk for me.'' He straightened in his saddle
for a moment. '' 'Tis the last time I am like to talk to
ye like this, for we are men, ye know.''

"Aye."

"But ye can call me whatsoever ye'd like."

"E'en Papa?"

"And ye want."

"Nigel dinna like me."

"He dinna like me either, so we are even there. And
I can tell ye, Hell will turn cold ere we visit him again.
But for now, 'tis your mother I'd see above any. No
doubt she's worried until she's sickened herself o'er
us.''

Chapter Thirty-Six

In the nearly dark room Arabella sat alone in the shadows, waiting for word from William. Those of the castle who'd not ridden out were all abed save she and Ena, who was below tending Ewan. At least the other woman had her love before her. For Arabella the hours crept slowly, making the night unbearable. From time to time she bowed her head, to repeat prayers said so often that God must surely have wearied of them: *Please, Father, for the love of she who bore your Son, I'd ask that my son survive.* Her lips moved silently, saying the words that echoed in her heart: *Holy Mary, Mother of God, answer this mother's prayer.*

Nay, but William would bring Jamie back safe, she knew it. She closed her eyes, seeing again her son's face as he'd walked. It had in truth been a miracle. Even now she could hear Jamie's voice saying, " 'Twasna God, Mama—'twas Lord William." As long as she lived, she would remember those words.

And her heart was filled with what she felt for her husband. It did not matter that he'd never given her a stone for her chain—he'd given her far more precious things. He'd given her a son who could stand and take

steps, he'd given her a son who no longer cried and
cringed, he'd given her a husband who disputed with
his words rather than his hands, and he'd given her
another babe to cherish. But more than anything he'd
given her his love and his kindness, making her un-
afraid.

She heard the steps on the stairs and she turned
around, seeing him. He was alone, and for a moment
her heart beat painfully in her chest. Then he smiled.
"The boy is below, palleting with Wat, for he is too
tired to know where he is. He is all right, Bella." He
turned to shut the door, then barred it.

"And you, my lord?"

"I am all right also, and nearly as tired as he is."

"And he does not take a fever from the wound,
Ewan will mend," she offered.

"Aye, I spoke with Ena. She'd nae wait, ye know—
she'd have the banns cried as soon as there is a priest."

"And what of Father Edmund—this Walter, I mean?
Did you . . ?"

"Nay, but God gave him justice, Bella. He
drowned." He moved closer, towering over her. "But
I'd speak of none of them this night, Bella. I'd just
come home to you. Before, I had not the time to tell
you how much I missed you."

Her heart beat rapidly beneath her breastbone. "And
I you, William."

"Jesu, but I am saddle-weary this night." He started
to remove his mail, then felt the pouch that hung from
his belt. Despite the awful fatigue that seemed to gnaw
at his very bones, he managed to smile again. "I
nearly forgot," he murmured, reaching inside the
leather sack. "I'd meant to give you this when we rode
in earlier." He held out his palm, revealing the green
stone. " 'Tis for your chain."

Her throat ached and her eyes misted as she took it
turning it over in her hand. "Sweet Mary, but 'tis
lovely," she whispered.

"Not half so lovely as you, Bella. Look at it—look
at the loop that goes over the chain."

She carried it closer to the fire to study it. " 'Tis a rose—the stone hangs from a golden rose," she marveled aloud.

"I have had the stone awhile," he admitted, "but I had the other made for you in Edinburgh. 'Tis fitting, is it not—one rose for another?" Coming up behind her, he lifted her braids to brush his lips over the nape of her neck. "On the morrow I'd hang it on the chain for you, Arabella of Byrum. And when I am rested, I'd see you with naught but this on you."

She felt weak with the promise. "You give me too much, my lord."

"Nay, but I have just begun. Ere Jamie is grown and we have a household more also, you'll have a box full of jewels, Bella. I have but to win them for you."

Jamie. She'd nearly forgotten the letter from Hugh. "Uh—a message comes to you from Woolford, William. I could not read most of it."

"I saw that ye'd been learning to write when I got your letter," he teased, smiling at her. "If ye'd wanted to learn, ye had but to ask me. I'd teach ye as well as Walter FitzHamon did."

But she was too worried to smile back. "I'd like that, my lord. Uh . . . when do you mean to look at Hugh of Woolford's letter?"

He wanted to say he'd read it on the morrow, but he did not. He could tell by the anxious way she said it that she feared what Hugh might have written. "Where is it?"

She moved to the box where she'd placed the rolled parchment, then returned to hand it to him. "Would you that I lit a lamp?"

"Nay, I can read it by the fire." As bone-weary as he was, as stiff as his body was beneath his heavy mail, he sat to unroll it and read aloud to her:

To William, Lord of Blackleith, I give greetings from Woolford.
    On the 29th of January just past, Donald, brother to me and lord to Woolford, was carried

from this earth by a fever, and with him were taken his three sons and two daughters, leaving me heir here. King Stephen confirms my right to rule Woolford, and it is as head to mine family that I write to you concerning the child James, sired upon Arabella of Byrum by Elias, my father.

As the said Arabella is a chaste woman, and as James was born within the bonds of wedlock, I am willing to accept him as brother here at Woolford, taking all responsibility for one born of my blood. As for the mother, the said Arabella of Byrum, she is most welcome to journey here also whensoever she wishes to see the boy.

Knowing him to be malformed and lame, it is my desire to place James within Holy Church, paying whatsoever monies are required for his instruction and keeping, at such time as he is of an age to go there. More than this I cannot offer, for there are my sons, and those of Milo of Woolford also, before him in this patrimony.

To the Lady Arabella I offer mine good wishes, for she suffered greatly in her years at Woolford and at the hands of mine family. May God grant her happiness and peace with you.

Subscribed for me, by the hand of Bertram, a scribe.

> Hugh, baron to Woolford,
> witness his mark.

For a long moment there was silence between them, then Arabella could stand it no longer. "What do you answer him?" she asked. "Would you send Jamie there?"

"Nay. I will write this Hugh on the morrow, saying that I'd keep the boy." He laid aside the extraordinary parchment that acknowledged the legitimacy of his stepson. "I mean to see him walk, Bella. When James of Woolford gains his spurs, I mean to be the man as buckles them on him."

He looked up at her, seeing the loveliest woman of his memory, and the knowledge that she was his nearly overwhelmed him. As tired as he was, he'd still feel her body against his. Rising stiffly, he held out his arms to her, smiling crookedly. "And I swear I'll nae touch ye wrongly, would ye give me a kiss, mistress? I'd lie with ye and no other, I promise ye."

"You'll have to get out of your mail first," she reminded him, moving into his arms. "And I'd bathe you also."

"Aye. And this night, 'tis you as will have to ride."

As he enveloped her in his embrace she leaned into him, heedless of the cold hardness of the metal links that pressed into her, and savored the strength of the big man she'd wed. From his body to his heart to his soul there was naught small about William of Dunashie, and as she lifted her lips to his, her own heart swelled with pride. He was in truth a giant among men—and she loved every inch of him.

Epilogue

Blackleith, Scotland: August 27, 1139

It seemed as though Arabella had labored forever, and yet when Ena finally came down from the solar she was smiling, saying the birth had been an easy one. Not waiting to hear whether he had a son or a daughter, William ran up the stairs eagerly. At the door he hesitated, wondering if she would wish to see him, if she would yet curse him for the pain he'd given her.

Ena followed him, her own body swollen with Ewan's child. "And ye dinna go in, she'll think ye are displeased," she muttered behind him. "The least ye can do is admire the babe she gives ye."

"Aye."

His mouth felt nearly too dry for speech, and his whole body was taut as he approached his bed. Arabella lay back, her face drawn and her hair wet from the labor, but her eyes opened when she heard him. He dropped down on one knee to take her hand.

"Art all right, Bella? Sweet Jesu, but I worried."

" 'Twas easier this time." Moving slightly, she shifted the swaddled babe from the crook of her arm to her chest. Her eyes filled with tears and her lip trembled as she looked on the small bundle. Choking from the emotion she felt, she pulled the cloth from his babe, "Thanks be to God, but she is whole—she is whole, William! There is naught about her that is not perfect!" Lifting her eyes to his, she added tremulously, "Sweet Mary, my lord, but her hair is redder than yours."

Relief washed over him. He had a daughter. He looked across at the wee, wrinkled babe born of his flesh and hers, and despite its redness he thought it so beautiful that he could not speak for the lump in his throat. Arabella's hand smoothed the orange down against the small head.

"Ena says 'twill darken," she offered. "We have hopes 'twill be as yours." She looked from her babe to him. "You truly do not mind that she is not a son?"

He squeezed her fingers. "Nay. I told ye I'd have a girl like ye." With his free hand he gingerly touched his tiny daughter's face, tickling it with a fingertip. "She is as soft as the petal on a rose," he managed reverently. The slate-colored eyes blinked at him. "Aye, and ye know your sire, don't ye, wee one?"

"Now that you have seen her hair, would you still name her Rose?" Arabella asked softly.

"And ye dinna mind it, I'd name her naught else."

"Not Rosamund or Rohese? Just Rose?"

"Aye—she'll be the Red Rose of the Border when she is grown."

"God willing, the next one will be a son we can name Giles for your brother."

"Mayhap, but if 'tis not, there are other flowers I like also." He leaned over to brush a kiss against her lips, then he stood. "Thank you for loving me, Bella."

" 'Twas nae hard task, Will o' Dunashie," she answered, smiling. "But I'd nae hae ye leave me yet."

"Och, but I'd hae one of us speak right, Bella," he chided, grinning. "Ye'd nae have the bairns speak like border louts, would ye? As for leaving ye, I'd but get Jamie that he may see the wee one also. He's prayed